VALENTINE'S BILLIONAIRE AUCTION

A FAKE FIANCÉE ROMANCE

WESTON PARKER

STAR KEY PRESS

Valentine's Billionaire Auction
A Fake Fiancée Romance

Copyright © 2025 by Star Key Press

All rights reserved. This book or any portion thereof may not be reproduced or used in any manner whatsoever without the express written permission of the publisher except for the use of brief quotations in a book review.

The novel is a work of fiction. Names, characters, places and plot are all either products of the author's imagination or used fictitiously. Any resemblance to actual events, locales, or persons – living or dead – is purely coincidental.

First Edition.

Editor: Eric Martinez
Cover Designer: Ryn Katryn Digital Art

FIND WESTON PARKER

WESTON PARKER
EVERY *good girl* DESERVES *a bad boy*

www.westonparkerbooks.com

1

KAIRA

"So glad this weighs eight thousand pounds." I grunted and shoved a ridiculously heavy box toward the open door of the van. "Does anyone look at me and see a dainty woman? No. What do they see? A donkey. Someone meant for hard labor."

Talking to myself was so normal for me I barely knew I did it. If I didn't talk to myself, I would spend most of my days in silence.

Okay, maybe that wasn't entirely true. I had Carla, my roommate, to talk to. But she wasn't always there by my side to indulge my chatter.

"Move, bitch!" I shouted at the stubborn box.

The thing finally moved, sliding toward the ramp. That would be another challenge, getting it on the dolly and down the ramp without squishing myself in the process.

When I took this job out of sheer desperation, I didn't know I'd be the mule. I envisioned myself serving champagne and mingling with the rich and powerful. I imagined I would be blowing up balloons and setting up tables and putting finishing touches on floral arrangements. At the end of the night I thought I'd be getting praise and compliments instead of boob sweat and lower back pain.

But this gig? It was so *not* the vibe.

I was the sucker in charge of toting all the shit into the venue and my boss and coworkers were the ones inside making things look pretty. It was a temporary gig, so I shouldn't be surprised. I wasn't one of the cool kids. I had zero experience with event planning. I had taken the job because I needed one, but I had no clue how much physical labor it would require.

I paused to slump against the box and catch my breath. Blowing a strand of sweaty hair off my forehead, I leaned forward and braced my hands on my knees.

"Pro?" I muttered to the asphalt beneath my feet. "Possible weight loss. Con? Thousand-dollar orthotic insoles. Super sexy."

I'd spent the last fifteen of my twenty-nine years trying to achieve a slimmer physique. Spin classes had resulted in dizzy spells, vomiting, and the humiliating experience of a hot paramedic handing me a bottle of water and gently telling me I wasn't made for spin class.

That one stung for a while.

I'd tried lifting weights to great protest from all my joints and my bank account. Gym memberships were no joke these days and canceling mine had been so frustrating, it would have been easier to burn the place down.

I'd done every diet under the sun, tried every weight loss tea, and even succumbed to wearing a corset to try to "reshape" my waist. Lunacy.

Maybe all I really needed to drop the extra pounds and softness was this backbreaking job.

"This is it," I said with a laugh. "This will be the thing that finally works."

I lifted another box with a grunt and carried it to the back.

"Unless I just end up so buff I look like a female Hercules. That would be my luck."

I leaned against the van, panting, and surveyed the mountain of boxes still waiting to be unloaded. Each one seemed larger and more intimidating than the last. A bead of sweat trickled down my spine, racing straight for my butt crack. I pressed my shirt to my skin to soak it up but it was too late.

The little bastard had already disappeared into the dark crevasse, tickling me in an unpleasant way.

So much for my break. I loaded up the dolly with more boxes and wrestled it down the ramp, each bump threatening to topple the precarious load. Inside the venue, voices echoed across the large, ornate hall that was slowly transforming into tonight's event arena. I didn't stop to take in the sights. My arms were screaming at me, so quickness was key.

I wheeled the empty dolly back outside and groaned when I looked toward the open door of the van. Boxes of brochures, centerpieces, and every random object needed for the evening's fundraiser were stacked haphazardly, daring gravity to send them toppling.

"Come on," I muttered, my breath puffing out in the cool night air. "Muscle up."

It wasn't much of a pep talk but it got me moving. And my old personal trainer, Marshall, used to call me "uncoachable."

Suck an egg, Marshall.

I climbed back into the van and got back to work. It wasn't just the manual labor that had me so frazzled. It was *The Kelly Hotel*. I couldn't help but stare every few seconds at the towering beauty of the seventy-five-year-old building. It was like something out of a storybook—ornate stone carvings framed massive arched windows and soft golden lights glowed from inside.

I'd always thought the place was romantic, somewhere two soulmates could find each other and start their happy ever after. I could almost see two young lovers coming together for a blazing kiss, swept away in each other.

To my dismay, the woman in my little daydream wasn't me. Even in my fantasies, love like that was for some other lucky girl. Never for me.

Still, as an aspiring romance writer, it would be a great setting for a book.

"Kaira! Move your ass! You're on the clock!"

The sharp bark of my manager's voice shattered my musing. I

jumped, nearly tripping over the dolly, and yanked myself back into reality.

"Right, sorry!" I called, scrambling to stack another load.

I pushed through the back entrance and into the kitchen, struggling. The rest of the staff moved like a well-oiled machine. They weaved around one another as plates clinked and voices rose over the hum of industrial appliances. The air smelled faintly of butter and rosemary and my stomach rumbled like a famished lioness. *Easy, girl.*

I hustled through, careful not to bump into anyone, and emerged into the grand ballroom. And oh, what a ballroom it was.

The chandelier was breathtaking, a massive cascade of crystals catching every glimmer of light and refracting it across the marble floors. The ceilings soared three stories high, and the entire far wall was made of glass. Beyond it, the landscaped gardens sparkled with twinkling lights in the cool, dark evening. It was pure magic.

For a second, I forgot I was sweaty and awkward and out of breath, feeling like maybe I'd stepped into one of my own stories.

But then the dolly hit a crack in the marble and the boxes wobbled. I lunged forward to steady them. The event planner, a sharply dressed woman with a clipboard that seemed permanently attached to her hand, glanced my way.

Her eyes narrowed as she took in my near disaster. "Keep it moving, Kaira," she said briskly, her voice carrying the sharp edge of authority and impatience. "These boxes aren't going to unpack themselves."

"Yes, ma'am," I replied, wincing at the stiffness in my back.

I quickly unloaded the dolly and rushed back out to get the next haul. Each trip from the van to the ballroom felt longer as fatigue set in, my muscles pleading for reprieve. I stole moments, brief seconds to breathe in the beauty of the Kelly Hotel's majestic architecture and the event slowly taking shape within it. Tables draped in rich velvet cloths were arranged meticulously around the room, each one crowned with elaborate floral arrangements bursting with colors—deep red, pink, and gold.

I wondered if this was like a pre-Valentine's thing. I was noticing a trend in the colors and there was a shit ton of heart-shaped everything.

I was not a fan of the Hallmark holiday. Maybe I would be if I had a Valentine or any hope to find one. Valentine's Day was all about singling out the poor souls who were all alone. It was like the universe's way of saying, "Look at all these happy couples! Isn't it too bad you're not one of them?" Or, in fewer words, "loser."

The ballroom transformed before my eyes. The setup crew had moved to positioning elegant golden chairs around the tables. Giant heart-shaped balloons were being affixed to the walls, and strings of fairy lights added a magical touch to the scene.

By the time the van was empty, my back ached and sweat stuck my hair to my neck. I snatched a bottle of water and gulped it down, although I was tempted to pour it over my head. It wasn't hot out, but after that kind of physical labor, it felt like it was a hundred degrees. In reality, January in LA was pretty comfortable. The parts that weren't on fire, anyway.

After dabbing away the sweat and adjusting my uniform so I didn't look like a total slob, I made my way back inside to see what else they needed me to do. The event would be starting soon. I would probably be dismissed and rushed out of the place.

My manager waved me over. "Kaira, if you're done with the van, help out with the lighting adjustments. They want a more romantic vibe, some kind of dim ambiance. I guess it's easier to fall in love in the dark."

"Got it," I replied, though the very idea of tweaking mood lighting felt miles above my pay grade.

He pointed me toward a tech guy who was fiddling with a control panel bristling with sliders and buttons.

"You know how to work one of these?" he asked without looking up.

"Not really," I admitted, "but I can follow directions."

He didn't look convinced. "Just go stand there on the stage so I can get the lighting right."

I shrugged. "I think I can handle standing."

I climbed up on the stage and stood on the tiny white X that had been placed on the floor. Suddenly, bright light blasted me and I immediately shielded my eyes.

"How about now?" the lighting guy called out.

I opened my eyes, but all I saw were stars. And red, shiny hearts. The lights were much dimmer now. I blinked a few times and gave him a thumbs-up. For the next fifteen minutes, he had me moving around the room like I was a pawn in a chess game.

When it was done, I escaped back to the kitchen and found a spot with a great view of the ballroom. The string quartet played and the lights twinkled like distant stars. The space had been transformed into something spectacular.

The balloons bobbed gently in the air currents stirred up by the bustling event staff. Servers dressed in black and white began circulating, bearing trays of champagne flutes and bite-sized hors d'oeuvres.

The guests arrived in a parade of living art—impeccably dressed, glowing with confidence, and utterly out of my league. My practical work clothes, black on black, only made me feel more invisible. My fingers twitched at my side. If I were them—if I had even a fraction of their poise and beauty—what would my life look like? Would every night be this glamorous?

"Kaira!" My manager again. He was at my elbow before I could turn, clipboard in hand. "We need you to cover for Sarah."

"Who is Sarah?" I asked, suddenly wary. I wasn't a server. There was no way I was coordinated enough to balance a tray of champagne flutes, especially after lugging boxes around all night. My arms were dead.

"She was supposed to wrangle the billionaires backstage for the auction."

I blinked. "Wrangle the what?"

He gave me a look like I was a particularly dense piece of furniture. "Do you not know what's happening here tonight?"

"No one told me," I said, feeling embarrassed.

"Well, it's a fundraiser. For Valentine's Day, they're auctioning off dates with the three billionaires. You know, for the Children's Cancer Society?" He handed me a note card with a bunch of writing on it. "Those are all the details. All you have to do is fetch them, bring them backstage, and review the stuff on that card with them. Easy."

My mouth opened, but no sound came out. Three men.

"Who?"

He gestured to a table. My eyes followed until I was looking at the men I was supposed to "wrangle." I didn't even know what that meant. *Isn't that what cowboys do?*

I sized up my cattle. *Or would they be steers?*

The first was a man in his fifties with a round face and kind eyes. He looked like someone's indulgent uncle. Second, a wiry man with sharp features and hands heavy with rings, his posture impeccable. And then... *him.*

Roman Kelly.

I'd known his name before I'd even known this job would bring me here. His family owned The Kelly Hotel and half the skyline of Los Angeles. He was tall—insanely tall—with broad shoulders that carried an air of absolute authority. His suit, dark as midnight, looked as though it had been poured over him. His chiseled jaw was lightly shadowed. I had a feeling he was one of those guys that would have to shave three times a day to avoid the five o'clock shadow.

He was looking down at his phone. He looked bored, like he wanted to be anywhere else but at that table.

My stomach flipped.

I couldn't do this.

"Kaira," my manager hissed, nudging me with his clipboard. "Get wrangling."

I swallowed hard and adjusted my shirt. With every ounce of courage I could muster, I approached the first billionaire. He followed me with a smile, chatting to his assistant as we walked backstage. The second man was a little more aloof, but he followed without issue. And then it was time.

Roman Kelly was standing now but still engrossed in his phone.

For a moment, I just stood there, frozen, trying to figure out how to form words with my mouth. My hands clenched at my sides.

I raised one, hesitated, and finally tapped him on the shoulder. He was so damn tall I had to practically go up on my tiptoes to do it. The moment my finger brushed the fabric of his jacket, he turned and I was hit with the full force of his gaze. He had to look down—way down—to meet my eyes.

"Yes?" he asked.

Dear God yes.

"Uh," I stammered. My voice felt too small. "I need you."

His brows lifted slightly. "Do you?"

2

ROMAN

The woman stood there, hands clasped tightly in front of her, knuckles white. Her cheeks were a vibrant shade of red, and her wide brown eyes practically screamed *terror*. She was short, curvy as hell, and clearly intimidated to address me.

"Come with me," she blurted out, the words tumbling out so quickly they barely made sense.

"Why?" I asked, tilting my head slightly.

"Auction," she said, her voice barely audible.

Right. The fucking auction.

Her desperate eyes held a silent plea for cooperation. Something about her vulnerability, her clear discomfort, piqued my curiosity. She looked like a terrified rabbit staring at a grizzly bear. Poor thing.

"You don't think I can get there on my own?"

"I was told to show you the way," she said, her voice a little more certain.

My jaw tightened as I straightened. I felt like throttling my PR manager for pushing me into this. For nearly two decades, my family's hotel had hosted this fundraiser, and for nearly two decades, I had managed to avoid getting involved. Normally, the third auction slot was reserved for some fossilized old billionaire whose name alone brought in outrageous bids. But six weeks ago, he'd gone out in true tabloid style—an overdose on his yacht, surrounded by coke and escorts. That left an inconvenient little opening for *me*.

Billionaires willing to be auctioned off were apparently in short supply.

I exhaled sharply, shoving my irritation down. None of this was her fault. "Lead the way then," I said, finally relenting.

Her shoulders sagged slightly in relief as she turned, expecting me to follow. She threaded through the throngs of glittering guests with more grace than her nervous demeanor let on.

The crowd wasn't so inclined to weave around her.

She moved quickly but apologetically, muttering "sorry" and "excuse me" every time she brushed past someone. People barely glanced at her. A man bumped into her shoulder hard enough that she stumbled a step, and when someone stepped backward onto her foot, she actually toppled sideways.

Before she could hit the floor, I caught her, one hand steadying her elbow and the other at her waist. "You okay?" I asked.

She looked up at me, stunned, and nodded. Around us, the partygoers turned to see what had happened. A few gave me polite smiles that faltered when they glanced at her. I knew the rules my station in life dictated. The help was never to be seen or heard.

I ignored them and turned my attention back to her. "Are you okay?" I asked again.

"I'm fine," she said.

"Excuse me," a woman's voice rang out. One of the more overdecorated guests waved a near-empty wineglass in the air. Her many diamonds caught the light, which I had a feeling was intentional. "Could you get me a refill?"

The woman in black, my escort, faltered. "Oh, I'm not—uh, I don't—"

"Relax, Vera," I said smoothly to the guest, cutting her off. "I'm sure someone will be along with wine soon enough." I turned to the woman I had just steadied. "Lead the way, miss?"

She was looking up at me like I was her knight in shining armor. I was definitely not that. I was no one's knight.

Her mouth opened, closed, then opened again. "It's Kaira," she said finally, her voice small.

"Kaira," I repeated, then gestured for her to continue. "Shall we?"

This time, I moved in front of her, acting like a linebacker protecting his quarterback. The crowd parted easily for me, guests stepping aside without hesitation. Behind me, I could hear her murmuring a quiet "thank you" or "sorry" as she slipped through. She only stepped around me again when we reached the backstage hall, where the other two "bachelors" were already waiting.

They greeted me with terse nods, neither bothering to look at Kaira. I couldn't explain it, but for some reason, it really pissed me off that she was so easily dismissed. Was I like that? Was I an asshole that ignored people who weren't in their social circles?

"All right," she began nervously, glancing at a note card she'd pulled from her pocket. She gnawed at her bottom lip, acting like she had been thrown into the lion's den and was afraid we were going to attack her. "You'll be called to the stage shortly. I'll give you your cues. Once you're bid on, you'll join your winning bidder in the crowd and spend the evening with them." She shifted awkwardly as she read the card, clearly uncomfortable. "You'll leave at ten for your planned date, which ends at two in the morning. Transportation is included."

The other two men chuckled, trading amused glances.

I leaned back against the wall, crossing my arms. "The sooner this is over, the better."

Kaira pressed on, explaining the logistics of the dates. The two men talked over her as if she didn't exist, swapping stories about previous fundraisers and speculating on who might bid on them. She was still trying to explain what was expected of them, but they were ignoring her like she was an annoying fly.

I watched her retreat into herself. Her shoulders hunched slightly. She turned away from them and peeked out through the door into the ballroom. I followed her gaze, though my eyes didn't linger long on the stage or the gathering crowd. Instead, they wandered back to her.

She was curvy in a way that was impossible to ignore, even beneath the utilitarian black uniform. Her posture was stiff, but it didn't hide the fullness of her hips. I wondered what she would look like in something elegant, something that matched the sparkle of the ballroom beyond the door.

"When are we getting this show on the road?" I asked irritably.

Kaira glanced back. She looked nervous, like she would give anything not to be stuck with the three of us. "They should start calling you out in about ten minutes," she answered. "I think. I don't know. I just got told to gather all of you back here."

"Was someone worried we weren't going to follow through?" I shook my head.

She shrugged. "I don't know. Maybe. I was told to wrangle you."

"I'm not sure I've ever been wrangled before. Were you going to use one of those electric cattle prods?"

"A what?" She gasped, looking horrified.

I sighed and shook my head. "Never mind."

"I'm only using the word I was told. I would never shock anyone."

"Consider me wrangled."

She sighed, like she was relieved. "Then I guess I did my job."

"Unless I make a break for it."

I saw the fear in her eyes. "Please don't."

I smirked. "Wouldn't dream of it. I'm sure I would be *wrangled* back here. Potentially with the prod."

She frowned like she couldn't decide if I was joking or not.

I sighed and pulled out my phone again to scroll through the news. I wasn't necessarily reading anything but just wanted something to do. The other two were carrying on about their yachts and when they had last been in Saint Tropez. I hated the snobbery. I had grown up in the world and was very familiar with the typical behavior of people who believed their financial status elevated their humanity. I hated it more because I knew there was a time when I would have joined right in, not thinking twice about it.

Kaira nervously glanced past me toward the two boasting men. "I should make sure they know the schedule," she murmured, more to herself than to me, but made no move to interrupt their conversation. "I don't think they heard me while I was explaining."

"Let them talk," I said low enough so only she could hear. "They seem to enjoy hearing their own voices."

She gave a small, appreciative chuckle and her shoulders relaxed slightly. "Not you?"

"I prefer silence."

"Sorry," she said. "I'm sure they'll be calling you soon."

"Stop apologizing."

"Sorry, what?"

"That. Stop apologizing. What are you apologizing for?"

Kaira blinked, unsure how to respond. "I... I guess it's just habit. When you're used to making sure everything goes smoothly, you tend to apologize for anything that might not be perfect."

I nodded, understanding the predicament of someone who constantly felt the need to prevent any ripples. "Your job doesn't seem easy."

Her lips twitched into a wry smile. "I'm just the setup team. I was supposed to be out of here already. I got caught gawking at all the fanfare and got roped into handling you all."

"Is this a punishment?" I was genuinely curious.

"Um, no. I don't know. I don't think so."

"But you don't know for sure?"

I was making her uncomfortable, which actually made me want to laugh. She looked like she wanted to be anywhere else but in front of me. I was used to people trying to get into my orbit, not away. It was a refreshing change.

"I should check and see when they need you," she murmured and hurried away.

I glanced out at the party, enjoying the anonymity of the wall and darkness that shielded me from the crowd. My eyes took in all the Valentine's decor in the ballroom. The walls were draped in deep red curtains, adorned with gold and silver heart-shaped garlands. The floor was scattered with rose petals. Tables were covered in red velvet tablecloths with flickering candles and arrangements of red and pink roses. The air was filled with the sweet scent of flowers and strong, expensive perfume and cologne.

I hated all of it.

The auctioneer's voice boomed through the microphone, pulling my attention back. Kaira came rushing back. "It's time," she said, her voice a little steadier now. She nodded toward the first billionaire, who grinned as he straightened his tie.

"Do I look like a million bucks?" he asked her.

She hesitated before offering him a small nod. "Yes, sir."

He winked. "If only I was twenty years younger, sweetheart."

I almost laughed when I saw her disgust written across her face. He didn't seem to notice or care about her reaction. Men like him rarely did. He walked out onto the stage. The second followed shortly after, adjusting his cufflinks as he went. The cockiness level in the two of them was admirable. Neither were exactly catches. The only thing going for them was their money.

Not that I was any better, but it amused me they thought they were irresistible to women.

Finally, she turned to me. "You're next," she said softly.

For a second, I just looked at her. Her lips curved into a small, nervous smile, and something in me softened—just a fraction.

Without a word, I brushed past her and strode onto the stage, ready to get the whole farce over with. But as I stepped into the spotlight, I couldn't quite shake the image of Kaira's wide, nervous eyes and that shy, fleeting smile. I glanced back and saw her watching the whole stupid charade.

The applause pulled my attention back to the stage and the crowd. I waved before taking my seat next to the other two. I hated this. I would prefer to just write a check than suffer through this humiliation ritual.

3

KAIRA

The lights from the stage were blinding, but I could still make out his silhouette as he took his place beside the other two men. My heart thumped erratically. Part of my unease stemmed from being in such close proximity to Roman Kelly. He was a god-like fixture in this town. Really, all of California. But to my surprise, Roman, unlike the other two men, seemed unwilling to participate in this pompous display, yet here he was, subjected to the same pageantry.

From behind the curtains, I watched the event unfold. I had never seen anyone be auctioned off. Although, back in high school, we did have those silly fundraisers where you could "buy" a day with the most popular kids to raise money for prom or some class trip. It felt strangely similar, except the stakes were infinitely higher, and the bidders weren't giggly teens but adults with deep pockets.

And the money was going to kids with cancer. That was definitely a worthy cause.

The auctioneer introduced each participant with great flourish, and when it came to Roman, his introduction was met with a mixture of cheers and murmurs—his reputation clearly preceding him.

Roman Kelly didn't smile or even glance in my direction. *Why would he?*

I stood frozen for a moment before shuffling out of the way, lingering with the other staff to the right of the stage.

"Good work," my manager said as he passed by, barely pausing to look at me. "It all went off without a hitch."

"Thanks," I muttered.

I knew I should leave. Go find something to clean or a box to carry. I really had no reason to be here. But I couldn't tear myself away. I was intrigued by the whole glitz and glam thing. This was probably going to be the one and only time I ever saw anything like this up close and personal. I would never be in the same room again with this much money and power.

Not that I wanted to be, but it was like watching a soap opera. It was a glimpse into a life I would never have. I listened to the auctioneer talking about the plans once a bidder won their billionaire. I couldn't stop looking at Roman, who was staring blankly at the crowd.

I wondered if he had a girlfriend or someone he was hoping would buy him. My gaze drifted to the crowd, trying to follow his line of sight to see what or who he was looking at.

I saw a sea of beautiful people wearing jewelry that was worth more than the typical car. Then again I was looking at the sheer luxuriousness of the room in general. I couldn't help it—this place was like stepping into a dream. My imagination took over, painting scenes of star-crossed lovers beneath the glittering chandeliers, their whispered secrets lost among the soaring marble arches. It wasn't exactly the Eiffel Tower, but I could imagine a romance unfolding within these walls.

It would be a real Cinderella scene. The woman who came from nothing falls in love with the handsome rich guy. Beauty and the beast, rags to riches, fairytale love that transcends societal boundaries —all of it made me swoon. It was difficult to keep my mind from wandering in that direction when I was standing in a room full of glitz, watching Roman Kelly being auctioned off like some irresistible hunk of man meat.

The auctioneer continued with his enthusiastic descriptions, each one more outlandishly lavish than the last. The crowd had turned into a sea of bobbing heads and excited chatter.

"Are you ready!" The auctioneer's voice boomed across the room.

The first billionaire stood and did a silly dance before the bidding started. It was a performance designed to open wallets and loosen inhibitions. But as I watched, my thoughts lingered on Roman Kelly, who sat with an impassive face, his eyes occasionally scanning the crowd with a detached curiosity.

The first billionaire was "sold" for a staggering thirty-five grand. I couldn't believe it. I knew the people in the room were rich, but I didn't realize just how much.

The second billionaire and his birdlike features stood. He reminded me of a peacock strutting back and forth across the stage. He was clearly relishing the attention. The bidding for him started high and only climbed higher, spurred on by his theatrical antics. But despite all his posturing, he was sold for the same thirty-five grand.

It was ridiculous. Seventy thousand dollars in just two bids, not including ticket sales or the ludicrous markups on the food and drinks. The charity was going to be rolling in dough. I wasn't jealous or envious, but it was pretty impressive to see these people all willing to fork out so much money without batting an eye.

And then there was me, standing here in my black-on-black uniform, earning sixteen dollars an hour and praying my car wouldn't break down again this month. Or that I wouldn't twist an ankle or, God forbid, get sick enough that I wouldn't be able to work.

When only Roman Kelly was left, the energy in the room shifted. I could practically feel the women perking up and paying attention. I glanced into the crowd and saw several women had casually moved to the front. If I was him, I would be feeling like a prime cut of meat. A prized horse. A valuable antique going up on the block.

For a moment, I felt bad for him. He looked so uncomfortable. And angry. I didn't understand why he would agree to do it if he didn't want to. He was a billionaire. And a grown-ass man. Couldn't he say no?

"Last but certainly not least, we have Mr. Roman Kelly, the owner of the Kelly Hotel itself, not to mention a few other *minor* business ventures." The crowd chuckled, clearly in on the joke. Roman's business empire was legendary. As was his wealth and his prowess. He was the stuff of legends. "Let's make it count and really fill that charity pot, shall we? We'll start the bidding for Mr. Kelly at a modest fifty thousand dollars!"

My mouth dropped open at the amount of money. My boss was standing next to me. Clearly, he was not immune to the excitement.

"Is the date just for a few hours?" I whispered.

He scowled at me. "Yes."

That was more money than I made in a year. Two years if I didn't get another job. Fifty grand to hang out with the man for a few hours? Was it sex? Was this some kind of legal prostitution?

The response was immediate and chaotic. Hands shot into the air faster than I could track. Bidding erupted into a cacophony of shouts and waving hands, the numbers climbing with dizzying speed.

Each bid was met with cheers and applause, as if the higher the number, the more exhilarating the spectacle. I watched as one particularly determined bidder—a woman in a shimmering gold dress—pushed her way to the front, her credit card held high like a warrior's sword.

I had suggested using bidding paddles earlier, thinking it would add some order to the madness, but my idea was shot down. My job was to move stuff, not think. Chaos encouraged competitive bidding, I was told, and no one here could claim they couldn't afford it.

Still, watching the numbers climb higher and higher, I couldn't help but gape. Fifty thousand. Sixty. Seventy-five. The bids flew faster than I could keep up, climbing toward a hundred grand.

A hundred thousand dollars. For one night with this man.

What could I do with that kind of money? Pay off my credit cards, fix my car, maybe even afford to take a real vacation for the first time in years. I could buy new shoes. Buy some magical weight loss pills.

And then celebrate with a meal that would counteract the pills. But boy would it taste good.

"Ninety thousand!" a woman shouted loud enough to shake the chandeliers.

The activity on the floor was actually stirring the shimmering hearts and balloons hovering overhead. These women were worse than sharks going after chum in the water.

I glanced back at Roman. He was standing stalwart. No expression. His broad shoulders were back, and he appeared to be looking at something on the back wall. I knew that look. When I was trying to be invisible, that was what I *hoped* I looked like.

As I let my mind wander, a woman in an elaborate feathered dress brushed past me. I didn't know who she was or where she came from, but she was on a mission.

She left a trail of tiny feathers in her wake. It looked like a pillow fight gone wrong, like she was shedding. The little feathers floated through the air and tickled my nose. I rubbed my face, but it just made it worse. It felt like I was wallowing in feathers.

I tried to hold it in, but there was no stopping it. The sneeze came out loud and sudden, echoing like a firecracker.

"Sold over here to the woman in black for one hundred and ten thousand dollars!"

The gavel struck, and the room erupted into applause.

It took a moment for the words to register. I blinked, stunned, and looked around, sure there had been some kind of mistake. My manager was staring at me. His face was a mask of horror and fury.

"What?" I squeaked, but it was too late.

"You just won the bid," my manager hissed.

"No, I didn't!" I said, panicked. "I sneezed!"

"Then go up there and tell them it was a mistake!" His voice was low but sharp, each word laced with irritation and a warning.

I froze, unable to move. My mind raced. I couldn't just walk up there in front of everyone and announce that I couldn't afford to bid, that I wasn't even supposed to be bidding in the first place. My stomach churned as chaos erupted in the ballroom. Everyone was trying to get a look at the woman who just won Roman Kelly for the night.

I tried to slink away. All my life I felt like people didn't see me. The one time I wanted to be invisible and it wasn't working.

The other two billionaires were already being whisked away by their winning bidders, women who looked like they'd stepped out of a fashion magazine. The lights dimmed slightly as music began to play, signaling the start of the evening's first dance. The crowd began to disperse, couples moving toward the dance floor.

And then I saw him.

Roman Kelly was stomping toward me like a dark shadow, his towering frame moving with purpose. He was coming straight for me.

My throat dried up as he stopped in front of me, his hazel eyes locking onto mine. The sheer size of him made me feel impossibly small, like a mouse caught under the gaze of a hawk.

He extended his hand, his expression unreadable.

"We're leaving," he said, his voice low and gravelly, sending an unexpected shiver down my spine.

"What?" I stammered, shaking my head vigorously. "No. No, I—I didn't bid! It was a mistake! I sneezed! I have to tell them what happened. I can't pay for you!"

"Now," he said, ignoring my protests entirely.

Before I could say another word, his large hand closed over mine, his grip firm but not painful. He turned, guiding me through the crowd with an authority that left no room for argument.

I stumbled along behind him, my heart hammering in my chest. What had I just gotten myself into?

4

ROMAN

Well, that could not have gone worse.

She wasn't even supposed to bid. She wasn't supposed to sneeze, either, but here we were. The naïve event staffer had just cost herself money she clearly didn't have. Now I was going to be on the hook to cover her ass. I had already given three hundred thousand.

Fuck it. What's another hundred grand for charity? For someone like me, it was pocket change.

I led her out the back before anyone caught on to the absurd mistake. She hustled to keep up with my long strides, her smaller frame practically jogging as I navigated the maze of hallways that only I knew about because, well, I owned the damn place. Her shirt and pants clung awkwardly to her curves. I wondered if the bland, ill-fitting uniform was the company's idea or hers. We passed through a hallway with a poster covered in red and pink hearts taped to the wall. I caught a glimpse of the words announcing a staff Valentine's party.

"I need to go back," she said, her voice tight with panic. "I need to explain to them that this was a mistake. They need to auction you off again."

I couldn't help but let out a bitter laugh. "That's not happening. I'm not going through that bullshit again. Fuck that."

"Why not? It's the only way to fix this!" she argued, sounding frantic. "We'll default to the last bidder. I have a feeling she would be willing to pay double to have you."

"Absolutely not."

"It wasn't my fault!" Kaira protested. "Some lady was wearing all these feathers. When she brushed by me, I was swarmed by the damn things. It's her fault I sneezed. We have to go back. Why won't you let me fix this?"

"Because you're the lesser of all evils in that room. Trust me, I'd rather cover your bid than end up spending the night with one of those desperate, single socialite women who've been circling me like hyenas."

She yanked her hand out of mine, forcing me to stop and turn to face her. Her face was flushed with determination, her brown eyes sparking with defiance. She had looked all sweet and meek, but I was seeing another layer of her. In a crisis, our true selves came out, the inner core we keep hidden from the world. It was like I was seeing her for the first time.

Her warm eyes had real fire behind them now, from a glow to a blaze. Her pouty lips and full face gave her a cherubic appearance but I saw the steel beneath all her softness. She wasn't angry, just passionate.

Nice to meet you, Kaira.

"You're not paying for my mistake," she said with a little shake of her head. "Just let me go fix it. I can clean up my own messes."

I leaned against the wall and eyed her more closely. Most people came to me with their hands out, trying to get something from me. Here I was, offering her a lifeline and she wanted nothing to do with it.

"There's no mess to clean up."

"Oh yeah there is," she replied.

"Let's call it a happy accident. Serendipity."

"That sounds like something you'd need antibiotics for."

I smiled. She had a sense of humor, even with the tension crackling off her. "Let me ask you this. Do you think I can't afford to cover your bid?"

"You can afford to do a lot of things." She shrugged. "Doesn't mean you should do them."

"I promise it's not a big deal. That kind of money is a drop in the bucket."

Her lips thinned into a tight line, unimpressed. "It's four years of salary for me."

I scoffed. "Yeah, can you imagine?"

She stared at me, her gaze steady and unflinching. If she was trying to give me an x-ray with that gaze, she was doing a damn good job. I couldn't figure out why she was pissed at me. I didn't do anything.

And then it hit me.

She wasn't joking.

I had insulted her. That explained the clothes, I thought, and the way she let people in that ballroom look right through her. She was truly that broke.

Damn. My net worth had probably gone up a few million while we were talking. What a world.

"Let's go," I said, jerking my head toward the end of the hallway. "We're getting out of here."

"I don't go anywhere with strange men I don't know," she snapped, crossing her arms over her chest.

I laughed, the sound echoing in the empty corridor. "Feel free to read my wiki page. You know, some of those women out there *intentionally* bid on me. They willingly wanted to pay just to be alone with me."

She rolled her eyes. "Ever heard of some of the most infamous serial killers? Lots of women chose to spend time with them too."

My mouth dropped open. "I'm sorry, are you calling me a serial killer?"

"No, but the same principle applies. People choose to do dangerous things all the time. It doesn't mean I have to."

"Every woman that has been alone with me has lived to tell the tale."

"So far," she said, arching a brow.

I stepped close enough that she had to look up to meet my eyes. "Are you always this stubborn with people who are trying to help you?"

Her jaw clenched, and her features pinched in anger, making her look like a puffed-up kitten trying to take on a lion. It was adorable.

She jabbed a finger at my chest. "I know men like you."

"Do you?" I asked, amused.

"Well, erm, no, not really. Not in real life," she stammered. "But I know what you're made of."

"Not in real life?" I repeated, smirking. "What else is there?"

"Don't twist my words," she said, exasperated.

"Maybe I should be afraid of being alone with *you*," I said.

"No, I'm a writer," she said breathlessly, her earlier fire extinguished in an instant. Her shoulders slumped, and she looked away. "Or I'm going to be one, one day. I was talking about books. That's what there is besides real life."

"Fine," I said with a shrug. "Judge me however you want. I'm just trying to offer a simple solution to the problem."

"I thought it was a happy accident?" she asked sourly.

"Well, you seem distinctly *un*happy. So now it's a problem." I took a breath to steady myself. "Here's the way I see it. You can let me pay or you can go back and tell them you don't have the money and they have to redo the whole thing over again—which isn't happening because I'm not going back. Not a fun conversation."

She stared at me. "This one isn't that fun either."

"I'm giving you an out," I said, my voice lowering to a harsh whisper. "Would you really put yourself through that rather than accept a little help?"

Her face contorted as if she was about to cry, but instead, she inhaled deeply, steeling herself. "It's just not right," she muttered. "Just throwing money at a problem doesn't fix it."

I rubbed the back of my neck, feeling frustrated. "It totally does.

Like ninety-nine percent of the time, money can fix anything. And this money is for kids. Kids with cancer."

"But—"

"Okay, what's your plan then?" I asked, interrupting.

She bit her lip. After a moment's hesitation, she squared her shoulders and met my gaze with newfound resolve. "I need to come clean and apologize. Then face the consequences, whatever they may be."

I nodded. "Or come with me, grab a bite to eat at a fairly fancy restaurant, and take a ride in a really nice car. Then, the only consequences you'll face are a full stomach and a fun story to tell your friends." I cocked my head, studying her. "Final offer."

Her gaze flicked back down the hallway toward the ballroom. For a moment, I thought the crazy woman might actually turn around and leave.

Then she let out a soft sigh and nodded. "Fine," she muttered. "But only because I don't know how else to fix this mess."

"I swear, I've never seen anyone so against having a fun night," I said, already walking again.

She followed. We exited through one of the back entrances, where my car was waiting. The sleek black car gleamed under the soft glow of the hotel's outdoor lighting. My driver looked surprised to see me. He hopped out of the front seat and rushed to open the door for us.

I motioned for her to get in. "Ladies first. Or are you going to argue with me about that, too?"

She scowled at me before sliding into the leather seat, looking both out of place and oddly enchanting as she fidgeted with the seatbelt.

I jumped in beside her. As soon as the door shut, the driver got in and pulled away from the hotel. A bottle of champagne was waiting in the console, along with two crystal flutes. I popped the cork with practiced ease, pouring the sparkling liquid into the glasses.

"To letting yourself have some fun tonight," I said, handing her a glass.

She accepted it, taking a small sip.

"I just want this night to end," she said quietly, staring out the window.

I chuckled, leaning back in my seat. "You don't know what you want."

Her head whipped around, and she glared at me. "Excuse me?"

"You heard me," I said, unbothered. "You've got indecision written all over you. It's practically a second skin."

Her mouth opened and closed, her cheeks reddening with indignation. "I know exactly what I want, thank you very much!"

"Do you?" I asked, raising a brow. "Because from where I'm sitting, it seems like you have no idea."

She sputtered, clearly offended, but I didn't care. If nothing else, this night was going to be interesting.

She bristled and shot me a dirty look. "What I want is to rectify my mistake, not to run away from it. Not to hide behind champagne and flashy cars and your big-ass wallet."

I smirked, swirling the champagne in my glass, intrigued by her. I didn't really understand why she was so averse to spending time with me. She couldn't be getting a lot of offers like this.

I had grown up sheltered in a world of luxury and money. Money bought people and power. I rarely interacted with anyone outside my social circle. Something about this woman drew me in. I wanted to know what made her tick.

If nothing else, it seemed like a good way to shake things up. My life was all very planned. Nothing happened I didn't want to happen. Even the stupid auction. I could have walked away if I really wanted to.

For the first time tonight, I was starting to think it might not have been the worst choice ever.

5

KAIRA

This guy was the definition of a Grade-A asshole. Roman Kelly radiated entitlement, as if the world should bow down at his feet simply because he graced it with his presence. He probably expected women to fawn over him, to throw themselves at his feet—and probably other parts of him, too—showering him with adoration.

But I was not one of those women. I had agreed to accompany him, yes, but only because I saw no other option. It wasn't as if I could simply saunter away from the consequences of that insane auction.

Damn that woman and those stupid feathers.

"Sir?" The driver looked at Roman in the rearview mirror.

"Dinner."

"Yes, sir."

It felt like they were speaking in shorthand. Or Roman was just too damn good to have a conversation with the lowly driver.

That irritated me.

The champagne in my hand was untouched after that first obligatory sip. I did not want to get drunk. Not around him. I didn't think I was in any danger of him trying to get in my pants, but I had read enough books and had seen the true crime shows. Men weren't exactly picky about who they banged. It was more about getting a little piece of every pie and nothing about the person they were having sex with.

I was not going to be one of those women who slept with some rich guy because I had some wild Cinderella fantasy. He was not going to fall in love with me and pull me out of the poverty I wallowed in.

Roman watched me. I could feel his eyes on me even as I continued to ignore him. He had this way of observing that felt almost invasive. And then he pulled his phone out.

It was my turn. I wanted to watch him.

Who was Roman Kelly?

From where I was sitting, all I could see was a spoiled, overgrown man-child who had clearly never been told "no" in his entire life.

But why did he have to be so hot?

It was infuriating.

I caught myself staring. The sharp cut of his jawline, the tousled hair swept effortlessly back, the stubble on his face that was just the right amount of rugged. And those hazel eyes, intense enough to pin you in place.

And that body. He didn't just look strong; he looked powerful. Like he could toss me around with ease if he wanted to.

Not that he would. Men like him didn't go for women like me. And thank God, because I couldn't stand his cocky attitude, like he could do whatever he wanted. He might be physically attractive, but he was so irritating. Obnoxious. A jerk. Although he hadn't technically been a jerk to me, I was sure he was a jerk in general. He had that air of a true snob. An elitist.

Roman glanced up from his phone, maybe sensing my gaze. Our eyes met for a flash of a second, but in that moment I saw something flicker there. Maybe curiosity, maybe amusement, it was hard to tell with him.

"Yes?" he asked.

"Where are you taking me?"

"To eat."

"Can you be more specific?" I asked.

"Yes." He smirked and turned his attention back to his phone. "But I'm guessing you probably won't know it. You'll see when we get there."

I opened my mouth to retort that it was a total asshole statement but then snapped it shut. He didn't care about my opinion of him, and sadly, he was probably right. The fanciest place I went to regularly had golden arches out front.

I sipped my champagne. Now that the reality of my situation was sinking in, I needed the bubbly or I was going to start panicking at any second. Behind me was an angry boss, who I had left dangling without explaining what was going on. Ahead of me was a night with a man who might as well be an alien for how different we were.

What a mess. How did I always manage to get myself into such disasters? I wasn't just physically clumsy. I was a disaster. Some people were born with poise and grace; I was born with the uncanny ability to stumble into the most complicated situations possible.

"I don't think we were supposed to leave," I said quietly.

"Supposed to?" he asked. "I don't need anyone's permission."

"Right, but I was working."

He didn't say anything.

"I laid out the schedule."

"And we're mostly following it," he said.

I took a deep breath. "I didn't even tell my boss I was leaving."

"Do you want me to call someone?"

The way he said it had me clenching my teeth. He truly was insufferable. He didn't *see* me. I was an escape hatch. That was it. He didn't really want to do the auction. I was his way out of an obligation he signed up for.

"Did you know her?" I asked.

"Who?"

"Feather Lady."

"Yes."

I nodded. "Did you two… you know?"

He paused whatever he was doing on his phone and turned to look at me. "Are you seriously asking me that?"

I shrugged. "You seemed very averse to going to dinner with her. I got the feeling there was some history. Maybe you ruffled her feathers once."

He put his phone down, a hint of amusement behind his irritated expression. "I have not had sex with her. She's nearly twenty years older than I am."

"She didn't look that old."

He shook his head. "Wait, do you think I'm her age?"

"I don't know. Men tend to hide their years better."

"I'm thirty-three, Kaira. Damn. And Mrs. Wilson is a friend's mom. Plenty of people have called me a motherfucker but never literally."

I burst into laughter. "Oh."

"How old did you think I was?"

I shrugged. "I don't know. Thirty? Thirty-five."

"Yeah, right. You're a terrible liar."

"She doesn't look fifty," I said. "Not really."

"Thanks to the fine hands of her skilled surgeon," he muttered.

"I guess I don't know how to spot the same things you do. In my world, we age the way we age. We don't get to spend thousands of dollars on surgery. We're lucky to buy a drug store cream to stop the wrinkles."

I could feel him studying me. It was very disconcerting. "How old are you?"

"You should never ask a woman that."

"You should never ask a guy if he's banged his friend's mom, but you whipped that right out at me." He smiled, like the sun breaking through the clouds. "So maybe we don't have to be so formal."

"I guess," I said, pretending that smile hadn't made me feel anything. My mouth hadn't gone dry and my heart wasn't hammering in my chest.

"You don't have to answer, of course. It's your choice. But then I'll have to make my own assumptions."

I couldn't stop my curiosity. "And if you were to guess, what would you say?"

He reached for my hand, shocking me, and ran his thumb over the back of it.

"Are you a palm reader?" I asked nervously.

"No, but my grandmother said you could always tell by a woman's hands. I'm guessing twenties."

I laughed and pulled my hand back. "There is a huge difference between twenty and twenty-nine. A whole lifetime."

"And by that statement, I'm guessing you're on the high end of the twenties."

I nodded. "Twenty-nine."

He squinted his eyes at me like he wasn't sure he believed me.

"I'm twenty-nine, you ass," I said.

He nodded and grinned. "Good. I find anyone under twenty-five to be insufferable. Not enough life experience. Well, usually."

I took another sip from my glass and told myself I just needed to get through the next hour or two. Then it would be over. I would go back to my life, and he would do whatever it was he did. For the moment, Roman lounged in his seat like he owned the world. He probably did, at least the expensive bits of it.

When we pulled to a stop, I nearly gasped. The restaurant was breathtaking, perched right over the ocean with floor-to-ceiling windows offering views of the moonlit water.

"I'm not dressed for this!" I exclaimed.

"It's fine," he said calmly.

"Oh, sure, you're in a suit. You're fine. You're not the one who's going to embarrass themselves."

He held up a palm. "No, I mean no one is here. You can go in wearing a garbage bag if you want."

"What?"

"I reserved the whole restaurant for whatever date I was going to be forced to be on. It's just us."

"Of course," I sighed.

He smiled again. "You have the weirdest reactions to good news."

Without another word, he got out of the car and came around to open my door. Ugh, the show-off. Grumbling under my breath, I allowed him to help me out and he led me toward the entrance, two big silver doors that looked like the gates of heaven.

The staff greeted Roman like royalty. I followed him in, trying not to feel too self-conscious in my boring black outfit, knowing I had been sweating in it earlier. True to his word, the place was completely devoid of customers and even the space was wide open. A single table in the center was covered with a red tablecloth and two flickering candles, and it was just for us.

The restaurant was decked out for Valentine's Day in red, white, and pink. It was all very elegant and pretty, staying just this side of tasteful. It softened some of the anxiety plaguing me since I sneezed and turned my whole world upside down.

We were seated and a waiter presented a bottle of wine for Roman's approval. He nodded but said nothing. Our glasses were filled and then the feast began.

It was a steady stream of dishes, each more elaborate than the last. Roman ate with gusto, completely at ease, while I worried about every little thing I put in my mouth. Was I eating too fast? Too slow? Did he think I was a slob? I honestly didn't even know what most of the dishes were. I could be eating frog eyes, and I wouldn't know any better.

If they were, they were tasty as hell.

At one point, he leaned over and nudged a plate toward me. "Try this," he said, his voice smooth and confident.

I hesitated, but the look on his face made it clear he wouldn't take no for an answer. I took a small bite. "Good," I said. "What part of the frog is it?"

"What?" he asked, blinking. "It's risotto with truffles." He watched as I took another bite, this time more confidently.

"It's delicious," I admitted, warming to the flavor as I allowed myself to relax a little.

He nodded approvingly before returning to his own food. We barely talked while we ate. The food stole the show, lighting up my mouth like fireworks. Was this what rich people ate? It was a far cry from ramen noodles with cut-up hot dogs, which was one of my specialties. The chefs here were slightly more talented than I was, every mouthful a delight.

As yummy as everything was, each bite was also a reminder of the giant gulf between Roman and me. He was like a king and I was the mule lugging boxes around and taking orders. This moment was fleeting, like smoke in wind.

After tonight, our paths would never cross again. I would remember this night for the rest of my life but he would probably forget about it by the end of the week.

After dinner, Roman leaned back in his chair, clearly relaxed. I, on the other hand, couldn't stop spiraling. The evening, the luxury, my clothes, my everything—it was all wrong.

"So," he began, his tone conversational. "Isn't this better than getting yelled at by your boss and the auction people?"

I nodded. "It's not the worst evening ever."

"High praise from you," he said, chuckling. "This is my life. Luxury cars, private jets, multi-million-dollar deals. The works."

"And?"

He went on, telling me about his hotel empire, the businesses he'd acquired, the obscene amounts of wealth he'd amassed. He barely paused to take a breath. I didn't know if he was trying to impress me or just talking. He spoke like it wasn't a big deal. Like he was talking about the weather.

At one point, he shifted the conversation to the auction. "Do you know they forced me into this?" he said, shaking his head. "I didn't want to do it, but my PR team wouldn't let it go. Now look where it's gotten me."

That stung, even though I knew he wasn't trying to insult me.

As he snapped his fingers to get the attention of a nearby server, something inside me snapped, too.

"Don't do that," I said before I could stop myself.

He turned his head slowly, his brows raised. "Do what?"

"Snap your fingers at them," I said, gesturing toward the server. "It's rude."

For a moment, I thought he was going to unleash his wrath. I had heard stories about Roman Kelly's temper. But instead, he just stared at me, his expression unreadable. Then, to my surprise, he started laughing.

"You think you're in a position to tell me what I can and can't do?" he asked, his tone mocking.

"Yes," I said, refusing to back down.

He snapped his fingers again, this time with a smirk, and instructed the server to clear the table and refill our drinks.

I couldn't stop myself. "I'm so sorry about that," I said to the server, my voice gentle.

Roman's head snapped toward me, his amusement fading. "What are you doing?"

"Apologizing," I said, glaring at him. "Because clearly, you don't know how to behave yourself."

"Excuse me?"

"You heard me," I said, my voice steady. "Men like you think the world revolves around you. You think snapping your fingers at someone is acceptable just because you're rich? You have no idea what kind of day they've had. You don't know what they've been through before starting their shift to serve some entitled jerk who thinks he's better than them."

My heart was pounding. I couldn't believe the words coming out of my mouth. But I wasn't done.

"For the record, you're not. Better than them, I mean."

Roman stared at me, his hazel eyes burning with something I couldn't quite place. For a moment, I thought he might actually lose it. But then he leaned back, a cold smile curling his lips.

"You know what?" he said, his voice low. "I was wrong. Going on a date with one of those desperate socialites would've been a much better idea than spending the night with some self-righteous goodie two-shoes on her high horse trying to teach me a lesson."

I swallowed hard, his words cutting deep. But I refused to let him see how much they hurt.

"Glad we're on the same page," I said, forcing my voice to stay steady.

6

ROMAN

The mood was ice cold as we stepped out of the restaurant. My driver pulled up almost immediately. I opened the door for her and watched as she climbed into the car. Kaira didn't look at me. That was fine.

I wasn't about to start a conversation. She hated my guts, and honestly, I wasn't a fan of hers either. Sure, she had the kind of outside packaging that could turn heads—mine included—but the high morals and endless preaching? That was a hard pass. I didn't need a mother to tell me when to say thank you. And I certainly didn't need a date with Miss Manners. I was a grown man. I could do what I wanted. I could talk the way I wanted.

Didn't she know who the hell I was?

The tension in the car was thick as the driver pulled away. I stared out the window, my jaw clenched so hard it was giving me a headache.

"Where are we going?" she asked with a sigh.

"I planned for a four-hour date, per the auction rules," I said. My tone was flat. "We're going to a museum. Nice and safe. No chance of romance."

"Can you just take me home? Let's skip the rest of the date. We don't need to go to a museum. It's not like I actually won the bid. You don't want to do this any more than I do."

I couldn't help it—I laughed. "I'm paying over a hundred grand for this date, and you want to bail?" I turned to look at her. "Do I need to remind you I'm the one saving your ass?"

She rolled her eyes, crossing her arms. "Fine. Whatever."

Typical.

Why in the hell was I insisting she stay with me? I could go home and enjoy the rest of my evening. I could call up someone else. But something about this infuriating woman made me want to push her buttons even more. Maybe it was the way she stood up to me, or maybe it was just the challenge of it.

"We won't go to the museum," I said.

I gave the driver the next address. I knew it was only going to piss her off more. I didn't care. She was stuck with me for a couple more hours. I didn't think I was all that bad.

The nightclub was my kind of place—exclusive, swanky, the kind of spot where everyone knew my name and bent over backward to keep me happy. I didn't have to ask for anything. They just knew.

The second we stepped out of the car, the doorman gave me a warm welcome. The people in line were already whispering and pointing. I saw the flashes from the pictures. Kaira looked up at me with shock and horror.

"I can't go in there."

"Sure, you can."

"I'm not dressed for the club."

"Get out of the car." I left no room for argument.

She groaned and climbed out. I led her to the velvet rope and waited to be allowed in.

The doorman's eyes fell on Kaira, his expression shifted.

"Mr. Kelly," he said hesitantly. He looked stressed like he would prefer to be anywhere else. "I'm afraid your guest doesn't meet the dress code."

I looked down at her. Black pants, a plain shirt, and sensible flats. Not exactly nightclub material.

She shrank under the scrutiny, and for the first time all night, I felt something resembling guilt. I should've seen this coming. She told me she wasn't dressed appropriately.

Yes, that was a dick move. Even I could see that.

Without a word, I took her hand and led her across the street to a diner.

"What are we doing?" she asked. "This is stupid. Just take me home."

"No." I pulled open the door and gestured for her to go inside. She sighed and walked in. I followed behind her and froze. I could honestly say I had never been in such a place.

She looked around as if she belonged, like she was finally comfortable for the first time since she and I met. I, on the other hand, felt like a fish out of water. The place was clean but simple—chrome stools, laminated menus, the smell of fresh coffee and grease hanging in the air.

It was all very kitsch.

We slid onto two stools at the counter. I tried to hide my discomfort as my eyes took in the sight. Kaira turned over a white mug.

"Why did you do that?" I asked.

"If you want coffee, turn over the cup."

I hesitated but flipped my cup as well, signaling to the waitress bustling about that we were ready for service. She came over with a smile, pouring out steaming coffee into our cups without asking.

"You planning on ordering food, or just here for the coffee?" she asked, tucking her order pad into her apron.

"Food. I think." I wasn't sure I wanted to eat but I was curious what they offered.

The waitress handed us each a menu.

"Be back in a few," the waitress said and hurried away.

"This better?" I asked, watching her as she scanned the menu.

"Much," she said with a small smile.

The sight of that smile caught me off guard. She looked different here. Comfortable. Natural. She had been very nervous and uncomfortable most of the night. But here, she looked like she could finally breathe.

"I'm not hungry," I said. "I happened to like my meal."

"No one's forcing you."

"What are you going to order?"

"Apple pie. A la mode."

"A la what?"

"Ice cream on the side. It's one of my favorite late-night treats. Coffee and ice cream."

I had no idea but when in Rome.

Kaira ordered and I asked for the same. The waitress walked away and returned a few minutes later. I tried not to look put off by the simple serving of pie on a plate with a scoop of ice cream.

The coffee tasted like burnt tar, but whatever. I could prove I wasn't a snob. I could eat regular people food. My personal physician was on-call twenty-four seven. I took a bite and was pleasantly surprised.

It reminded me of a custard with poached pears I had in Paris. She and I weren't so different.

I decided to try and make conversation. "So, Kaira, what do you do when you're not sneezing your way into six-figure auctions?"

She stiffened but didn't look up. "We don't have to do this."

"What? Sit here in seething silence? I was trying to move past it."

"It's fine, alright? We don't have to pretend to like each other. Or care. After tonight, you go back to your life, and I go back to mine. Order restored. Let's just have some quiet pie together. Eat up. Diner pie is good for the immune system."

Her words caught me off guard. Not the part about the pie. I fully expected it to turn on me, despite how good it tasted. It was the other part.

Most people fell over themselves to make a connection with me, to stay on my radar, to insert themselves into my life. But Kaira? She acted like she hated me, clearly wanting nothing to do with me.

It was a very odd feeling, rejection. It got under my skin like itching powder, which was ridiculous. She was no one to me, a minor detour in life's long journey.

And yet... I couldn't help but like it.

She'd stood up to me. She'd called me out. She didn't care about my name, my money, or the power I held. Even my most charming smile couldn't win her over, and I had been on several magazine covers where it was featured prominently.

Kaira had spoken up because her values mattered more to her than I did. She didn't care if I liked her or not. She had an opinion, and she wasn't afraid to share it.

That was rare. And, to my surprise, I respected it. I also respected her request for quiet pie. We finished in silence. Whatever it did to my guts, the pie was worth it. Lost in a sugar daze, when the waitress brought the check, Kaira grabbed it before I could.

"Are you out of your mind?" I asked. "I'll buy the pie."

"No, it's the least I can do," she said, dropping a twenty on the table.

I stared at the bill, then at her. "Cash?"

She shrugged. "Some of us don't carry black cards."

I almost laughed at the comment. Almost. Instead, I said, "Thank you for the dessert."

She said nothing but I thought I caught the edge of a smile as we walked back to the car. She climbed in and gave the driver her address without asking me if we were finished for the night. Technically, we still had some time left on our date but I didn't think it was a good idea to push the issue.

The night was far past its peak. We both had enough. As we pulled up to her building—a modest rental in LA—I couldn't help but feel underwhelmed.

I climbed out and walked her to the front door. "What are you doing?" she asked.

"I'm walking you to your door."

"You don't need to do that."

"But I'm doing it anyway."

She stopped at the entrance of the building. "This is good."

"You don't want me to know where you live?"

"Hell no."

Not just no but hell no. Ouch. I nodded, having to respect that. But it didn't mean I was ready to let her go.

"Thanks for dinner," she said stiffly. "I'm glad it's over and you didn't suffer so horrendously."

Her words were sharp, but her cheeks were pink, her arms crossed protectively over her chest.

As she reached for the door, I stopped her. "You owe me, you know."

She froze, then turned to glare at me. "Why?"

"One hundred and ten thousand dollars. That's why."

Her face turned red as she sputtered for a response.

Before she could say anything, I leaned in closer, dropping my voice to a low rumble. "Don't worry, sweetheart. I'll find a way to collect."

She let out a frustrated huff, yanked the door open, and disappeared inside without another word.

"I fully intend to cash in, Kaira!"

The door shut, and I found myself standing there with a stupid grin on my face.

I had dodged a bullet tonight. But I couldn't shake the feeling that Kaira might not be out of my life for good. There was just something about her I couldn't simply walk away from. In the back of my mind, I knew I should. The last thing I needed to do was chase after a woman who hated me.

I got back into the car and shut the door. "Home," I said, slumping into the seat.

Kaira's indifference was like a breath of fresh air in a life otherwise filled with sycophants and yes-men. It was unsettling but intriguing. As much as I tried to dismiss her from my thoughts, curiosity gnawed at me. What made her hate me so much? What had shaped her into the fiercely independent creature that sat across from me earlier, scoffing at my attempts at civility?

By the time the car pulled up in front of my building, a plan was already forming in my mind. I needed to see her again.

Just let it go, Roman.

But I knew me. I knew the way I worked. I never just let anything go.

7

KAIRA

I woke up to the smell of coffee and the sound of Carla singing an off-key rendition of some pop song in the kitchen. Carla was probably in the category of one of the older Swifties. I had never personally cared for the music, but Carla loved Taylor. Which meant our Alexa playlist was filled with her music. It grew on you after a while.

Dragging myself out of bed, I shuffled into the small but cozy kitchen of our two-bedroom condo. Carla was flipping pancakes with one hand and scrolling her phone with the other, her oversized sweatshirt hanging off one shoulder.

"Morning, sunshine," she said, flashing me a grin.

I groaned in response, heading straight for the coffee pot. "I need caffeine before I can deal with people."

I grabbed a mug and filled it up.

"How was your night at the ball, Cinderella?" she asked.

"It was an auction—and you wouldn't believe it if I told you."

She slid a pancake onto a plate. "Wait, is this a real story or an idea for a story you want to write?"

"All this happened, more or less."

Carla leaned against the counter, her interest piqued. "Spill."

I took a sip of my coffee, the bitterness waking me up before the caffeine did. "I went on a date with a billionaire."

Her eyebrows shot up. "A billionaire, huh?"

"Yep."

"How big was his dick?"

"I don't know, but *he* was a pretty big dick."

She frowned at me. "Wait, you're serious?"

"He was one of the rich guys at the auction I worked last night. I was standing and very innocently watching a bunch of rich ladies frothing over the billionaires, bidding insane amounts of money."

"Wait, we can buy one? How much do they cost?"

"Well, the one I bought cost about a hundred thousand dollars."

"Damn, I better start saving up my pennies."

"No, listen. I was watching the auction and some woman walked by me wearing half a dead bird on her dress."

She cocked an eyebrow and flipped another pancake. "Is this one of those faerie books you like?"

I rolled my eyes. "No, I'm being serious. Feather Lady, who was just a regular human lady with poor fashion sense, walked by me and the feathers tickled my nose. I sneezed and the auctioneer counted it as a bid, which I won. So I bought a billionaire."

She stared at me. "Then I hope *you've* been saving up your pennies."

"It happened, Carla. It was very real."

"So is he in your bedroom?" she asked nonchalantly. "Can I borrow him when you're done? Anoint him in oils and send him to my room."

"This isn't funny."

"It's a little funny." She sipped her coffee. "You're broker than me and I'm really fucking broke. So I know you didn't buy any billionaires."

"No, I actually bought the guy for a hundred and ten thousand."

"Come on."

"Yep. I'm serious."

"Where the hell did you get that kind of money? Did you rob a bank? Without asking me?" She looked hurt.

"No, obviously I don't have a hundred thousand dollars to piss away." I sighed. "Are you seeing the problem?"

Carla shook her head, trying to process what I'd just told her. "So, what happened next?" she asked.

"I was going to explain the mistake, even though I'd probably get fired, but the billionaire I bid on grabbed me and pulled me out the door to go on our *date*."

"How are you going to get that money?" She smiled and wagged her brows at me.

"We're not robbing a bank," I said, appreciating that she still had a sense of humor. I was having trouble finding mine. "He said he's going to cover the bid. I tried to get him to let me straighten everything out but he wasn't having it. The guy is insufferable. Like, peak billionaire jerk. He made me sit through an entire dinner listening to him brag about himself. And don't even get me started on the nightclub fiasco."

Carla's eyes lit up. "Oh, please, *do* get started. Someone had quite the adventure last night."

I sighed, pulling out eggs and bacon from the fridge. "He rented out an entire restaurant. Like a really, really nice place. Just the two of us."

"Sounds like a romantic date."

"Well, it wasn't actually a date," I protested.

"It sounds like a date. And you called it a date. I mean, it still counts even if you have to pay for it."

"Hey!"

"What did you eat?" she asked.

"All these fancy dishes. Like seven courses. I have no idea what any of it was but it was good. So then he takes me to this super exclusive club, right? Only, he dragged me out of work. I was in my uniform, which did not meet their dress code. He didn't even think about that ahead of time! Anyway, we ended up at a diner eating pie. Pie, Carla!"

"Pie sounds nice," she said, grinning.

"Not when it's with Roman Kelly," I muttered, cracking eggs into a bowl.

Carla froze, the spatula in danger of melting against the pan. "Wait a second. Roman Kelly? Hold on." She flipped the pancake and furiously typed something into her phone, then spun it around to show me.

There he was, shirtless on some beach, his abs looking like they'd been carved from marble.

"This guy?" Carla asked, her voice dripping with incredulity. "You spent an entire night with this guy?"

I rolled my eyes and whisked the eggs. "Not the whole night. And let me tell you, those abs? Completely negated by his personality."

Carla was zooming in on the photo. "I'm sorry, Kaira, but I don't feel bad for you in this moment. Look at that smile. I'm not entirely convinced this isn't some sort of AI. Is it? Does he really look like this?"

"He kept his shirt on."

"But he was hot, right?"

"I need more than a handsome smile, Carla!" I protested.

She looked up at me, smirking. "So you admit he's got a nice smile? No further questions, your honor."

I groaned and moved to refill my coffee. "He's as good-looking as he is a total douche bag."

Carla raised an eyebrow. "Bet he'd make a fun lay, though."

My mouth fell open. "Stop it!"

"What?" Carla said, all innocence. "I'm just saying. Can you imagine his core control? I bet he can fuck like a jackhammer."

"Carla!"

She burst out laughing, nearly spilling her coffee. "I'm just saying, Kaira. You missed an opportunity! I would drop my panties in a heartbeat for a man like that."

I shook my head, trying not to laugh with her. "Yeah, but you're kind of a ho."

Carla posed prettily, chuckling. "Guilty as charged when it comes to a man like that," she admitted, leaning back against the counter. "You can't tell me you don't think he's hot."

"The second he opens his mouth, his physical appearance fades. He's an ogre."

"Plug your ears and ride him off into the sunset."

"No thanks. I would never sleep with a guy like him. And he'd never sleep with a sloppy nobody like me."

Carla's smile vanished, and she turned to face me, hands on her hips. "What did we talk about?"

I looked away, embarrassed. "Carla, I didn't mean—"

"Nope," she interrupted. "You be nice to my friend Kaira. She deserves the fucking world, you hear me?"

I couldn't help but smile. "Sorry."

"That's better." She grinned, taking a big bite of her pancake.

I pulled out another pan and stood next to her to make the eggs. It was a routine for us. Cooking together while dissecting the absurdities of my disastrous night, hashing out life's dramas over spatula and stove.

Living with Carla for the past three years had been the best decision of my life. When I couldn't afford the rent on my condo, I'd put out an ad for a roommate. Carla had been the first to respond, and from the moment she walked in the door with her infectious energy and bright smile, I knew I had hit the jackpot. She wasn't just a roommate—she was my best friend.

I finished the eggs while she nuked the bacon. We chatted as we ate, talking about our plans for the day.

"I'm heading into the office," I said, sipping my coffee. "Debriefing from the event and starting on the next one."

"Hot yoga for me," Carla said, stretching dramatically. "Then a quick shower before my shift tonight. Tips better be good—rent's coming up."

Carla worked as a bartender. Her beauty and bubbly personality were a win-win combination. She was the kind of woman a guy like Roman would typically date. Carla was tall, slender, and had immaculate skin. Her blonde hair and blue eyes just added to the total package.

We finished breakfast and got ready for work. I grabbed my purse and headed out, opting to take the bus. I chose not to drive as often as I could. I hated LA traffic.

The office was buzzing with the usual post-event chatter when I arrived. I didn't even get the chance to get some of the cheap coffee and check the job assignment board when my manager appeared in front of me.

"Kaira, can I see you in my office?"

His tone made my stomach drop. I knew I was probably in trouble after abandoning them without telling them I was leaving. Technically, I was done with my job, but my shift hadn't been over.

I followed him into the office. He closed the door behind me and gestured for me to take a seat.

He sat down and looked at me. I saw pity on his face, which was my second clue this was not going to go well for me.

"Sorry about running out last night," I said.

"Kaira, I'm sorry to do this, but we have to let you go."

My heart sank. "What? Why?"

He sighed, rubbing his temples. "The auction. Your false bid—it's a bad look for the company. Roman Kelly had to cover it, and we can't afford that kind of scandal. We'll start losing gigs."

"It was a mistake," I said, my voice shaking. "I sneezed. I didn't bid!"

"Be that as it may," he said, sliding a check across the desk, "this is your final paycheck. We wish you the best."

I stared at the check, my mind racing. "That's it? No severance?"

"We're a small company, Kaira. We don't have the budget for that. You were hired on a trial basis. It didn't work out."

I was stunned, my hands trembling as I took the check.

"But Mr. Kelly insisted on covering the bid. I told him I wanted to fix it, but he wouldn't let me go back. He dragged me out of there!"

My manager's face softened slightly, but there was a finality in his eyes that told me the decision was already made. "I understand it was a complex situation, but we have to consider the company's reputation. We can't be associated with unpredictability or accidents like this. There were a lot of complaints. One woman in particular was very upset that she did not win the bid."

I felt defeated. It seemed so unfair—punished for something I hadn't even intended to do. Suddenly, the office felt incredibly small, the air stiff and suffocating.

"Thank you for the opportunity," I managed to say, my voice hollow. I stood up, clutching the check like a lifeline, but feeling it was just another reminder of yet another failed job.

He practically shooed me out of the office. I didn't bother looking at any of my former coworkers. Stepping outside, the bright Los Angeles sun did little to lift my spirits. I felt small surrounded by people indifferent to my plight, each person absorbed in their own routines and dramas.

I walked aimlessly for a while, letting the noise of traffic and snippets of overheard conversations wash over me. My thoughts kept circling back to the unfairness of the situation. I hadn't meant to bid at the auction, and yet here I was, jobless because of a simple mistake. If anyone should get fired, it was the damn auctioneer who couldn't tell a bid from a sneeze.

The thought of going home and facing Carla with this news was daunting. She had her own worries about money; adding mine would only burden her further.

"Shit, shit, shit!"

Why couldn't I get a job and just keep it?

8

ROMAN

The flash of cameras started the second my car pulled up to the curb outside my downtown LA office tower. I didn't even have time to straighten my tie before a wall of reporters surged toward me, their microphones and smartphones thrust forward like weapons.

I stepped out of the car, my polished leather shoe hitting the pavement with practiced precision. A sunny January day in LA should've been glorious, but not when you're fending off vultures.

"Mr. Kelly! Any comments on the recent acquisition rumors?"

"Are you dating a secret Kardashian?"

"Will you be selling your hotel?

"How was your date last night?"

"Was that woman homeless?"

I ignored the questions, finding them utterly ridiculous. It was nothing new. My every move was under a microscope. They always asked me inane stuff about my personal life, from who I was dating to what I was wearing. The attention was obnoxious.

I pushed through the crowd, making sure I didn't use my actual hands. I didn't need a fucking lawsuit.

Been there, done that.

"Roman, what do you have to say about the allegations of workplace misconduct in your Paris office?"

"Are the profit margins on Kelly Industries legitimate or just clever accounting?"

The last question made me pause for a fraction of a second. That question was the main reason I was here today. The numbers coming out of that division were absurdly good—so good they'd started raising eyebrows. But I wasn't going to address their bullshit. Not until I got to the bottom of it myself.

"Roman! Roman!" one overeager reporter shouted, darting in front of me and stepping squarely on my shoe.

I stopped dead, glaring down at him. "You've got to be kidding me."

"Sorry—"

"No, you're not sorry. If you were sorry, you wouldn't be so desperate to shove a mic in my face that you'd trample over my Ferragamos. Move."

The man stammered an apology, backing away, but not before someone's phone captured the exchange.

I strode into the lobby of the tower, my blood simmering. Behind me, the crowd buzzed louder, no doubt already composing their dramatic headlines. Thankfully, security kept the vultures outside.

I noticed the people in the lobby looking my way. Some knew me, some didn't. Thankfully, they had a little more decorum and didn't try to ask me anything. They all minded their own damn business.

Why couldn't everyone do that?

I strode across the shiny floor, nodding once at the security guard. I hit the button for the elevator and made the mistake of looking toward the windows where the vultures were still circling. As soon as I stepped into the elevator, I looked down at my shoe.

A scuff. A dark mark on the pristine leather that would need more than a simple buffing to remove. My jaw tightened as I stared at it. The scratch wasn't just a scratch. It was a representation of the morning's aggravations. The reporters needed to recognize personal space. I had smelled more bad breath and B.O. from pushy reporters than I would smell in a crowded, seedy bar.

It was annoying. Nothing about my life was that interesting.

As the elevator doors slid shut, cutting off the muffled sounds of the reporters outside, I exhaled slowly, trying to release some of the tension that had built up. The ride up was silent, except for the soft hum of the elevator and the faint tapping of my foot. By the time I reached my floor, I had managed to compose myself somewhat.

The doors opened to reveal the sleek interior of Kelly Industries' headquarters. The moment I stepped out of the elevator, I felt the vibe change. The atmosphere was calm and professional, not chaotic like the world outside those glass doors. As I passed by the rows of cubicles, my employees nodded respectfully or offered a brief smile —simple acknowledgments of my presence without the invasive questions or frantic scrambling.

I made my way directly to my office at the end of the hall, a spacious room with a view of the city skyline that never failed to remind me why I had climbed to this height in the business world. The walls were adorned with awards and recognition plaques, each one marking a milestone on my climb to the top.

If my mom could see me now.

She'd probably say I was working too hard, or that the office could use a woman's touch—something about the lack of plants making it feel too sterile. She was always worried about me. As a preteen, I thought it was annoying. But damn, I would give all my billions for another week with her.

I dropped into the high-backed leather chair behind my desk. If I had an assistant, she, or he, would come running in to give me coffee and announce my schedule.

But I didn't have an assistant because they kept quitting. I really didn't understand what the problem was. I didn't think I was that big of an asshole. I liked things done a certain way and I liked them done right. If you got a job, why wouldn't you do what was asked?

My phone beeped, distracting me from my thoughts. I pulled it out to check the screen. It was a reminder for the meeting that started in ten minutes. Without an assistant, it was up to me to be on time. I set another reminder and quickly turned on my computer to check email and the latest reports.

It wasn't long before the reminder alarm started chiming again. It wasn't the worst thing to have to get myself to meetings on time. It was either my chiming phone or someone bugging me with reminders. The phone was looking better and better.

I stood and took another look out the window from the twenty-fifth floor. I adjusted my tie and strolled out of my office. I made my way to the conference room where everyone was already seated. I was still pissed and irritable. The room was full—executives and analysts seated around the sleek, glass-topped table, all of them flipping through quarterly financial reports. The conversation paused as I entered, but I didn't acknowledge it, grabbing the file in front of my chair and flipping through it before I sat down.

"If it sounds too good to be true," I muttered, scanning the report, "it probably is."

The room stayed silent for a beat too long, the tension palpable.

Finally, one of the senior analysts, a graying man named Frank, cleared his throat. "The numbers are... unusual. But the team assures us everything is above board."

"Uh huh." I didn't look up, still skimming the line items. "Tell the team I want a full breakdown by end of day. And if this is smoke and mirrors, I'll make sure whoever is blowing the smoke regrets it."

The meeting continued, discussions shifting to projections for the next quarter, potential new ventures, and a handful of minor mergers. But the air changed halfway through when one of the junior execs slid his phone across the table to the VP.

The VP frowned at the screen, then pushed it toward me.

"What now?" I snapped, taking the phone.

The screen showed a video clip of my exchange with the reporter outside. My voice—sharp and dripping with disdain—played on a loop. I looked like a real prick. Like a guy who hated the little people, even though it was mostly the asshole on my shoe I didn't like.

The VP leaned forward. "That's already on three major news outlets. We need to talk about your... approachability."

I laughed bitterly. "Approachability? I'm running multimillion-dollar businesses, not a daycare. I don't need to be approachable. If anything, I need to be less approachable. He stomped on my foot but they don't show that in their damn video."

"You're running the businesses now," Frank said carefully. "But, Roman, your reputation is starting to hurt your future ventures. Your legacy businesses will thrive—they're established, reliable. But nobody wants to take risks on new projects with—"

"With what?" I challenged, my eyes narrowing.

"An asshole," Frank said bluntly, his hands clasped on the table.

The room went still.

No one talked to me like that.

Except Frank.

I leaned back in my chair, staring him down. "Careful, Frank. You're on thin ice."

"I'm on reality," he replied evenly. "You're brilliant, Roman, but you're not relatable. People don't trust you. And if you don't fix that? This might be the peak of your career. From here, it'll be a slow regression. You are going to be harassed even further. They will get you to do more than just yell at them. You're going to snap in a way that can't be undone, and when that happens, you'll lose everything you've built. You will be sued into oblivion and canceled for good."

I was silent for a long moment, feeling every eye in the room on me. My usual response would be to fire back, defend myself, assert dominance. The words hit harder than I expected. I hated them—but I couldn't dismiss them outright.

My mind flashed back to my mother's gentle scoldings about my stubbornness. How she'd deal with me not by throwing my attitude back in my face, but by pointing out the truth with a soft but firm honesty.

"I'm a Kelly," I said, my voice like steel. "Kellys don't peak. We persevere."

"Then prove it," Frank said, leaning back.

I tapped the table, considering. "Fine. I want proposals—real, actionable solutions. No fluff. No motivational posters. By the end of the week."

The room nodded in agreement. I stood, buttoning my suit jacket. "Meeting adjourned."

I had no desire to sit in the office another minute. I didn't really need to be there. Any work I needed to do could be handled from my phone or laptop at home. I stopped by my office and collected a few things before strolling right back to the elevator.

I heard the whispers and knew the video was making its rounds. It wasn't the first time I had been the subject of a viral video, and I knew it wouldn't be the last. People loved to hate me. There wasn't a damn thing I could do about that. They were going to call me an asshole no matter what I did.

When the elevator opened, the usual hustle and bustle in the lobby quieted when I stepped out. Some people were looking at their phones. I heard my own voice telling the reporter not to shove his phone in my face. Fame could be the most isolating thing in the world. I ignored the looks and strolled toward the door. Outside, the mob of press seemed to have doubled in size. I stepped out and was greeted once again by the persistent shouting of questions.

"*Mr. Kelly, do you have anything to say about the viral video from this morning?*"

"*Will you be issuing a formal apology?*"

"*Do you have an official statement?*"

"*How much are those shoes?*"

I flashed my most dashing smile. "My official statement is you all smell like desperation."

The cameras clicked furiously as I climbed into my car, slamming the door behind me. I started the engine and revved it up. They were doing their best to lock me in, but they were just scared enough about what I might do and backed up.

I pulled away and hit the gas once I made it onto the street. I leaned back in my seat, loosening my tie. The board's words echoed in my mind: *Nobody wants to take risks with an asshole.*

Fine. I would clean up my act. Or at least, I'd find a way to make people think I had.

For now, though, I'd stick to what I knew. Which, apparently, was being the villain.

9

KAIRA

I got home, feeling incredibly guilty for being at home in the middle of the day. Carla was working two jobs, and I had none. Zero.

I was dead weight. Once again, I was unemployed. I didn't think I was a total failure, but I couldn't seem to find a job that worked well for me.

I changed into cleaning clothes. I was going to be the house bitch for at least a couple days. While my roomie worked, I was going to scrub the apartment from top to bottom. Maybe by then, I'll have figured out what I was going to do.

And I would make her a late dinner. She typically got off at nine or ten on the weeknights. I pulled my hair up and started with the fridge. I pulled out a few containers of Chinese food and gave them the sniff test.

"Good Lord." I nearly gagged. "Who ordered the poopoo platter?"

I kept cleaning and tossing stuff in the trash. By the time I finished, it looked like we were impoverished. I supposed we were.

Well, I was.

I continued my cleaning spree in the kitchen, even cleaning the dishwasher before I loaded it. The place was sparkling clean and ready to be cooked in. But it was still early. I busted out the Pledge and dusted the living room before vacuuming and mopping.

By the time I was done, I collapsed onto our couch, breathing heavily. The apartment smelled faintly of citrus and soap.

"Maybe I should become a housekeeper or something," I mumbled to myself, eyes resting on the spotless kitchen.

With a sigh, I pushed myself up from the couch and walked over to our small bookshelf. There were a handful of dusty cookbooks there that Carla and I kept promising each other we'd try cooking from one day. Maybe today was the day.

Pulling out a book titled *International Delights*, I started flipping through the pages, each one containing exotic dishes from all around the world. As I skimmed through, one dish caught my eye—Spanakopita, a Greek spinach and feta cheese pastry.

"Why not?" I murmured to myself. My pencil traced down the list of ingredients I'd need. Flour, feta cheese, spinach. Most of them already in our pantry or fridge.

I put on an apron and got to work. I thought about last night. How ridiculous was it that a single stupid sneeze cost me my job? Utter bullshit.

I could not say the night had been worth it, either. Hanging out with the insufferable Roman Kelly was not worth being jobless. If he would have let me go back and apologize and fix things, I would still have my job, crappy as it was.

But there was no going back, only forward. I chopped the spinach. Carla would appreciate this meal, I hoped. It was a small thing, cooking dinner, but it was better than just springing the bad news on her.

If life kept tossing me out of jobs because of absurd reasons or bad luck intersecting with bizarre circumstances, maybe I should stop relying on traditional jobs. Maybe I could do some kind of freelance stuff.

Carla texted and let me know she was heading home early and offered to pick up pizza. I quickly replied and told her I made dinner.

She stopped almost immediately when she walked through the door. She looked around and then at me.

"Wow," she said.

"I cleaned up."

"Is the pope coming over or something?"

"I had some time on my hands."

"Uh oh. That's the face of a woman who needs a glass of wine. What happened?"

"I got fired."

Her eyes widened. "No. Way. Those bastards!"

"It was my fault," I admitted. I grabbed the bottle of wine from the fridge and opened it.

"What did you do?" she asked.

"That whole auction bid thing—it wasn't a good look for the company. They said it jeopardized their reputation."

"Ugh, reputation-schmeputation. Did you explain what happened?"

"I tried, but they weren't hearing it. I had just started anyway."

"Did you get severance?" she joked.

"Nope. Just my last check." I laughed bitterly. "Guess that'll make a nice going-away card when I frame it next to my unemployment notice."

"Okay, okay. Let's figure this out. How much do you have in savings?"

"Less than three thousand."

"Rent's due in two weeks," she muttered, doing mental calculations. "Look, don't stress. I'll cover your share this month. You'll find something by then—I know you will."

Her confidence in me felt warm and reassuring, but it didn't fix the pit in my stomach. "I hate this," I said, tugging at my hair. "I hate feeling like I'm going to let you down. Or myself. I'm dragging you down. It's wrong. You shouldn't have to support me."

Carla smiled. "Kaira, stop. People fall in love with you the second they meet you. Employers are no different. You'll get a new gig, probably one that doesn't suck. You didn't even like that job!"

"That's not the point," I sighed. "Everyone needs money, and not everyone needs to like their job. Few people go to work because it's fun. Besides, the one thing I love doing isn't profitable."

"You don't have to tell me that," she said. She took a drink of her wine.

"I made dinner," I said. "Spanakopita"

"Did you just sneeze again?"

I grinned. "Just wait. It looked good. I just hope it tastes as good."

We dished up and chose to eat in front of the TV. After our meal, she stretched out. Her long legs flexed as she kicked one foot into the air, the delicate anklet on her ankle catching the light. Her job as a yoga instructor kept her nice and flexible.

"Maybe this is the universe's way of telling you to go for something you actually want. Like, I don't know... writing?"

I rolled my eyes. "Here we go."

"I'm serious! You've been talking about writing for years, Kaira. If you're not going to take a shot at it now, when will you?"

"Writing doesn't pay bills," I said, the words bitter on my tongue. "Do you know how hard it is to get a book in front of an agent? And then the agent has to get it in front of a publisher. But before any of that can happen, I have to actually write a book."

"You wouldn't know how hard it is. You've never tried." Carla's tone was gentle but firm, as it always was when she decided to nudge me toward a truth I didn't want to face. "You just write these stories in your head and claim you *want* to be a writer. One of these days, you've got to take a chance on something you care about."

"I care about being able to pay rent," I muttered, but her words sank deep. "I don't have time to write a book because I have to work a job that actually pays the bills."

"You will. I'll help you." She shrugged like it was the easiest thing in the world. "But come on—this is your chance. Don't waste it. Tomorrow morning, you get your ass up and start writing."

I didn't have a good response. "We'll see," I said. "I'm going to read. I'll see you in the morning."

I stood and retreated to my bedroom. Carla was right, as usual, but hearing it was exhausting. I felt like a loser. She saw something she wanted, and she went after it. She was fearless. Nothing held her back. I wanted to be like that.

I grabbed the book I'd been reading from my nightstand and curled up under the covers. It was a sweeping romance—the kind that made me laugh, cry, and wish I had half the talent it took to write something so good.

The story pulled me in, but my thoughts kept drifting back to Carla's advice. My old laptop sat on the desk in the corner, its scratched silver surface practically taunting me. *You wouldn't know. You've never tried.*

With a groan, I shoved my book aside and dragged the laptop onto my bed. It whirred to life, louder than I remembered, as I opened a blank document.

I stared at the blinking cursor for a full minute.

"This is stupid," I muttered. But my fingers hovered over the keys anyway.

I closed my eyes and let my mind drift to that story that had been percolating in the back of my mind for months. It was the story that haunted me when I was sleeping or when I was in the shower. It was like the characters were screaming at me to get it on the page.

And then, as if a dam had burst, the words started pouring out. My fingers started flying over the keyboard.

By the time I glanced at the clock again, it was three in the morning. My hands were stiff from typing, my shoulders ached, and my thighs were numb where the laptop had been sitting. But none of that mattered because for the first time in years, I felt *alive.*

The characters I'd carried around in my head for so long were finally on the page, breathing and living and falling in love. I couldn't stop. Every time I tried, a new scene or line of dialogue would pop into my head, demanding to be written.

It was the most exhilarating feeling I'd had in ages.

I knew I should go to bed, but there was a little voice in the back of my head telling me it wasn't like I had a job. I didn't have to wake up early. I could work all day and night.

I started typing once again. I didn't want to think about how many typos I was making. I would fix them later. I just needed to get the story down.

The next thing I knew, sunlight streamed through my curtains. There was a horrible kink in my neck. I yelped as a sharp, stinging heat flared across my thighs.

"Holy crap!" I scrambled to push the laptop off my lap, but the damage was done. The fan had gone into overdrive during the night, overheating the machine and leaving an angry red mark on my skin.

My chest tightened as I tried to turn it back on. Nothing.

"No, no, no," I whispered, pressing the power button frantically. The screen stayed dark.

I flipped it over, yanked out the battery, and tried again. Still nothing.

"No!" My voice cracked as I clutched the laptop to my chest. Hours of work—of *magic*—gone in an instant.

Carla burst into the room, her hair wild and her eyes wide. "What happened? Did someone break in?"

"My computer died!" I wailed.

She crossed the room and plucked the laptop from my arms, inspecting it like a doctor diagnosing a patient. "Did you overheat it?"

I nodded miserably.

"Well, shit." She set it down and turned to me. "Is everything backed up?"

I shook my head.

"Kaira!"

"I didn't think I'd need to! It was my first time writing in a while."

Carla groaned, running a hand through her hair. "Okay. First of all, don't panic. Second, this is why we use Google Docs, babe."

My hands clenched the sheets, tears burning at the edges of my eyes.

"Kaira, hey." She crouched in front of me, her hands on my knees. "It's okay. You're okay. We'll figure this out."

"I can't believe I did this," I whispered. "It was finally happening, Carla. I felt like... like I found something real. And now it's gone."

She pulled me into a hug, stroking my back. "Listen to me. You wrote it once, and you'll write it again. You've got this. Okay?"

I nodded, but the sting of losing something I'd poured my heart into was unbearable.

For the first time in a long time, I'd let myself dream. Now I had to figure out if I could find the courage to start over.

The story was gone. There was no way I could write it the way I did the first time.

10

ROMAN

The end of the week came fast, but not fast enough for my liking. The stupid video of me scolding the so-called reporter had blown up even more.

Of course.

People were posting pictures of my shoes, suits, my car, everything. They were splashing my private life all over the internet, picking apart every detail as if I were a character in a movie rather than a real person with real feelings.

I saw one video with dollar signs on everything I was wearing along with my Starbucks cup of coffee. It was supposed to be shaming me for being wealthy. I didn't know why it mattered. Yes, I was rich. Big fucking deal. I liked nice things. I could afford it.

And Starbucks wasn't even fancy.

I knew they were trying to prove a point. I didn't need to get pissed the asshole stepped on my two-thousand-dollar shoes because I could buy more.

I sank into the leather chair in my office. I had another board meeting shortly. I wasn't looking forward to what they had to say. I didn't feel like I owed them an explanation about my personal life, but they sure as hell expected one. It wasn't any of their damn business.

But that wasn't going to stop them from giving me their two cents. With the way the ridiculous story blew up the last few days, I had a feeling they were going to have lots of opinions.

There was a knock on my door. I didn't say anything.

The door opened. "Mr. Kelly?"

I sighed and looked toward the door. "Yes?"

My new temporary assistant was standing there. She started yesterday and I already knew she wasn't going to last longer than a week.

She hesitated, fiddling with the edge of a file folder she held tightly against her chest. "The board members are starting to gather in the conference room. They've asked if you could join them a bit earlier today."

"Did they bring doughnuts or something?"

Her eyes widened and she shook her head. "I don't know, sir. I can ask."

"No, that's alright." I leaned back in my chair and pinched the bridge of my nose. "Tell them I'll be there in five minutes."

"Sure thing, Mr. Kelly." She nodded quickly and almost stumbled as she hurried out, closing the door quietly behind her.

It wasn't that she was a bad assistant, but she was too timid. I knew it was only a matter of time before she declared I was impossible to work for. I would inevitably hurt her feelings with my gruff demeanor. It was the same thing every time.

By the time I walked into the boardroom, I was already irritated. I probably woke up that way if I was being honest. The sun blazed in through the massive windows, reflecting off the polished table where the board sat waiting, their stiff expressions a reminder of how much they loved playing the role of moral compass for Roman Kelly, the man they swore up and down was too much of an asshole for his own good.

"Let's get this over with," I said, taking my seat at the head of the table. The air felt too formal, too expectant. It made my skin crawl.

My eyes drifted to the windows. I wanted to be out there, away from everyone's opinions.

Charles, one of the senior members of the board and a guy who rarely spoke unless he had something important to say, leaned forward. "We've put together a few strategies for addressing your public image concerns."

I gave him a flat look. "My *public image concerns* aren't my top priority, Charles. The financials for three of our newer ventures are. But sure, let's hear how you think I can stop the media from painting me as a villain. Maybe you are all in the wrong line of work. You should be working for a PR company. There are plenty of celebrities that could benefit from your expertise."

Charles was unfazed by my sarcasm, arranging his glasses on the bridge of his nose and referring to his notes. "Well, Roman, whether you prioritize it or not, your image directly impacts our company's reputation and, by extension, its financial health. It's all interconnected."

I turned to look at my VP. "Are you involved in this image repair?"

"I've made some suggestions," he said.

I leaned back, not bothering to hide my disdain for the whole process. I folded my hands behind my head. "Let's have it."

They proceeded to pitch their ideas one by one.

First up was a suggestion to "shmooze the public." I shot that one down before they could even finish.

"I'm not kissing babies at grocery stores or showing up to weddings uninvited like some Hallmark movie character," I said. "What else?"

The second idea involved some kind of charity tour. A detailed map of events I would attend, complete with photo ops and press releases about how much money I had personally donated.

"No," I snapped. "I already donate to charity. I just don't use it as a marketing stunt. I may be an asshole, but even I know better than to brag about my charity. Isn't there a proverb or something about being humble?"

"But there are plenty of ways you can show your charitable side without getting into all the details."

I shook my head. "Not happening. I'm not exploiting the charities or the work they do. Next."

A younger board member looked like he had something to say but was too terrified to speak.

"Just spit it out," I said. "I don't think your idea could be any worse than what I've already heard."

He cleared his throat. "I would suggest you try to be 'warmer' to the media."

I laughed. "Let me get this straight: you want me to roll out a welcome mat for the same people who stand outside my building at six in the morning and shove cameras in my face? The same people who've gone out of their way to smear my name this week. What have they done for me? Nothing. They've done nothing but made my life hell. Pass."

The silence that followed was heavy. The board members exchanged desperate glances, like a pack of deer realizing their last path to safety was blocked. They could all give me their opinions but each of them knew I was the one that made the final decisions. I was Roman Kelly. I was the company. I could take my toys and go home. I'd still be rich. No skin off my nose.

And then they all looked at Mary.

Mary had been on my board longer than almost anyone. A shrewd, silver-haired woman who didn't mince words. She was the type who could politely tear you apart in a way that made you thank her for it. I respected her. She was one of the few people I did respect in this world.

She was their secret weapon.

She cleared her throat. "Roman, there's one option we haven't discussed yet. It's unconventional, but it could be the answer to your image problem. It would solve many of your issues, not just the personality."

I arched a brow. "Oh, this should be good."

It was just a little insulting to have all these people pointing out my flaws like I was damaged goods. If I was an insecure man, I might have taken offense. But as it was, I could only be intrigued by what Mary thought could polish my tarnished reputation with a single stroke.

"You need to settle down," she said simply.

The room went dead silent.

"Settle down?" I repeated, leaning back in my chair. "Mary, I'm not a child acting up. What exactly do you mean *settle down*? Because I know you aren't suggesting I behave myself."

"Actually, yes," Mary said. "That is what I'm suggesting. You need to settle down and act like a grown man. Do what grown men do."

"Like, buy a house in the suburbs and get a dog?" I scoffed.

"No, Roman." I saw the stern look. It was like getting reprimanded by my grandmother. "You need to find a woman. Someone grounded, approachable, kind. Someone who can balance you out."

I laughed, a deep, genuine laugh that echoed off the walls. "You've got to be kidding me."

But when I looked around, I realized she wasn't. None of them were. Their expressions were somber, like they were talking about the details of a funeral.

"You're serious?" I asked, incredulous.

"As a heart attack," Mary said. "Your public persona is abrasive, Roman. People see you as detached, selfish, and cold. Having a partner—a real, steady relationship—would soften your image considerably. It would show the public a different side of you."

"And help rebuild trust with potential investors," Charles added.

"You're insane," I said. "You think a woman's going to magically fix all of that?"

"She won't fix it," Mary said. "But she'll make you look more relatable. More human. Soften all of your hard edges. Women tend to do that."

I stared at her, shaking my head, but the longer I sat there, the more her words started to make sense. As much as I hated to admit it, she was on to something.

An idea began forming in the back of my mind.

I thought about Kaira—the woman who'd bid on me at the auction. Or, more accurately, sneezed. She was a little spitfire, that one. I could still see the flash of anger in her eyes when she'd called me out for being rude to the server. She wasn't someone who would roll over just because of my name.

She was grounded, approachable, kind. She was also a sympathetic person. She wasn't some rich snob. People would see me with someone like her and think I wasn't a pompous prick. I could be normal.

But it wasn't like I knew how to find Kaira. And she despised me. I didn't see her willingly agreeing to be my wife—real or otherwise.

But she owed me.

"How are we going to find someone like that?" I heard one of them ask.

"She exists," I said out loud, more to myself than to the room.

"What?" Mary asked.

"The woman you're describing. I know someone who fits the bill. I know the woman that would soften my image, as you say."

They looked intrigued but skeptical.

"She's not a professional, is she?" Charles said.

I smirked. "No. She's perfect. Sweet, normal, and, most importantly, she's got the guts to call me out when I need it."

"And she's willing to play along with this?" Mary asked.

"She will be," I said.

"That sounds ominous," one of the younger members muttered.

"I'll have her here for your consideration on Monday. I just need to talk to her first."

Mary chuckled. "Roman, we don't need to approve your choice of partner. This isn't an arranged marriage."

"I think it is a good idea we meet her," Charles said. Mary frowned, but the two of them exchanged a look. "Just to be safe."

I nodded, the gears in my mind spinning. "Fine. Let's make it official then. I'll bring Kaira here on Monday, and you can see for yourselves how well she balances me out."

That seemed to make everyone happy. There were nods all around.

"Then it's settled," I said. "I'm off to bag me a woman."

When I left the meeting, my mood was split between smugness and irritation. Smug because I had a plan. Irritated because it meant dealing with the media circus outside.

Again.

The second I stepped out of the elevator and into the lobby, I could feel the tension. Just beyond the doors was the waiting feeding frenzy. I could go out the back, but I wasn't one to shy away. I wasn't about to let them send me running into the shadows.

I pushed open the doors and stepped into the LA sunshine. The buzz of cameras and voices met me. By the time I reached my car, they were swarming.

"Mr. Kelly, have you attacked anyone else today?"

"Roman, how much is too much for a pair of shoes?"

"Is it true your steroid use is making you rage?"

"Do you have a love child with Miley Cyrus?"

I stopped by the car door, fixing them with my most dazzling smile. "I'd love to stand here and chat, but I've got places to be. Stay tuned for Monday, though. I have an announcement to make. You're *warmly* invited to cover it."

The flash of cameras lit up like fireworks as I climbed into the car.

By Monday, I would need to convince Kaira to play her part. And if she said no?

Well, she owed me one. She'd have to say yes.

11

KAIRA

Job hunting sucked.

By the end of the week, I had sent out more resumes than I could count, each one tailored to perfection, and I hadn't gotten more than a single, half-hearted callback. I knew what that meant. It was the equivalent of patting me on the head like a good dog.

Now, it was late and most people were enjoying their Friday night with friends or out on dates. I was at home alone searching for a job.

My old contacts—the people I thought might at least toss me a bone—either ghosted me or politely reminded me they weren't hiring. No one was willing to vouch for me. It stung more than I wanted to admit.

Carla kept telling me something would work out. "You're too good not to get snatched up," she said over coffee that morning, her confidence in me like a lifeline. But the truth? My bank account was shrinking, rent was looming, and my stomach was tying itself into tighter knots with every passing day.

I sat cross-legged on our couch, with Carla's laptop balanced precariously on a cushion, scrolling through another job board.

I had all this time to write, and I couldn't because I fried my laptop, and I couldn't afford to buy a new one. Carla insisted I could use hers, but I wasn't about to break hers too. I couldn't afford to buy her a new one. With an uncanny knack to break shit without trying, it was dangerous for me to even use the laptop to job hunt.

I saw a job listing for a housekeeper at a local hotel. That was a job I was qualified for. I was about to click on the link to fill out the application when the apartment buzzer startled me out of my focus.

Frowning, I got up and pressed the intercom button. "Hello?"

"Ms. Foster, I'm here to pick you up," a man's voice said, calm and professional.

I laughed. "Are you sure? I'm kind of heavy."

There was a pause. "Um, ma'am, I'm your driver."

"Yeah, sure you are."

"Miss, my boss all but insists I bring you back."

"Who's your boss?"

"Mr. Roman Kelly," he replied.

The name hit me like a punch to the gut. I clutched the wall for support, my heart racing. "Go away," I said, my voice sharp.

The man sighed. "Ms. Foster, Mr. Kelly asked me to bring you to him. I'll leave if you want me to but he has an offer for you—one that could change your life. Please come with me. If it helps, I drove you around the other night. Watched you two have awkward pie in that diner."

It did help. The man wasn't a total stranger at least. But that wasn't the part I was focusing on.

"Change my life?" I repeated, narrowing my eyes. "By making me another notch on his bedpost? No thanks. Kindly tell Roman to choke on his own ego."

"I'll probably leave that part out," he said. "But come with me and you can tell him whatever you want. If you don't like what he has to say, I'll bring you right back. No questions asked. You have my word on that."

I hesitated, chewing my bottom lip. I hated Roman Kelly. At first, he'd been sort of charming and fun but he turned out to be arrogant and entirely too pleased with himself. The man was like a perfect chocolate chip cookie but then you take a bite and it's raisins. Tragic.

But the mention of an "offer" gnawed at me, especially in my current, less-than-stable state. If there was a job on the table, I wanted it.

"Fine," I snapped. "Give me a minute. You could have called first."

I threw on a sweater and my comfiest pair of sneakers—no way was I dressing up for this—and headed down to the car. The driver held the door open for me like I was Roman.

"That's not necessary," I said.

"Manners are always necessary," he replied with a polite smile. "And I'm going to stand here until you get in."

I didn't want to be mean to him. He did nothing wrong. He was only doing what his boss asked him to do. "Right, fine. Let's not keep Roman waiting. God forbid."

His smile was more real this time and he quickly smothered it. I hopped in and leaned my head back against the seat. This offer better involve a way to pay my rent. Knowing my luck, he wanted me to work off the hundred grand for the bid. He would probably have me scrubbing floors or cleaning his precious shoes.

Of course I had seen the video making the rounds online. And I was not surprised in the least. That was the Roman Kelly I had the misfortune of meeting.

"So where are we going?" I asked. We were stuck on the highway, and I was impatient.

"We're about ten minutes away," he said.

He sounded unfazed by my frustration. That wasn't a surprise. He worked for Roman who was always grumpy. At least from what I had witnessed. I watched the changing scenery out the window. We were off the highway and moving into the suburbs.

Suburbs.

No.

These were mansions. This was the Pacific Palisades area. I knew of it because one of my many temp jobs had been working for a caterer. I had been a server at some swanky house party. Soon, the driver pulled up to a gate and used a clicker to open it.

The estate was ridiculous.

As we drove up the palm-lined driveway, I gawked at the sprawling property. It had everything—pools, ponds, perfectly trimmed hedges and a fountain. The house itself looked more like a luxury hotel than a home.

The white two-story house was huge. There were columns lining the front entrance. Large windows with sheer curtains blurred the view but I could see the soft glow of lights from the many rooms. Perfectly manicured gardens surrounded the property.

As we stopped in front of the grand entrance, the driver exited and opened my door. "We're here, Ms. Foster."

I stepped out, taking in the magnificence of the place. No wonder Roman Kelly strutted around like he owned the world—he practically did, or at least this little corner of it.

The driver escorted me as far as the front door, where an attendant greeted me with a smile and offered me slippers in exchange for my shoes. Slippers. Was I going to be given a housecoat as well? Was he putting me to bed?

I followed her through grand hallways and cavernous rooms until we reached a solarium at the back of the house. It was humid but cozy, the kind of space designed to make you feel like you were lounging in a tropical paradise without ever leaving LA. Lush green plants filled the room. Vines and flowers spilled over the edges of large pots, adding bursts of color.

I had never been to a tropical rainforest, but I had a feeling this would be how it smelled. The air was humid and heavy with the scents of moist earth, damp leaves, and floral blooms. It was sweet and musky. I had never seen anything like it.

I was about to sit in one of the chairs at a bistro-style table when I noticed a gardener in the corner, awkwardly pretending he wasn't there. He left in a hurry when a woman wheeled in a tray of liqueurs, set it up neatly, and disappeared without a word.

I was alone. The only thing missing was the sound of tropical birds or crickets. Anything. It was just silence.

Then he walked in.

Roman looked infuriatingly relaxed, his slacks hanging perfectly on his hips, his Henley rolled up to reveal strong, corded forearms. I hated that I noticed, but it was impossible not to. I thought about the picture Carla had shown me. The one with the abs. I had a feeling it was very accurate. He moved to the tray of liquor, fixing two drinks without saying a word.

"Glad you came," he said, handing me a glass.

"I didn't have much of a choice," I muttered and took a sip. It was good. Annoyingly good. "I was afraid you would fire your poor driver if he didn't do your bidding."

"No, I'd just dock his pay."

My mouth dropped open. "You're horrible."

Roman sat across from me, ignoring my comment. "I need you to hear me out before you say no."

"When you put it that way, I feel like I should walk away right now."

"If you don't like my offer, you're free to walk away."

"Fine." I crossed my arms. "Let's hear it."

He leaned back, his expression calm but calculating. "Here's the deal. My board thinks I need to clean up my image. They've pitched every ridiculous idea under the sun—charity tours, media schmoozing, the works. But one idea stuck. I need a fiancée."

My jaw dropped. "What?"

"You heard me," he said, his tone maddeningly casual. "A fiancée. Someone normal. Someone who can balance out my reputation and make me look a little more... human. A man of the people."

I stared at him, waiting for the punchline.

"I've chosen you," he continued, like it was the most logical thing in the world. "You owe me a favor. And we already have a backstory—our public date at the auction. We'll claim we've been seeing each other for a while and that you bid on me as part of some romantic gesture."

"You're insane," I said, putting my drink down with a loud clink.

"You haven't heard the terms yet." His smirk was infuriating.

"Yeah, everything kind of blanked out after the word *fiancée*."

"For six months, you'll live with me, attend events with me, and convince the world we're in love. In return, you'll have access to my lifestyle—money, connections, whatever you need to get back on your feet. I'll pay you a hundred thousand dollars at the end of the arrangement. After six months, we'll go our separate ways. Done and dusted."

I blinked at him, dumbfounded. "There's no way. Absolutely not."

"You don't need the money?" he asked bluntly.

In the back of my mind, there was a little voice pushing me toward him. *You're jobless, your contacts have dropped you, and you're one missed rent payment away from losing your apartment. This could solve all of that.*

The audacity of this man. He didn't even try to soften the blow.

"There are expectations," he added. "You'll need to move in with me, attend social functions, and convince people you actually like me." His smirk deepened. "Perhaps the most difficult part."

"You think this is funny?" I snapped. "This is my life you're talking about. Six months of it."

"And this is my business," he said, his tone serious now. "I need you as much as you need me."

I opened my mouth to argue, but the words wouldn't come. "Why me?" I asked finally.

"Because you're perfect for this," he said simply. "You're kind, grounded, and real. You stood up to me in a way no one else has in years. People will believe it."

I leaned back in my chair, my mind racing. This was insane. Completely, utterly insane.

"What's in it for you?" I asked, narrowing my eyes.

"A clean slate," he said. "A chance to rebuild my image and secure my future. We both get what we want."

I hated that his logic made sense. I hated that I was even considering it. But most of all, I hated that he was right—I didn't have any other options at the moment.

"Six months," I said, my voice shaky.

His smirk faded. "That's all I'm asking."

I exhaled slowly, the weight of my decision settling on my shoulders. "Fine. I'll do it."

Roman raised his glass, a glint of triumph in his eyes. "Here's to a mutually beneficial arrangement."

I clinked my glass against his, my stomach churning with nerves.

Had I just found my salvation or had I made a deal with the devil?

12

ROMAN

Victory tasted as sweet as the bourbon I swirled in my glass. She agreed. I knew she would, of course—I always won. Still, watching Kaira wrestle with her decision and finally come to the inevitable conclusion had been entertaining. I leaned back in my chair, letting her simmer in the quiet for a moment.

"Excellent," I said smoothly. "You've made the right choice."

"That is yet to be determined," she muttered.

"Here's what happens next. You'll meet my board on Monday morning. They'll want to put a face to the arrangement and finalize the terms. We'll have a contract drawn up, which we'll both sign. You'll receive your payment when the contract is fulfilled."

She nodded cautiously, like she was bracing for impact.

"In the meantime, I'll cover all your expenses. Rent, bills, living costs—anything you need. Just send me an invoice."

Her brows shot up. "An invoice? For my rent and bills? My... living expenses?"

"Everything," I confirmed. "Down to your birth control costs."

Her cheeks flushed so deeply I thought she might combust. It was hard to tell if she was embarrassed, offended, or both. She opened her mouth, probably to yell at me, but shut it again. Instead, she crossed her arms and looked at me like I was an alien.

"I have a roommate," she said. "I can't leave her high and dry."

"I said I will pay your expenses. I'll cover your half of the rent and bills and what not."

Kaira gave me a long, measured look. "Why are you doing this? Why go to such lengths?"

I swirled the bourbon in my glass again, watching the liquid catch the light. Honesty wasn't always my first choice, but perhaps with Kaira, it would be a different kind of weapon.

"There's more at stake than just my reputation," I confessed. "Business deals, potential partnerships—my future—it's all on the line. You being by my side, convincing the board and investors that I'm a stable, committed man changes the narrative."

Kaira's eyes narrowed slightly. "You're using me to secure your empire."

"I prefer to think of it as mutual assistance," I countered smoothly. "You help me stabilize my image; I pull you out of financial quicksand. We both emerge stronger."

She studied her hands for a long moment. Then, looking up, she said, "And what happens when this contract ends? When these six months are over?"

"You go your way, and I go mine. Period."

"Why me?" she asked again. "Why not one of the women that fawn all over you?"

I smirked slightly at the question, setting the glass down with a soft clink. "Fawning women are too easy to read, too predictable. They enter the room, and everyone knows what they're after. But you? You challenge me. You keep them guessing, and that's exactly what I need right now. My board will not approve of a woman that's been out there and is known. Not that they need to approve, but they would have an issue with someone that would not be taken seriously by the public."

"And I will?"

"Yes. We'll make sure they do."

She sighed. "So, I'm just a strategy to you?"

"Isn't that what I am to you?" I shot back gently. "This is nothing more than a business deal."

Kaira bit her lip, clearly contemplating her next move. "And if I decide, at any point, that this isn't what I want—what then? Can I just walk away?"

I leaned forward, elbows on the table, fixing her with a steady gaze. "There will be stipulations in the contract for both of our protections. But yes, you can walk away. However," I paused, letting the weight of my next words sink in, "breaking a contract comes with penalties. They're designed to discourage either party from backing out prematurely."

She was silent, her mind clearly racing through the implications. Finally, she looked up and met my eyes, her expression resolute but wary.

"Okay," Kaira said slowly. "I'll do it. But I want something in writing that details every aspect of this arrangement—what you'll cover, the penalties, everything. And I want my lawyer to look over it before I sign anything."

"Of course," I replied. "You'll have your contract by tomorrow morning. Your lawyer can go through it with a fine-tooth comb."

We both knew she didn't have a lawyer, nor could she afford one. But I would let her pretend she did. She downed her bourbon, surprising me just a little. She didn't even flinch.

"Can I leave now?" she asked flatly.

I smirked. "I was going to give you a tour first. You'll be moving in Monday night."

"Monday?" she yelped, her eyes wide. "That's only three days away! I can't do that! I have... I have..."

I waited for her to finish her sentence. "Yes?"

"Well, I have nothing scheduled but why so soon?"

"This has to move quickly," I explained. "Monday is final—so long as the board approves, of course." I rose to my feet and gestured for her to follow. "Come on. Walk with me."

The solarium transitioned seamlessly into the indoor pool area.

Warm light glimmered off the water's surface. I pressed a button on the wall, and a partition slid open, revealing the outdoor pool beyond.

"You can swim inside or outside, depending on your mood," I said casually. "The outdoor section is heated year-round and big enough for laps. And I have rafts and stuff if you just want to float around."

She took it all in, her arms wrapped tightly around herself like she was trying to keep from reaching out and touching the ridiculous luxury. My place was a lot. I knew that. But what was the point of being filthy rich if you didn't treat yourself?

"Next, the spa." I led her through a side door, where sleek massage tables and treatment rooms awaited. "The staff is on speed dial. You can book any service you like while you're here. There's a sauna and a hot tub and literally the softest towels you'll ever use."

Her narrow-eyed expression didn't change but I noticed her eyes linger on the cozy treatment chairs.

"And here's the gym," I said as we stepped into a state-of-the-art facility. "Top of the line equipment. Plus, I have access to trainers and nutritionists who the celebrities go to." I grinned and gave her a playful smack on the ass. "Though I'd rather you not spend too much time in here, to be honest."

She yelped, whirling around to swat my hand away. "How dare you!"

"What?" I held up my hands in mock innocence. "You're my fiancée."

Her eyes narrowed to slits. "That doesn't give you the right to touch me. Just because there's a contract doesn't mean—"

"I apologize," I interrupted, still grinning. "You're right. But for the record, your curves are something else. It'd be a shame to lose them. In fact, I might just lock this room. I don't ever want you in here."

Her lips parted like she wanted to argue, but she clamped them shut, her cheeks tinged pink. "I do exercise. Trust me, my curves are more stubborn than you are. They aren't going anywhere."

"Good."

I took her through the kitchen, with its gleaming marble counters and a fridge that could feed a small army, then through the dining room and dining hall.

"This is absurd," she muttered.

"Thank you," I shot back. "That's sort of the point."

Smirking, I led her into the ballroom.

"Of course there's a ballroom," she said, throwing her hands up. "You throw a lot of balls, Roman? You a big ball man?"

I chuckled. "Not so much, but my parents used to throw lavish parties here," I explained, glancing at the polished dance floor. "It's mostly unused now, but who knows? Maybe we'll host something while you're living here."

"Don't hold any balls on my account," she said with a glimmer of amusement in her eyes.

"Noted," I said, wondering if she was warming up a little.

Finally, we reached the staircase that spiraled up to the second floor. Before we ascended, she stopped, her gaze locking onto a pair of double doors on the other side of the foyer.

"What's in there?" she asked.

Curious. I liked that. "Some would call this the crown jewel of the entire estate."

I pushed the doors open, revealing my library. The room was a masterpiece—floor-to-ceiling shelves lined with books of every kind, rolling ladders to reach the higher levels, and a massive window that overlooked the grounds. The window was covered with a protective film to keep from damaging the book covers. Some were hundreds of years old.

The library was filled with dark wood and leather furniture that looked soft as a cloud, a perfect spot to relax and get lost in the pages of a book. There was a fireplace in one corner, with more padded chairs surrounding it. The smell of old books was something I'd always appreciated. It was warm, inviting, and utterly breathtaking.

Kaira stepped inside like she was in a trance. "This is heaven."

"Well, it's yours to access anytime you like," I said. "While you're living here."

She didn't say anything, but the way her fingers brushed over the spines of the books spoke volumes. Finally, something had caught her interest. She pulled out a tattered copy of "Wuthering Heights" and traced the embossed title with her fingertip. "How did you get this many books?"

"Some were my father's," I explained, watching how the dim light played over her face, softening her initial displeasure into something more like wonder. "Others, I added over the years."

Kaira turned to face me, her earlier defensiveness fading into the background. "You must love reading a lot."

"I do." I stepped closer, pointing to a section of the shelves painted in a slightly darker shade. "That's my favorite area. It's filled with first editions and rare manuscripts. Feel free to explore them, just handle with care. They're irreplaceable."

Her eyes widened as she stepped toward the section, gently pulling out a leather-bound volume. "I've never seen so many first editions in one place," she whispered, almost to herself.

I chuckled softly. "I suppose it's just one of those passions that's easy to feed when you have the means."

"I don't even want to think about how much value is in this room," she murmured.

"Shall we move on?" I said. "You'll have plenty of time to explore the collection."

She nodded and gave one last longing look at the room. I closed the doors and led her back to the staircase. We climbed up to the next floor and turned down the wide hall toward the room she would be occupying. Her suite was the last stop. It was one of the finest rooms in the house—a private retreat with massive windows, a fireplace surrounded by plush sofas, and a walk-in closet bigger than most apartments.

"You'll have your own bathroom and a coffee bar," I said as she stepped inside, her wide eyes taking it all in. "I'll have the closet stocked with clothes. You'll need to look the part of my fiancée."

She turned to me, her arms crossed again. "And what exactly does that mean? You're going to dress me up like a little doll?"

"It means elegant," I said, leaning against the doorframe. "Classy. Confident."

"Expensive," she added, rolling her eyes.

"That too. But you'll have plenty of options and you can tell me if you want anything in particular."

She walked to the window, looking out at the grounds, then back at me.

"Will this do?" I asked, spreading my arms.

She hesitated for a moment, then nodded slowly. "It'll do."

Victory. Again.

13

KAIRA

The weight of the week hit me all at once, like a dam breaking. Roman stood before me in the most beautiful room I had ever seen, asking if it would *do* for the next six months—as though I were somehow making a compromise by staying here.

Did he have any idea what my tiny bedroom back home looked like? How often Carla and I ate ramen noodles dressed up because we paid rent and bills and had little money left for food? But no, he didn't have any idea.

He had grown up rich and he'd made a solid fortune of his own in the past decade. He'd never had to check his account balance before buying groceries, not that he did any of his own shopping. It was such a different life than the one I knew.

We lived in the same world, the same country, the same city, but he was a god while I was an ant just trying not to get stepped on.

I nodded mutely, unable to force words past the tightness in my throat. I wouldn't cry in front of him. I *couldn't*. Not in front of a man who would never understand going to bed hungry. No, I was going to keep myself composed, though my head swam with the opulence around me.

He must have sensed my mood shift because he took a step closer, frowning slightly. "What's wrong?" he asked, his voice softer than I'd expected. "Did I say the wrong thing?"

I shook my head quickly, my jaw clenched against the emotion threatening to spill over.

His frown deepened. "Can I get you something? Sparkling water?"

I shook my head again, looking away. I was going to turn into a blubbering mess at any second.

Then, suddenly, his hand was on my shoulder. The contact immediately had my attention. I was no longer thinking about crying. It was like getting zapped by electricity. His thumb tipped my chin up gently, forcing me to meet his gaze. His hazel eyes locked onto mine, disarming me completely.

"Tell me what you need, Kaira," he said, his voice low and intimate.

That was all it took for a tear to escape. I cursed myself silently, but before I could pull away, he caught it with his thumb, brushing it away with a tenderness I didn't think he possessed.

I turned my face, trying to put distance between us, but his hand remained steady. Instead of letting me retreat, he stepped closer, and before I realized what was happening, his arms wrapped around me in a steadying embrace.

At first, I was too shocked to react. But then the exhaustion, frustration, and relief of the past few days broke through my defenses. I sank into his arms, resting my head against his chest. His cologne was warm and woodsy, comforting in a way I hadn't expected. I felt the tension in my body start to unravel, even as tears soaked his expensive shirt.

"I'm sorry," I muttered, my voice muffled. "I'm being such a baby. I just, well, I guess I really needed life to give me a break, and it finally did."

He held me. "Sounds like we found each other at the right time."

"Thank you," I said softly.

His hand moved up my back, a slow, soothing motion that sent a rush of heat through me. My breath hitched and I tilted my head back to look at him. His eyes searched mine, something softer and more vulnerable than I'd ever seen flickering there. I had to look at him to make sure it was really him offering such comfort. The man I was convinced was nothing but solid ice under the hard body was acting human.

Maybe he had some chocolate chips in him after all.

My heart pounded. My body felt too warm, too aware of the man standing so close. His gaze flicked to my lips.

What was he doing?

"Roman…" I whispered, unsure if it was a warning or a plea.

And then he kissed me.

His lips were warm and firm, his touch commanding yet careful. I melted into him, my body responding instinctively as his arms tightened around me, pulling me closer. A part of me screamed that this was a terrible idea, but I couldn't stop. His kiss ignited something deep and primal inside me, something I hadn't felt in years.

This can't be happening.

I let myself fall into the sensation for a moment longer before reality crashed back down. What was I doing? I couldn't let myself get carried away by *him* of all people.

I pulled back abruptly, pressing my fingers to my tingling lips. "I… I have to go," I stammered.

"Kaira—"

"I *have* to go," I repeated, stepping away before he could stop me.

I turned and fled. My footsteps echoed through the massive house as I passed the library without sparing it a second glance. My heart raced for an entirely different reason now.

Roman's driver was waiting by the sleek black car and he opened the door for me without a word. I climbed in, slamming the door harder than I meant to.

As we pulled away from the estate, I leaned back against the seat and let out a shaky breath. My lips still tingled from the kiss, and my chest felt tight with a mix of anger, confusion, and something I didn't want to name.

"You're quiet," the driver said, glancing at me in the rearview mirror.

I crossed my arms. "Just processing."

"Are you okay?"

I heard the concern. This guy worked for Roman and was probably used to women running out of his boss's house in tears.

"I'm fine. I just... I don't know."

"Did you accept the offer?" he asked.

"I accepted," I said. Saying it to someone else made it real.

He chuckled softly. "It'll be nice to have someone new around for the next six months. Driving Mr. Kelly around can get... interesting."

I snorted. "Interesting? Or infuriating?"

The driver's eyes twinkled with amusement in the mirror. "A little of both."

"Yeah, he can be a total asshat," I said before I could stop myself.

The driver burst out laughing. "On some days."

I smiled faintly despite myself. "How do you put up with him?"

He shrugged. "I understand him, I guess. He's lost a lot."

That made me pause. "Lost? He has more than anyone I've ever met."

"From the outside looking in, sure," he said, meeting my gaze briefly in the mirror.

I frowned, filing that away for later. There was clearly more to Roman Kelly than met the eye, but I wasn't sure I wanted to unravel that particular mystery. This was a temporary business arrangement. No sense in getting my feelings tangled up in it. Better for Roman to remain a locked puzzle box.

For now, I needed someone to talk to. Carla was at work, so I asked the driver to take me there. I didn't want to go home and spin out thinking about what I had just agreed to. I needed Carla to tell me I wasn't crazy. Or that I was crazy and needed to tell him hell no, it was never going to happen.

"Of course," the driver said.

He flipped the turn signal and maneuvered through the traffic. My mind was a whirl of emotions—frustration, longing, fear, excitement—all tangled together like a messy ball of yarn. Part of me was still thinking I was caught in some wild dream and I was going to wake up at any second. This was not the kind of thing that happened to people like me.

"I'm Anthony, by the way," he said. "I'm sure we'll be spending some time together."

"It's nice to meet you, Anthony. I hope you'll call me Kaira."

"Of course."

When he pulled to a stop at the bar, I thanked him and hurried out, not giving him a chance to open the door for me this time. The bar's familiar noise greeted me. It wasn't exactly swanky. It was all very casual with blue-collar people hanging out. The music was just loud enough to drown out the noise, but not too loud that you couldn't have a conversation.

I found Carla behind the bar chatting with a couple of other people. When she saw me, she looked at me with surprise. "What are you doing here?"

"I needed to talk to you."

"Is everything okay?" she asked.

"I don't know."

"That sounds like a no. What happened?"

I slid onto a stool and slumped over the bar. "I'll tell you if you get me a soda."

She smiled. "Going right for the hard stuff?"

"I need caffeine but no booze. My brain is fried enough as it is."

She poured me a Coke with extra ice and set it in front of me, leaning on the bar with an expectant expression. "Spill. What fried your brain? Not meth, right?"

I barked out a laugh. "No, Carla, I didn't do meth for the first time today. I'm not breaking bad."

I told her everything—about the ridiculous proposal, the stunning mansion, the library, the room that was too perfect to believe. I even told her about the kiss, though I skimmed over how much it had affected me.

Carla's jaw dropped. "You kissed him?"

"He kissed *me*," I corrected, my cheeks burning. "And it was a mistake. A huge, stupid mistake. Talk about complicating our business arrangement."

"But you're doing it, right? The whole fake fiancée thing?"

I hesitated, taking a long sip of my soda. "I think I have to. It's a lot of money."

"Not just for the money, although that's a huge perk," Carla said. "You deserve six months of luxury, seeing how the one percent lives. And think of it as a writing retreat! You could finally finish that book you've been talking about."

I laughed weakly. "I don't know if I can write while dealing with Roman Kelly every day."

"You can handle him," she said confidently. "As long as you keep it in your pants. If you catch feelings for this guy, you're setting yourself up for heartache."

"I'm not going to fall for him," I said.

"And yet, you two are already locking lips and you haven't even moved in yet."

I shook my head. "A momentary lapse in judgment. Don't worry. His personality will keep me from falling for him. I can assure you of that."

"Maybe he's not as bad as he seems," Carla said.

I raised an eyebrow.

"Okay, he's probably worse," she admitted, smirking. "But you'll survive. And who knows? You might even enjoy it."

I doubted that. But as I sipped my soda and listened to Carla ramble about all the ways I could take advantage of the situation, I couldn't help but feel a glimmer of hope. Maybe, just maybe, this would be the opportunity I needed to get my life on track.

"Think about the material you'll gather for your book. All those eccentric rich folks? It's gold!" She wiped down the bar, then leaned closer as if sharing a secret. "Plus, you'll be living there. You can snoop around—legally. I bet he's got a fancy toilet. The kind with buttons and a seat warmer."

I chuckled, but her words stuck with me. It was true. Living in that mansion offered a rare window into a world I had never known and would never know again. It was a chance to observe the quirks and secrets of the wealthy. How they spoke, what they valued, their everyday dramas—it was a rare chance to experience it, and experience was what writers turn into stories.

"You're right," I conceded. "It's an opportunity. I just have to keep my head clear." My cheeks burned just thinking about that kiss. "He chose me because I'm disposable. When he tosses me to the curb in six months, his world won't be affected since I'm not a part of it and I never will be."

She shrugged. "Maybe so, but it's not like you're not getting something out of this."

I sighed, playing with the condensation on my glass. "This is so weird, right? Like who hires a woman to pretend to be his fiancée? Especially when he could have any woman."

Carla grinned. "The women who want him will also want to stick around after six months. With a business arrangement, things should be less complicated. In theory."

I took another sip of my soda, the bubbles tickling my nose. "Still weird."

"Hey, it's not every day you get to play Cinderella."

"Cinderella didn't have to deal with paparazzi and social media, though," I countered, feeling the weight of the public eye on my shoulders already.

Carla laughed. "True, but she did have to deal with a wicked stepmother and stepsisters. You just have to handle one wealthy businessman. How hard can it be?"

"I guess when you put it that way," I said, trying to find the humor in the situation.

"So, when do you move in?" Carla asked, breaking me from my thoughts.

"Monday."

She looked just as stunned as I felt. "Holy shit."

"Yeah. Maybe pour me something stronger than soda."

14

ROMAN

The weekend was supposed to be a chance to regroup before the whirlwind of Monday hit, but instead, it had spiraled into an unrelenting storm. The headlines were ruthless: "Kelly Conglomerate Under Fire for Fraudulent Practices," "Roman Kelly's Business Empire Faces Scrutiny," and my personal favorite, "Kelly's Empire: Built on Lies?"

It didn't matter that the accusations weren't directly tied to me. It didn't matter that I'd already worked with my lawyers to confirm I wasn't legally responsible. The damage to my reputation was done. By the time I disbanded the company, reimbursed every wronged party, and fired the guilty employees, the internet had turned my name into a meme synonymous with corporate greed.

No one gave two shits that it wasn't me. They didn't care that I had no idea it was happening. Did they not understand how many irons I had in the fire? I couldn't possibly scrutinize every accounting report and dissect it. I had people that did that for me. They were supposed to be the ones that handled that kind of thing. I was only looped in when there were problems too big for my people to handle.

But that didn't matter. It was a chance for the media to rake me over the coals. And now, as I sat in the expansive silence of my home office, I realized just how fragile my station in life was. They wanted to take me down because they didn't like me. They didn't know me, but they didn't like me because of the ten-second clips they had seen of me. They didn't know what precipitated my reactions.

I scrubbed a hand down my face, feeling the stubble rasp against my palm. This was not how I had envisioned this weekend going. Instead of restful solitude at my estate, I was here grappling with crisis management and preparing for an impending media siege.

I stared at the email from my PR team summarizing the fallout, feeling the familiar thrum of anger under my skin. A glance at my reflection in the office window confirmed it: my jaw was clenched so tight it looked like I was auditioning for a toothpaste commercial.

My ears actually hurt from all the clenching. I needed a distraction, something to pull me out of the media-fueled panic and back to some semblance of strategy. My gaze drifted to the corner of my desk where a photo frame stood. It was a candid shot taken at a charity ball ten years ago, one of those rare moments when I actually looked happy. Maybe it was the company, the ambiance, or the fact that no one at that ball knew enough about me to judge. But now, looking at that photograph felt like gazing through a window at a foreign land.

My phone buzzed with another notification. I didn't need to look to know it was bad. The PR team was doing their best to control the narrative, but it was like trying to put out a wildfire with a water pistol.

The house was eerily quiet as I paced the hallways, phone in hand, ignoring the carefully curated art and the floor-to-ceiling windows that made the place feel like a palace.

The staff knew better than to get in my way when I was in a mood like this. My chef had quietly left a plate of something I hadn't touched on the kitchen counter hours ago. Even Anthony, my driver, had texted instead of calling when he'd checked in.

I tossed the phone onto the sleek gray sofa and ran a hand through my hair. I needed Kaira now more than ever. This mess was proving exactly why the board was right. My image needed a redemption arc, and Kaira was the key. If we played this right, the narrative would shift from *"heartless billionaire"* to *"reformed man in love."*

The thought of her brought a flicker of something I hadn't felt all day: anticipation.

Maybe it was the challenge. Or maybe it was the fact I was lonely. The house had been feeling empty since she left. Clearly, a part of me craved companionship, someone to share all my good fortune with. She might not like me, but at least I knew she and I could have a conversation. It might get heated, and she would definitely call me an asshole among other things, but it would be human connection.

Most people just agreed with me, whether they liked me or not. It was impossible to know who was being genuine and who just wanted something from me. I often wondered what it would be like to have a true friend. Someone that wanted to hang out with me because they wanted my company and not for what I could do for them.

This could be my chance to start fresh, to show a different side of myself, one that people could actually relate to, maybe even like. It meant vulnerability, something I wasn't very familiar or comfortable with, but desperate times called for desperate measures.

The thought of letting down my guard made me less than comfortable. I was not the warm and fuzzy type. Letting my guard down opened me up to getting exploited. But what if behind my gate and within the safety of my home, I could relax and be myself around Kaira?

I groaned, not wanting to think about that. The fake relationship was vital to changing the narrative around me and my companies. Things needed to go smoothly. No matter how much I kept thinking about the kiss we'd shared, I couldn't do that again. This whole thing would blow up in my face if I blurred the lines between business and pleasure.

I was going to drive myself crazy if I kept thinking about her lips. I needed a distraction.

I went upstairs to my room and changed into a pair of shorts and put on my tennis shoes. I headed to the home gym to work out all my frustrations. Starting with the punching bag, I threw punches harder and faster with each thought that raced through my mind.

The bag swung back and forth, absorbing the impact of my fists and the weight of my troubles. Each hit was a release, a way to clear the fog of stress and anger that clouded my judgment.

Sweat dripped down my forehead, stinging my eyes. I ignored it, focusing instead on the rhythm of my breath and the sound of leather colliding with leather. My heart pounded in my chest.

After the punching bag had taken its fill, I moved onto weights, pushing myself with each lift. The clink of metal on metal reverberated through the large, empty room. The physical exertion helped; it always did.

As I set down the heavy dumbbells with a final clank and wiped the sweat from my brow, I realized that my body felt less tense, my mind slightly clearer. I moved to the treadmill to finish up my grueling workout. I knew people, women, admired my body. Most people assumed it was vanity that kept me in such good shape. The washboard abs and defined muscles were a side effect... not the goal. The more stress I was under, the more I worked out.

It wasn't vanity; it was survival.

The treadmill hummed beneath my feet. I settled into a steady jog. The thoughts began to pour back in, but this time they were more controlled, less chaotic.

I thought about Kaira living under the same roof. She had fire, that much was undeniable. Maybe it was that fire that drew me to her, made me believe she could be the key to changing public perception of me.

Kaira didn't mince words, didn't smile just because it was expected of her, and certainly didn't play nice for the sake of appearances. She was real. That would go a long way toward getting the public to see me differently.

A plan began to form in my mind as I jogged. By the time I was cooling down, stretching my limbs, the outline was clear. I needed to approach this delicately. Any misstep with Kaira could send this whole house of cards tumbling down.

I grabbed a towel and headed upstairs to get in the shower. The water was almost scalding, the steam filling the room in seconds. I leaned my head against the cool tile, letting the spray beat against my back.

Kaira's face swam to the forefront of my mind. The way she'd looked at me when I'd shown her the library—a mix of wonder and disbelief. She'd been trying so hard not to let me see how overwhelmed she was, but I saw it.

I shouldn't have kissed her. I knew that even as I leaned in. It had been reckless, impulsive—a moment of weakness I couldn't afford to repeat. But even after my exhausting workout, the memory of her lips was burned into my mind. Soft, hesitant, and then hungry. Like she'd been as surprised by her reaction as I was.

I reached for the shower gel and started to wash. I ran my hand down my stomach, and before I knew it, my hand was wrapping around my cock.

I couldn't focus on anything but her. Every touch, every caress I imagined was her touching me. And God, it felt good.

I tugged harder, the fantasy of her fingers doing the work instead of my own propelling me toward the edge. The suds from the shower gel provided just the right amount of slick as my grip tightened. I closed my eyes, letting her image consume me—the curve of her smile, the challenge in her eyes, her fiery spirit manifesting in every fantasy touch.

My breath came out in ragged gasps, the sound of the shower drowning out everything else. I let out a groan as the pleasure grew more intense. My cock throbbed in my hand as the climax built, until I could barely stand it.

With a final thrust against my own hand, I released, my knees nearly buckling under me from the intensity. I braced myself against the wall, water cascading down as I caught my breath.

I rinsed off, hoping to feel better, but I only wanted her more. Even though it wasn't her hand on me, in my mind, it had been. I was able to very easily imagine what it would feel like to sink into her wet heat.

I shut the water off abruptly, the silence in the bathroom deafening. Wrapping a towel around my waist, I stepped out, catching my reflection in the mirror. My expression was unreadable, my eyes darker than usual.

"Get it together," I muttered to myself.

I didn't need complications. What I needed was a clear head and a plan to salvage the disaster this week had turned into. Kaira was a strategic move. Nothing more.

But even as I told myself that, I couldn't shake the memory of the way she'd felt in my arms. Like she belonged there. Like maybe, for the first time in years, I wasn't completely alone.

I turned away from the mirror and headed into the bedroom. Monday couldn't come soon enough.

15

KAIRA

I opened my eyes and stared at my ceiling. It was Monday. I didn't want to move. It was confusing. I was excited and terrified, plus a little sad. Last night, Carla and I had spent our last night together enjoying pizza and splitting a bottle of wine.

I was going to miss hanging out with her. I knew I would still see her, but with me in the Pacific Palisades and her working two jobs, it was going to be hard to catch up as often. We weren't going to have wine and pizza nights in our jammies.

When I agreed to accept Roman's offer, I didn't really think about what it would mean for me. I was leaving my life behind to step into his.

The thought left a knot in my stomach that even the morning sunshine couldn't unravel. Yet, despite the anxiety, a part of me thrummed with anticipation. This was a unique opportunity—stepping into Roman's world could open doors I'd never even dared dream of before.

Dragging myself out of bed, I walked to the kitchen to make myself some coffee. There was a note from Carla wishing me good luck and promising to text me all the time.

Blinking back tears, I took my cup of coffee and left it on the counter to cool while I showered. The board wanted to meet me today. I didn't really know what that meant, but I wanted to look nice. And normal. Roman made it clear I was the grounding force in this fake engagement.

I packed a small suitcase with my things. Roman said he would provide a wardrobe, but some things I preferred to take with me, like underwear and comfy lounging clothes. Hopefully, he wouldn't object to my peasant rags when we were just at his house, alone.

There was so much about this arrangement I didn't know. I was jumping into dark waters with no idea what waited below the surface, but I had no choice but to keep myself afloat, come what may.

I pulled on a pair of jeans and a lightweight sweater, then did my hair and makeup and pulled on my favorite boots with the heel that gave me a little extra confidence. If I was going to be standing next to Roman's giant ass, I didn't want to look like a helpless child.

My makeup and toiletries went into my suitcase and I looked around my room, wondering if I was forgetting anything. I grabbed the photo of me and my parents and added it to the suitcase as well.

I checked the time. Roman had texted me and told me he would be sending Anthony to pick me up at ten. I had thirty minutes. I wiped my sweaty palms on my pants and paced. I grabbed a notebook and quickly wrote Carla a note.

I told her how much she meant to me, that it wouldn't be the same without our impromptu dancing in the living room or our late-night confessions over margaritas and chips and queso. I folded the note and left it on the kitchen counter where she'd surely see it.

The door buzzer cut through my thoughts. It was ten o'clock. Showtime. I took a deep breath, squared my shoulders, and grabbed my suitcase and purse. Anthony was waiting for me downstairs.

"Are you ready?" he asked with a smile.

"I don't know how to answer that," I said with a nervous laugh.

Anthony's smile widened with understanding. "Well, I'm sure there's nothing to worry about. Let me get your bags. No arguments."

I let him take my things and he led me to the sleek black car parked outside. It was different than the last car he'd picked me up in. I wondered how many vehicles Roman had. Probably a whole fleet.

The ride was silent except for the hum of the engine and the occasional blip of traffic noise. Anthony seemed to sense I wasn't in the mood for small talk. My stomach was a ball of nerves, twisting tighter with every mile closer to downtown.

When the car pulled up to the high-rise, I couldn't help but gape. The building gleamed under the morning sun, all glass and steel. A beacon of wealth and power. I shouldn't have been surprised. Of course, this would be the place where Roman worked. Just like his big house, the office building was a statement.

Anthony opened the door for me, offering a reassuring smile as I stepped out.

"You'll do fine," he said quietly, as though sensing my hesitation.

"Thanks," I murmured, though I didn't believe him. "I just wish I knew what I was supposed to actually do up there."

"Just go in with your head held high. The rest will fall into place."

"Thank you, Anthony."

I noticed some people milling about, chatting with each other and loitering in general. I didn't pay them much attention and pulled open the door to go in.

Inside, the lobby was just as grand as the outside. Marble floors, towering ceilings, and a chandelier that looked like it belonged in a museum. I walked to the elevator and pressed the button for the top floor.

Roman had given me instructions on what to do when I arrived. A gentleman would have met me in the lobby. But Roman Kelly was not a gentleman.

I knew that and I was still going through with this ridiculous agreement.

The elevator ride felt like an eternity. My reflection stared back at me from the polished walls, and I couldn't help but second-guess every detail of my appearance. Was my sweater too plain? Not plain enough? My makeup too minimal? Too much? Would they laugh me right out of the office before I even said a word?

I had done a little research and saw some of the women Roman had been photographed with. I was not even a little like them. They were all tall with legs to their ears and beautiful. Like really, really beautiful.

When the doors slid open, I stepped into Roman's world. His office was as extravagant as I had expected.

A pretty young woman sat behind a tall reception desk wearing a headset.

"Welcome to Kelly Industries. Do you have an appointment?"

"I'm here to see Roman. Roman Kelly."

"Ms. Foster, of course. He told me to take you to his office. Follow me."

I followed her through a maze of cubicles in the center of the room and doors along the perimeter. She opened a door and let me inside a massive office.

"He'll be right with you," she said and quickly walked away.

I was in a room with floor-to-ceiling windows offering a panoramic view of Los Angeles, modern furniture that looked more like art than anything functional, and an atmosphere that screamed power.

"You're right on time," Roman said from behind me.

I turned around to see him stride into the office with his usual confidence. He was wearing a navy suit that fit him like a second skin.

"Being on time is easy when you have someone driving you around. And you made it clear I wasn't allowed to be late."

"They are waiting for us," he said.

"Great. I was hoping you would say that." I was being sarcastic. He wasn't giving me a chance to settle in or even get a drink of water for my suddenly dry mouth.

"Let's get this over with," he said.

I walked by his side through the office. I could feel everyone looking at me. They probably thought I was a new employee. In a way, I was.

We entered the boardroom and I was convinced I was going to pass out from the nerves. It was massive, with a long table surrounded by men and women in nice suits. Their eyes were sharp, their gazes assessing. I felt like a bug under a magnifying glass.

"This is Kaira," Roman announced, his tone all business.

The scrutiny began immediately. They looked me up and down, not bothering to hide their judgment. One woman leaned back in her chair, folding her arms. "Her?"

"Yes," Roman replied without hesitation.

Another man adjusted his glasses and glanced at a tablet in front of him. "We pulled up her background. Middle-class upbringing. Public school education. A degree from a state college. Father was a mechanic. And her old Facebook page says her mother was a domestic engineer."

I stood with my mouth hanging open. I looked at Roman, but he was looking at them. Domestic engineer? That wasn't on my Facebook page.

But it was on my mom's.

"You stalked my mom!" I gasped.

They ignored me.

"And no connections to the social elite," someone else added. "Quite the plain Jane."

I swallowed hard, forcing myself to stay composed even as my chest tightened. My palms were clammy, and I wished for the thousandth time that I hadn't agreed to this insanity. They were talking about me like I was a cow on the auction block. I had a flashback to Roman's expression when he'd been auctioned off and I completely understood how he felt in that moment.

"Nobody is going to believe this," one of the board members said bluntly.

"Definitely not one of the models he's known for," said another, who was no runway model herself, the judgmental bitch.

Heat rose to my cheeks, humiliation bubbling just under the surface. I wanted to disappear, to shrink down to nothing and escape the room, but Roman's voice cut through the tension.

"You're all wrong," he said firmly.

I glanced up at him, surprised by the conviction in his tone. He stood tall, his jaw set, his hazel eyes locked on the group in front of us. He wasn't the least bit intimidated, in total control.

"Kaira is perfect because she isn't part of my usual world," he continued. "She's genuine, not plastic. Normal. A good woman worth settling down with. Building a life together."

His words touched me, making me feel warm in a different way.

There was a pause as the board members seemed to be considering it. "And let's not forget—everyone loves a rags-to-riches story," Roman added.

Rags. The word stung, even though I knew he didn't mean it as an insult. Plus, technically, I was a few missed paychecks away from being homeless when he'd made this job offer. I hadn't exactly been living high on the hog.

I looked down at my hands, feeling a mix of gratitude and resentment. He was defending me, but at the same time, he was reducing me to a narrative—something marketable. There I went again, getting my feelings involved. He'd chosen me *because* I fit the narrative. It was what this whole thing was about. I couldn't pout about agreeing to it.

The board exchanged glances, murmuring among themselves. Finally, the woman at the head of the table nodded. "If you think she's the right fit, we'll honor your unconventional choice."

Screw you too, lady. I smiled sweetly at her.

Moments later, like magic, a contract appeared in front of me. It looked identical to the draft agreement Roman had emailed to me. I would have to read the whole thing again to be sure but I wasn't going to do that.

I stared at the pages, my mind racing with a hundred reasons to doubt this. But as I glanced at Roman, who was watching me with an unreadable expression, I knew there was no turning back.

I picked up the pen and signed my name.

Roman signed below it.

The tension in the room eased slightly as the board members began gathering their things, but I felt like I'd just signed away a part of myself.

"Let's go," Roman said. "We're all set here."

We left the boardroom together and walked back to his office.

"Now what?" I asked with a resigned sigh.

"Now, we face the sharks."

"Didn't I just do that?"

He smirked. "Those were guppies compared to what we're about to deal with."

"Is it too late to back out?" I asked sullenly.

"Yep," he said with a grin.

We walked back to the elevator.

"Just let me do the talking," he said when we stepped out into the lobby.

I frowned, not fully understanding what he was talking about. Chaos erupted in the lobby. Cameras flashed, reporters shouted questions, and microphones were thrust in our direction. The press tended to report on every detail of Roman's life but I just didn't understand how this was news.

Then again, he wanted people to know about our "engagement." The board had probably invited them all here.

Roman's hand settled on the small of my back, guiding me forward with an ease that suggested he had done this a thousand times before. I tried to keep my head down, but the noise was overwhelming.

"Who's the lucky lady, Roman?"

"Mr. Kelly! Is she the secret Kardashian?"

"Is that the homeless woman from the auction?"

Were they referring to me? Did people think I was homeless?

Roman stopped abruptly, turning to face the sea of reporters. He pulled me closer to his side and I froze, trying to give off non-vagrant energy.

"Kaira has been in my life for some time now," he said smoothly, his voice cutting through the commotion. Everyone stopped talking, hanging on every word he said, getting it all on their cameras. "We wanted to keep things private, but you jackals are never going to give me privacy. So we're ready to share our happiness with the world."

He turned to me, his eyes locking onto mine. There was a flicker of something—an apology, maybe? Before I could wonder what he was sorry for, he leaned in and kissed me like he fucking meant it.

The world tilted on its axis. The flash of cameras faded into the background as his lips moved against mine. My brain was too stunned to respond but my body knew exactly what it wanted. I leaned into him, my hands clutching the front of his suit jacket as I deepened the kiss.

For a few seconds, there was no crowd, no cameras, no reporters. Just him and the magical kiss.

When we finally broke apart, I was breathless, my heart hammering in my chest. Roman's hand lingered on my waist. He flashed a small, almost imperceptible smirk.

"Let's go," he murmured, guiding me toward the waiting car.

As we slid into the back seat and the door closed, muffling the noise outside, I turned to him, still reeling. "What the hell was that?"

He raised an eyebrow. "That was our first public appearance as a couple. It went perfectly."

"You could've warned me!" I hissed.

"And missed the opportunity to make it genuine?" His smirk widened. "You looked like you enjoyed it."

I opened my mouth to argue, but no words came out. Because, dammit, he was right. And after all the bruises to my ego today, it was nice to feel wanted.

I wasn't about to admit that to him, though.

16

ROMAN

"The jewelry store?" Anthony asked.

"Yes."

Kaira was sitting quietly looking just a little shell-shocked. The kiss might have been unnecessary. I could have just told the vultures she was my girlfriend. But once I saw her and the opportunity presented itself, I couldn't resist.

Anthony eyed me with skepticism thinly veiled behind his otherwise impassive expression but he drove to the Beverly Hills area. There were paparazzi waiting outside the jewelry store. Someone had tipped them off, just like in the lobby. It was all part of the marketing push.

"Ready?" I asked her.

"I don't know. What are we doing here?"

"Getting your engagement ring, my love."

Once again, I shocked the hell out of her. "Seriously?"

"Can't be engaged and not have a ring," I said. "What kind of man do you think I am?"

She let out another loud, exaggerated sigh. "I don't know if I'm ready for all this."

"Just remember that none of this is real. Just try to have fun with it. I'm going to come around the car and get you out, okay?"

She nodded. "Okay."

I stepped out of the car, smoothing my suit as I rounded to her side. The cameras began clicking immediately, capturing every move. I opened the door, offering Kaira my hand like a proper gentleman. She took it, her hand trembling slightly. As she stepped out, the flashbulbs intensified.

We walked together into the jewelry store. The manager, recognizing me instantly, hurried forward. I had called ahead and made sure we would have privacy while we browsed.

"Mr. Kelly, what an honor! How can we assist you today?"

"I need an engagement ring," I stated, my voice calm and clear.

The staff greeted us warmly, their smiles polished to perfection as they welcomed us into the showroom. There was someone waiting to help us standing behind every case.

The store was well stocked with amazing pieces—glass cases lined with exquisite diamonds, emeralds, and rubies.

Kaira's eyes widened as she took it all in, her lips parting in an unspoken gasp. For a moment, she looked like she might turn and bolt.

"You okay?" I asked, leaning in close.

"This is a lot," she admitted, her voice barely above a whisper.

"It's supposed to be," I replied with a smirk. "Come on. Let's find something befitting your beauty, huh?"

She rolled her eyes but I thought her cheeks reddened a bit. I led her to a counter where the jeweler had already prepared a tray of rings for her to choose from. The diamonds sparkled under the bright lighting, each one more dazzling than the last. Kaira hesitated, her hand hovering over the display.

"These cost more than I've made in my entire life," she murmured, her tone somewhere between awe and disbelief.

"Nothing but the best for you," I said, picking up a ring with a center diamond so large it could blind someone in direct sunlight. "Try this one."

She hesitated but eventually let me slide the ring onto her finger. The diamond caught the light perfectly, throwing tiny rainbows across her skin. Kaira stared at it, her brow furrowing as though she couldn't comprehend what she was seeing.

"It's too much," she said, her voice shaky.

"Nothing is too much," I replied firmly. "Pick the one you like."

"But—"

"No 'buts.' This is part of the deal, Kaira. You're going to wear my ring, and if I have to choose it for you, it's going to make a statement."

Her gaze darted between the ring and the others on the tray. Finally, she pointed to one—a more conservative design, though still worth an obscene amount of money. The solitaire diamond was elegant and understated, just like her.

"Are you sure?" I asked as I picked it up.

She nodded. "That one is more *me*, compared to that other beautiful monster."

I slid the more elegant ring on her finger and stepped back, taking her in. She looked radiant. It wasn't just the way it sparkled under the light. It was the way her eyes softened when she looked at it, the way her lips curved into a small, hesitant smile. It felt so real.

"It looks good," I said, my voice softer than I intended. "It suits you."

Kaira stared at the ring, her fingers trembling slightly. "I can't believe this is real."

"It's real," I assured her, taking her hand in mine, playing along. She was a better actress than I had expected. "And now, let's give them a real show, shall we?"

I gestured toward the windows, where the media was still buzzing. Without waiting for her response, I leaned down and pressed a kiss to her knuckles, holding her gaze as the cameras went wild.

I pulled back. "Alright, let's buy this."

I pulled out my black card and quickly paid for the ring.

"Shouldn't we put this in the box?" she asked.

"No, you should wear it."

She looked down at her hand. "Are you sure?"

"Yes."

"What if I get mugged?"

I had to bite back my laugh. "For one, you're with me. And we're in Beverly Hills. You're not getting mugged. Just try not to leave it on a sink somewhere and you'll be fine."

We left the jewelry store and continued our shopping adventure. I took her to one of the most exclusive boutiques in the city, available by appointment only. The staff greeted us with champagne. There were no price tags on anything because, if you had to ask, you couldn't afford it.

She was hesitant, fidgeting nervously as the salespeople brought out racks of clothes for her to try. Good thing about the price tags. If she had any idea how much these outfits were worth, she'd run away screaming.

"Either you pick what you want, or I do it for you," I said. "We talked about this. I figured you'd prefer to choose. You said you didn't want me to dress you up like a doll."

"I did."

"See? I listen."

"I just feel so silly, so much fuss just for me," she said quietly. "I'm not used to it."

"Just ignore everything but the clothes. Find yourself something nice." I sat in one of the plush velvet chairs and shooed her away. "Or I'm just going to choose the shortest dresses with the lowest necklines."

Kaira scowled at me. "Okay, okay. I'll look."

She pulled a few items and disappeared behind the velvet curtains of the fitting room. Meanwhile, I sipped on the cold champagne, trying to appear disinterested while my heart raced with every movement I heard from behind those curtains.

I had been joking before, but the thought of choosing slutty outfits for her to wear seemed appealing. Shopping was tedious on the best of days, but if she would do a little dress-up for me, I could sit here all day.

Minutes ticked by slowly until finally, Kaira emerged. The transformation was nothing short of stunning. The blouse draped elegantly over her, paired with a tailored skirt that accentuated her round hips and flowed gracefully around her legs. She looked refined and powerful.

"I vote yes," I said, sitting up. "Add it to the pile and try on the next one."

Kaira's cheeks flushed. She looked away quickly. "Do you really think so?" she asked, her voice small. "Just like that?"

"Absolutely."

With a timid smile, she looked at herself in the mirror again and nodded. Then she scampered off to try the next one, already more comfortable with the process. Good. No reason we couldn't enjoy ourselves.

As the hours went by, I watched her transform. Her posture straightened, her eyes lit up, and she started smiling more—genuine, unguarded smiles that made my chest tighten in a way I didn't entirely understand. She was getting used to the idea of dressing like she truly was my fiancée.

We moved on to the next store and it was the same process. I sat and waited while she carefully chose piece after piece.

"You look incredible," I said as she stepped out of the fitting room in a sleek black cocktail dress that hugged her curves perfectly.

She frowned, tugging at the hem. "It's too tight."

"It's perfect," I countered, standing to adjust the fabric slightly. "Trust me."

"It's too short. I don't wear things that show so much thigh. I look better in loose skirts."

"The hell you do," I said. "That's perfect."

"I don't know, maybe I should look for something a little less— well, a little more."

"No. That goes on the pile." I gestured to another dress waiting on the rack outside the dressing room. "Try that one."

She scrunched up her nose. "I don't think girls like me should be wearing dresses like that."

"What the hell does that mean?"

"I'm not a model, Roman. I don't have the legs or the butt for that. More like, I have too much of both."

I gave her a slow, deliberate look, my eyes tracing over her form. "You're exactly the kind of woman who should be wearing dresses like that," I said firmly. "You're real. You've got an ass and hips. Try it on. For me. Please."

Kaira bit her lip, looking uncertain. "Fine. You don't have to beg. Jeez."

She turned to head back into the fitting room. I didn't miss the fact there was a new sway in her step that hadn't been there before.

As she disappeared behind the curtain once more, I leaned back in my chair and realized I had found a crack in her confidence. She was self-conscious about her body. Maybe everyone in the world was, at least a little bit.

Still, I didn't like that. She had a rocking body. So, what if she wasn't a size two. Watching Kaira grow into herself, buoyed by the expensive clothes and my occasional encouragement, felt like a victory.

When she emerged again, the dress she wore was a bold blue that clung to her in all the right places—the sort of dress designed to make a statement in any room it entered. As she stood there in front of me, nervously tugging at the edge of the sleeve, I had to wipe the drool from the corner of my mouth.

"It's not too much?" she asked.

"Keep it on. You're leaving in it." I got up and paid for the dress and the other outfits that made her look like the confident, stunning woman I knew she could be.

By the time we left the last boutique, Kaira was practically glowing. Her arms were full of shopping bags, and her smile hadn't faded.

"You're spoiling me," she said as we climbed into the car.

"That's the idea," I replied, unable to hide my satisfaction. "Now, how about we get some food?"

"I don't think I should eat anything while I'm wearing this dress."

"If you get something on it, we'll just buy another one."

"This dress cost four-thousand dollars!"

"So?"

She shook her head. "It's going to take a minute for me to get used to your way of living."

"I have a feeling it will happen faster than you think."

Anthony drove us to a swanky restaurant. It was the kind of place where celebrities went to be seen. The maître d' practically tripped over himself to seat us. I couldn't help but notice the envious looks I got from other diners as we walked through the room.

Kaira looked stunning in the dress, and I wasn't shy about showing her off.

We sat and she seemed more focused on the menu, her eyes widening at the prices.

"Roman, this is insane," she whispered, leaning toward me.

"Just order what you want. Or I'll order you a plate of snails. I mean, they're delicious here, but not everyone's a fan."

She caved and ordered the branzino. I even managed to convince her to order dessert, on the condition we share it. By the time we finished the sticky toffee pudding with ice cream on top, the restaurant staff had all but rolled out a red carpet for us. I left a generous tip before guiding Kaira back to the car, where Anthony was waiting. He'd eaten his steak in the car.

When we finally returned to my house, Kaira let out a long breath and leaned against the doorframe of the grand foyer. Anthony had helped carry in the many, many shopping bags. They were now all over the hall, adding splashes of unfamiliar color to my life.

"That was overwhelming," she admitted.

"Good overwhelming or bad overwhelming?" I asked.

She smiled, and it was so genuine that it made my chest tighten again. "Good. Definitely good."

"Good," I echoed, my voice low.

"Thank you."

"Only the best for my favorite gal." I had said it as a joke, but they weren't untrue. I had enjoyed spending time with her, making her smile and checking her out in different outfits.

Maybe it was a good thing I was attracted to my fake fiancée but I suddenly felt like I was in trouble.

17

KAIRA

The day had been a whirlwind of luxury and unfamiliar splendor. Roman had been like my fairy godmother, only sexy as hell in his tailored suit. He took me from shop to shop in a surreal dream. From the soft slide of silky dresses over my skin to the attention from the high-end boutique clerks, it was all so foreign yet exhilarating. But now, standing in Roman's expansive foyer surrounded by bags stamped with designer logos, I felt a tingling realization of the new world I was stepping into.

I didn't know if I was cut out for this kind of life. My meager suitcase was among the bags. It stuck out like a sore thumb.

"So, uh, I guess I'll take the bags to my room," I said. "I can't wait to get out of this dress."

"We're not done yet," he said.

"I think we've done enough," I replied, trying to sound lighthearted but failing to mask the exhaustion creeping into my bones.

I didn't want to be alone with him. There was something about him that made me feel like I was dancing with the devil. I didn't trust him. More like I didn't trust myself. He had worn me out. The shopping marathon had been fun, but I never knew how draining shopping could be.

He shook his head, an amused smirk on his lips. "We need to update our socials. If the world is going to believe this, we've got to sell it. Nothing is official until we're Insta-official."

I raised a brow. "And by 'sell it,' you mean…?"

"Photos," he said matter-of-factly. "Something convincing. Something that shows we actually spend time together. That all of this is real."

"We could have taken photos at the restaurant," I said. "Not that we needed to. I saw all the people trying to pretend they weren't taking our pictures. Or there is the announcement you made outside your building. And the jewelry shop."

He chuckled, the sound terrifying and a total turn-on "Oh, those were just appetizers. Now comes the main course. That is easy to fake, and people will definitely call us out for that. We need something intimate."

The way he said "intimate" made my skin prickle. If he thought I was making a sex tape with him, he had another thing coming. "Like what?"

He didn't answer right away. Instead, he walked over to one of the bags and pulled out a tiny bikini. He held it up with a grin. The fabric was so minimal it might as well have been a napkin. I had no idea when that got in there.

"How? When?" I stammered.

"I have a pool. You'll be living here. You'll need a bathing suit."

"That's dental floss!"

He laughed, clearly enjoying this. "It's fashion, Kaira. Haven't you heard? Less is more."

I couldn't believe this was happening. The transition from an ordinary day to this extravagant lifestyle was too abrupt. And now, he was suggesting—no, almost insisting—that this threadbare piece of cloth was a bathing suit? I crossed my arms, trying to maintain a semblance of control over the situation.

"If you like it so much, you wear it," I declared firmly. "And I'm sure as hell not taking poolside pictures of myself and posting them to Instagram. I saw the mob after you. Those pictures will make it to mainstream media and spread around the world. My ass—literally—will be on display for the entire world. No thank you."

Roman's expression didn't change. He simply placed the bikini back into the bag and shrugged nonchalantly. "Alright, we'll revisit that one," he said casually as he dug around. I balked in horror when he brought out another one.

This one, while marginally more substantial, was still less of a swimsuit and more of a suggestion. Its vibrant blue color was really pretty. He dangled it before me like a challenge.

"You must have something against fabric," I muttered, eyeing it skeptically.

He flashed a cocky grin. "I think you'll look stunning in it. And it's perfect for a casual poolside photo. Very 'girl next door goes Hollywood.'"

The thought of plastering such an image on social media made my stomach churn. "Or very 'girl next door sells her soul,'" I retorted.

"Do I need to remind you of the contract?"

I wanted to throw something at him. Anything.

"No way," I said, backing up a step. "Absolutely not."

"Yes way," he countered, his smirk turning into a full-blown grin. "We're going in the pool. You can put that on or get in naked. I don't care, but we're getting the pictures. We need to sell this thing hard."

Before I could protest further, he stripped off his jacket. And then he started unbuttoning his shirt.

"What are you doing?" I gasped.

I couldn't look away. He tossed his shirt onto a nearby chair. Any further protests caught in my throat as I took in the sight of him—broad shoulders, chiseled abs, and a confidence that was impossible to ignore. He shimmied out of his pants, leaving him in nothing but black boxers that clung to him in a way that felt borderline illegal.

"Your turn," he said, nodding toward the bikini.

"I'm not—" I started, but the words faltered as he turned and headed toward the pool, his back muscles rippling under the low light. He didn't even look back to see if I was following.

"I guess those abs are real after all," I murmured to myself. I was tempted to take out my phone and snap some pictures to send to Carla. She had been the one wondering about his abs being photoshopped. They were legit but that was just the half of it. The arms. Back. His legs.

And the most exciting part of him barely hidden by those tight little boxers.

I still wasn't sold on taking pictures, but suddenly, the idea of showing off my body to him was growing on me. I wanted to see what I could make grow on him.

With a deep breath, I snatched the bikini and disappeared into the bathroom to see if it even fit me. It took me longer than it should have to work up the nerve to come out. The thing barely covered anything. I couldn't shake the feeling that this was some elaborate joke he'd set up to mess with me. I had a flashback to middle school when someone had switched out my gym uniform with one that was way too small. I had no choice but to put it on. When I walked into the gym with the shorts riding up and my belly hanging out, everyone laughed. That same sense of dread pooled in my stomach now. If he was doing this to humiliate me, I would never forgive him. I would never forgive myself for being dumb enough to fall for this stupid game.

When I finally emerged, I followed the sound of splashing to the pool. Roman was already in the water, floating lazily on his back. The water lapped gently at his skin, and his hair was slicked back, making him look like a damn model in a cologne ad. It was unfair that one person got all the good looks.

"Finally," he said, straightening and turning to face me. His eyes roamed over me as he slowly treaded water. For a moment, I thought I saw something flicker in his expression—something hungry. There was no way he was looking at me trussed up like a turkey, feeling vulnerable, and thinking I looked good. But he had that glint in his eye that suggested otherwise.

"Jump in," he beckoned with a wave of his hand, as if it were the most natural request in the world. The water shimmered under the moonlight, and for a split second, the idea of cooling off didn't seem so bad. But stepping closer to the pool's edge, I hesitated.

I crossed my arms over my chest. "I feel ridiculous."

"You look amazing," he said simply, gesturing for me to join him. "Come on. The water's perfect."

I dipped a toe in, then eased my way down the steps, hyper-aware of his gaze on me the entire time. The water was nice but it did little to calm the nerves buzzing under my skin. I couldn't believe I was virtually naked in front of him. Talk about blurring the lines of our agreement.

Roman swam to the edge of the pool and picked up his phone. He started snapping pictures. "Just relax," he said. "Pretend it's just us."

"It *is* just us," I pointed out, though I couldn't help the small laugh that escaped.

"Exactly," he said, his voice softer now. "You don't need to worry about anything."

Easier said than done. But as the minutes ticked by, I started to feel less self-conscious. Roman guided me gently, asking me to lean on the edge of the pool or let the water ripple around me. His compliments came freely.

"That's perfect."

"You look stunning."

"You're a natural."

I started to believe him. For the first time in a long time, I felt... attractive. He made me feel pretty. And the lighting was flattering. I took comfort knowing my butt was under the water. My bit and boobs were mostly hidden.

At one point, he moved closer, lowering the phone to adjust the strap of my bikini, which had twisted awkwardly. His fingers brushed my skin as he straightened it. I found myself face to face with his chest. His skin was warm and damp, the ridges of his muscles so close I could feel the heat radiating off him.

My hand moved before I could think better of it. I placed it gently on his ribs, marveling at the firmness of his body. I supposed part of me was still wondering if it was all real. If there had been airbrushing, it would have melted away. His body was just as hard as it looked, like granite wrapped in silk. He stilled, his gaze dropping to where my hand rested. Emboldened by the fact that he didn't pull away, I placed my other hand on him, just below his collarbone.

He put the phone down on the edge of the pool. His body was so close now. He cupped my face in his hands and looked into my eyes. There was a silent question in his gaze. I didn't know how he understood, but he did because, a second later, his lips crashed into mine with a force that stole the breath from my lungs.

I sank into him, my hands sliding up to his shoulders as he pulled me closer. The kiss was desperate, all-consuming. His lips moved against mine with a hunger that sent heat coursing through my veins. One of his hands slipped to the small of my back, pulling me flush against him, while the other tangled in my wet hair.

"Roman," I gasped when we broke apart for air. My heart was pounding, my chest rising and falling.

"If the world thinks you're mine, then fuck it," he growled. "You're mine."

His words sent a shiver down my spine that wrapped around and landed right in my lower belly. I barely had time to process them before his mouth found mine again. His hands roamed my body, slipping under the thin fabric of my bikini to caress my skin. I felt like I was on fire, every nerve ending alive with sensation.

"Should we really be doing this?" I managed to pant between kisses, though my body betrayed me by pressing closer to him.

"I don't care," he murmured, his voice rough with desire. "I need you, Kaira."

His words undid me. I melted into him, letting myself get lost in the moment. The contract and the expectations faded away until there was nothing left but the feel of his hands on me and the taste of his lips. The water lapped against our bodies as he deepened the kiss. My hands slid down his chest. I groaned at the contact. He truly was a magnificent creature.

Roman's hands slid down my back and cupped my ass, pulling me against him. I could feel his erection against my belly. A thrill raced through me—I was making him hard. It was intoxicating. I wrapped my legs around him, pulling him closer as we bobbed in the water.

His tongue swept into my mouth. I moaned against him, the sound muffled by the hungry press of his lips.

The smooth tile of the pool edge pressed into my back as he pinned me there. Roman's kisses trailed down my neck, each one sparking fireworks behind my closed eyes. I tilted my head back, giving him more access, lost in the sensation. His hand moved from my hair, tracing a searing path down my spine and then around to cradle my breast. His thumb brushed over my nipple. I arched into his touch, a sharp gasp escaping me.

My body was wet in more ways than one. I could feel heat spiraling in my very core. Every touch set me on fire.

18

ROMAN

I couldn't pull myself away. The feel of Kaira's soft skin under my fingers, the taste of her lips, the way her body responded so eagerly to my touch was overwhelming. I had seen beauty in numerous forms, but nothing compared to the electric connection that surged through me in that moment. My body was screaming with need. My dick was throbbing with want for this woman.

Every rational thought urged me to stop, but all caution slipped away. She was fire and need and everything I suddenly craved viciously. With every touch, every kiss, it was as though I was marking her as mine. The thought made heat curl even tighter in my gut. I was consumed by the desire to claim her.

She tangled her fingers in my hair, pulling me closer, deeper. The sensation of her hands on me stoked the flames inside me. My hands explored her body with a mind of their own, tracing every curve and memorizing the feel of her against me. She was soft in all the right places. I just knew riding between her legs was going to be like climbing the stairway to heaven.

Her hips moved against mine, mimicking the act I was so desperate to complete. My hand slid lower, grazing the edge of her bikini bottom, teasing her. I could feel her heart racing, her body trembling under my touch. This wasn't just desire—it was a blazing need that consumed us both. I pressed her harder against the pool edge, my hips pinning hers, making it clear that I was locked in.

"Roman," she whispered, her voice a desperate plea laced with lust and longing. It was all the encouragement I needed. My name, falling from her lips, fueled my desire further.

I responded with a deep, possessive kiss, as if I could somehow capture her soul between our entangled breaths. Her fingers tightened in my hair, nails slightly scraping my scalp in a way that sent a shiver down my spine. She was everywhere, all around me, and I never wanted this to end.

"We need to stop," she breathed out, her words contradicting the movement of her body against mine.

"Why?" I asked, brushing kisses along her jawline to her ear, delighting in the way she shivered at my touch. "Tell me you don't want this as much as I do."

"It's not about what I want," she murmured, her breath hitching as I traced a fingertip along her collarbone.

"But it should be," I countered softly, pressing my forehead against hers. "It should be exactly about what you want. It feels good. This is just the tip of how good it will feel."

She looked at me and I saw the moment the lust faded, and reality crashed in. She pushed against my chest. "I can't," she said. "We can't."

The moment Kaira climbed out of the pool and wrapped a towel tightly around herself, I knew I had screwed up. She looked at me, water dripping down her body, her cheeks flushed with a mix of anger and embarrassment.

"We can," I insisted, using my arms to lift myself out of the water.

She stared at me, eyes wide. Her eyes drifted down my body. I knew she was feeling the same thing I was. I saw her staring at my rock-hard cock, standing proudly and unashamed, straining against my underwear.

"No," she groaned, conflicted.

Then she bolted inside without a word.

I followed, dripping wet and without a towel, leaving a trail of water across the marble floors. I didn't care about the mess, although I had to step carefully to keep from slipping and going ass over elbows. The rest of my focus was on Kaira, who was practically sprinting away.

As hypnotizing as she was, bouncing around in her towel, showing off her sweet curves, I didn't want her afraid of me or uncomfortable around me. She had been meeting me kiss for kiss, as into me as I was into her—until she wasn't.

"Kaira," I called after her. "Wait a second. Talk to me."

She stopped in the middle of the foyer, whirling around to face me, cleavage spilling over the top of the towel. Too bad the look in her eyes was nothing short of lethal.

"I need space, Roman," she snapped, pulling the towel tighter around herself, hiding her sweet tits. It was like blocking out the sun. "I can't breathe when I'm around you."

"What does that mean?" I asked, confused by her sudden shift in tone. Moments ago, she'd melted in my arms. I had been seconds away from plunging into her wet heat, just like I had been dreaming about the last couple nights.

I knew she wanted me. I couldn't get my head around why she was running away from me like I was the devil incarnate.

"This wasn't in the contract!" she spat, her voice rising. "None of this was. I'm not your real fiancée. I'm not your real anything! We're not going to do this. We're not going to have sex. It's too weird."

Her words stung more than they should have. "You're taking this way too seriously. What's wrong with having a little fun?" I tried to keep my tone casual, but her reaction only intensified. I kept blundering forward regardless. "We're under the same roof and we both want what almost happened. I can see it in your eyes."

"I'm not here for fun, Roman." She shook her head. "I'm here because you made me an offer I couldn't refuse. I'm here because I was broke and desperate and had just been fired because of that stupid auction debacle. I'm here because I have no other options—

not because I want to be your girl, fake or real. This thing between us isn't real. I don't like you."

Her words hit me like a punch to the gut. I opened my mouth to argue, but she wasn't finished.

"You think you can do whatever you want because you're rich," she continued, her voice trembling with emotion. "But newsflash: not everyone is at your beck and call. I'm not one of your staff, Roman. I'm not here to make your life easier or more entertaining. I'm here because I didn't have a choice."

Her words were sharp, cutting through the ego I usually wore like armor. "That's not fair," I said, my voice tight with anger. "I've done nothing but treat you well. You think I forced you into this? You signed that contract on your own."

"Oh, give me a break," she shot back, throwing her hands up. "I'm not stupid. I know there's nothing about me a man like you could possibly find attractive. And you know what? I can make my peace with that. But I can't make peace with being used by a man who thinks he can have anything he wants."

She turned and marched toward the stairs.

"Well, you can't have me," she called over her shoulder. "I'm not yours."

I stood there, frozen, as her words echoed through the foyer. *What the fuck?*

No one ever spoke to me that way. And even if they did, I wouldn't care. So why the hell did it piss me off so much? She was just the woman I was paying to pretend to be my fiancée. I should not care what she thought about me. I shouldn't care that she didn't want me. There were a thousand other willing women that would crawl into my bed.

I stormed into the study, my chest heaving up and down. I rarely allowed myself to lose control, but I felt my hold on it slipping away. It was shredding and there was nothing I could do to stop it.

I grabbed a vase off the table and threw it against the wall. Red-hot fury bubbled up inside me, demanding release. The vase shattered, pieces scattering across the floor. Not the smartest move for a barefoot man but I wasn't thinking clearly.

I went for a book and threw it. A stack of papers went flying as I swiped them off the desk. The destruction felt good, liberating even, but it did nothing to really make me feel better. I kicked a chair and then punched it, splintering the wood. My rampage spun out of control. I didn't stop until the room was in disarray, until every ounce of rage had been spent.

Then came the shame.

I stood there in the wreckage, breathing heavily, my hands shaking. I could hear the sound of footsteps in the hallway—the cleaning staff, no doubt, already on their way to tidy up the trail of damage I had caused.

They would reset everything. By morning, it would be as if nothing had happened.

But the mess wasn't just in the room. It was in me.

I went back to the foyer and caught a glimpse of one of the housekeepers hurrying away. With the rage fading, I was suddenly very aware of my state of undress. I stormed up to my bedroom and slammed the door hard enough to make the wall shake.

Kaira's words replayed in my mind on a loop.

I'm not yours.

The conviction in her voice stung, getting right through the gaps in my armor.

There's nothing about me a man like you could possibly find attractive.

How could she believe that? How could she not see how magnetic she was, how her fire and passion drew me in like nothing else ever had?

But maybe she was right about one thing: I'd been using her. Maybe not intentionally, but I had. She'd been a solution to my problem, a way to fix my image and distract from the chaos in my life. I had convinced myself it was harmless—that she'd benefit from this arrangement as much as I would. I had seen her as just another commodity. And wasn't she right? Hadn't I thought I could just buy her compliance and affection because I could afford to?

Why did Kaira's words matter so much to me? Was it just because I wasn't used to being denied? No, there was something else, something deeper that her defiance stirred in me. It wasn't about ownership or control. It wasn't frustration born out of rejection or unmet desires. It was shame, mixed with a raw vulnerability.

My mother's face flashed in my mind, unbidden.

"What would she think of me now?" I muttered under my breath.

She'd raised me to be better than this. To treat people with respect, to work hard, to earn everything I had. She'd been my compass, even in death. Everything I had done—every deal I closed, every business I had built—had been for her.

And now?

Now it felt like the carefully constructed life I'd built was in danger of unraveling, one loose thread at a time. I hadn't felt true emotional pain in years. The world I operated in didn't allow for such weaknesses. Emotions were liabilities, best managed or entirely avoided. But here I was, pacing the length of my bedroom, wrestling with thoughts I had long buried.

Maybe it was because, for the first time in a long while, someone hadn't backed down from telling me the truth about myself.

19

KAIRA

The next morning, I woke to the sound of a vacuum. It took me a second to remember where I was. I stretched my arms wide and stared up at the ceiling of my new room. The massive bed was beyond comfortable. I felt like I was being cradled in a cloud.

Despite the opulence surrounding me, there was a heaviness in my heart that even the plush comfort couldn't erase. Last night's confrontation with him had left me shaken. I said things I wasn't sure I should have. Was I too harsh? Did I cross a line? Was he going to tear up the contract and send me packing?

I wouldn't blame him. In fact, that might be the best thing for both of us. My rent wouldn't get paid but my heart wouldn't get twisted into knots either.

I sat up and wrapped the silky sheets around me, catching sight of myself in the ornate mirror across the room. The woman staring back seemed stronger than I felt—the same woman who had stood her ground against him. But under it all lay an undercurrent of fear and uncertainty. What would happen next? Could there be any coming back from what was said?

I got out of bed and walked over to the window, pulling back the curtains to let in the light. The sun was up, casting a warm glow over the sprawling estate grounds. It looked peaceful and so inviting. If I wasn't kicked to the curb in the next hour, I wanted to take a walk and check out all of the plants and that little nook in the back of the property.

I had thought about everything said and done for most of the night. I wanted to be stubborn and tell him to kiss my ass, but I needed to be a realist. The truth was, I needed this job. Not just for the money, although that was crucial, but because this role, this environment, were supposed to be stepping stones for me. I wanted to study the rich and famous in order to accurately write them.

There was a soft knock at the door. I didn't think it was Roman. I didn't think he knew how to do anything softly. "Yes?" I called out.

"Ms. Foster, there's a delivery for you downstairs. And a visitor."

I frowned, unsure who or what that would be. And then it hit me. *Oh, shit.*

"I'll be right there," I said.

Last night, I had texted Carla and asked her to pack up more of my things and bring them over. I had been pissed and wanted to stick it to him by adding my cheap throw pillows, candles, and my own worn clothes to his big fancy house.

I didn't know why I texted her. That had been stupid. If she really brought it over, I was just going to have to pack everything up and take it home when he kicked me out.

I climbed out of bed and was about to go to the bathroom when I saw a note sitting on a table near the door. I picked it up, my heart stopping as I realized Roman had been in my room without me even knowing it. I read the brief note.

Stay. Went to office. Be back later.

I guess that was a good thing. I wasn't kicked out. Yet.

I quickly washed my face, piled my hair on top of my head, and pulled on a pair of jeans I had brought with me. I wasn't interested in wearing any of the new clothes from yesterday. The bags were haphazardly tossed in the corner of the room, waiting to be unloaded. That could wait.

I rushed downstairs just as several staff members carried in boxes. Carla walked in behind them.

"Kaira!" she squealed, running toward me.

"You're here," I said with relief.

"Of course, I'm here. Are you okay? I texted you back when I got home but you didn't answer."

"I'm fine," I said.

Her eyes widened as she looked around, taking in the grandeur of the foyer. "Oh my God, girl. You're living in a *palace*."

I gave a nervous laugh. "I'm not sure I'm even allowed to have people over."

Carla rolled her eyes, grabbing my hand. "Screw that! You're not spending six months in solitary confinement in this oversized dollhouse."

"Do you want some coffee?" I asked.

"Do you have a bell you ring?"

She was joking, but she had no idea just how close to the truth it was.

"Honestly, there probably are little bells all over this place. Let's go to the kitchen and see what we can find. Roman left me a note and said he would be back later. We are on our own."

She gave me a dry look. "On our own minus the twenty or so staff."

"Miss, do you want these things in your suite?"

I turned to see an older man that had no business hauling boxes up and down those stairs. "Just leave them here," I said. "I'll take them up later."

He looked horrified. "We can't leave them in the foyer."

A little rebellious side of me bubbled up. "I live here, and I say it's fine."

He nodded, clearly torn between following my instructions and tidying up the clutter. "Yes, ma'am."

"Now coffee," I said to Carla.

She followed me as I made my way to the kitchen, barely remembering my way. When I walked in, I was not surprised to see an older woman cleaning what was already an immaculate kitchen.

Just then, a staff member approached us, his eyes flickering between me and Carla. "Ms. Foster, will your guest be staying for breakfast?" he asked, his tone impeccably neutral yet somehow still managing to convey a hint of judgment.

"Yes!" Carla answered.

"Will you be taking your breakfast in the dining room or breakfast room?" he asked.

I felt like Alice in Wonderland. "Uh…"

"The breakfast room, clearly," Carla answered. "We're not savages."

"Can I make some coffee?" I asked the man.

He looked insulted. "I will bring in coffee service."

"Thank you."

He turned to walk away.

"Sir?"

"Yes?"

"Where is the breakfast room?" I asked sheepishly.

Carla laughed.

He gave a small, patient smile, the kind reserved for a teacher talking to a particularly slow student. "It's just next to the conservatory, madam. I can have someone guide you there if you wish."

"No, that's alright. We'll find it. Thank you." I nodded, trying to mask my growing embarrassment with a weak smile.

"Kaira, this place is insane."

"I know," I said with a small laugh. "They need to put up maps like at the mall."

We sat down at the small table that was in a room flooded with sunlight. A coffee service was brought in seconds later.

"Breakfast will be ready in five minutes," the man said and glided away.

"You're being waited on hand and foot," she said.

"I didn't ask them to do that," I said defensively.

"This is their job. Don't look down on them or try to be independent. They are earning their paychecks."

I nodded. "You're right."

"So, I saw the pictures of you two yesterday. Let's see the ring."

I raised my left hand to show her the sparkling ring that Roman had slipped on my finger. The diamond caught the morning sun, throwing specks of light across the pristine walls of the breakfast room.

"It's gorgeous," Carla breathed, her eyes wide as she leaned closer to inspect it. "Roman really did go all out, didn't he?"

I couldn't help but smile, despite the whirlwind of emotions I had been feeling since arriving at Roman's mansion. "He did. It still feels surreal."

Before we could say anything more, two plates covered with silver domes were delivered.

"Can I get you anything else?" the man asked.

"Can I know your name?" I asked him.

"Tony."

"Tony, I'm Kaira and this is Carla."

"Very well, ma'am."

"Please, call me Kaira," I said.

He nodded and walked away. Carla eagerly lifted her dome and gasped when she saw the fluffy omelet and a side of golden hash browns laced with fine herbs. Beside it, slices of ripe avocado and a vine-ripened tomato salad completed the picturesque breakfast.

I lifted my own dome and found a similar dish. The aromas mingled in the air, creating a delightful scent that seemed almost too luxurious for an early morning meal.

"This is like eating at a gourmet restaurant every day," Carla exclaimed, forking into her omelet with a pleased sigh. "You could get used to this."

I took a bite of my own meal, the flavors rich and perfectly balanced. It was delicious.

"So, what happened yesterday?" she asked. "Don't say nothing, because I can tell there is definitely something."

I took a deep breath and gave her the rundown, skipping over the most salacious details.

"Are you going to stay?" she asked.

"Yes. For now. But we can't cross the line. I don't want this to get confusing."

She nodded. "I think that's a good rule. You don't want to fall in love with the guy and have him dump you in six months, which is the plan."

"Exactly. It feels so real sometimes, it's hard to remember the ticking clock hanging over our heads."

"Just keep your eyes on the prize," Carla said, shoveling up more hash browns. "In six months, it's payday."

I knew she was right. This was a business deal, a transaction. My heart wouldn't get broken if I kept my head on straight and didn't let myself fall under his spell.

We finished our breakfast and then took ourselves on a tour of the mansion. Carla and I giggled and twirled around in the ballroom. After finishing our impromptu dance number, we were greeted with a round of applause.

Several of the staff were leaning against the wall and watching us.

"It's nice to have laughter back in the house," one of them, a middle-aged woman named Marta, said with a kind smile.

That caught my attention. "Back in the house?"

She nodded, her expression softening. "It's been a long time since this place felt warm. Or like a home."

I didn't know what to say to that, so I just nodded and followed Carla as she dragged me toward the next room.

The library was easily my favorite. Carla's jaw dropped when we walked in.

"Okay, *this* is where I'm living now," she declared.

"It's amazing, right?"

After exploring the shelves in depth, we found ourselves in one of the sitting rooms. Carla threw herself onto one of the oversized sofas and leaned back.

I laughed and joined her, sinking into the plush cushions. The kitchen staff brought us a tray of snacks—fresh fruit, cheese, crackers, and some kind of fancy sparkling water. Carla immediately dove in while pulling out her phone.

"So," she said around a mouthful of cheese, "let's Google your fiancé."

"Carla," I groaned, but she ignored me, her fingers flying across her screen. "The less I know, the better."

It didn't take long for her to find a treasure trove of information.

"Roman Kelly," she read aloud. "Billionaire entrepreneur. Started his first company at eighteen. Forbes 30 Under 30, blah blah blah. Ooh, listen to this: 'Known for his sharp business acumen and ruthless approach to deal-making.'" She paused, raising an eyebrow at me. "Ruthless, huh?"

I rolled my eyes. "You have no idea."

She kept scrolling, her expression shifting from amused to curious.

"Oh no," she said softly, her voice losing its playful edge. "Oh my gosh."

I looked at her, my stomach twisting. "What?"

She glanced up at me, her eyes full of sympathy. "His parents were killed in a car accident when he was twelve."

The air seemed to leave the room. "What?" I whispered.

Carla handed me her phone to read the article. His parents had died in a head-on collision, and Roman had been in the car when it happened. He was the only survivor.

My heart ached for him. I couldn't imagine how horrifying that must have been, how it must have scarred him. Suddenly, so many things about him made sense—his need for control, his aloofness, the way he kept people at arm's length.

"It doesn't excuse him being a jerk," Carla said, as if reading my thoughts. "But it explains a lot."

I nodded, giving her the phone. "Yeah. It really does."

"Can you imagine growing up in a house like this?" Carla said. "The games of hide and seek?"

The darkness of the conversation shifted. We talked about our own childhoods and found ourselves laughing. A couple of the staff added their own stories. I felt like I was finally settling in.

A while later, the staff, who had been chatting and laughing with us, suddenly scattered like leaves in the wind. Like they could sense a change in the air. The sunlight that had been streaming through the windows seemed to dim, and a heavy silence settled over the air.

Carla and I were still lounging on the sofa when I saw him.

His presence was like a physical force. He filled the room with it, his broad shoulders and sharp suit commanding attention. His gaze landed on Carla, and his brow furrowed.

"Who is this?" he asked, his tone even but carrying an edge.

Carla sat up straight, her usual bravado faltering under his scrutiny. "I'm Carla," she said, holding out her hand. "Kaira's best friend."

Roman didn't take her hand. Instead, he looked at me, his expression unreadable.

"Did you invite her here?"

"I didn't think I needed permission," I said, crossing my arms.

His jaw tightened. "This isn't a college dorm, Kaira. It's my home."

"And I'm living here," I shot back. "Which means I should be able to have a friend over without being interrogated like a criminal."

The tension in the room was palpable. Carla cleared her throat.

"Maybe I should go," she said, standing up.

"No," I said firmly, grabbing her arm. "You're staying. Roman, if you have a problem with that, we can discuss it later."

He looked like he wanted to argue, but then his eyes flicked to Carla, who was watching the exchange with wide eyes. He exhaled sharply.

"Fine," he said, his voice clipped.

With that, he turned and walked out of the room.

Carla let out a low whistle. "Damn. He's intense."

I sighed, sinking back onto the sofa. "I told you so."

20

ROMAN

The moment I walked into the house, I knew something was off.

I couldn't put my finger on it right away, but the air felt different. Warmer, somehow. Livelier. Voices and laughter drifted down the hall, a stark contrast to the usual quiet that greeted me when I came home. Usually, one of my staff would be waiting to take my briefcase or offer me a drink.

I heard them talking in the kitchen, which seemed odd. But it wasn't their voices that had me going down the other hall. It was Kaira. She was talking to someone, which confused me.

I paused at the doorway, watching the two of them reclined on the sofas with a tray of snacks between them, laughing about something. My staff, usually composed and efficient, were lounging in the room, enjoying drinks and food with smiles and even a chuckle or two.

It was like walking into someone else's home.

When I finally stepped into the room, the staff jumped up and rushed out. I wasn't thrilled about the intrusion, but I let it go. For now.

After being dismissed in my own home, I walked back to the foyer with the intention of going to my study when I noticed a couple garbage bags and boxes in the corner. *What the hell?*

It was like I walked into the wrong house. My staff had been put under some spell. I stared at the things and knew where they came from—Kaira, obviously.

I stared at the clutter, my irritation growing. This wasn't acceptable. My home was a place of order, of structured calm, not this. I took a deep breath, trying to control the flare of anger. I couldn't help but overhear more laughter coming from the sitting room. The sound grated against my nerves. It wasn't that I despised joy or laughter; I just didn't know what to do with it.

I walked to my study, not surprised to see it had all been put back to rights. I did feel a little guilty for the mess I left the staff to handle. It had been quite a bit worse than the mess in the foyer. I knew I was going to have to talk to Kaira at some point, but I wasn't doing it in front of an audience.

After a couple of hours, I emerged from the study and noticed the clutter in the foyer was gone. I was informed dinner would be served in twenty minutes. I went upstairs to change before returning to the dining room, wondering if our guest would be joining us.

Kaira was already there, chatting with one of the staff. They were acting like they were best friends. When I entered the room, they stopped talking. The staff member, Jessica maybe, quickly poured me a glass of water before leaving the dining room.

Kaira looked at me but said nothing. Her friend must have left at some point, for which I was grateful.

Dinner was served. I noticed it again. The staff who served us seemed to share secret smiles and easy chatter with Kaira. She laughed, thanked them warmly, and even joked about the impeccable presentation of the dishes. They were charmed by her. Everyone was charmed by her.

Everyone except me at that moment.

I couldn't pinpoint why it irritated me so much. Maybe it was the way she so effortlessly connected with people, how she made my staff —*my* staff—feel more at ease than I ever had. Or maybe it was the nagging sense that this was no longer my house. It was hers, somehow.

The thought burrowed into my chest like a thorn. I took another bite of the beef that I technically knew tasted great, but in my mood, it tasted like betrayal.

"I had some of my things brought over," Kaira said, breaking the silence.

"I noticed."

"I've taken the bags and boxes to my room."

"Good. You could have had your buddies do it."

"My buddies?"

I waved a hand. "My staff that you seem to have befriended."

Kaira tilted her head slightly, her expression unreadable for a moment before a soft smile played on her lips. "Roman, they're not my buddies. They work here, yes, but they are people too. Friendly conversation doesn't cost anything."

"I'm aware," I replied curtly. "But this is my home, not a social club."

Her smile faded and she looked down at her plate, her fork playing idly with the food. "I understand this is what you're used to. However, loosening up a bit wouldn't hurt. They seem happier."

"Happier doesn't necessarily mean more productive," I countered.

She shook her head and went back to her meal.

By the time dinner was over, I had enough.

"Can you get the staff in here?" I demanded of Jessica.

"Yes, sir."

They filed into the dining room.

"Your work today was less than impressive," I said curtly. "I will not tolerate mediocrity and inefficiency."

The atmosphere shifted immediately. Kaira's smile faded, replaced by a look of confusion and maybe a touch of disappointment. And anger.

"Don't let it happen again." I stood and tossed my napkin on my plate. I didn't stay to explain myself. I headed back upstairs to change into my workout clothes. I needed to get rid of the frustration without trashing my house.

The gym was my refuge.

I went for the punching bag again. I wrapped my hands and started throwing jabs at the heavy bag. My mind replayed the scene over and over. The looks on their faces—the mixed expressions of surprise and hurt, the sudden drop of morale. I punched harder, each blow a futile attempt to shut out the guilt gnawing at me.

Kaira had been right; they were people, not just cogs in my meticulously maintained machine. But acknowledging that felt like loosening a grip I wasn't sure I was ready to release. The sound of my fists against the bag was the best music I'd ever heard.

I finished with the bag and moved to the weights, letting the familiar rhythm of lifting and lowering distract me from the storm brewing in my mind. The clink of the dumbbells and the rush of blood in my ears were grounding, a stark contrast to the chaos I had been feeling.

"Did you have a bad day?" Kaira's voice cut through my spiraling thoughts. I lowered the weights and turned to see her leaning against the doorframe, arms crossed over her ample chest.

"No," I said, grabbing a towel to wipe the sweat from my face. "It was fine until I came home to find you getting chummy with my staff."

Her eyebrows shot up. "Chummy? Seriously?"

"They're employees, Kaira. Not friends or family. They have work to do, and you can't be distracting them."

She rolled her eyes. "They're people, not furniture."

"What?" I snapped.

"You'd rather your staff spend their time shining your already shiny marble floors again instead of letting them enjoy themselves for half an hour?" she asked, her voice dripping with disbelief. "This place is cleaner than a hospital. It's not like they were sitting around watching soap operas. Do you want them to clean what's already clean?"

"Yes," I said automatically. "That's what I pay them to do."

Her jaw dropped, and for a moment, I thought I had finally managed to silence her. But then her eyes narrowed, and I saw the anger flash in them. She took a step closer, fists clenched at her sides.

"I don't understand you," she said, her tone low and biting.

"That makes two of us," I shot back.

Her defiance only seemed to grow with each word I threw at her. Most people would have backed down by now, but not Kaira. Her determination was infuriating—and, annoyingly, a little admirable.

"You live in this beautiful house," she said, gesturing around us, "but it feels like a tomb. Cold, lifeless. Your staff are good people. They deserve to enjoy their work, Roman. And if you can't see that, then I don't know how to help you. Spend five seconds getting to know them and you'll have their loyalty forever."

Her words hit harder than I cared to admit.

"This is my house," I said, my voice hard. "I don't need their loyalty. I pay them. They signed NDAs. Period."

She met my gaze head on, her eyes blazing. "And you're the one making it miserable."

I clenched my fists, struggling to keep my temper in check. "You don't know anything about me or this house."

"I know enough," she said, her voice softening slightly. "I know you're unhappy here. And I think that's the real problem."

Silence stretched between us, heavy and uncomfortable. She shook her head and turned on her heel.

"I'm going to the library," she said over her shoulder. "At least that room doesn't feel like it's suffocating me."

I watched her go. Part of me wanted to call her back, to argue, to prove her wrong. But another part—the quieter, more vulnerable part—knew she wasn't entirely wrong.

The gym wasn't a refuge anymore. She'd ruined that.

I sat on the bench, staring at the floor, my mind racing. Kaira's words replayed in my head.

She was right about one thing: I was unhappy here. This house, with all its grandeur and memories, was a prison of my own making. The ghosts of my parents lingered in every room, their laughter and warmth haunting me but always just out of reach. I had spent years trying to fill the void they left behind, but nothing ever seemed to fit.

Kaira had brought something new to this house—life, warmth, laughter. And I was ruining it. For her, for the staff, for myself.

I leaned back against the wall, closing my eyes. What would my mother think if she saw me now? If she heard the way I spoke to Kaira, the way I let my anger and insecurities consume me? And the staff?

She would be disappointed. And that thought hurt more than anything else.

For years, I had worked to prove I was worthy of my mother's pride, her love. But somewhere along the way, I'd lost sight of what really mattered. And now, with Kaira here, I had a chance to bring something good back into this house.

If only I didn't keep getting in my own way.

21

KAIRA

The library was by far my favorite spot in Roman's sprawling house. He said he liked the library, but this was the one room that felt untouched by him. It was warm, unlike the rest of the place. It was cozy and inviting. It wasn't just the furnishings that were different. It was the whole vibe.

I closed the doors and took a moment to soak it all in. With so many options, I had no idea what I wanted to read first. If I had had the ability, I would read several books at once. Unlike a typical library, this one wasn't organized by genre. The books weren't alphabetical from what I had seen either.

I didn't mind. It would give me the chance to explore all of the titles. Despite the messy organization, or perhaps because of it, I found myself drawn to a particular shelf where books were stacked haphazardly in no apparent order. I reached out and pulled out a book with a leather spine that looked as though it hadn't been touched for years. The title was embossed in fading gold letters, "Echoes of the Heart."

Curious, I opened the book to a random page and read a bit to see if it was something that piqued my interest. It was definitely a possibility. I put it on one of the small tables and started to scan more of the titles.

I wanted something romantic, but not quite Jane Austen. Preferably something a little more modern. Given the owner of the library, I had a feeling romance was not really his thing. He probably liked books about polo and yachts and how to properly chastise your butler.

I found something vaguely romantic and curled up on one of the cushy armchairs, my legs tucked beneath me as I held the book in my hands. I opened it and started to read.

Rather, I tried to read.

My eyes scanned the same sentence for the tenth time, but the words blurred together as my mind drifted, drawn away by a daydream I couldn't seem to shake. It wasn't unusual for me to get lost in the world of my own characters—hell, I did it all the time when I was writing—but lately, the male lead in my imagination had started to take on an infuriatingly familiar shape.

Roman.

Not cool.

I shook my head and tried to focus on the story. But the memory of his hands on me in the pool last night was impossible to ignore. The heat of his touch, the intensity in his eyes, the way he looked at me like I was the only thing in the world that mattered—it had been intoxicating.

But then, there was the other side of him. The moody, sharp-tongued Roman who could suck the energy out of a room with a single comment. The man who saw the world as a battlefield and everyone in it as either an opponent or a pawn. He was a hammer looking for a nail.

Why was he like that? What made him so cold and guarded?

I wondered about his parents, the people in the pictures Carla and I had found earlier. I couldn't imagine losing my parents, let alone so young and in such a tragic way. What kind of mark did that leave on someone?

I forced my attention back to my book, determined to shake off these thoughts. But just as I was starting to lose myself in the story, the soft creak of the library door pulled me back.

Roman walked in, freshly showered and dressed in gray sweatpants and a simple black T-shirt. His dark hair was damp, and he looked more relaxed than he was.

I quickly returned my gaze to my book, pretending not to notice him as he approached. I wanted to ignore him and pretend he was nothing more than an obnoxious insect.

But Roman was not the kind of man you could simply ignore. It wasn't just his size—it was his whole aura. He walked into a room and demanded the attention of everyone in it whether he meant to do it or not.

"Wine?" he asked, holding out a glass.

"No, thank you," I said without looking up.

He surprised me by putting the glass on the small table beside me instead of walking away. I glanced at him, expecting a sharp remark or a sarcastic comment, but instead, he stood there quietly for a moment.

"Should you be drinking in here?" I asked.

Truthfully, I didn't really trust myself. He might be fine, but I wasn't sure I wouldn't spill my glass on an irreplaceable tome.

"It's furniture," he said. "It can be cleaned. Or replaced."

I raised an eyebrow, unsure how to take his nonchalant response. Was he trying to tell me he didn't care about the furniture, or was it a test to see how I would react? Either way, Roman was standing here, in his library, offering me wine and speaking softly, almost gently.

He pulled up another armchair, positioning it so that it faced mine, and sat down with his own glass of wine.

I could feel a standoff coming. Again. I picked up the glass of wine and took a drink. I was going to need the liquid courage to deal with him.

"I was out of line earlier," he said.

I blinked, lowering my book. That was the last thing I expected him to say. "Which time?"

He nodded and took a sip from his glass before licking his lips. I nearly moaned when I saw him do it. It reminded me of him kissing me. That tongue that promised pleasure.

I shook off the thoughts and gave him my full attention.

"This house has been too quiet for too long. It could use a little laughter. You were right." He shook his head. "I've been living here a certain way but that doesn't mean it's the right way."

His honesty caught me off guard. Roman didn't apologize, at least not in the time I had known him. But there was something in his expression—an openness I hadn't seen before—that made me believe he was sincere.

I put my book down, leaning forward slightly. "I didn't think you'd admit that."

He smirked faintly. "Neither did I."

We sat in silence for a moment before he continued.

"I've spent so many years in my business world, treating everyone like they're trying to take something from me. It's become a reflex."

"Like if you don't get them first, they'll get you?" I asked gently.

He nodded, his gaze dropping to the floor. "Yeah."

"That sounds like a lonely way to live," I said, keeping my tone soft.

His jaw tightened, and for a moment, I thought I'd pushed too far. But then he let out a quiet breath and looked back at me.

"It is," he admitted. "But when you're in it, you don't really notice. It's second nature to me." Then he paused, looking into his glass as if it held some hidden truth that he was reluctant to share. "Until someone comes along and makes you see things differently," he added quietly, almost to himself.

I felt my heart do a quick skip. Was he talking about me? I wanted to press him, to ask who had made him reconsider his fortress-like existence, but I feared destroying the fragile truce we had just built. Roman was a wounded animal. I had to tread lightly. If I started asking questions or imposing my thoughts and beliefs on him, he was going to bolt.

Instead, I chose a safer question. "So, what are you going to do about it?"

Roman glanced up at me, his eyes searching my face as if trying to decide how much to reveal. There was something in his gaze that made my chest ache—a vulnerability I hadn't expected to see. For the first time, Roman wasn't the arrogant, guarded man who infuriated me. He was just... human.

I reached for the glass of wine and took a small sip. It wasn't much, but it was enough to make the corners of his mouth lift into a faint smile. I wanted him to feel relaxed.

"Thank you," he said.

"For what?"

"For not giving up on me entirely," he said, leaning back in his chair. "I know I'm not the easiest person to be around."

I laughed softly. "That's an understatement."

His smile widened, and I saw a hint of humor in his expression. "Fair enough."

We started talking after that, our conversation flowing surprisingly easily. Roman asked me about the book I'd been reading. I teased him about the fact that his library was filled with books I doubted he'd ever read. He didn't deny it, laughing when I called him out on the pristine condition of the spines.

"Do you collect the books just to have them?" I asked. "I didn't even get to see a quarter of your library. It's truly one of the biggest personal libraries I've ever seen. Well, let's be honest, I've never actually seen a personal library."

Roman chuckled, a sound I was quickly learning to appreciate. He didn't laugh enough. He didn't smile enough. "I suppose, in a way, yes. They are part of the aesthetic I desired for this place—a symbol of knowledge and culture. But maybe it's time I actually started reading more of them."

"Which book would you start with?"

"I don't know," he said. "I'm a very black and white guy. I don't know if I'm the kind of guy that can read fiction. I would pick it apart too much."

I studied him. "What about biographies?"

"I don't care enough about people."

I giggled softly. "Honest."

"That probably sounds like a dick thing to say, but I think we all have our own stories. What makes any one person any more interesting than the next?"

It was evident he valued his own privacy and solace over understanding others' lives—a trait I found both frustrating and intriguing.

"Maybe, it's not about one person being more interesting than another. It's about seeing how someone else has navigated their unique challenges. You might find pieces of yourself in their stories, or you might learn something completely new."

Roman looked pensive. "Maybe," he conceded after a moment. "But I've always felt like we should deal with our own shit. It feels like telling one's story is inviting people into your life. Like you need the attention or accolades. Or pity. That's the last fucking thing I want."

It was all very valid. "I get it. I guess I never really thought about it like that."

"Do *you* like biographies?"

"Some. I do like to read about people living through extraordinary events. I find some to be inspirational. I couldn't give a shit about politicians or—"

"People like me," he said with a twitch of his lips.

I grimaced. "Sorry."

"Don't be. I wouldn't read my story."

I didn't want to tell him that I knew a little about his story and I did find it intriguing.

"I'll let you get back to your book," he said.

I didn't want him to leave just yet. "Would you like me to recommend a book?" I asked. "Something juicy."

He chuckled. "I don't want to bother you."

"How about you turn that fireplace on, and I'll find you something? I bet you would like a good true crime thriller."

"That sounds dark. Are you sure it's a good idea for a guy like me to read a book like that? It might give me ideas."

"Ha. Ha. Just get that thing going."

I had seen a few books by Dean Koontz that I had a feeling would hold his attention. I picked up the book and took it back to the sitting area.

The fireplace was on. "It's just a remote," Roman said. "Just push the button, set the temperature, and you're good to go."

Roman took the book from my hands. A slight frown creased his brow as he flipped through the pages, scanning the blurbs and the author's note.

"What's this one about?" he asked.

"Murder, mystery, a bit of psychological twist. It's gripping, pulls you into the mind of both the detective and the killer. Thought it might be something you'd appreciate—the strategy, the analytical side of it."

"Sounds good."

We settled in with our glasses of wine, the warmth from the fireplace and a newfound peace between us.

22

ROMAN

I glanced up from my book. It was so strange to be sitting with a woman I was physically attracted to and not be all over her. We had been sitting in the library for two hours, drinking wine and reading in mostly silence. Occasionally, I would ask her about my book or hers.

She seemed to enjoy discussing the plot twists and the characters' motives, her eyes lighting up each time she unfolded a new layer of the story. It was a different sort of interaction than I was used to, one that didn't involve pressing for more physical intimacy or showcasing my usual charm. Instead, it felt genuine, like we were actually connecting on a level beyond surface attraction.

I had to admit, it was refreshing not to play the part I usually played around women. With her, it felt like I could just be myself—whatever that was. As I turned another page, I found myself wondering about her life outside of these walls. Who was she before she showed up in my life?

I glanced up from my book and smiled.

Kaira had fallen asleep on the chaise in the library. Her book had fallen onto her chest, her lips slightly parted. I sat and watched her. The golden glow from the fireplace cast a soft light over her features.

Her breathing was even, peaceful. I didn't have the heart to wake her. She looked like she belonged.

I felt an attraction to her, but it wasn't like the same pull I felt last night. Yes, given the chance, I would take her to bed right now. But this felt different. There was something profoundly serene about this moment, watching her sleep. It stirred something within me that I hadn't felt in a long time—if ever. It wasn't just desire, it was respect, admiration even, for the way she carried herself, for her intellect, her passion for the stories she read.

She wouldn't be able to sleep so peacefully if she didn't trust me. My eyes lingered on Kaira's sleeping form. Maybe she was right; perhaps there was merit in sharing parts of our own lives to forge true connections.

I quietly got up and walked to the bench in the corner. There were blankets neatly folded for those that might want to cuddle up while reading. The blankets were essentially new. I grabbed one and carefully covered her. She stirred slightly, murmuring something unintelligible before settling back into her dreams.

I picked up our empty wine glasses and made my way to the kitchen with the half-full bottle of wine.

The kitchen was alive with quiet conversation. A few members of the night staff were gathered around the island, sipping on cups of coffee and laughing. They stopped the moment I entered, their voices cutting off mid-sentence as their eyes darted to me.

I wasn't usually in the kitchen. Not like this. My presence made them uneasy. I hated that I had created an environment where they felt like they couldn't relax in their own space.

I probably never would have noticed their behavior but now that I had seen them with Kaira, I saw the stark contrast in their attitude when I was around.

They scrambled to make themselves busy, wiping down already spotless counters and organizing the coffee station.

I nodded toward the coffee pot. "Any left?"

Marilyn, my head of cleaning staff, nodded cautiously. "Yes, sir. Would you like me to pour you a cup?"

I shook my head, putting the wine glasses in the sink. "No, I've got it."

I could feel them all watching me like they were waiting for me to yell at them or start screaming orders. Their uncertainty was palpable as I poured myself a mug and added a splash of cream. I leaned against the island, stirring the coffee slowly, aware of the furtive glances they were exchanging.

"Do you want something to eat?" Marilyn asked. "I can make you a sandwich or I believe there are some leftovers in the refrigerator."

"I should go make sure things are locked up," Tim said.

"Please, stay," I said. "Everyone, have a seat."

I saw the looks of fear. Tim looked resigned to the lecture. Marilyn looked irritated, but she held her tongue.

"I need to apologize," I said, my voice cutting through the tense silence. "To all of you."

Marilyn straightened, her expression unreadable. The others froze before exchanging glances with one another. Their reactions were telling. I was such a dick, they couldn't believe I was apologizing.

"My house guest—Kaira—she's made me realize some things." I took a sip of coffee and considered my next words. "I've been a shitty employer."

A couple of the younger staff members exchanged wide-eyed looks, clearly startled by my bluntness.

"I'm sorry," I continued. "This house hasn't been a welcoming place to work for a long time, and that's on me. I want to change that. I want to make it better. Like it used to be."

Marilyn's eyes softened. She stepped forward, her hands clasped in front of her. "The bones of this house still have all the memories of your parents and the life they built here, Roman. It was a house full of love and laughter once. It's about time we all breathed some of that back into it."

Her words hit me hard. She was right. This house had been a home once. A real home. And somewhere along the way, I'd let it become something cold and impersonal. Marilyn had been with the family for my entire life.

Marta walked into the kitchen with a bright smile, but the moment she saw me, it fell away.

"I'm sorry," she murmured.

"Stay," I said. "I was just telling the rest of the staff things are going to change around here."

"He was just saying he wants this cold mausoleum to be a home again," Marilyn said with a smile.

Marta grinned. "Really? That's wonderful. We've missed the old days."

"From now on, I want you all to feel free to use the common areas after your shifts. Read in the library, watch TV in the lounge, make yourselves a meal—this is your home too while you're here."

There was a collective exhale throughout the room, as if a pressure valve had been released. Tim's shoulders dropped slightly from their usual tense position.

"Kaira is a bright, beautiful woman on the inside and outside," Marilyn said.

I glanced back toward the library, where Kaira was still sleeping. "Having her here—it's been different. But good. She's not afraid to stand up for what she thinks is right, even when it scares her. And she speaks her mind." I shook my head, a small smile tugging at my lips. "I didn't expect that from her."

Marilyn smiled knowingly. "She's something, isn't she?"

I nodded, sipping my coffee. "Yeah, she is."

The other women in the kitchen exchanged sly smiles, and I felt the atmosphere shift, becoming lighter.

"She told us she loves to write," Marta said. "She and her friend had a good time in the ballroom. They thought it was like stepping into a fairytale."

"I think it might be time we used that ballroom for more than just storing old furniture," I mused, the idea forming as I spoke. "Maybe we could host some events here—charity galas, art shows. Bring some life back into this place."

The staff nodded enthusiastically at the idea.

"Your parents used to love throwing parties." Marta sighed. "I will never forget the first time I was tasked with serving. I dropped a whole tray of appetizers. Your mother was very kind. I had just started working for the family. I expected to be fired. Instead, she helped me clean up, laughing and telling me stories of her own mishaps when she was younger. She made me feel like I belonged here, not just as an employee, but as part of the family."

I smiled at Marta's memory and felt a pang of longing for my parents. "I want to bring that feeling back," I declared. "I don't just want this house to be a place where you work; I want it to be a place where you feel at home, too."

"I remember the time I was vacuuming and tripped over the cord," Marilyn said with a shake of her head. "Your father didn't even flinch. He just came over, turned off the vacuum, and made sure I was okay before he got it untangled. He always had a way of making the small disasters feel like nothing more than tiny bumps in the road."

The room filled with gentle laughter as others began sharing their anecdotes as well. It seemed that each memory unearthed another. The staff were part of my life. I realized I had been treating them like furniture or art on the wall instead of the extended family they really were. They were the closest thing to family I had beyond my aunt.

"You know, Valentine's Day is coming up," Marilyn said, her tone casual, but I was picking up on a hint. "Maybe you should think about doing something nice for Kaira. It seems like she's brought joy into your life. You could do something to show her how special she is."

Her suggestion caught me off guard. And not in a good way. I couldn't explain why, but something triggered me. I straightened, my usual defenses going back up. "This isn't real. You know that."

Marilyn shrugged. "Maybe not. But the media doesn't know that. And a good fiancé plans something special for his bride-to-be."

The others murmured their agreement, nodding along.

I was immediately defensive. "This is a PR strategy. That's all. I don't want to lay it on too thick."

Marilyn raised an eyebrow. "Of course, sir. But even a PR strategy could use a little romance."

I finished my coffee in silence, half-listening to their many suggestions. I was preoccupied with thoughts of Kaira.

Was I really considering doing something for Valentine's Day? For her?

It was so out of character for me.

But the more I thought about it, the more I realized that Kaira had changed the dynamic of the household. I probably did owe her a little more than just the money and fine things I was buying her. She would probably enjoy a nice gesture.

"I'll think about it," I finally conceded.

The kitchen fell silent for a moment, everyone likely just as surprised as I was.

Marilyn smiled. "She would appreciate it, even if it's just a small gesture."

"I'll think about it," I repeated. "I'm going to bed. Goodnight."

I walked out of the kitchen and stopped by the library once again. She was still sound asleep. I left her where she was and headed upstairs.

The staff had given me a lot to think about.

23

KAIRA

I woke up with a start, my heart pounding and my skin tingling. My cheeks flushed as the remnants of my dream lingered in my mind—Roman's hands on me, his mouth tracing a line down my neck, his voice low and demanding in my ear.

God, get a grip, Kaira.

I let out a shaky laugh and glanced around the dimly lit library. The soft glow of the fireplace was the only light. There was a soft blanket draped over me, one I hadn't grabbed myself. My lips curved into a small smile. *Roman.*

I stretched, the dream still clinging to the edges of my consciousness. It had been one hell of a ride. The erotic dream had been a combination of reality and straight fantasy. Elements of the pool situation mingled with the book I had been reading and my own very vivid imagination.

My body was still tingling. Taking a deep breath, I lifted the blanket off and rose from the plush chair. The floor was cold under my bare feet. I quickly slipped them into my discarded shoes.

My relationship—or whatever it was—with Roman had turned into something I couldn't quite classify. Was it just a ploy for the public? Or was there something more, something that could be expanded upon?

I stretched, trying to work the kink out of my neck. I wondered how long I had been asleep. And why hadn't Roman woken me up?

I couldn't decide if it was really sweet or callous. Then I looked down at the blanket. I was going to give him the benefit of the doubt. It was a kind gesture.

I spotted my phone on the table along with the book I had been reading. I checked the time, knowing it had to be late.

It wasn't just late, it was the middle of the night. I couldn't believe I had slept so hard. I chalked it up to the craziness of the last few days. The exhaustion had finally caught up with me.

I found the remote for the fireplace and turned it off. Then I laughed quietly to myself. "Like he's going to be worried about the electric bill."

But still, I couldn't leave it on. Just because he could pay the electric bill, it didn't mean I needed to just blow it. I picked up the blanket. I wasn't sure where it belonged and decided to take it with me. I would ask Marilyn where it belonged in the morning.

The house was eerily quiet when I stepped out of the library. The staff that lived on the premises stayed in a group of rooms downstairs. It was a little antiquated, but it wasn't like they were living in squalor.

I wandered down the hallway. It was the kind of silence that amplified every tiny little sound. I could hear a soft humming noise. It could be the refrigerator or any one of the many gadgets in the kitchen. I made my way up the grand staircase, running my fingers along the polished banister, and stifled a yawn.

As I reached the landing, I nearly jumped out of my skin when a door at the top of the stairs opened abruptly. Roman stepped out, pulling the doors closed behind him with a soft click of the lock.

He froze when he saw me, his expression unreadable in the low light.

"Did I wake you?" he asked, his voice low and smooth, like velvet brushing over my senses. It stirred up memories of the dream. I visibly shuddered but it had nothing to do with the chill in the air.

"No," I said, shaking my head. "I just woke up on my own. I'm on my way to bed."

His gaze flicked to the blanket still draped over my arm. A faint smile tugged at the corner of his lips.

"Thanks for this," I said, holding it up slightly. "And for letting me sleep."

He nodded. "You looked comfortable. I didn't want to wake you."

"I don't even know when I passed out." I laughed softly. "Obviously, the book wasn't that good."

"It was probably around eleven," he said.

"Did you enjoy your book?" I asked.

"I haven't decided yet. It's one of those that makes you think, and I'm not sure if I'm in the mood to think that hard."

He paused for a moment and scrutinized my face. It was like he was trying to read something in my expression, or perhaps sensing the remnants of my dream that lingered around me.

God, what if I had the dream when he was still in the library? What if I moaned his name?

I could feel my cheeks burning.

"Are you okay?" he asked, stepping closer. The space between us seemed charged with an unspoken tension. It was just like the moment before he kissed me in the pool.

I forced myself to settle down. There was no way he knew about the dream.

I glanced at the door he'd just locked. "What were you doing in there? It's three in the morning."

His eyes darkened, a shadow passing over his features. "Work," he said curtly. It was clear from his tone that the subject was closed.

I didn't press further. It wasn't my business, and honestly, I wasn't sure I wanted to know.

"Heading to bed?" he asked, his voice gentler now.

"Yeah," I said, brushing a stray hair from my face. I couldn't even begin to imagine what my hair looked like. And I probably had a crease mark on my face from where I was lying against the armrest.

"I'll walk you," he offered.

I nodded, my throat suddenly dry. It wasn't like I had a long way to go, but it was a nice gesture. I wasn't going to reject any kind gesture he offered. They were very few and far between. I wanted to encourage more of them.

He fell into step beside me. I could smell his body wash or shampoo. It had a fresh scent to it. It was very crisp and masculine, almost like he had just stepped in from a hike in the mountains.

The hallway seemed longer than I remembered. His presence made the space feel smaller, more intimate.

When we reached my room, he opened the door for me, holding it just wide enough for me to slip past. I murmured a quiet "thanks" as I walked through, but the moment I moved, my body brushed against his.

It was barely a touch—just my hip grazing across the front of him, but it was enough to feel the unmistakable hardness pressing against his sweats.

My breath hitched. I froze, turning to look up at him. His jaw was tight, his eyes burning with something dark and dangerous that sent a thrill down my spine. Again, it was that same look in his eyes I had seen that night in the pool.

"Kaira," he said, his voice strained, like he was barely holding himself together.

The air between us crackled with tension, thick and electric. I knew I should step away, should say goodnight and shut the door, but I couldn't make myself move. He was the one that had said it. We both wanted it. We were both craving sex. There was a running dialogue in the back of my mind going through all the pros and cons of sex with him.

"You should go to bed," he said, his tone more a command than a suggestion. "Before I do something we'll both regret."

I swallowed hard and knew I was staring down a big decision. It was the kind of decision that could change everything. Something told me there was no simple one-nighter when it came to Roman. I would be living under the same roof as him.

I shut down the voice in the back of my mind. "Regret is a problem for morning," I said.

His control snapped. One moment, he was standing there, composed and restrained, and the next, his mouth was on mine, his hands tangling in my hair as he kissed me like he'd been holding back for years.

I gasped against his lips. He took advantage, deepening the kiss, his tongue sweeping against mine. Heat surged through me, pooling low in my belly as I clung to him, my fingers digging into his shoulders.

He backed me into the room, kicking the door shut behind him. I didn't care about the rules, the contract, or the line we were so clearly crossing.

All I cared about was the way he made me feel—alive, wanted, and utterly consumed.

"Tell me to stop," he murmured against my lips, his voice hoarse and full of need.

"Don't stop," I whispered, pulling him closer.

His hands slid down to my waist, gripping me firmly as he kissed me again, slower this time, but no less intense. Every nerve ending in my body felt like it was on fire. I knew there was no going back from this.

Roman wasn't just under my skin—he was in my veins, my heart, my soul. And for the first time, I didn't want to fight it.

Not anymore.

He backed me against the wall. His large, oh-so-hard body pushed against me, pinning me with a delicious pressure that stole my breath away. Our lips separated for a mere moment as he looked down into my eyes, his gaze intense and searching.

"You sure?" he asked, his voice laced with both concern and desire. "I don't know if I can stop a second time."

In response, I reached up, putting my hand on the back of his head and pulling him back down to me. "Absolutely."

That was all the confirmation he needed. His lips crashed against mine once again, hungry and urgent. As we kissed, his hands slid down my sides and slipped between my ass and the wall. He squeezed hard, jerking my pelvis against his erection.

I groaned at the contact, my body burning for more. I didn't want to take it slow anymore. I wanted him now, hard and fast.

Too bad he had other ideas.

He pulled back slightly, his eyes dark with lust as he looked down at me. He slid his hands up, cupping my breasts through the thin pajama top I was wearing. His thumbs grazed my nipples, causing them to pebble under the fabric.

"You're so fucking beautiful," he muttered against my lips before capturing them once again.

His kisses were slow and sweet now as he continued to tease my nipples through the fabric of my shirt. My brain screamed at me to stop, but my body refused to listen.

He broke the kiss again and looked down at me before sliding his tongue along the sensitive skin between my ear and collarbone.

"Say you want this," he whispered breathlessly against my skin. "Tell me you need this."

"I need this," I said, gasping as he nibbled on the tender spot under my ear. "I want you."

His hand slid down between our bodies again, traveling between us until it found the hem of my shirt. With a quick movement, he lifted it over my head, tossing it aside before running his hands up my bare stomach and chest once more.

I gasped at the contact, arching into him as he trailed his fingers down toward the waistband of my pajama bottoms. Unlike in the pool when he touched me, there was no hesitation or restraint in his movements now.

His fingers slipped under the fabric, tracing over my mound through my panties. I bit my lip, his touch sending shockwaves through me. I could feel the dampness gathering between my legs as he teased me mercilessly.

"Roman," I moaned, rocking into his hand.

He pulled back slightly, a small smile playing on his lips. "Tell me," he said softly. "Tell me what you want."

"Please," I breathed. "I need you to fuck me."

Without another word, he slid two fingers inside me, thrusting deep and hard, hitting that spot that made me gasp out loud. It felt so good. It was everything I had wanted and more. He kissed me again as he rubbed his thumb against my clit in time with his fingers.

Moans of pleasure escaped me as he brought me closer and closer to the edge. I knew I wouldn't last long, not with his fingers inside me and his mouth on me.

When the first orgasm crashed over me, it was like nothing I had ever felt before. It took my breath away and left me shaking.

He pulled away from the kiss, getting on his knees before pulling down my bottoms and panties in one swift motion. He looked up at me, heat burning in his eyes.

Oh God. There was no way I would survive what I thought he was going to do.

24

ROMAN

As soon as I knelt down and saw the look of anticipation on her face, I felt a low growl rumble in my chest. Her scent filled my nostrils, intoxicating me and driving me to lose control. I had to hold myself back from taking her too fast. I needed to make this moment memorable for both of us.

I looked up at her, a seductive smile on my face. I licked my lips in anticipation. My mouth replaced the spot where my fingers had been moments before. The taste of her was intoxicating. Sweet and musky, with just a hint of vanilla from her body wash.

I ran my tongue from her entrance to her clit and back again, pressing firmly against the bud that made her writhe in pleasure beneath me. Her moans filled the room, fueling my desire even more.

I licked her over and over, pushing two fingers inside her once more while circling her clit with my tongue. She gasped and arched into me, her body quaking with another orgasm.

"Roman!" she cried out, her voice trembling as waves of pleasure coursed through her body. Every spasm, every twitch was reflected by a tightening around my fingers, spurring me on to keep going.

I added a third finger into the mix, stretching her further and hitting that spot inside her that made her cry out in pleasure. I felt the walls of her core clench tightly around my fingers, effectively warning me that she was close to another orgasm. I didn't know her past sexual experiences, but I had a feeling she never let herself go like this. I wanted to give her the best orgasm of her life.

My tongue continued its relentless assault, lapping at her swollen clit, tasting her sweet juices that were practically flowing out of her. Her scent filled the room. I was like a predator drawn to its prey. I continued to devour her, groaning in pleasure as she tasted so damn good.

When I felt fingernails dig into my shoulder blades, I knew she was close. I doubled down my efforts, and just as predicted, a few seconds later she was crying out. I could feel her knees bending and knew she was about to collapse into a heap on the floor.

I leaned back on my haunches and looked up at her. I wiped my mouth with the back of my hand. She was half-standing, half-leaning against the wall. Her chest heaved up and down.

I slowly got to my feet. "I need to get a condom. Get on the bed and wait for me."

She looked at me, but I wasn't sure she was really seeing me. I swatted her ass. "Go. Now."

With a laugh, she pushed herself off the wall and stumbled to the bed. I watched her collapse onto the mattress, her naked body splayed out like a feast ready to be devoured. I ignored the throb in my pants and went to rummage in the bathroom for a condom.

I found one and quickly walked back to her bedroom. She was watching me. Her eyes roved over my body as I stripped off my clothes. Once naked, I joined her on the bed.

Her fingers danced over my chest and down to my stomach. Her touch was like a flame against my skin. I felt myself harden even further as she wrapped her fingers around me. She moved her soft little hand up and down. I was already so close to losing control I had to push her hand away.

I ripped open the condom and slipped it on. I positioned myself over her body, supporting my weight on my elbows. She looked up at me. There was no hesitation.

"Ready?" I asked.

She nodded. "Yes."

I positioned myself at her entrance and slid inside slowly, groaning at the tightness that surrounded me. She was so wet and hot, it felt almost too good to be true.

The long, soft moan that escaped her lips nearly undid me. Each inch of me sinking into her felt like heaven and a surge of possessiveness washed over me. Closing my eyes, I took a deep breath, relishing the sheer pleasure that came from being buried inside her.

Her small hands clutched my biceps as I began to move, creating a rhythm that was both slow and torturous. She cried out each time I pulled back, only to push back in just as slowly. Her body arched up to meet mine.

The trembling had started again, harsher this time, radiating from her inner thighs and along the curve of her hips. Her legs squeezed around me so tight I couldn't move.

Sweat trickled down my spine. The lust in her eyes matched perfectly with the wild intensity I was sure she could see in mine.

I slipped my hand down and pushed her left thigh open. She gave a small whimper at the sudden change in position. I grunted in response, my pace quickening as the new angle allowed me to slide even deeper into her. It was pure pleasure, the feel of her heated, slick walls squeezing me tightly as I thrust in and out of her.

Her fingers dug into my back as her body started to tense around me. "Roman... I'm..." she gasped out.

"I know," I replied gruffly, fully aware of how close she was to tipping over the edge. Her walls clenched around me again, tighter this time, and it was everything I could do to hold back, wanting to make sure she went over that edge first.

I leaned down, capturing her lips with mine as I continued my rhythmic onslaught inside her. I could taste the salty tang of our mixed sweat on her lips. My heart pounded in my chest as it raced to keep up with the pleasure.

The sound of skin slapping against skin filled the room as I settled into a rhythm that sent us both spiraling toward oblivion. Every stroke inside her felt like heaven on earth—the way she wrapped herself around me, the way she moaned my name.

I wasn't going to stop. This was one of those experiences I wanted to last for as long as humanly possible.

Her cries grew louder, and her body shook with each thrust. I could tell she was close to the precipice again. Her eyes were closed and her head rolled back and forth. The pleasure was making her crazy. I was almost there too, but I had to hold on. For her. It wouldn't be much longer, I promised myself, as her inner muscles squeezed me once more.

"Roman," she purred, pulling me back to reality. Hearing her say my name sent waves of hot pleasure surging through me.

"Let go," I whispered into her ear.

All at once she shattered beneath me, writhing beneath me. Her loud cries echoed around the room as wave after wave of pleasure crashed over her. There were no words to describe what it felt like at that moment. The intimate connection between us was impossible to be expressed in language. I savored every moment of her orgasm.

Feeling her fall apart under me was my undoing. With a grunt, I tipped over the edge, my euphoria echoing hers as I let myself explode. Each spasm was a jolt of sheer ecstasy. It was overwhelming and satisfying at the same time.

Eventually, our bodies stilled. Spent and satisfied, I collapsed on top of her, burying my face into her neck. She was panting heavily but made no move to push me off. Her soft curves were like lying on a comfy pillow.

Her fingers gently ran up and down my back, calming my erratic heartrate. We lay there in silence, basking in the afterglow. I wanted to stay put and give myself time to recover and take her again.

But I wouldn't.

I rolled off her and walked into the bathroom, disposing of the condom. I glanced at my reflection in the mirror and immediately felt self-loathing.

Kaira had pulled the blankets over her breasts. She was looking at me with a soft smile. I pulled on my briefs.

"Where are you going?" she asked.

"Bed."

She said nothing as I picked up my pants and shirt. I walked out of her room without saying another word. I started back toward my room, pausing as I passed the double doors at the top of the stairs. I shook my head and continued to my bedroom.

It was almost four and I knew I should get my ass in bed, but I wasn't going to be able to sleep with the scent of her on me. I could still taste her. It was an aphrodisiac. I wanted more, but something told me I couldn't. I knew it was wrong.

To keep myself from caving into temptation, I walked to the shower. I had to wash her off me. The water was scalding, almost painful against my skin, but I forced myself to stay under the spray until the feel of her seemed less imprinted on my body. It was crazy, but I needed this pain. Each drop that hit me was a punishment for the way I had lost control, a penance for enjoying it too much.

I stayed under until the water ran cold. The chill helped clear my mind, sharpening the thoughts that were previously blurred by lust and desire.

Toweling off, I couldn't help but look at myself in the mirror once again. This thing between Kaira and me? It wasn't supposed to be complex or emotionally charged. It was a slip, a moment of weakness that could potentially unravel both our lives if not controlled.

I grabbed my toothbrush and started brushing vigorously, trying to scrub away the lingering taste of her. I needed to forget the memory of her moans, the feel of her skin under my hands.

I caught my reflection staring back at me with a mix of frustration and resignation. I turned off the bathroom light and headed back to my room, the towel hanging loosely around my waist. I dropped the towel and collapsed in my bed. I closed my eyes and hoped like hell I had not just made a huge mistake.

I didn't want Kaira to leave, but I also knew I couldn't keep doing this with her. She was dangerous because she was so easy to like.

There was no way in hell I could let myself catch real feelings for her. Something told me she was the one woman in this world that I was in danger of falling for.

25

KAIRA

I could see the sun was out, nice and bright. The start of a beautiful day. I should be up, enjoying the nice day with a walk or coffee on the patio. But I couldn't bring myself to leave my little cocoon.

I stayed curled up in my bed, staring at the ceiling. My mind was replaying the events of the previous night on an endless loop, tormenting me with every moment of weakness.

What had I been thinking? One night of Roman being considerate and suddenly I was throwing myself at him like some starry-eyed fool. I should've known better. I acted on the crush like the band geek in high school that finally got a little attention from the star quarterback.

Now, I was wrapped in silent regret.

We had shared something amazing. At least, I thought it was amazing. The man had rocked my world. My body was his to control. I wondered if he felt the same, if last night meant as much to him as it did to me. Or was I just another name on his list?

I knew the answer and it was killing me. I knew what he thought. It was evident in his reaction after the deed had been done.

He had gotten up and left afterward like it meant nothing. No hesitation, no lingering glances, no soft words. Just gone, as if nothing had happened. It made me feel cheap. Nothing more than a pincushion.

I tried to shake these thoughts from my mind but they clung to me. My fingers nervously tugged at the edge of the blanket, twisting the fabric as I let out a deep sigh. How could I have been so naive? How could I not see the signs that were probably as clear as day to everyone else?

I buried my face in the pillow and groaned. It was ridiculous. Roman had shown me exactly who he was time and time again. One night of kindness didn't erase the rest of it. I'd been stupid to think otherwise, even for a second. How was I going to last all six months when I couldn't make it through the first week without jumping his bones?

I knew I should get up, wash off the remnants of last night, and face the day with whatever strength I could muster. But every motion felt monumental, weighed down by a mix of longing and dread. I couldn't stop thinking of his hands, strong yet gentle. I didn't want to want him. I wanted to be like him and just pretend it was no big deal.

Eventually, I summoned the will to rise. My legs swung over the side of the bed, where I sat and stared out the window for a few seconds. I needed to decide what I was going to do. Did I stay? I was committed to a contract, so running out with my head hung in shame didn't really feel like an option.

Was I supposed to just ignore him? Roman was way too big to ignore, literally and metaphorically. Did they still sell chastity belts? If so, I needed to buy one and throw away the key.

I stood up, stretching the stiffness out of my muscles, and walked to the bathroom. I stared at my reflection in the mirror, searching for some sign of the strength I used to think I had. Instead, all I saw were the remnants of yesterday's makeup.

I turned on the shower, cranking it up nice and hot. I wanted to melt away any reminders of him. I needed to rid myself of his smell. His touch. All of it.

As the shower heated up, the steam clouded over my reflection, mercifully obscuring the disappointment on my face. I stepped under the hot spray, letting it wash over me as if it could cleanse away not just the physical but also the emotional residue from last night. The water slid down my body. I closed my eyes, allowing the warmth to wash over me, hoping that when I opened them again I would feel like a new, confident woman.

Unfortunately, the shower wasn't quite the renewal I had hoped for. I still felt a level of self-loathing that was new to me. I had plenty of things to hate about myself, but this was different. Last night, he had made me feel so beautiful. So wanted.

And I dropped my pants and opened my legs for him.

The self-recrimination was brutal, and yet, there was a part of me that was still clinging to the attraction that had driven me to him. I was going to drive myself crazy. The only way to get out of anything was to go straight through it. That's what I was going to do.

"It's going to be rocky, but I can still make this work."

I wrapped a towel tightly around myself, and stepped out, determined to get dressed and face the day like nothing happened. If Roman could brush it off, so could I. He was probably already gone anyway. The mirror was still fogged over, and in a way, I was grateful for that. I wasn't ready to face myself just yet.

I padded back into the bedroom, avoiding the bed where it had all happened. Instead, I walked into my closet to find something to wear. I looked at the fancy clothes the staff had hung up for me. I didn't want to wear any of that. I wanted my comfortable clothes. It took a second to find my old, worn things, but I did. I dressed in jeans, a hoodie, and my old-school knock-off Uggs. It was the perfect outfit for lounging around the house.

"Please don't be home," I murmured before I opened my bedroom door.

I hated that I felt like I had to hide.

The sound of a loud commotion downstairs startled me out of my self-loathing spiral. A woman's voice rang out—laughing, crying, yelling? I couldn't tell if she was furious or ecstatic, but she was definitely loud.

"What the hell?"

Was he bringing a woman home? Oh hell no. I would drive one of his precious cars into the pool if he thought he could disrespect me like that.

I was about to rush out when I remembered my comfy clothes and makeup-free face. I did not want to meet one of his other women like this. Maybe it was silly to care about something like that but I did. So I paused in my open door, listening.

The woman was loud. I couldn't make out what she was saying but clearly she was either really pissed or really excited. What if Roman was married? Oh shit. What if the woman of the house came home and learned I was here?

No, Kaira. Pump the brakes.

My writer brain was sweeping me away in its madness. The dark side of having a vivid imagination was jumping to the worst-case scenario when anything happened in my life.

Got a flat tire? It wasn't a random nail. Someone let the air out so they could abduct me from the side of the road.

Lose a sock? Stolen by my long lost twin who wants to steal my identity.

Find a quarter? It's probably rare and valuable and I'll get stuck in the crossfire between two ruthless coin collectors.

Then again, a simple sneeze had purchased a night with Roman, gotten me fired, and resulted in me living in his house, freshly fucked within an inch of my life. So sometimes little things ended up being a big deal.

But a simple female laugh didn't mean he was married or had a girlfriend. He wouldn't need me to fake it if that was the case. A prostitute then.

Kaira, stop.

Whatever was happening, standing up here and hiding in my room was not going to answer my questions. Curiosity won out over my desire to stay holed up and I walked to the top of the staircase, peering down into the foyer expecting to see some supermodel or some other stunning woman.

That's not what I saw.

I saw an older woman dressed in vibrant, mismatched colors rushing into Roman's arms. Her silver hair was piled into a messy bun. Her wrists jingled with dozens of bracelets that clinked as she moved.

She kissed Roman on both cheeks, leaving purple lipstick marks that he rubbed at with an exasperated expression. She handed off several large bags to the house staff, who looked delighted to see her. One of them even hugged her. She returned it enthusiastically.

"Home at last!" the woman declared with a flourish.

Home?

Who *was* this person?

As if sensing me watching them like a gargoyle, the woman's gaze snapped upward and landed on me. Her eyes lit up, her mouth broke into a huge smile, and she threw her arms wide.

"Ah!" she exclaimed, bracelets jangling. "You must be Kaira! I've been *dying* to meet you. Come on down, dear. Let's have a cup of tea and get to know each other."

I glanced at Roman, who was pinching the bridge of his nose as if he already had a headache. He caught my eye and shrugged, silently telling me to just go with it.

Reluctantly, I descended the stairs.

The moment I reached the bottom, the woman enveloped me in a cloud of floral perfume and warm hugs. I nearly suffocated. The perfume was something expensive and incredibly strong. But the hug was nice.

"You're even prettier than Roman described!" she said, holding me at arm's length to appraise me. "He's such a terrible storyteller, but when he mentioned your eyes, he got it exactly right."

I blinked, my face heating. Roman had *described* me? Was he selling me to her?

"This is my Aunt Ruby," Roman said. "My mom's sister. She spends most of her time traveling abroad, but she's staying here for a few weeks."

Ruby beamed. "Until Valentine's Day," she clarified with a wink.

"But I'll be out of your hair before the romantic day. Wouldn't want to ruin the love boat you two are sailing on."

My stomach dropped. So, she thought our engagement was real. Of course, she did—why wouldn't she?

Ruby looped her arm through mine and led me toward the sitting room. "Come, dear. I want to hear all about how my stubborn, impossible nephew finally found someone to put up with him."

I glanced over my shoulder at Roman, who gave me a tight-lipped smile that clearly said, *Good luck*.

I gave him a look that begged for help, but he had already turned away. He was feeding me to the wolves.

"Roman, join us!" Ruby called out.

I almost laughed. He thought he was going to escape. Well, not so fast.

The house staff rushed to set up a tea tray in the sitting room, complete with an assortment of pastries and finger sandwiches. I had a feeling they might have known this visit was coming. Or maybe they were just amazing at their jobs.

Ruby settled in like she owned the place—which, given her familial connection, she sort of did. "Sit, sit," she gestured.

I did as she asked, watching as she poured us each a cup of tea. She held her dainty cup with the perfect pinky pose and stared at me over the rim. Roman took his seat and propped his foot up on his knee, the picture of calm.

"So," Ruby began, her eyes sparkling with curiosity. "How did you two meet?"

I opened my mouth, scrambling for an answer, but Roman spoke first.

"It's not a particularly interesting story," he said smoothly. "Business acquaintances, mutual friends, that sort of thing."

Ruby wrinkled her nose. "Nonsense. Every love story is interesting. Kaira, you tell me. What was your first impression of Roman?"

I hesitated, my mind racing. If I told her the truth—that I had thought he was arrogant and insufferable—it might raise some red flags.

"He's…" I began searching for a diplomatic answer. "He's certainly confident."

Ruby let out a peal of laughter. "That's a polite way of saying he's a pain in the ass, isn't it?"

Roman cleared his throat, clearly unimpressed with the turn the conversation had taken. "Nothing wrong with a man who knows what he wants."

Ruby leaned forward, her expression softening. "I'm glad he has you," she said, her voice filled with genuine emotion. "I've always worried about how alone he is in this big house. He's worked so hard, but it's not the same as having someone to share it with."

I glanced at Roman, who was staring into his tea.

"Roman told me you two were close," I lied.

"Oh my, yes. After my poor sister passed away, I took him under my wing. I raised him like he was my own. I love him like a son, always have. I worry so much about him. I'm so glad I don't have to worry about him being alone."

That made me love her almost immediately. I loved that he had family. I was beginning to think he had no one.

"I'm fine, Aunt Ruby," Roman said.

"You did a good job raising him," I said. "He's a good man."

There was an uncomfortable, awkward silence. I sipped my tea and looked anywhere but at him.

"Okay," Ruby said suddenly, sitting back with a sharp look. "Spit it out. What's going on?"

I froze, my teacup halfway to my lips.

"What do you mean?" I asked, my voice higher than usual.

Ruby pointed between Roman and me. "You two are as stiff as boards. Did you have a fight? Are you pregnant? What is it?"

Roman sighed, setting his cup down with a clink. "It's nothing, Aunt Ruby. You're overthinking things."

26

ROMAN

I looked at Kaira, desperately hoping she'd pick up on my silent plea to tread carefully. In all honesty, Ruby had an uncanny knack for sniffing out secrets. I was more than a little concerned about how much she could glean from our awkward exchanges.

"Nobody's pregnant," I said, attempting to paint over our unease with a brush of fatigue. "It's just been a long day, that's all. We weren't expecting company."

Ruby studied me for a moment, her sharp eyes narrowing slightly as if trying to see through to my soul. I knew that look well. It was the same one she'd given me countless times when I was sixteen and got caught coming home drunk.

And she was not stupid. When I was younger, I used to believe she was clairvoyant. She had this eerie ability to see the truth despite all the smoke screens. She was doing it again now, searching my face for a hint, a clue that would give us away.

I shifted uncomfortably, feeling like a teenager under her intense scrutiny. "Really, Ruby, it's just been one of those days," I reiterated. My voice sounded strained even to my own ears.

"Roman Jameson Andrew Kelly."

I grimaced. Yep, it was a flashback to the night she found me passed out cold in the front yard after I failed to make it all the way inside.

I glanced at Kaira, who looked terrified. And amused.

"Aunt Ruby—"

"Don't you dare try and Aunt Ruby me. What's going on? Did you cheat on her?"

"No!" I answered quickly.

Aunt Ruby turned to look at Kaira. "Tell me, sweetie. What did he do? You tell me and I'll set him straight."

Poor Kaira had a deer in the headlights expression.

There was no point in denying the truth. Aunt Ruby would sniff it out eventually.

"What we aren't saying is that our engagement is not real."

She frowned. "Excuse me?"

"The engagement isn't real. We're faking it. It's just for show."

She looked at me like I was crazy.

"What do you *mean* it's not real?" she shrieked, flinging herself backward onto the couch as if I'd just confessed to robbing a bank. "You're *engaged*! You're having a wedding! There's supposed to be a *cake*! With layers, Roman! *Layers!* I want the little bride and groom on top of the cake!"

I rubbed the back of my neck, fighting a grin. She was eccentric, but she always managed to make me smile.

Kaira was holding her cup in front of her mouth, clearly trying to hide her own smile.

"Aunt Ruby," I began, attempting to calm her, but she cut me off with a dramatic gasp.

"Does she know it's not real?" she demanded, sitting upright and pointing an accusatory finger at Kaira, who was perched on the edge of her seat looking utterly bewildered.

"Yes," I said, chuckling despite myself. "She knows."

"Oh, thank God," Ruby said, throwing a hand over her chest in mock relief. "I thought you'd tricked the poor girl into pretending to be your fiancée. Although honestly, that would've been less insane than *both* of you willingly going along with this madness!"

Kaira finally found her voice. "It's just for six months. Roman needed help, and I... well, I agreed."

"Six months?" Ruby repeated, her bracelets jangling as she gestured wildly. "This is lunacy! When it all implodes in your faces, don't come crying to me. Playing with the media like this? With *your* reputation, Roman? Have you lost your mind? And Kaira." Aunt Ruby put her teacup down. She turned to Kaira with a frown on her face. "Have you thought about how difficult it might be to go back to your normal life after this? The media doesn't just *let go* once they've got their claws in you. Not when it comes to our family. Do you really know what it's like to be associated with a man like Roman?"

Kaira stiffened. "I'm not sure I'll miss any of this," she said, gesturing to the grand sitting room. "I like my home. I might not be a Kelly and have a big mansion, but that's not always a bad thing."

Ruby's expression softened. "I don't mean the house or the lifestyle, darling. I mean the *public eye*. You think they'll leave you alone just because the engagement ends? Think again. You'll be 'Roman Kelly's former fiancée' for years. Paparazzi, tabloid rumors, the works. Are you ready for that? Anytime you're out getting a cup of coffee they'll make a headline out of it. If it's a slow news week, the sharks will circle."

Kaira's eyes widened as the realization sank in. It was clear neither of us had considered that angle. We had been so focused on *now*, we never thought about *after*.

Ruby stood, brushing imaginary dust from her skirt with an air of finality. "Well, it's your lives. You can do whatever you want. Just don't say I didn't warn you." She winked at Kaira. "Now, if you'll excuse me, I have a date with a charming gentleman who happens to own a vineyard in Napa. I've got a rich, handsome suitor in every corner of the world, you know. Keeps me young."

With that, she sashayed out of the room, leaving us both sitting in stunned silence.

Kaira finally broke the quiet. "Your aunt is... a character."

I laughed, shaking my head. "She's always been like that. Larger than life. My mom was nothing like her."

Kaira leaned forward. "Oh yeah, what was she like?"

"She was Ruby's opposite in every way," I said, my voice softening at the memory. "Soft spoken, conservative, gentle. Normal."

"What was her name?"

I hesitated, caught off guard by the question. It had been so long since I'd spoken her name aloud. "Rowena," I said finally, the name feeling foreign on my tongue.

"That's a pretty name," Kaira said, smiling. "Unique."

I nodded, but the conversation was starting to make me uncomfortable. I got to my feet. "We have things to do today. I'll have some clothes sent up to your room."

"I have a ton of clothes up there already," she said. "I haven't even worn them."

"I want something else."

She rolled her eyes. "You're ridiculous."

"It's the job."

She gave me a dirty look. "We should probably get more specific about what the job is," she muttered. "And what it isn't."

I knew exactly what she was referring to. Yes, it was worth a conversation, but I wasn't ready to have it just yet.

"The job is exactly what I said it was. I have a delivery arriving soon. You'll want to do the hair and makeup thing."

"Why?"

"Because we're going into the city and there will be photographers."

Kaira groaned. "I'd rather not."

"Do I need to I remind you of the terms of our agreement?"

"No. I'm your pawn. Someone you can dress up like a doll when you want to."

"I'll meet you in the foyer in an hour," I said. "Maybe you'll be less sulky by then."

She shot me a glare before sulking all the way up the stairs.

I exhaled and rubbed my hand down my face. This was getting

messier than I had anticipated. The boundary lines of our agreement kept blurring into something more personal and less contractual.

I got up walked to the window. We had jumped headlong into this farce of an engagement without fully considering all its implications. The media was a beast I was accustomed to but Kaira was not. She had the innocence of someone unscarred by the sharp claws of public scrutiny. I could shield her here on the estate, but once this was over, she was on her own.

Earlier that morning, I had done a lot of thinking. There was a dress we hadn't bought during our shopping excursion, but I realized that was a mistake. I had called the store and ordered it to be delivered along with whatever accessories the salespeople thought would work with the dress.

The delivery arrived fifteen minutes later. I gave it to a staff member to take up to her. I hated that I was anxious to see her all dressed up. Was I treating her like a doll?

Either way, I liked spending time with her but last night had messed things up. The sex was one thing, but the way I acted after was abysmal. I had left the room without a word. I knew that was cold. She did not deserve to be treated like that.

I left the sitting room and walked to my study. I paced the small space feeling caged. Kaira had been a pleasant distraction when this all started. We had a simple agreement, business-like and mutually beneficial. But last night had changed something fundamental between us. The lines were hazy, our roles confused, and now I found myself in uncharted emotional waters.

I wasn't just her faux fiancé anymore. There was something more, something deeper that I hadn't anticipated. It was why I had gotten so distant after we rocked each other's worlds. She made me feel things that scared me.

There was no way in hell I could act on those feelings.

I quickly changed into another suit and went to the foyer to wait for Kaira. I didn't think she would stand me up but I wouldn't be surprised if she made me wait as a way to pay me back for my rudeness earlier.

Later, when she descended the grand staircase, she looked incredible. The dress I'd chosen for her fit her perfectly. She had left her hair down and put on just enough makeup to enhance her natural beauty. The sight left me momentarily speechless.

"You clean up well," I said, my tone light but sincere.

She gave me a dry look, clearly unsure whether or not to accept the compliment. "Wouldn't want to disappoint the photographers."

"I mean it," I added, stepping closer. "You look stunning. I don't know why we walked away from this dress the first time."

Her cheeks flushed slightly. "Thank you."

"Please tell me you're comfortable in it."

She smoothed her hands over the front of the dress. "Yes. It's not something I would normally wear, but it's okay."

I chuckled. "It's better than okay."

"I can't believe you remembered it."

"I haven't been able to get it out of my mind."

She seemed surprised by my confession.

"Shall we go?" I asked.

"Do I have a choice?"

"No."

We headed out to the car where Anthony was waiting. The drive into the city was quiet but not unpleasant. Kaira seemed more at ease than usual, though I couldn't quite tell if it was genuine or a performance. After the way I'd walked out on her, she had every right to be upset with me.

Then again, why would it have bothered her? She wasn't falling for me the way I was for her. I couldn't hurt her feelings if she didn't have any.

When we arrived at the restaurant, the maître d' greeted us with an overly enthusiastic smile, clearly recognizing me. I made the necessary introductions to a few friends already seated at our table, and Kaira stayed close to my side without me having to say a word.

Almost like she wanted to be there.

She charmed them easily, answering their questions with poise and laughing at their jokes as though she'd known them for years.

For a moment, I let myself relax. I could almost believe this whole thing was real.

As the evening went on, I found myself watching her more than I should have, captivated by the way she carried herself. She was blending in better than I could have imagined.

With every passing second, I was falling harder for my fake fiancée.

27

KAIRA

The restaurant exuded luxury, from its shimmering chandeliers to the gold cutlery. It was a lot like the first one he'd taken me to. It was fancy and meant to impress. The staff were all well-trained and knew how to be invisible while keeping their customers fed with a steady supply of drinks. Roman's friends, dressed in designer suits and dresses that could pay for a new car, sat around the table with an effortless charm. It was the kind of wealth I had only seen in movies or on magazine covers.

And now I was part of it—temporarily, at least. I was getting an up-close and personal view of how the one percent lived. I had been incredibly nervous but it wasn't so bad.

The group was already deep in conversation when we arrived, but Roman's hand on the small of my back kept me grounded. He introduced me as his fiancée, and I was met with a mix of curiosity and intrigue. They seemed more surprised by me than disgusted. In the back of my mind, I had worked myself up to think they were going to point and laugh the moment they laid eyes on me.

"So, you're the mystery girl," one of them said, a dark-haired man with a British accent and a smile that seemed too perfect to be real.

"Am I a mystery girl?" I replied with a smile.

"No one saw you coming."

I smiled nervously, unsure how to respond. They weren't what I expected. Not cold or dismissive like I feared. Instead, they welcomed me into their conversations. They didn't leave me out or ignore my comments.

"I've got to know," another chimed in, a stunning woman with sharp cheekbones and a laugh that turned heads from nearby tables. "How does someone keep Roman interested? The man is like a cat. Aloof, temperamental, and impossible to pin down. I know many women that have tried and failed."

Just get him to sign a contract. I laughed awkwardly, hoping Roman didn't hear. He was deep in conversation with another guest. He glanced over every now and then like he was checking on me, which I found to be very sweet. Or he was just making sure I didn't sneeze my way into another crisis.

I found the woman's question unnerving because I heard the question she wasn't asking. Or my own insecurities were making me read more into it. She was wondering how a man like Roman managed to get captivated by a woman like me.

"Stop, Chloe," another woman said. "Look at her. Do you really have to ask how she keeps him interested?"

I smiled, but again, I was reading between the lines.

The same woman turned her attention to me with a warm smile. "You are a scrumptious slice of pumpkin pie."

She seemed genuine. I was going to give her the benefit of the doubt.

"Thank you, I think."

"Easy, Sara," Chloe said with a laugh. "She's not on the menu."

I sipped my cocktail and listened as the conversation moved on to yachts and villas in the south of France. They talked about stories of summer escapades. As I listened, a part of me grew more aware of the differences in our lives. It wasn't just about having money, but how one carried themselves within these circles. They all had impeccable manners and seemed to know everyone.

"Kaira, have you ever been to Monaco?" asked the man with the British accent, now known to me as Simon.

"No," I admitted, slightly embarrassed. "I've never left the States."

Their surprise seemed mixed with a tinge of admiration rather than judgment.

"You'll have to get Roman to take you to the Maldives," Chloe said.

"Private of course," Sara said.

That started another conversation about Simon's new private jet. I listened intently, taking mental notes on everything. They would be useful to have filed away, in case I needed the details for a story. Yet despite feeling like an outsider in this opulent world, their openness made it less intimidating.

They weren't bragging. They were just talking about their lives. I didn't blame them or find it snobbish. It was their world. They didn't know any different. It would be the same thing if Carla and I talked about our favorite thrift store and the amazing finds. That kind of thing would be foreign to anyone else.

"Kaira, you must tell us about yourself," Simon prompted after a lull in the conversation. "Where did you grow up?"

"Philadelphia," I answered.

"Wow! How did you get all the way out here?"

I smiled. "I always dreamed of living in the City of Angels. I wanted the sunshine and beaches and all the beautiful people."

"You found us," Sara said and everyone laughed.

"Is your family still in Philadelphia?" Simon asked.

"Yes." I smiled and nodded. "I try to get out there to visit as often as I can."

"Where did you go to school?" Chloe asked.

They weren't asking about my high school. I knew they were all Oxford and Ivy League. "I didn't go to college."

Simon grinned and held up his hand for a high-five. "Me either. Well, I tried, but I kept getting kicked out."

"I got a degree in art history," Chloe said with a giggle. "I can tell you the difference between a Monet and a Manet, but otherwise, it's useless."

Everyone laughed, and the tension I felt eased a bit. It was refreshing to hear someone from their circle admitting to something so ordinary, so human.

The conversation shifted naturally from one topic to another, and soon I found myself sharing funny stories of my misadventures in Los Angeles, which seemed to delight and intrigue them as much as their tales of exotic travels did for me.

I couldn't help but notice how different this was from my usual life. I was used to being invisible—overlooked in grocery store lines, passed by on sidewalks, ignored at bars. But here, with Roman's friends, it was like I mattered. If only it wasn't because I was his fiancée. Or maybe because I was so different from all of them. I doubted they ever sat down and actually talked to someone like me before. But I didn't hold that against them. It wasn't like I went out of my way to talk to their type either.

"Do you remember that time Roman got arrested in Monaco?" Simon asked with a smile.

"Oh my God," Chloe groaned.

"What happened?" I asked. I wanted to hear more about Roman, behind the stiff, serious man I knew him to be.

Chloe rolled her eyes playfully before starting the story. "It was absolutely ridiculous," she began, shaking her head. "We were all at this fabulous party on a yacht, right in the heart of Monaco during the Grand Prix. The champagne was flowing, music was pounding—just a crazy night."

"Roman was in high spirits, to say the least," Simon said. "Started bragging about how he could outswim anyone back to shore."

Chloe laughed. "And before we knew it, he stripped down to his trunks, dived into the water, and started swimming. It was dark, and everyone was cheering him on."

Simon picked up the story, his eyes glittering with mischief. "He nearly made it too. But then, out of nowhere, the coast guard pulls up. Apparently, swimming back to shore at night during the Grand Prix is not exactly legal."

Everyone burst into laughter, and Chloe shook her head again. "They pulled him out of the water and onto their boat. Roman was so charismatic, even then. He ended up charming the officers with his broken French."

"He managed to get off with just a warning."

"We happened to be in London and he tried to climb the statue at Piccadilly Circus for a dare," Simon continued. "The police weren't quite as charmed that time."

"Ended up spending the night in a cell," Chloe added. "As you can imagine, there was copious amounts of alcohol involved that time as well."

I was enthralled by these tales of Roman's wilder days. This was a side of him I never saw—carefree, reckless, even daring. It made me see him in a different light.

They continued to tell stories about Roman's drunken escapades when he was younger. They talked about how he once bought an entire bar a round of drinks after winning big in Vegas.

I glanced at him, still engrossed in the conversation, and tried to reconcile the version of Roman they described with the man I knew.

"Speaking of celebrations," someone said, turning to me. "Do you have something planned for next week?"

I blinked. "Next week?"

"For his birthday, of course," the woman said, her diamond earrings catching the light.

My stomach sank. His *birthday*? No one in the house had mentioned it. I pasted on a smile and nodded as if I'd known all along. "Of course. We've got it covered."

Later, when the women suggested a bathroom trip, I hesitated. But before I could decline, they were already rising, taking me along like I was one of their own. That was one thing that was the same in my world. Women went to the bathroom in packs.

Roman glanced my way as the ladies led me away. I offered a small smile, letting him know everything was okay.

The restroom was nicer than my entire apartment. Marble counters, gold fixtures, and a lounge area with plush chairs and mirrors framed by soft lighting. There was an attendant standing discreetly at the door, ready to provide a fresh towel or whatever.

The women lined up at the vanities, expertly touching up their makeup. I sat down and opened my clutch, my drugstore lipstick suddenly feeling out of place among their designer brands.

I unscrewed the cap, hiding the label in my palm as I applied it. If they noticed, they didn't say anything. They were too busy chatting about career updates, social dramas, and, surprisingly, Roman.

"He's a hard one to figure out," Sara said, examining her reflection. "I don't know how you managed it. I tried once, and he shut me out faster than I could blink."

"Same," a girl named Barb added, smoothing her perfect hair. "There must be something special about you." She winked at me, her tone light but sincere.

I swallowed, unsure if they were teasing me or not. My insecurities flared. These women were stunning—movie-star gorgeous with Botox and filler, flawless skin, and bodies that could make anyone feel inadequate.

"How did you manage to get that rock on your finger?" Chloe asked, lifting my hand to admire the ring. "It's absolutely gorgeous."

"You're a lucky girl," Barb chimed in. "We all know Roman can be a bit... what's the word?"

"Abrasive?" Sara suggested.

"Exactly. Abrasive. But we also know he has a good heart. He just guards it fiercely. But not with you." Barb smiled warmly. "You must have some sort of superpower. We've all been hoping someone like you would come along to remind him who he really is."

Their kindness surprised me. I'd expected them to be dismissive, maybe even cruel. But instead, they seemed genuine, even hopeful. I felt bad for judging them before I ever met them.

"Thank you," I said softly. "I'm not sure why it works, but it just... does."

They nodded approvingly, and soon we headed back to the table.

Roman met me halfway. I could see the concern on his face. "You okay?"

I nodded. "I really like your friends. They're nice."

"You sound surprised."

I smiled up at him, letting the moment linger before replying. "I was expecting stuck-up rich assholes like you."

The table burst into laughter. I hadn't meant for anyone to overhear the comment, but they did. Even Roman cracked a smile, shaking his head at me.

It was surreal, feeling like I belonged here, even for a moment.

Just wait until Carla hears about this. She's going to lose her mind.

28

ROMAN

I was pleasantly surprised to see Kaira fitting in with my friend group. I really thought she'd recoil from all of them. When I first met her at the auction, she looked like she would have preferred to be anywhere else. She tried to disappear, and truthfully, she did. I saw the way people ignored her.

But here, they were talking to her and she was sharing stories about her life back in Philadelphia. We had not talked about her life before the moment we met at the auction. I realized that made me a bit of a dick. I never took the time to get to know her.

Her laughter mixed with the rest of the group's. I found myself drawn to her in a way I couldn't explain. It was a rare feeling for me. As Kaira settled back into her chair next to me, she glanced over at me and smiled.

Dinner was served with the conversation still flowing all around us. I chimed in on occasion, ready to jump in and help Kaira out of a sticky question about our relationship and engagement. She wasn't a natural liar. I didn't know what it meant that I seemed to be able to lie easily about our so-called relationship.

My growing affection for her wasn't a lie, just everything else.

I noticed Kaira's drink was never empty. I didn't feel like she was getting trashed and chose not to say anything about it. She was a grown woman. As the night wound down, I felt like I could call it a success. I had introduced her to my social circle and they accepted her. When the press inevitably tried to ask them about her, they would be able to talk about how amazing she was. And no one should have any doubts that we were serious.

"Ready to go?" I asked her.

She smiled, looking very relaxed and at ease. "Yep."

"There will be photographers outside," I warned her.

"And that's what you expected, right?" she asked.

She didn't say it in a snotty way. She was far more astute than I gave her credit for. I knew with the lingering dinner, other diners would send texts to TMZ and other tip lines. My friends were all stars in their own right. Having all of us together in one room was a big deal.

She pulled out a little mirror from her purse and used a finger to rub at the corner of her eye.

"You look fine," I assured her.

"Fine isn't the goal."

"You don't need to fix your makeup. It's just as good as it was when you walked down those stairs."

"Thank you."

I led her through the restaurant and ignored the looks from other patrons. I was used to being stared at. The flash of cameras greeted us as we stepped out of the restaurant. Even though it was the whole point of the evening—to give the tabloids something to chew on—I still hated it. The shouting of reporters and the pops of bright lights made my jaw clench, but Kaira seemed unfazed. She turned her face toward me, linked her arm through mine, and smiled like she was born for this.

Good. It was convincing, at least.

The night had gone better than I expected. My friends loved her, and Kaira had been a hit with everyone at the table. More importantly, she seemed to have genuinely enjoyed herself. Anthony had the car waiting. She slid in and gave one last wave to the photographers.

"That was so much fun," she said for the tenth time, her voice light and almost dreamy. "I haven't laughed like that in... God, I don't even know how long. Your friends are amazing."

"They like you," I said simply, though I couldn't help the small smile tugging at the corner of my mouth.

"Good. They are really nice."

She told me some of the stories my friends told her about me. I laughed most of it off. They were just doing what they did.

When the car pulled to a stop in front of the front door of the house, I helped her out of the car. She walked fine, but there was a lightness to her.

"Tonight was fun," she said as I walked her to the stairs. I kept my arm around her. "I was so dreading it. I liked your friends."

I wasn't sure if she remembered telling me that earlier, but whatever. "They like you as well."

"They like me?" She stopped on the stairs and turned to look at me, the movement nearly sending her off balance. I reached out instinctively to steady her. "Do *you* like me?"

"I tolerate you," I corrected, fighting to keep the amusement from my voice.

She giggled, leaning into me as I helped her upstairs. She stumbled a couple of times, clutching at my arm. I pulled her against me and practically dragged her up the stairs. Once we reached the landing, she bent forward and kicked off her heels.

"I'm going to break my ankle," she said with a laugh. "I probably should have taken them off before I started upstairs."

She stood up with her heels in her hand and looked at the doors in front of her. She walked toward them, one hand outstretched toward the handle.

"What's in here?" she asked, her fingers curling around the polished brass knob.

"Nothing," I said quickly, my tone sharper than intended. I stepped forward, covering her hand with mine to stop her.

She giggled again, clearly unconvinced. "It's not nothing. I can tell. Come on, tell me! I'm great at keeping secrets. I saw you in here. What is it?"

"No," I said firmly, my hand still over hers. "This room isn't for indulging curiosities. No one is allowed in there. Please, respect my privacy."

She tilted her head, her playful smile fading slightly as she searched my face. For a moment, I thought she might press further, but then she nodded. "Fine," she said, her voice softer, almost apologetic. "I'm sorry. It's your home."

"Good." I let go of her hand and gestured toward the hallway. "Let's get you to bed."

"How come you didn't tell me about your birthday?" she asked. "I'm your fiancée," she said dragging out the word. "Isn't that something I should know?"

God, she was drunk. It was kind of adorable. "It's not a big deal," I said. "I don't celebrate."

"What?" she gasped. "How do you not celebrate your birthday?"

"I just don't. I haven't since I was a kid."

She stopped abruptly and turned to face me. "Because of what happened to your parents?" she asked softly.

I froze. Normally, a question like that would have me shutting down or lashing out. But the way she looked at me—with genuine sympathy, not pity—caught me off guard.

My throat tightened, the words stuck there. I didn't talk about them. I didn't *want* to talk about them. But she stepped closer, her hand resting gently on my chest.

"I'm sorry," she said, her voice barely above a whisper. "I can't imagine the grief you've carried. I wish I could make it better."

The sincerity in her eyes chipped away at the walls I'd so carefully built. It wasn't just sympathy—it was understanding. She wasn't trying to fix me or dissect my pain. She was just *there*.

"Thanks."

"I probably wouldn't want to celebrate either. I get it. I won't push it."

Her hand lingered on my chest, and before I could stop myself, I leaned down and kissed her. It was soft, unhurried—an unspoken thank you.

She leaned against me, on the edge of collapse. "Let's get you tucked in."

I guided her into her room. She dropped her shoes and began fumbling with the zipper of her dress, giggling when it got stuck.

"Here," I said, stepping forward to help.

She let me, standing still as I unzipped the back and slid the straps off her shoulders. She stepped out of the dress clumsily and fell onto the bed, burying her face in the pillows with a contented sigh.

"You good?" I asked.

"Mhm," she mumbled, already half-asleep.

I pulled the blanket over her, shaking my head at the soft giggle she let out before passing out. I leaned down and brushed a kiss against her temple.

I walked out, closing her door behind me. I loosened my tie and removed my cufflinks as I walked down the hall. The house was quiet as usual.

When I reached the double doors to the room I told her to stay out of, I hesitated. The urge to keep walking was strong, but something pulled me back. I turned the knob and stepped inside.

The room smelled faintly of oil paint and varnish, though it had been years since any work had been done here. Moonlight filtered through the stained-glass window, casting fragmented patterns of color and shadow across the floor.

There was a feeling in my chest. The same feeling I always got when I stepped inside. It was a form of self-torture.

I reached over and flipped on the light. Canvases were scattered throughout the space—some finished, others abandoned midway. At the far end of the room, the largest canvas leaned against the wall.

I approached it slowly, my chest tightening as the image came into focus. It wasn't like I didn't know what it was, but there was always this feeling of shock, longing, and pain when I saw it. It was a family portrait, or at least it was supposed to be. The background was richly detailed, as were the clothes. But the faces were incomplete, their features left as shapeless nubs of paint.

My mother had started this painting the summer before she and my father died. She never got the chance to finish it.

I closed my eyes, and the memory washed over me like a tide.

I was eleven, running into the room with the carefree joy only a child could muster. The space was alive with color, sunlight streaming through the stained glass and painting rainbows on the walls. It was a gorgeous summer day but my mother was inside.

"Mom!" I called, skidding to a stop near her easel.

She turned, her smile so warm it could have melted glaciers. "There you are! I thought you'd gotten lost."

She looked at me like she hadn't seen me in ages. She bent down and kissed my forehead before leaning back, both of us turning to look at the painting.

"What do you think?" she asked, tilting her head.

"Why are the faces funny?" I asked, frowning.

She gasped, mock offended. "That's what you look like!"

"None of us have mouths! Or eyes!"

She clamped a hand over my mouth and eyes, laughing. "There, now you match!"

I laughed so hard I could barely breathe, her giggles mixing with mine.

"Mom! I have a face."

She released me and ruffled my hair. "Of course you do, my love. And such a handsome one at that." She turned back to the canvas, her brush poised delicately between her fingers. "These faces will have to wait, though. They need to be perfect, and perfection needs patience."

I watched as she dipped her brush into a swirl of colors, and with gentle strokes, she filled in more of the background.

The memory faded, leaving me standing in the silence of the studio.

I opened my eyes and stared at the unfinished painting. The laughter, the warmth, the safety—it was all gone, replaced by a cold, hollow ache. I always wondered what the faces would have looked like had she finished them. She said they needed to be perfect, but what was her idea of perfect? Would she have painted us smiling or maybe looking at each other.

I would never know.

Running a hand through my hair, I turned and left the room, closing the door behind me. Some spaces weren't meant to be shared, even with someone like Kaira.

29

KAIRA

The sunlight streaming through the café window was not my friend this morning. I squinted against it, nursing my coffee like it was a lifeline while Carla smirked at me from across the table. She looked entirely too put together for me.

I was really regretting that last glass of champagne. It had all gone down way too easily. I rubbed my temple and contemplated my life choices as one did when they suffered from such a serious hangover.

"You look like shit," Carla teased.

"Thanks," I muttered, trying to summon the energy to glare at her. "That's better than I feel."

Carla snickered and took a sip of her mimosa. "Rough night?"

I couldn't stop the grin that spread across my face. "The best kind of rough night."

"You said you rubbed elbows with the rich and famous," she said. "Tell me more. Tell me all of it."

The sunlight shifted as a cloud moved lazily across the sky, momentarily relieving my eyes from its harsh glare. I was two seconds from putting on my sunglasses. Carla would think it was my living arrangement making me feel like I could wear sunglasses indoors like the rich and famous.

I leaned back in the booth and began recounting the night before. "It was crazy," I said. "I was so nervous but they welcomed me with open arms. The champagne never stopped flowing. Although there were plenty of other options to drink. Thankfully, I stuck with champagne or I would be in far worse shape."

She laughed. "You've never done well with champagne."

I groaned and rubbed my head. "I know. Because it's so good and so easy to drink."

I launched into a rundown of the evening. I knew she wouldn't think I was bragging as I described everything we ate and the stories they told me about their travels around the world.

Carla looked truly interested. "So, they weren't all stuck-up rich jerks?"

I shook my head. "Not even close. They were kind. Like, genuinely interested in getting to know me." I paused, a little embarrassed. "Imagine that. Me, feeling comfortable with people like them."

"That's awesome," Carla said with a warm smile. "You deserve that. I'm so glad you got to have the experience."

"Thank you for not thinking I'm bragging," I said.

"Are you kidding? I'm living vicariously through you." She pulled out her phone.

"What are you doing?"

"I want to see the pictures from last night," she said. "You said you got papped, right?"

"Oh yes. I mean, not in those words, but yes."

Her mouth dropped open. "Oh my gosh! You looked hot! That dress is just bam. Damn, girl."

I laughed and instantly regretted it when my head felt like it was going to split in two. "Ow."

"I can see why you blended in with the rest of the group. You look like a socialite, all hot and sexy."

"Stop." I smiled. "But thank you."

The waitress set down our plates—pancakes for me and an omelet for Carla. Brunch with Carla was a familiar ritual. It grounded me in ways I needed more than ever. I knew when I moved out it was going to be hard to abandon our lazy breakfasts. I was so glad we were still getting the chance to have these moments.

Between bites of syrup-drenched pancakes, I shifted the conversation. "Roman's birthday is next weekend."

"Really?" Carla asked, cutting into her omelet. "What's the plan?"

"He doesn't celebrate," I said, my fork pausing midair. "For good reason. But I think... I don't know, I'd like to do something nice for him. Nothing big, just something thoughtful. Something that makes him feel like it's okay to celebrate his birthday."

"Why doesn't he celebrate?" she asked.

"His parents."

"Oh," she said with a nod. "Harsh. Poor dude."

"Exactly."

"That sounds sweet. What are you thinking? B-Day BJ?"

I snorted a laugh and shook my head. "Not quite. I was going to talk to the house staff and see if they have any ideas. They know him better than I do, and—" I stopped mid-sentence, noticing Carla's expression shift. "Hey, is everything okay?"

She shrugged, her fork picking at her food in a way that wasn't like her. "I'm fine."

"Carla," I said gently. "What's going on?"

Her shoulders rose and fell again, but this time she sighed. "It's nothing. It's stupid."

"It's not stupid if it's bothering you," I pressed. "Come on, spill. I've been rambling. What's going on?"

She hesitated, then finally looked up at me. "It's just... you've been so wrapped up in this whole Roman thing. You never call to check in on me. You don't ask about my life. It's like I've been relegated to the background while you play house with your fake fiancé."

My heart sank. "Oh, Carla... I didn't mean to make you feel that way. I asked if you were okay with everything. I'm so sorry. I didn't know. I mean, I did, but, dammit, I'm sorry."

"I know you didn't," she said quickly, but her voice was tight. "It's just... I miss you. It feels like I've been left behind while you're off living this glamorous new life."

I reached across the table and took her hand. "You're right. I've been so caught up in all of this, and I've been a terrible friend. I'm so sorry."

She gave me a small smile. "You're not a terrible friend. Just a distracted one. I know you have a lot on your plate. I told you to do this. We both knew it was going to be hard with you trying to live a double life."

"I'm going to make it up to you," I promised. "Starting today. Let's spend the day together. No Roman, no mansion, no paparazzi. Just us."

Carla's smile grew. "What did you have in mind?"

"How about what we would normally do? We're stuffing our faces and going to see a movie. I'm sure there's a rom-com out for Valentine's."

"Don't pity me," she said. "I feel ridiculous for even bringing it up."

"You're not ridiculous. I'm sorry I've been neglectful."

"You haven't been neglectful. I am really happy for you. And you did look hot last night."

"Thank you."

While we ate, I looked up movies playing. We found a romance flick and headed over for a matinee showing.

We chose seats in the middle row, far enough from the screen to avoid neck strains but close enough to catch every detail. The theater slowly filled, the murmurs of other moviegoers blending into a soft background noise.

"Thanks for doing this," Carla whispered. "I really needed it. I don't think I fully understood how much I was going to miss you."

"Me too. We should do this more often. It's not like he needs me on hand around the clock. Honestly, I don't even see him during the day usually."

The lights dimmed, signaling the start of the film. On screen, a clumsy meet-cute unfolded involving a stray cat and a spilled cup of coffee. As the characters on screen navigated their blossoming yet awkward relationship, I found myself thinking about romance. I wanted that. I wanted to stumble into the man of my dreams.

I could almost picture Roman as that man, but he was so far out of my league, I knew it wasn't meant to be. I was only getting to play make believe.

After the movie, we wandered into a tapas bar. We shared a dozen tiny, delicious dishes and gossiped about everything and nothing.

"I should let you go," she said.

"Hell no. I'm not done hanging out with you. Are you trying to ditch me?"

Carla laughed, her eyes crinkling at the corners. "Not a chance. It's just getting late, and I figured you'd have to rush off to some high-profile event or another."

"Not tonight," I said firmly, popping an olive into my mouth. "Today is about us. Besides, playing dress-up for the cameras gets old fast. This," I gestured between us, "this is real life."

"I guess it can't be easy, living like that. Always in the spotlight, having to pretend all the time."

"It's exhausting," I admitted. "But fun. Don't pity me. I want to get some makeup. You have to help me pick some stuff out. I need that photo stuff."

"I will help you get what you need. Let's hit that boutique on Seventh. They always have the most amazing makeup selection. It's all the leftover designer stuff, but it works the same."

She helped me pick out a few pallets and a new lipstick. They were a step above drugstore brands.

From there, we indulged in some retail therapy, trying on clothes we couldn't afford and splurging on matching bracelets we both swore we'd wear every day.

By the time Anthony picked us up, the tension between us had completely melted away. We were back to being Kaira and Carla, best friends against the world.

"Come home with me," I said.

She grimaced. "I don't want to get you in trouble. Last time Roman came home and saw me there he didn't look very happy."

I waved my hand. "Who cares? He probably won't be home until late. And trust me, I think he'll be happy that you're there. Things are a little awkward between us. It will be nice to have someone to break up the tension. He'll probably just hide in his study or his room."

"Are you sure?"

"Positive."

When we got back to the mansion, the idea struck me as we walked into the kitchen. "Let's cook dinner."

Carla raised an eyebrow. "Here? In this kitchen? After we ate tapas?"

"Why not?" I grinned, pulling open a cabinet to inspect the contents. "We'll make our famous mac and cheese."

"Won't the cook get mad at us messing around in his kitchen?"

I shrugged. "It'll be fine. I am supposed to be the lady of the house."

She looked around the massive space. "I wouldn't even know where to start."

"The staff can help us find what we need."

As if on cue, one of the kitchen staff appeared, eyeing us warily. "Miss Kaira, what are you doing?"

"We're making dinner," I announced cheerfully. "For everyone. Something nice and homey. No offense, but not every meal needs to be elaborate and fancy."

The woman's eyes widened. "I don't think Mr. Roman—"

"Don't worry about Roman," I said, waving her concerns away. "I'll take the heat if he's upset. Now, where do you keep the cheese?"

Carla and I led the charge, searching through the three refrigerators and huge walk-in pantry for everything we would need.

"I cannot believe people live like this," Carla whispered. "Seriously, this kitchen is amazing. And it's like a mini grocery store."

"It is very impressive."

We got to work grating cheese and boiling pasta while the staff offered tips and occasionally stepped in to fix our amateur mistakes. The stove wasn't like the basic stove in our condo.

It had buttons and dials that seemed to require an engineering degree to operate properly. But soon, the aroma of melting cheese filled the air.

Carla turned on her playlist while we cooked. It felt like one of our dinners in. The massive house felt like a home instead of the cold, lifeless mausoleum.

"I think anyone could be a gourmet cook with all of the fancy gadgets and gizmos in here." Carla laughed.

I stirred the bubbling pasta and looked around the kitchen. A couple of the staff had come in and were sitting at the kitchen island, watching us.

"It's nice to see someone other than the cook enjoying this kitchen again," Marilyn said. "It's been too long since we've had a lady in the kitchen making a meal for Roman."

That made me feel good. I hoped Roman would appreciate it as well. It was hard to know which Roman was going to walk through the door. The Roman that tucked me into bed last night all sweet and gentle or the Roman that barely looked at me. I hoped it was the first.

30

ROMAN

I sat behind the wheel of my Porsche and counted to ten. The temptation to lay on the horn and scream at the cars in front of me was very, very strong. My day at the office had been horrible. We were still getting raked over the coals about the stupid profits. Yes, I knew it was impressive, but shit, I was good at what I did.

We were going to have every government regulator on our ass. No one could believe we were legally making the money we were. They were convinced I was laundering money for the mob. I chuckled bitterly as I sat on the I-10. The mere idea that anyone would even think I needed to resort to crime. I had built my empire from nothing; integrity was engraved in its foundation.

The cars around me inched forward. I should have had Anthony drive me today. LA traffic could either be really good or really fucking bad. Today, it was brutal. We were moving at a snail's pace. Cars were all vying for a spot in the never-ending line. Billboards and signs flashed with advertisements, adding to the chaotic scenery. People in neighboring cars honked and yelled, their faces strained with frustration. The constant start-and-stop motion was pissing me off.

I wanted to be home. My comfortable mansion with the woman that was driving me crazy in a very different way.

I turned up the radio, hoping the music would drown out my thoughts about Kaira. The last thing I needed was to get distracted thinking about her while in this ridiculous traffic. Our relationship—if you could call it that—was complicated enough without me getting lost in mental tangents about her.

The phone mounted on my dashboard buzzed. I tapped the hands-free system.

"Kelly," I answered curtly.

"Sir, we have a situation," my head of security said without preamble.

My jaw clenched. Those were never words you wanted to hear. "What kind of situation?"

"A couple of young ladies tried to break into the office. They thought you were here."

"What the hell did they think they were going to find in my office?"

"You. They wanted you." There was a moment of silence. I waited for him to explain. "They're, um, well, they aren't fully clothed. They were, or are, wearing coats. Not much else. I don't think ribbons and hearts the size of my pinky count for clothing."

I pulled my phone away and stared at the screen. I wasn't sure if I was being punked or not. "They were wearing ribbons?" I repeated.

"Yes, sir. They said they were your Valentine's gifts."

"Sent from who?"

"I don't believe anyone sent them. I would venture to guess they took it upon themselves to uh, gift themselves to you. What do you want me to do with them?"

I shook my head. This was about the last thing I needed. I inhaled deeply. "Let them go. Trespass them and please remind them I am engaged. The only Valentine's gift I need is from my fiancée."

"Yes, sir."

I ended the call and almost smiled. This fake engagement thing might not be the worst thing in the world. It was like a shield. I just hoped other young ladies saw it as such. I was very used to being the subject of affection for women. They all wanted the sugar daddy. They wanted to be on the inside of LA's rich and famous.

Which was exactly why I needed Kaira. I needed her to keep me from women like that. I needed her to save me from the onslaught of unwanted attention. Traffic started to move. Not anything above a fast crawl, but at least it was moving.

Cheese. I smelled cheese. Not like stinky, feet cheese, but something gooey and yummy.

The rich aroma hit me the moment I stepped into the house. It wasn't the usual sterile cleanliness or the faint lemon scent the cleaning staff favored. No, this was different—warm, indulgent, and vaguely familiar. It tugged at a thread deep in my memory, pulling me back to a time I hadn't revisited in years. Decades to be more accurate.

I stood in the foyer, loosening my tie and letting the scent wash over me. My mother used to cook on rare occasions when she wasn't painting. I could almost hear her soft laugh as she whisked something on the stove, humming under her breath. She wasn't a great cook and often burned her attempts, but she always laughed at her failed meals.

I remembered the grilled cheese. She insisted they were easy and no one could screw it up. But somehow the ones she served me had black around the edges. I knew now she had in fact burned the sandwiches and scraped the charcoal before serving it to me. That thought startled me. I hadn't thought of her in the kitchen for a long time. The memory didn't hurt as much as I expected it to. Instead, it made me smile.

That was new.

Curious about the smell and what was happening in my house, I followed the cheesy aroma to the kitchen. As I rounded the corner, the scene before me stopped me in my tracks. The normally orderly, quiet kitchen was alive with music and laughter. Kaira, Carla, and half the house staff were gathered around the counters, surrounded by bowls, spoons, and what looked like a battlefield of shredded cheese and breadcrumbs.

Kaira was at the center of it all, her cheeks flushed, her hair slightly messy, and a smear of something suspiciously cheesy on her wrist. She was laughing at something Carla said, her voice rising above the low hum of conversation and the faint beat of a pop song playing in the background.

The rest of the staff froze the moment they saw me, the laughter dying as if someone had hit pause. Carla turned, her expression shifting from carefree to cautious. Even the music seemed to dull.

Only Kaira remained unaffected. She turned, her bright eyes landing on me, and smiled like she hadn't just disrupted the entire dynamic of the household.

"Roman!" she called, weaving through the now-stiffened group toward me. Before I could say a word, she grabbed my hand and tugged me further into the chaos. "You have to try this."

She led me to a baking dish that had just come out of the oven. The golden, bubbling surface looked almost too indulgent, the edges crisped to perfection. A fine crust on the top was perfectly golden.

I raised an eyebrow. "What is it?"

"Mac and cheese," she said proudly, scooping a steaming spoonful. She blew on it lightly before holding it up to my lips. "It's good. I promise. Go on, try it."

I stared at her for a moment, surprised by her audacity. Everyone else in the room stayed still as statues, watching us like it was a scene from a soap opera. This was not something I did. Well, many somethings. A woman didn't feed me. I didn't eat straight from a dish.

But Kaira had a way of disarming people. She marched to the beat of her own drum. I was just the guy she was dragging along in her little parade. And honestly, it wasn't the worst thing in the world. With a sigh, I leaned forward and took the bite.

It was divine. The sharpness of the cheese, the buttery breadcrumbs, the perfect amount of salt—it was comfort food elevated to an art form. A couple pieces of crunchy bacon completed the dish, making it perfect. It was indulgent and basic and nothing like I had ever eaten before. I had literally grown up with a silver spoon in my mouth. I didn't eat macaroni and cheese often.

I swallowed, meeting her expectant gaze. "It's... acceptable."

She rolled her eyes. "Please, Roman. You love it."

I allowed the corner of my mouth to twitch upward in the barest hint of a smile. "It's not bad."

That seemed to please her enough. She grinned, handing me a spoon. "Great. Then you can help."

I stared at her, genuinely surprised. "You want me to cook?"

"You're not exempt just because you wear fancy suits," she teased, shoving a bowl of lettuce toward me. "Now, mix."

I shrugged off my suit jacket, rolled up my sleeves, and did as I was told. It felt strange at first, stepping into the chaos instead of controlling it. But the longer I stayed, the more natural it felt.

The staff began to relax as Kaira coaxed them back into their previous moods before I stepped into the room.

By the time we sat down to eat, the dining-room table was transformed into a feast. Plates of mac and cheese, a fresh green salad, which I helped prepare, and fresh bread were passed around. The table was filled with the house staff. That had never happened before.

I couldn't stop watching Kaira as she interacted with everyone. She listened intently, laughed easily, and made every person at the table feel like they belonged. Some of the newer staff I had never exchanged more than a few words with. Others had been around me since I was a child. But I had honestly never sat and had a meal with any of them. It was strange, but in a good way. Kaira seemed very comfortable with the staff.

She reminded me of my mother in that way.

I remembered sitting at a table like this as a child, my mother holding court with her soft, commanding presence. Usually, it was her friends and not the staff. Although I could remember a few times I saw her sitting down to tea or dessert with Marilyn. My father used to watch her the way I was watching Kaira now, his eyes full of quiet admiration. I had always groaned, bored out of my mind, whenever my father waxed poetic about the beauty of the little moments. "One day, Roman, you'll understand. The greatest treasures in life are in the quiet moments."

Maybe today was that day.

I took a bite of the cheesy dish. It was good, but damn, was it rich. I was going to be spending some serious time in the gym to work this off.

"Do you like it?" Kaira asked. "Be honest this time."

I glanced up, catching her watching me intently. The staff around us had fallen silent, waiting for my response as well.

"It's excellent," I said simply.

Her face lit up. The smile that spread across her face was so genuine, so unguarded, that it caught me off guard. For a moment, she wasn't the carefully constructed fake fiancée, but just Kaira. A woman that made me feel things I had not felt in a long time. Some feelings I had never felt.

"We used to make this all the time back in our apartment," she told the table, gesturing to Carla. "It was our comfort food. When we were broke, stressed, or just needed a pick-me-up, we'd make mac and cheese. It was our go-to meal."

The staff listened as Carla told a few stories about their substitutions when they didn't have money to buy cheese, including a version with canned cheese. Even I found myself leaning in, curious about her life before our paths crossed.

"How did you two meet?" Marilyn asked.

Carla jumped in before Kaira could respond. "She needed a roommate and I was the lucky one to answer the ad."

Carla launched into a story about how they met and their first week living together. "I was trying to make it as a photographer, and Kaira was writing whenever she could get a moment."

There was something endearing about seeing their friendship—a mixture of fondness, respect, and genuine love. I had never had a friend like that. I was glad Kaira had her. I needed to do a better job welcoming Carla into the house over the next six months. I didn't want to ruin that relationship because, when this was all over, Kaira would be moving back in with Carla. Life would go back to how it used to be.

I wasn't sure I wanted it to, though.

31

KAIRA

I noticed Roman's gaze lingering on me during dinner, but I couldn't quite read his expression. Was he impressed? Annoyed? Amused? I couldn't tell. But he was participating, which was more than I expected.

After dinner, Carla gave me a look that said she was ready to head home. I walked her to the door, not wanting her to leave but knowing she had an early morning yoga class.

"Thanks for today," she whispered, hugging me tightly. "I needed this."

I hugged her back just as fiercely. "Call me anytime. Day or night. Just because we're not under the same roof doesn't mean I'm abandoning you. And I'll be back in five and a half months."

"I don't know," she said with a grin.

"What does that mean?"

"It means, he was looking at you like you were dessert."

I rolled my eyes. "I don't think so. He was probably thinking about what he's going to say to me once we're alone—if we're alone. He's going to yell at me for monopolizing his kitchen and serving him a meal that is way too indulgent."

"I think he can afford a few calories."

I laughed. "He's probably on his way to the gym downstairs as we speak."

"Oh, a hot and sweaty Roman is very, very intriguing."

I had to bite my lip. She had no idea how hot it was to see him go to town on a punching bag. Or between my legs. The thought made me blush.

I walked her to the car and waved as Anthony pulled out of the driveway to take her home. When she was out of sight, I went back inside and felt the shift in the air. The house was finally quiet. The staff had retreated to their quarters after I insisted they let me clean up my own mess. A few of them really tried to argue, but I insisted. I had to remind them I was currently the lady of the house.

I walked through the foyer and into the kitchen, which was still a mess. The night had been too perfect to end on a sour note of messy counters and piled dishes. I rolled up my sleeves and got to work.

The sound of footsteps startled me. I turned to see Roman leaning against the doorframe, his tie undone and his sleeves already halfway rolled up. He looked more relaxed than I'd ever seen him, and somehow even more intimidating for it.

"Can I help?" he asked.

"You don't have to help," I said, waving him off as he stepped into the kitchen. "I've got this."

He ignored me, walking over to the sink and grabbing a dish-towel. "I want to."

I blinked. Roman washing dishes? I wasn't sure if I should laugh or take a picture for posterity. But the way he set his jaw told me this wasn't up for debate.

"Okay," I said. "Don't say I didn't warn you."

"Why don't you just use the dishwasher?"

I sighed at him. "Her name is Gloria and I gave her the night off."

Roman's eyes widened and he laughed. "No, I know who Gloria is. I meant the actual machine that washes dishes."

"Oh, right," I said, feeling foolish. "This dish is too big and requires a little elbow grease."

The sound of water running and dishes clinking filling the room.

It was oddly domestic. I found myself smiling as I wiped down the counters.

"This was fun tonight," I said after a while.

Roman glanced over at me. "Cooking with my staff?"

"Yes," I said. "It felt like a home. Not just a fancy house where people work, but an actual home."

He was quiet for a moment, his hands moving methodically as he scraped a plate over the trashcan. "It's been a long time since this kitchen felt like that."

I wanted to ask more, but I gave him space to feel whatever he was feeling.

Until I blurted out, "You should let me throw you a birthday party."

Roman shot me a look that said he was very unimpressed with my suggestion. "I don't do birthdays."

"I know," I said quickly. "You don't celebrate. I get it. But tonight wasn't really about the mac and cheese, was it? It was about everyone being together. We could do something low-key, here at the house, with your staff and friends. Catered, so nobody has to work. Ruby would love it."

He paused, setting a plate in the drying rack. "Why would you think that?"

I shrugged. "I don't know. She's your family. She helped raise you. I would think she would want to hang out and celebrate with you."

He grunted. "Maybe."

"Where is she, anyway? I haven't seen her since the day she arrived."

"She's like an outdoor cat," he said with a faint smirk. "She comes and goes as she pleases."

That made me laugh. "Was she like that when she stepped in after your parents died?"

His smirk faded, and he nodded, his eyes distant. "She was good that first year. But Ruby's not built to stay in one place. She used to say she got itches in her britches. The world was always calling her. With me in school, she felt tied down. During summer break, she dragged me all over the place, but Ruby cannot stay in one place for nine months a year. I think it's impossible. When it's her time to say goodbye to this world, I have no doubt she's going to do it while on a cruise or flying over the Atlantic. There is no way she's going to allow herself to lay in bed and rot."

"I imagine her lifestyle keeps her young," I said. "What did you do while she was traveling all the time?"

"I spent a lot of time here, with the staff. They made sure I went to school, cooked dinner while I did my homework at the island, things like that. They all helped me with my math and offered plenty of opinions about what I should be reading for language arts. The gardener taught me how to care for the plants in the solarium, like my dad used to. And the cleaning staff? They were relentless about my bed and laundry. It was like having ten moms and a handful of dads. They kept me in check for the most part. When your staff is also raising you, it's hard to get anything by them."

I smiled at that, imagining a young Roman being scolded for leaving his clothes on the floor. "At least they tried to give you some normalcy."

He nodded, his voice soft. "I would have been lost without them."

I stopped scrubbing a pot and placed a hand on his wrist. "Well, I for one am glad you weren't lost. I'm glad you weren't left to raise yourself. I have a feeling you probably would not be where you are right now without them. Too many young people go wild and make some pretty shitty decisions that end up ruining their lives."

He looked down at my hand, then up at me, his eyes softer than I'd ever seen them. "Me too."

Something unspoken passed between us, a weight I couldn't quite name but felt deep in my chest. He cleared his throat, breaking the moment. "Enough about me," he said. "Tell me one of your dreams."

I blinked. "My dreams?"

He nodded, leaning against the counter, his full attention on me. He crossed his legs at his ankles and folded his arms across his chest. He looked very relaxed. Very normal. "Yeah. Tell me something."

I hesitated, but since he had told me a little about him, I felt like I needed to open up a bit as well. We did have to live together another five and a half months. We may as well try to be friends. "I want to write love stories."

"You said you wanted to be a writer the night we met, right?"

I laughed softly. "You remember that?"

"Vaguely," he admitted. "I feel like an ass for forgetting. I tend to get caught up in my own world. I know I'm a dick. Probably a narcissist. Some chick told me that once."

"It's fine," I said, waving it off. "It's not like I've written anything in a while. Just because I want to be something doesn't mean I'm going to. I've always loved books. Getting lost in the pages is my favorite thing in the world. One day, I'd like to give the world a chance to fall in love with one of my stories."

Roman tilted his head, studying me. "Why not now? You don't have a job. I'm not saying that to be a prick, but you don't have to work. You don't need to look for a job. You've got the time."

"Carla said the same thing," I admitted. "She told me I should use these six months to write."

"She's right. What's stopping you?"

I chewed my cheek, debating how much to tell him. "I started something a few months ago. I wrote half a book. I was on a spree, writing all night. It felt so good. It just flowed out of me. And then my laptop fried. I lost it all. It was devastating. It kind of stole my thunder."

"Get a new one," he said simply.

I snorted. "I can't just drop three thousand dollars on a new laptop, Roman. That's not how real life works for most people."

His expression shifted, a mix of surprise and something else I couldn't quite place. "I'll get you a new one."

"No," I said quickly, holding up a hand. "Absolutely not."

"Why not?" he asked, genuinely baffled.

"Because," I said, smiling despite myself. "That's not how this works."

"I don't think a laptop costs that much, and even if it cost ten grand, big deal," he said. "I can afford it. You need something to do."

"No, thanks." I flicked some bubbles at him. "Oops," I said innocently.

"You're playing a dangerous game, Kaira."

"Oh, I think I can handle you."

"Is that a challenge?" Roman asked, his eyebrows arching slightly.

I felt a spark of something—excitement, maybe a hint of danger—run through me. "Maybe it is," I replied, holding his gaze.

He took a step closer, and suddenly the kitchen felt much smaller. The playful tension between us shifted, becoming something more charged. I swallowed, wondering if he was going to kiss me again. I wanted him to kiss me. But I didn't want him to kiss me and run out on me again.

Instead, he stepped back and tossed a dish towel at me.

I caught the towel, my heart still racing from our near moment. The charged atmosphere dissolved as quickly as it had appeared, leaving me slightly breathless and confused.

"I have work to do in my study. I'll see you in the morning. Goodnight, Kaira."

"Goodnight, Roman."

I couldn't help but feel like we had just narrowly avoided something significant—or perhaps created more tension between us. By the time the kitchen was spotless, it was late, and I was exhausted. It had been a good night. Dinner was amazing and I felt like Roman and I had made big strides in our relationship. Not that it was a relationship, but we could at least be friends.

Roman was a prickly dude, but I did see his soft underbelly. Maybe I was a glutton for punishment, but I felt bad for the man. Yes he had money, power, and looks, but he was lonely. I wanted to try and bring him a little joy in this life. He deserved it.

I turned off the lights and climbed the stairs, briefly pausing at the double doors. I did vaguely remember him getting just a little testy when I asked what was in the room. It made me very curious, but I walked away. I didn't want to rock the boat.

32

ROMAN

The board meeting had gone better than I expected. For months, I had been under fire. People hated me and therefore hated my company. The numbers had been all over the place—volatile and uncertain. But today, the reports showed steady growth. Public perception was improving. Investments were back on the rise. It seemed that my engagement to Kaira and the accompanying media buzz were finally paying off.

I leaned back in my chair, taking a moment to appreciate the victory. In this world of corporate sharks, every win was hard-earned. A member from my PR team gave a recap about the latest positive media coverage surrounding our engagement. They were practically giddy about how well Kaira was playing her part.

As if on cue, my mind drifted to her. The woman who had somehow transformed my sterile mansion into something that felt almost like a home. The mac and cheese dinner. The way she'd engaged with the staff. Her dreams of writing. Her unexpected kindness.

I only half-listened to the other board members pepper the PR guy with questions about what was working and what wasn't. They were talking about putting Kaira and me here and there like we were actual chess pieces they were moving around on a board. I barely paid attention.

After the meeting, I officially excused myself and headed to my own office, where I closed the door behind me and sat behind my desk. I felt myself smiling. Like actually smiling. It was a little strange. I could tell myself it was the good meal the night before. I never ate like that.

My thoughts drifted back to Kaira. I wasn't sure what to make of her. She was unlike any woman I had ever met. There was a realness to her, a comfortable confidence, that made her stand out. She didn't try too hard, didn't put on airs. She was just... Kaira.

I found myself wanting to know more about her. To understand what made her tick. To see the world through her eyes, even if just for a moment.

I drummed my fingers on the desk, thinking about what I could do to show her how much I appreciated her. I still felt like shit after the night I walked out on her without so much as a thank you for rocking my world. She'd only been pretending to be with me for a couple of weeks and it was already having a positive impact on my public persona as well as in my life.

That gave me an idea. I turned to my computer and started my research. With my gift purchased on the way to my office, I found myself wanting to celebrate. I messaged Kaira.

On my way home. Got something for you. Feel like going out for dinner tonight?

Her reply came quickly: **What did you get me? Another dress? And yes, dinner sounds perfect.**

I quickly typed out a response. **I'll be home around five.**

I watched the little bubbles appear and waited. **Do I get dressed or did you get me something I'm supposed to wear?**

That made me feel a little guilty. I had been a little heavy-handed. It was our agreement, but tonight, I didn't want to worry about getting our picture taken and a flowery write-up in some stupid blog. Tonight, I just wanted to go out with her—Kaira. Not the fake fiancée.

Wear whatever you want. Something nice.

She replied with a happy face.

My office line rang. I glanced at the time. It was a scheduled call. I put on my game face and picked it up. Throughout the call, I forced myself to stay focused on the subject at hand. All I heard was blah, blah, money. Blah, blah, forecasts.

I finished up the call and quickly gathered my things, eager to get home and see Kaira. Thankfully, traffic was mild. I didn't think I could handle another gridlock kind of day.

When I got home, the house was quiet. Too quiet. I checked the kitchen first but she wasn't there. I went upstairs and knocked on her bedroom door. She wasn't there either. I headed back downstairs and found her in the library, sitting in one of the chairs with a notebook in her lap. She wasn't reading, as I'd expected, but scribbling furiously in the notebook. She looked so focused, her brow furrowed as she chewed on the end of her pen. I hated to interrupt her.

But I wasn't about to wait.

"Busy?" I asked, stepping inside.

She startled, then smiled up at me. Her hair was a bit of a mess. I had a feeling it started up, but with her frantic scribbling and obviously deep thought, it was now more down than up. It was cute. She had a spot of ink on her cheek, but I wasn't going to point that out.

"I've been outlining ideas for my story," she said. "I have all these ideas in my head. Characters are screaming at me. I can't think straight until I promise them I will write their story one day. For now, I'm just getting the basics on paper. I'm hoping that will quiet the voices."

"You hear voices?" I asked with just a little concern.

She laughed softly. "Not those kinds of voices. Just characters that want to be stars." She looked at me then frowned. "Is it five already? I'm sorry. I thought I set my alarm for four so I could get ready for dinner. I must have worked straight through it."

"It's not five. I'm home early."

"Oh. Is everything okay?"

"It's fine." I walked closer and held out the sleek black box I'd been holding behind my back. "I figured you might need something to help you with your writing unless you want to go back a few hundred years and write it all out."

Her gaze narrowed suspiciously. "Roman, what did you do?"

Without a word, I placed the box in her lap. She hesitated, her fingers hovering over the lid before she finally flipped it open. Her gasp was audible as she stared at the gift. Her eyes widened and she started to shake her head. She pulled out the brand-new laptop. Top of the line with all the bells and whistles.

"Oh my God." Her voice was barely a whisper. "Roman, this is too much."

"It's not," I said, sitting across from her. "You can't write your book without the right tools. Consider it an investment."

Her hands trembled as she traced the edges of the laptop, and then, to my utter shock, tears welled up in her eyes. "Thank you," she said, her voice cracking. "Thank you so much. I don't know what to say. This is so nice."

I wasn't sure how to respond to tears—happy or otherwise—but I reached out, awkwardly patting her shoulder. "It's just a computer."

"It's not just a computer," she argued, laughing through her tears. "It's... it's everything. It's a chance. It's an opportunity. I don't want pity, but I don't get a lot of opportunities in my life. This is so generous. So kind. I'm speechless."

I helped her set it up, watching as her excitement grew with each step.

"It's a touchscreen," I said.

"My last laptop was circa two thousand ten. It was a brick. This is amazing. I can't believe you did this for me."

"Well, you're going to need it," I replied. "You have a book to write."

"I promise I'll put it to good use."

"I know you will." I stood, gesturing toward the door. "Now, go get ready. I'm taking you to dinner."

We both headed upstairs to change. It only took me about ten minutes. I went back downstairs to wait for her. I worked in the study until it was time. When she wasn't in the foyer, I walked back upstairs to her room. The door was slightly ajar. I caught sight of her standing in front of the mirror, struggling with the zipper of her dress. The fabric clung to her curves. The sight of her made my throat dry.

I couldn't look away. God, she was beautiful.

She must have sensed me there because she turned her head, catching my gaze. "Roman?"

"Sorry," I said, stepping back. "I didn't mean to—"

She smiled at me and gestured for me to walk into her room. "It's okay. Actually..." She turned her back to me, sweeping her hair to one side. "Can you help me with this?"

I hesitated for half a second before stepping inside. My fingers brushed against the warm skin of her back as I tugged the zipper up. The urge to reverse the motion and let the dress fall was almost unbearable, but I clenched my jaw and focused. I promised her dinner. I could not keep ravishing her. It was confusing for both of us.

"All done," I said, my voice rougher than I intended.

She turned, her smile soft. "Thank you."

I nodded, stepping back. "You look stunning."

Her cheeks flushed, and she laughed nervously. "You clean up pretty well yourself."

I held out my arm for her to take. I led her downstairs and out to the waiting car.

Dinner was at a quiet, out of the way restaurant—a place I knew would offer us the privacy we needed. Kaira seemed surprised as we stepped inside, glancing around at the understated decor.

"This isn't your usual scene," she said as we sat at a corner table.

"No, it's not," I admitted. "This dinner is for us, not the media."

Her cheeks turned pink. "You're full of surprises tonight. I like this side of you."

I felt my lips twitch upward in a smile. "Don't get used to it."

She laughed, the sound music to my ears. "I'll take what I can get."

As we perused the menu, the conversation flowed easily between us. Gone was the stiff formality that usually characterized our interactions. Instead, there was a growing sense of comfort and familiarity. Like we were actual friends. She was so easy to be around.

"So, what's your plan for this new laptop?" I asked, taking a sip of my wine.

She inhaled. "Write. I plan on writing. I'll figure out how to use those programs, but usually, I'm just a Word girl. I don't mess with all the formatting and what not."

"Do you have a story in mind?"

She grinned. "I do."

"But you're not going to tell me."

"Not yet. I'm guessing you're not a fan of romance novels anyway."

I shrugged. "No, but it's different when I know it's a story coming from you."

"That makes it worse for me," she said.

"Why?"

"Because it's kind of embarrassing. It's very vulnerable."

"I won't read it if you don't want me to, but if you do want me to, I'd be happy to."

Our meals were delivered shortly after. We ate and talked a bit about the weather and the usual things. She never brought up the sex and my reaction. She either forgot about it or preferred to ignore it. I was grateful for that because I had no idea what to say about it.

"I can't believe it's almost been a month," I said as the server cleared our plates. "And Valentine's Day is next week."

"It doesn't feel like it's been that long."

"No," I agreed, my gaze lingering on hers. "It doesn't."

We sat in comfortable silence for a moment before she said, "Thank you, Roman. For tonight, for the laptop... for everything."

"Thank you. For teaching me how to let go a little. I'm looking forward to the next five months."

Her smile widened, and for the first time in years, I felt like I was exactly where I was supposed to be.

The rain started as we pulled into the driveway—a rare occurrence in LA. We stepped out of the car together, but instead of making a mad dash to the door, I glanced up at the sky, feeling the cool drops against my face.

Anthony pulled away, honking twice in his usual goodbye.

I stopped abruptly, grabbing her hand. She turned to me, her expression questioning.

"What's wrong?" she asked.

"Nothing," I said, pulling her closer. "Just this."

Before she could respond, I leaned in, capturing her lips in a kiss. She melted against me, her arms wrapping around my neck as the light drizzle turned into a full rainstorm. I barely noticed the rain. I was completely focused on her. Her lips were soft, warm, and tasted faintly of the wine we'd shared at dinner.

I deepened the kiss, my hands sliding to her waist, pulling her closer until there was no space between us. The rain fell harder, drenching us completely, but neither of us cared. Kaira clung to me, her hand sliding up to the back of my neck as we kissed. I had never felt a connection like this with anyone before. Something about Kaira broke down my carefully constructed walls, leaving me open and exposed.

When we finally pulled apart, she laughed breathlessly. "You're full of surprises tonight."

I smiled, brushing a strand of wet hair from her face. "Get used to it."

33

KAIRA

I stared up at Roman, breathless from the intensity of his kiss. The rain was pouring down around us, soaking us both, but I barely noticed. All I could focus on was the way his hands felt on my waist, the warmth of his body pressed against mine.

"We should probably get inside before we catch pneumonia," I said, my voice soft.

Roman nodded, reluctantly loosening his grip on me. He took my hand and we hurried inside, water dripping from our hair and clothes.

Once in the foyer, Roman reached out and gently brushed a raindrop from my cheek with his thumb. His eyes held a warmth in them that I hadn't seen before. Gone was the cold, ruthless man that only made moves that benefited him.

"I'm glad you agreed to dinner tonight," he said quietly.

"Me too," I replied, my heart still racing from our kiss. "Thank you for that. And the laptop. It was a very thoughtful gift."

He nodded, his gaze holding mine for a long moment before he cleared his throat. "We should probably get dried off."

"Yeah." I made no move to go up to my room. I just stared at him, waiting for something to happen. The kiss had left me wanting more.

"I think we should just get out of our wet clothes," he said, his voice husky.

"Yeah."

"Come with me."

He started up the stairs. I followed behind him, heading toward his bedroom instead of my own. He led me inside and closed the door behind him.

"Are you chilly?" he asked.

"A little."

"I think a nice, hot shower is exactly what we need."

I nodded but couldn't say anything. I had thought about this with him since the last time, but I truly didn't think it would happen again. After he got up and left without a word, I thought maybe he didn't like it. Like I wasn't good in bed. But the way he was looking at me now said otherwise.

Roman stepped closer to me, his gaze intense. "Let me warm you up."

He cupped my face, his thumb tracing my lower lip. I shivered at his touch, my heart racing. Slowly, he leaned in and kissed me again. It deepened as his arms wrapped around my waist.

I melted against him, my fingers tangling in his damp hair. The kiss was passionate, full of an underlying hunger that sent tingles down my spine. When we finally broke apart, we were both breathing heavily.

"The shower," Roman murmured, his voice thick with lust.

He didn't move. Instead, he reached behind me and pulled down the zipper of my dress that he had zipped up a couple of hours ago. It fell to the floor around my feet. I kicked off my heels and stepped out of it.

It was my turn to help Roman out of his damp suit. I gazed up at him, my heart pounding as my cold fingers started to undo the buttons of his shirt. His eyes were filled with desire as he watched me undress him, his fingers brushing against my skin in a way that sent shivers through me. Once he was down to just his boxers, he pulled me close and kissed me again, his hands roaming over my body.

Breathlessly, he pulled back. "The shower," he repeated, his voice low and rough.

He led me into the spacious bathroom, turning on the water and adjusting the temperature. Steam quickly filled the air, much faster than the water heated up at my apartment. He pulled me under the hot spray, his lips finding mine in a searing kiss. The feel of his wet skin against mine was electrifying. His hands ignited sparks of desire with every caress.

There was an urgency to the way he kissed me, like he couldn't get enough. I matched his fervor, my body arching into his as the water cascaded over us. His lips left mine, trailing a path down my neck. I let out a soft moan as his tongue swirled around one nipple then the other. He gently backed me up against the tile wall before he dropped to his knees in front of me.

The waterfall showerhead made it feel like we were back in the rain, but this time, very naked. He kissed my belly and moved lower.

I let out a shaky breath as Roman's hands slid up my thighs. His touch was electrifying, sending tingles through my body. When his mouth finally met my most sensitive spot, I cried out, my fingers tangling in his hair.

Roman worked over my clit. His tongue drawing out wave after wave of pleasure. My legs trembled, threatening to give out. I leaned against the wall, the shower pouring hot water over me and down his back. Just when I thought I couldn't take any more, he slid two fingers inside me, his mouth continuing its relentless assault.

The sensations were overwhelming. I cried out as Roman's fingers curled and stroked, his mouth never letting up. My body felt like it was on fire, every nerve ending tingling with pleasure. I was close, so close. He didn't let up. I moaned and squeezed my eyes closed.

"Roman," I murmured. I could feel the orgasm building in the tips of my toes.

His mouth and fingers worked relentlessly, pushing me higher and higher until the tension finally snapped. My body shuddered as the waves of pleasure crashed over me. I cried out, my fingers tightening in his hair as the climax ripped through me. Roman held me steady, his tongue and fingers coaxing every last tremor from my body.

When the last aftershock had faded, he slowly pulled away, gazing up at me with a satisfied smile. He stood and looked at me with that same predatory gaze. "I want you," he growled, crashing his lips back to mine.

My hands roamed the hard planes of his chest. Roman lifted me effortlessly, my legs wrapping around his waist. I could feel his arousal pressing against me and a fresh wave of desire coursed through my body. He kissed me hungrily, his hands gripping my thighs to hold me in place.

I ran my hands down his back, marveling at the flex of his muscles as he ground his hips against mine. A soft moan escaped my lips, swallowed by his searing kiss.

To my disappointment, he carefully lowered me to my feet and turned off the water. He stepped out and handed me a towel that was as tall as I as. It was warm and fluffy, straight from the towel warmer. I wrapped it around myself and watched him do the same. He opened a drawer and pulled out a condom. He held it up and smiled.

"Bed," he said.

Roman took my hand and led me back into the bedroom. Once by the bed, he pulled me close and kissed me, his hands roaming over my towel-clad body.

I felt a thrill of anticipation as he slowly unwrapped the towel, exposing my skin to his hungry eyes. His touch was electrifying, setting every nerve ending on fire. I reached for the knot of his own towel, eager to feel his bare skin against mine.

Roman watched me intently as I slowly pulled the towel from his waist, my gaze roaming over his sculpted physique. He was absolutely breathtaking. I let the towel fall to the floor and stepped closer.

He pulled me flush against him, his hands sliding down to grip my hips. I could feel his arousal pressing against me. He stepped back and rolled on the condom.

I was about to crawl on the bed when he stopped me. Without a word, he turned me to face the bed and gently placed his hand on my back.

I got the message. I bent forward, my hands on the bed. I looked over my shoulder at Roman, my heart pounding with anticipation. He moved up behind me, his strong hands gripping my hips. I shivered as he pressed against me, the tip of his arousal teasing my entrance.

Slowly, he pushed inside, filling me inch by delicious inch. I let out a soft gasp at the feeling of him stretching me. Roman paused, allowing me to adjust to his size before he began to move. His thrusts were deep and powerful, driving me higher and higher with each one.

I dropped my face to the bed, giving him deeper access. I cried out, the sound muffled by the bedding as Roman's hips slammed against mine. The pleasure was almost too much, like a livewire running through my veins. He set a relentless pace, his fingers digging into my hips as he pounded into me.

My toes curled as I gripped the sheets, my body trembling. Roman leaned over, his chest pressing against my back as his thrusts grew more erratic. His breath was hot against my neck.

"Kaira," he growled, his voice rough with need. "You're so fucking hot."

Roman's grip on my hips tightened as he drove into me with desperate, pounding thrusts. My body trembled with the force of his movements, the pleasure bordering on overpowering. I had to push back to keep from collapsing completely onto the bed.

One of his hands released my hip and went to my hair. He pulled just hard enough to feel good.

I gasped at the sensation, my body arching back into him. Roman's pace grew even more frantic, his fingers tightening in my hair. The new angle sent electric shockwaves of pleasure through me. I was so close, teetering on the edge.

"Roman," I cried out, my voice ragged. "Please."

He growled something unintelligible, his hips snapping against mine with bruising force. The coil of tension within me finally snapped. I shattered, crying out his name as the orgasm ripped through me.

With a low groan, Roman stilled, his hips grinding against mine as he found his release. My body clenched around him as waves of euphoria crashed through me.

He collapsed onto the bed face first. I turned to look at him. He offered a half-grin. "Damn," he said.

I waited for him to tell me goodnight. To kick me out of his bed and his room.

But he didn't.

He stood up and to my shock, slapped my ass. I shrieked and hopped up.

"Pull the blankets back, I need to throw this away," he said referring to the condom.

Was he inviting me to stay or was he asking me to turn down his bed for him?

I pulled back the blankets and adjusted his pillows. He came back into the room and stood beside the bed. "This is my side. You take the other."

And I had my answer.

I stared at Roman, surprised by his invitation to stick around. After last time, I expected him to quickly usher me out, or at the very least, keep a respectful distance. But here he was, casually gesturing to the other side of the mattress as if this was a normal, everyday occurrence.

"Are you sure?" I asked, my voice barely above a whisper.

Roman arched an eyebrow. "Do I look unsure?"

"No."

He climbed into bed and looked at me expectantly. I followed, keeping my distance just in case.

Roman didn't let me keep my distance for long. As soon as I settled under the covers, he pulled me against him, wrapping his arm around my waist. I tensed for a moment, unsure of how to react, but soon I was relaxing into his embrace. We lay there in comfortable silence, the only sounds the soft hum of the rain outside and our quiet breathing. I felt myself drifting off in his arms and let it happen.

34

ROMAN

When I woke, the first thing I noticed was the scent of vanilla lingering in the air. It wasn't my cologne or soap—this was her. Kaira. I turned my head slightly, and there she was, curled up beside me, her hair in a halo around her. She looked angelic and peaceful and most importantly like she belonged. Her lips were slightly parted as she breathed so softly I almost forgot she was in bed beside me.

It hit me like a brick: she was still here.

No one stayed. I never let them stay. Yet here she was, her presence filling the space with warmth I hadn't realized was missing. I clasped my hands behind my head and let my gaze trace her profile, soft in the morning light. For the first time in forever, I felt at peace. I closed my eyes briefly, letting the sensation wash over me.

This felt good.

The blanket had slipped down, exposing her bare shoulder. Instinctively, I reached out and gently pulled it back up, tucking it around her. Kaira stirred, murmuring something incoherent as she shifted closer to me. I leaned in and pressed a kiss to her temple, then to the corner of her mouth. Her eyes fluttered open, and a sleepy smile spread across her face.

"Good morning," she said, her voice husky with sleep.

"Good morning," I murmured, kissing her again, this time fully on the lips. Her hand came up to rest against my cheek. She pulled me in closer, her warmth drawing me in like a flame. I wrapped my arm around her and tugged her closer to me. Her silky, soft skin rubbed against mine.

This part of a sleepover was pretty new to me. I never stayed in a woman's bed long enough to experience the morning after and I sure as hell never invited a woman to stay the night in my bed. I realized I might have been missing out on something. There was a comfort to lying naked in bed the morning after, a closeness.

Kaira melted into my embrace, her fingers running over my chest. I savored the moment. My mind was all over the place. I liked this. A lot. Yes, I would happily fuck her again, but that's not what I was thinking about. This was what I believe they called intimacy. There was something very satisfying about it. It felt good in a different way.

Kaira let out a long sigh. That sigh held a lot of unspoken things. I knew what was coming. "So… what does this mean?" she asked. "I know that's not a question you want to hear, but I'm not a hit it and quit it girl. I'm not someone that does no strings. I get that you do, but I can't. So, I'm going to have to have some boundaries. Expectations."

I blinked, taken off guard by her directness. The meek little woman I met at the auction was not in this bed. This was a side of Kaira I liked and respected. I liked that she was willing to stick up for herself. But now I had to figure out how to answer that question because I honestly didn't know.

"I mean, I know this was never supposed to be serious, and we've been telling ourselves it's just for the cameras… but twice now, Roman. It's starting to feel like more than a contract. I'm sure this is all one-sided but this feels like more than fake. I'm just asking for some guidance here."

She had a way of cutting straight to the heart of things. I admired her for it. I took a deep breath, trying to find the right words. I wasn't quite as brave as she was when it came to facing my emotions.

"I don't know what this means yet," I admitted, meeting her eyes. "All I know is that I'm enjoying this. You. And I want more of it. Is that enough for now? I know it's not much and you deserve more but I'm starting from a different place in life. This is so far out of my comfort zone."

Kaira reached up and gently traced the line of my jaw. "I understand. I'm not asking for a commitment or anything like that. I know this started out as an arrangement, but it's clearly become more than that for both of us. I just want to make sure we're on the same page, that we both want the same thing, even if we can't put a label on it yet."

I covered her hand with mine, marveling at how perfectly it fit. "I want you, Kaira. I want to see where this goes, even if I'm not sure where that is."

"Can I ask one thing of you?" she asked.

"Sure."

"I don't know if you would or are, but if you want to sleep with another woman on the down low to keep the media from finding out, please tell me. I obviously can't stop you, but I can't be a side chick or a Tuesday girl."

"What the hell is a Tuesday girl?"

"Like you stop by my bed on Tuesday and another woman on Wednesday and so on."

I smirked. "You'll be my Sunday through Monday girl. I wouldn't do that. I'm not a saint, but I won't be bed hopping."

"Thank you," she said. "I never thought I'd be so happy that an asshole like you is into me."

I chuckled, brushing a strand of hair from her face. "And I never thought an angel like you would give an ass like me a shot."

"As long as you know what's up," she teased, leaning in for another kiss.

Kaira pulled back, a mischievous glint in her eyes. "So, what are your plans for the day?"

I grinned, my hands sliding down to her hips. "Well, Miss Kaira, I was thinking we could start the day right here in this bed."

She raised an eyebrow. "Oh really? And what did you have in mind?"

"I have a few ideas," I murmured, pulling her closer.

Kaira laughed. "I'm all ears."

I let myself get lost in her for a moment, savoring the way she tasted, the way she felt.

Eventually, we dragged ourselves out of bed and into the shower. It was a slow, teasing affair that had us both laughing and stealing kisses under the warm spray. I couldn't keep my hands off her. She didn't seem to mind. By the time we emerged, the tension in my chest —the tension I always carried—felt like it had melted away entirely. I felt like a whole new man.

Kaira grabbed one of my shirts to wear, the fabric practically swallowing her. She glanced at herself in the mirror, tugging at the hem. "This looks ridiculous."

"You look amazing," I said. "But if you go downstairs in just that, the staff will know exactly what happened."

She arched a brow at me, her lips curving into a smirk. "And do you care?"

The question hung in the air between us, and for a moment, I thought about it. Did I care? About the whispers or the knowing looks?

I surprised myself by shaking my head. "No. I don't. But I'd prefer I was the only one peeking at your ass."

She grinned and disappeared into her room, emerging a few minutes later wearing leggings beneath the oversized shirt. It wasn't much different, but it was enough to keep things relatively modest.

"Come on, I'll make you breakfast," she said.

"I have a cook."

"And I happen to know he doesn't come in this early," she said. "And if he is in there, I'm kicking him out. I'm making breakfast."

"Lead the way."

I managed to start coffee, pretty much the extent of my culinary skills. Kaira rummaged through the cabinets like she owned the place, pulling out eggs, bread, and a block of cheese. I sipped my coffee, leaned back, and enjoyed the show.

"We're making French toast and scrambled eggs," she declared.

"Are we?" I asked.

"Yes," she said firmly, pointing a spatula at me. "And you're helping."

She was mesmerizing.

Before I realized it, I was watching her the way my father used to watch my mother—like nothing else in the world mattered. That realization hit me hard, but instead of pulling away, I let myself sink into it.

This felt right.

"Tell me what to do," I said.

Kaira glanced at me, a soft smile tugging at the corners of her lips. "Why don't you start by grating some cheese for the eggs?"

I nodded, setting down my coffee mug and moving to the counter where she had a block of sharp cheddar waiting. As I began to carefully run the cheese over the grater, I couldn't help but steal glances at Kaira as she expertly cracked eggs into a bowl and whisked them together.

"Do you do a lot of cooking?" I asked.

"I wouldn't say a lot and I don't know if it's called cooking," she said. "Usually, it's whatever is in the pantry and typically involves pasta. Pasta is cheap and you can dress it up a hundred different ways."

I nodded, even though I really had no idea. I had never bought myself food beyond using my app to order something for delivery.

I couldn't help but feel a sense of wonder. This was so far removed from my normal routine, yet it felt so natural. There was an intimacy to it that I didn't want to analyze too closely.

It wasn't long before our breakfast was done. We sat at the kitchen island to enjoy our meal. The food was simple but delicious. The company was even better. Kaira told me about the plot of the book she was working on, her face lighting up as she spoke. I could see the passion in her eyes, the excitement that came with creating something entirely her own.

"You should've been a writer," I said, sipping my coffee. "I mean I know that's what you want to be, but I think you could have already had a couple bestsellers under your belt."

She laughed. "I don't know about that. It's a commitment. I haven't been ready to make that commitment."

"Trust me, I know all about the fear of committing."

We both laughed.

By the time we finished eating, I felt more relaxed than I had in years. Kaira looked at me.

"What are you thinking about?" she asked.

"Just how much I'm enjoying this. You. Us."

"Me too."

35

KAIRA

The next morning, I woke up in Roman's bed again, the scent of his soap lingering in the air. The fresh, clean scent mixed with the musky aroma of his cologne. I breathed it in greedily, reminded of our intimate moments shared in this very bed. He had left an hour ago, kissing me softly before he left the room. I rolled over and pulled his pillow against me.

It was becoming a dangerous habit, like I belonged in his bed. I lay there, reluctant to leave the warmth and comfort of his sheets. It was still early. I knew I should get up and start my day, but the thought of leaving did not sound appealing.

Yesterday, I felt like we made some progress in our relationship. And yes, it was officially a relationship. I still couldn't believe it. Me, little old nobody me was with Roman Kelly. Never in a million years would I have thought this would be my life. I knew this thing was tenuous. Roman still had a lot of baggage. I didn't want to let myself get too caught up too quickly.

But it was too late. I cared about him. Somewhere along the way, it happened. I wasn't going to just stop caring about the guy when he kicked me out of his bed. I pushed away the thought. I didn't want to dwell on the negative. Whatever happened, happened. It didn't mean I couldn't enjoy the ride.

I decided I needed to be productive today. After all, I had a birthday party to plan. The idea had come to me sometime yesterday. My thought was if he was open to being with me, something that was new to him, he might see the joy in celebrating his birthday. It was a special day. He just had a bad feeling about it, but it didn't need to be a bad thing. He just needed one good birthday to realize it was okay to acknowledge the occasion.

And I was going to give it to him.

I got up and walked down the hall to my bedroom. I quickly showered and got ready for the day. I was going to hit the ground running. I didn't have much time to get this organized.

On my way downstairs, I spotted Marilyn. "Can you have everyone meet me in the dining room in an hour?"

"Is something wrong?" she asked with concern.

"Nope, but I have big news and I want everyone there."

She nodded, still looking concerned. "Okay. I'll let everyone know."

I grabbed myself some coffee and a quick snack. There was a hum of energy coursing through me. I was so excited to do this.

An hour later, I had turned the dining-room table into a war room. The entire house staff sat around the table looking very skeptical and concerned. They probably thought they were getting fired. I knew convincing them wouldn't be easy.

"Thank you all for coming," I began, clasping my hands in front of me. "I have an idea, and I need your help."

A few wary glances were exchanged. "You know we're always here to assist, but what exactly are you proposing?" Marilyn asked.

"A birthday party for Roman," I said with as much enthusiasm as I could muster.

The room fell silent. You could've heard a pin drop. Then the murmurs started.

"He doesn't celebrate his birthday," one of the housekeepers whispered.

"Not since he was a kid," the gardener added.

"Oh, Kaira, that's a sweet idea, but he's just not the type to celebrate," Marilyn said. "I really don't think he would appreciate a party. I'm sorry to burst your bubble. It's a thoughtful gesture, but maybe something with just the two of you."

That was not what I wanted to do. Yes, I could be stubborn, but I was convinced this would make Roman really happy.

"I know, I know," I said, holding up my hands. "You guys have known him longer than I have. I get it. But hear me out. I've talked to him about it—well, sort of—and I really think this could be good for him. Roman works so hard, and he's done so much for all of us. Don't you think he deserves a little party? He doesn't think his birthday is worth celebrating, but I for one, think it is. I'm glad he's on this earth. I want to celebrate the day he was born."

They looked unconvinced.

"He's always so closed off, but I see how much you all care about him. I think this could be a chance to remind him he's not alone. That he's still surrounded by people who love him. Yes, he lost the two people that brought him into this world, but he's still here. He deserves to be celebrated."

That struck a chord. The murmurs shifted from hesitant to contemplative. Finally, Marilyn spoke up. "He's pushed us away over the years, Kaira. But you're right. We do care about him."

Relief washed over me as the staff began nodding in agreement. One by one, they started sharing ideas. A five-course dinner in the solarium, live music, personalized cocktails, and of course, a birthday cake. There was even talk of dancing and fun party games to lighten the mood.

"Do you think he'll actually enjoy this?" Marilyn asked. "I'm not going to lie; this makes me very nervous."

"I think he'll love it. Even if he pretends not to."

I was filled with restless energy as I paced back and forth in the dining room, listening as the staff came up with ideas for Roman's surprise birthday party. They seemed hesitant at first, but as we talked it through, I could see them getting excited about the prospect of celebrating their employer in a way they hadn't done in years. I could envision the whole thing coming together beautifully.

After figuring out what preparations needed to be made, the staff went back to their duties and I got started with the guest list. I had gotten a single phone number at the dinner with Roman's friends, and I used it.

I contacted Chloe, who was surprisingly eager to attend. "We've been dying to celebrate him," she said over the phone. "He never lets us."

"Well, this time, he doesn't have a choice," I replied with a grin. "He's going to love it once it's thrown for him."

"I'll contact some of his friends with the invite," she said. "People he actually likes."

I laughed. "You're a lifesaver."

After we said our goodbyes, I went on a hunt for Marilyn. I found her in one of the sitting rooms, making a list.

"Marilyn, have you seen Ruby?"

"No, I haven't."

"Where would I begin to look for her?"

Marilyn laughed. "Airport, harbor, or Grand Central would be my first guesses."

I laughed, understanding she was a rambler. "I really want to get her confirmation that she'll be here for the party. She's Roman's only living family. I know her presence would mean something to him. I need to find her."

"I'll make some calls," she said. "I'll talk to the young lady taking care of her room. She can leave a note at the very least."

"Thank you, Marilyn. I appreciate it."

As I got texts from Roman's friends replying to my invitation, it felt like a small victory. I was on a high, my excitement building with every passing hour. It wasn't just about the party—it was about Roman. About showing him that, despite everything he'd lost, he still had people in his corner. People who cared about him deeply.

Including me.

I grabbed my new laptop and started doing some shopping for

decorations. I wanted classy but maybe a little silly. As I shopped online for party supplies, I couldn't help but feel a sense of nervous anticipation. I wanted this birthday celebration to be perfect for Roman. He deserved to feel loved and appreciated, even if he didn't know it. I hoped that when he felt the love, he would be happy we went against his birthday ban.

I ended up ordering an elegant floral centerpiece for the dining table, along with some string lights to hang around the room. A few playful decorations like a large "Happy Birthday" banner and colorful balloons added a touch of whimsy. I wanted the atmosphere to feel warm and inviting, a far cry from the formal, solemn vibe that usually permeated the mansion. Roman mentioned he liked the sound of laughter in the house. I couldn't really buy him anything that he couldn't buy himself, but I could give him laughter and friendship. I could make him feel more human.

I put in the last order and felt like I accomplished all I could for the day. Marilyn appeared in the doorway. "Kaira, I have some good news. I was able to reach Ruby. She's thrilled about the party and said she'll be here. She'll be back in this hemisphere by then."

I felt a wave of relief wash over me. "That's wonderful! I'm so glad she's able to make it. Roman is going to be so surprised."

Marilyn nodded, a small smile on her face. "He is. We all know how much it will mean to him, even if he tries to play it off."

"Exactly. He may act annoyed or dismissive at first, but deep down, I know this will mean the world to him. I'm just glad you all were on board to help make this happen. I couldn't have done it without your support."

"We care about him, Kaira. Even if he's built up these walls, we see the man underneath. The one who is kind and generous, even if he hides it well. This party is the perfect way to show him that he's not alone—that he has a family here, even if it's not the traditional one he lost."

This wasn't just a party. This was a chance to show Roman how much he was loved and appreciated. By the time evening rolled around, I was exhausted but exhilarated. I retreated to the library with my new laptop and opened my manuscript, diving into the world I was creating. My fingers flew over the keys, the words pouring out of me faster than I could keep up.

Thank God for grammar checker.

I didn't even hear Roman come in until he was standing behind me.

"Hey," he said softly.

I turned in my chair, a smile spreading across my face. "Hey, yourself. I didn't hear you come in. You'd make a great cat burglar. What time is it?"

Before I could say another word, he leaned down and kissed me. It was the kind of kiss that made my toes curl and my heart race. When he finally pulled back, his eyes were full of heat.

"How was your day?" he asked.

"Good. Even better now."

"What have you been doing?"

"Oh, nothing," I said with a sly smile. "I've been here all day. Waiting for you. Working. Writing."

He kissed me again. "I've missed your lips since the moment I left this morning," he murmured against my mouth.

I giggled breathlessly. "Hang on. Let me write that down. That's a good line."

He chuckled, pulling back just enough to look into my eyes. "You're unbelievable."

"So I've been told," I teased, my cheeks flushing.

"I'm going to make myself a drink, want something?"

"Please," I said and closed my laptop. I left it in the library and followed him into what I was calling the lounge. It was basically another living room but it had a full bar in the corner. There were a few couches and chairs but no TV.

Roman went behind the bar. He pulled out two glasses and a bottle of scotch. "Do you want something specific or just something that isn't scotch?"

"I'll try the scotch," I said, surprising myself. "When in Rome, right?"

He raised an eyebrow. "Pun intended?"

I grinned. "Maybe. Depends how adventurous you are."

He poured two glasses, sliding one toward me. I took a tentative sip and immediately coughed. It burned going down, far more intense than any alcohol I was used to.

Roman chuckled, watching me with an amused expression. "Not quite what you were expecting?" he asked, taking a smooth sip from his own glass.

"It's like drinking smoke and dirt," I gasped, my eyes watering. "How do you drink this?"

"Practice," he said with a smirk. "Want something sweeter?"

I shook my head, determined. "No, I can handle this." I took another sip. It went down a little smoother. The gross taste was growing on me.

We moved to sit down, settling into comfortable silence.

I couldn't help but marvel at how much had changed between us. When this all started, Roman had been an enigma—a cold, calculating man who saw me as little more than a means to an end. But now? Now he felt like so much more.

I glanced up at him, my heart swelling with a warmth I couldn't ignore. Maybe I didn't need book boyfriends anymore. Not when I had a fake fiancé who ticked every box.

Minus the fake part.

36

ROMAN

The rest of the week felt like a dream. If I wasn't at work, I was with Kaira. She had a way of turning the mundane into something magical. Cooking together had become our ritual—a dance of teasing, stolen kisses, and laughter as we navigated the kitchen. My cook was fortunately not too upset that Kaira had kind of taken over the kitchen. She loved cooking and I had a feeling she loved cooking for me.

It was nice to come home to a beautiful woman cooking a meal in the kitchen. I never imagined I was the kind of man that would ever want that, and it certainly wasn't something I required, but it was nice all the same.

I smiled thinking about what could only be considered dessert last night. Last night, we'd finished what we started the last time we were in the pool together. The memory of her wet body sliding against mine nearly had me hard once again.

Every time I left my bed in the morning, I found myself counting the hours until I could return to it, to her. Even at work, where distractions were a given, I couldn't focus. She crept into my thoughts like a song I couldn't get out of my head. Except unlike an annoying song, I wanted this in my head.

It was like she was constantly with me. All day while I was at the office or sitting in meetings, I could feel her with me. I would think about something she said or the way she looked at me and I would find myself smiling. I knew people noticed. They probably thought I was drunk or losing my mind.

When the media bombarded me, it no longer bothered me the way it used to. Their questions and flashing cameras were mere static because I had someone waiting for me at home, someone who had become my refuge. I noticed that I felt that way about a lot of things. My mood was generally good. I didn't wake up pissed and ready to kick ass. I woke up with a smile on my face. Throughout the day, she would often text me. Nothing substantial, just little tidbits about her story or something she heard on the news. I did the same. I would text her about a meeting or something someone said.

I realized there had been an emptiness in me that Kaira had filled, and for the first time in years, I felt whole. I felt a giddiness I hadn't experienced in a very long time. The thought of seeing Kaira again after a long day at work filled me with a sense of anticipation. I found myself looking forward to our evenings together—the casual intimacy, the easy banter, the way she could make even the most mundane tasks feel special.

It was Friday evening, and I was driving home, but as happy as I was to be with her, there was a quiet voice in the back of my mind I couldn't ignore. Every time I felt myself really sinking into the not-quite-wedded bliss, there was a little doubt dragging me out of the warm glow and back into the chill of loneliness.

This thing between us had an expiration date. Five more months. That was the deal. What would I do when the contract ended and we went our separate ways? The thought left a sour taste in my mouth. I couldn't go back to how things were before her.

But could I really ask her to stay? Could I expect her to keep riding this roller coaster with me once her part of the agreement was fulfilled? Things between us were good right now but it was all new and fun and there weren't really any actual commitments. We lived together and were kind of role playing.

Part of me still very much understood this was make believe. It wasn't real. If I wanted to make it real, I would have to jump in with both feet. I just wasn't sure I was ready to do that. I was still a damaged guy that had never been in a serious relationship.

I shook off the negative, dark thoughts. I still had a few months with her. I didn't need to think about the end. I wanted to enjoy the time we did have. When I walked into the house, things were unnervingly quiet. No laughter, no music, no clatter of dishes from the kitchen.

I expected a member of the staff to greet me at the door, but the entryway was empty. Things felt off. Was the feeling of foreboding I had all day a premonition?

"Kaira?"

No answer.

A flicker of worry tightened in my chest. I checked the library, the kitchen, and the living room. Nothing. My pace quickened as I moved toward the back of the house. My heart stuttered when I saw a figure standing near the solarium door.

"Ruby?" I said, startled.

She turned, her red lips curving into a grin. "Roman, darling!" She swept toward me in a designer gown that sparkled under the hallway lights, her jewelry catching every glimmer. "You're just in time. I have someone I'd like you to meet."

I blinked, still trying to process the absurdity of her dressed to the nines. I assumed she must be on her way out with one of her princes or viscounts or whoever she was chasing after this week. "What are you doing here?" I asked.

She waved a hand. "I'm back for a couple of weeks, you know that."

"Yes, but I haven't seen you in a week. I wasn't sure you were still in town."

"I wasn't. Come along, come along!" She grabbed my arm and tugged me toward the solarium.

The second we reached the entrance, the room erupted in light.

Twinkling Christmas lights were draped from the ceiling and hanging down the glass walls.

"Surprise!" my friends all yelled in unison.

I froze in place, my gaze landing on Kaira standing in the center of the crowd that was packed into my solarium. There was a proud smile lighting up her face. She wore one of the dresses we had bought on our first shopping trip. The deep emerald fabric hugged her curves in all the right places. My breath caught in my throat as I took her in. I barely noticed the people surrounding her. I only had eyes for her.

She stepped forward, her hands clasped nervously in front of her. "I hope you don't mind," she said softly. "I might have gotten a little carried away."

Mind? I closed the distance between us. Without a second thought, I cupped her face and kissed her, a sense of gratitude swelling inside me that I hadn't felt in years.

"You're incredible," I murmured against her lips.

Her cheeks flushed as she smiled up at me. "Happy birthday, Roman."

The solarium had been transformed into a wonderland of soft lights, some gold and silver balloons, and a giant banner wishing me a happy birthday. The solarium was not a small room and it must have taken a fair amount of time to set this up.

"How did you do all of this?" I asked.

She laughed. "I've had some time on my hands. Go, greet your friends. There's a running bet between them."

"What's the bet?"

"Half think you're going to hate this and the other half? Well, they expect you to turn and run."

"People are about to lose some money," I said with a wink.

I mingled with friends I didn't get to see often. I was surprised by how many of them had come at Kaira's invitation. More than one of them had a lot to say about how charming she was. They were all impressed by how she'd pulled all of this together.

I tried the personalized cocktail she'd invented for me—whiskey-based, smoky with a hint of orange and vanilla. It was delicious, just like everything else about tonight. I couldn't believe the detail that had gone into planning the party.

The staff served dinner in the dining room. The food was exquisite, each course more impressive than the last. I found myself laughing more than I had in ages. The staff, my friends, even Ruby seemed genuinely happy.

But it was Kaira who held my attention. Whether she was laughing with a guest, dancing in her bare feet, or sneaking a taste of the cake before it was served, she was the gravitational pull of the evening. I couldn't keep my eyes off her. She was absolutely radiant, her joy and enthusiasm contagious. I watched as she moved through the room, chatting with my friends, giggling at their jokes, and making everyone feel at home. She was an incredible hostess.

At one point, she caught me staring and winked, a mischievous grin on her face. I had to resist the urge to pull her into my arms and kiss her senseless right then and there. Instead, I made my way over to her, capturing her hand and pressing a gentle kiss to her knuckles. "You've outdone yourself," I murmured.

Kaira's eyes sparkled with delight. "I'm so glad you're enjoying it. I wanted this to be special for you."

I gave her hand a gentle squeeze. "It is. More than you know."

She beamed up at me, and in that moment, I knew I was truly, irrevocably lost to her. This woman had worked her way past every single one of my defenses.

As the night wore on, the guests trickled out one by one, until it was just the two of us left in the solarium. The space was quieter now, the twinkle lights looking much brighter in the empty room.

She walked toward me, her emerald dress catching the light, a small smile playing on her lips.

"Dance with me?" she asked, holding out her hand.

I took it without hesitation, pulling her close as a slow acoustic ballad played softly in the background. We swayed together, her head resting against my chest, her warmth sinking into me.

"This has been the best birthday I can remember," I said quietly, my voice thick with emotion. "Thank you."

She tilted her head up to look at me. "You deserve it, Roman. You deserve all of this."

I didn't know how to respond to that, so I kissed her instead, letting the gratitude I couldn't put into words pour into the kiss.

When we pulled back, she smiled. "I have one more surprise."

I arched a brow, intrigued. "More? You've already surprised the hell out of me."

She took my hand, her excitement palpable as she led me toward the far corner of the solarium.

"What is it?" I asked, my curiosity piqued.

She grinned as she revealed a silver dome like the kind used to serve our meals. She revealed a small cake with the words *Happy Birthday, Roman* written in elegant icing. But that wasn't what caught my attention. Sitting next to the cake was a framed photograph—one I hadn't seen in years. It was of my parents, taken on one of their anniversaries.

"How did you..." My voice faltered as I stared at the picture.

"Marilyn," she said softly. "I thought it might mean something to you."

Emotion swelled in my chest as I reached for the frame, my fingers brushing over the glass. "It does. It means everything."

"I just wanted to remind you that you're not alone, Roman. You never have to be."

I turned to her, my throat tight with gratitude and something else—something deeper. "You're incredible," I said again, my voice barely above a whisper.

37

KAIRA

My heart swelled as I watched the emotions play across Roman's face. He looked both vulnerable and awestruck as he stared at the framed photo of his parents. The usually stoic and controlled man I had come to know was stripped bare, raw emotion shining through.

He pulled me into his arms, holding me tight. I melted against him. We gently swayed back and forth to the music. I couldn't begin to express how relieved I was that he enjoyed the party. I had been stressing out about his reaction. When I heard people were betting he was going to lose his shit and storm out, I came very close to canceling the whole thing.

But seeing the look on his face when he walked in, the pure joy and surprise, made it all worth it. He had clearly been touched by the gesture.

"Thank you for going through so much trouble for me," he said.

"It wasn't any trouble. I'm just glad you got to have a good birthday."

"I'll admit, it's been a while since I could say that. It was good. Really good."

"Well, it's not over yet," I said with a flirty smile.

"No?"

"No. I'm going to go upstairs and you're going to meet me in your room in five minutes."

He raised an eyebrow. "Oh yeah?"

I gave him a quick kiss. "It's my turn to give you my gift."

He chuckled. "I have a feeling it's going to be the best one yet."

I left him in the solarium and went upstairs to my room. I was incredibly nervous but also very excited to put on the lingerie I bought with this night in mind. The set was a deep red lace and satin number. It was snug and gave my boobs a nice lift, making my cleavage look amazing. The matching garter belt and thigh-high stockings added an extra touch of seduction. The panties were itty bitty. I grabbed the big red bow and stuck it to my chest. He was going to get to unwrap me.

Dressed and ready and feeling like a true seductress, I walked down the hall and waited for him in his room.

The anticipation built as I waited for Roman. My heart raced with excitement and a touch of nerves. I wanted this night to be perfect, to give him an unforgettable birthday gift.

When the door finally opened, Roman's expression shifted from curiosity to smoldering desire the moment his eyes landed on me. He slowly closed the door behind him, his gaze roaming hungrily over my lingerie-clad body.

"Kaira," he breathed, his voice thick with want. "You look… incredible."

I felt a thrill of triumph at his reaction. Slowly, I stood from the bed and sauntered toward him, the satin and lace caressing my skin with every step.

"Happy birthday, Roman," I purred, reaching up to trace the line of his jaw. "I have a very special gift for you."

His hands settled on my hips, pulling me flush against him. "I can't wait," he murmured, his lips finding mine in a searing kiss.

The giant bow squished between us. Roman stepped back and reached for it. "Can I?"

"It's your party."

He pulled it away, revealing the full scope of the lingerie. Not that there was a lot to see. He licked his lips. "Damn."

When he reached for me again, I stepped back and shook my head. "Nope. Tonight is about you."

I began to undress him, taking my time and rubbing my body against his as I slowly removed each article of clothing. His breath grew heavy as I teased him, my fingers trailing along his toned chest and abs. When he was finally stripped down to just his boxers, I pushed him back onto the bed.

He watched me with dark, hungry eyes. I climbed onto the bed, crawling up his body until I was straddling his hips. I ground against him, pulling a deep groan from him. His hands gripped my thighs, his thumbs caressing the satin ribbon that lined the panties. I kissed down his chest, sliding my body lower and down his thighs.

My tongue circled his navel before I slid off the bed once again. I reached for his boxers and pulled them down. I stared down at the large, naked man on the bed with his erection bouncing with every breath. I gulped down the lump of desire. I wanted to climb on him and ride him, but not yet. I wanted to drag this night out for him. He always gave me so much pleasure. I wanted to give him the same sense of euphoria.

Roman was magnificent, all toned muscle and rugged masculinity. My gaze drank him in, from his broad shoulders down to his thick, throbbing arousal. I felt an ache of desire between my own legs as I knelt on the bed beside him. My hand wrapped around his thick cock, gently rubbing from the base and sliding up. My thumb gently caressed the tip.

I felt a thrill of power as Roman's breath hitched, his hips lifting slightly at my touch. I leaned in, my lips grazing the sensitive skin of his inner thigh, my tongue tracing a path dangerously close to where he wanted me most.

His fingers tangled in my hair, gently guiding me. "Kaira," he growled, his voice strained with need.

I glanced up at him, holding his gaze as I slowly, deliberately, wrapped my lips around the tip of his cock. He let out a strangled groan, his hips bucking upward. I began to tease and suck him, keeping my movements languid and unhurried, savoring the way his body reacted to my touch.

Roman was putty in my hands, his usual control and composure completely unraveled. His fingers tightened in my hair, his hips shifting restlessly as I worked him over with my mouth. I loved seeing him like this, completely at my mercy.

"Kaira, I can't hold back much longer," he warned, his voice ragged.

I looked up at him and smiled. I slowly pulled back, my hand continuing to pump him gently. "I want you to let go, Roman," I said softly. "I want you to let go completely."

I returned my mouth to his cock and sucked him deep into my throat. With a primal groan, Roman hit his climax, and I felt his hot release fill my mouth. I swallowed each spurt, savoring the evidence of his pleasure as he shuddered and trembled in the aftermath.

Finally, when his breathing had returned to almost normal, I crawled up the bed and straddled him once more. "My turn," I purred, running my fingernails lightly down his chest.

He was breathing hard. "Two minutes."

"I'll occupy myself," I teased.

He rolled me off him, stretching out beside me. "I think I'd like to finish unwrapping my gift. Beautifully wrapped as it is."

His hands trailed up my bare thighs, gently caressing the satin ribbon bow. His fingers deftly untied it. My eyes closed as the air brushed against my heated skin. He repeated the process on the other leg, a small grin playing on his lips as he admired my lace lingerie. "You are the sexiest woman alive."

I blushed a deep red. "I wanted to surprise you."

"You've definitely succeeded in that. Now I can't wait to see how impatient I can make you."

I moaned as his talented fingers traced the lace along my thighs, dipping under the fabric. His fingers found my most sensitive spot. I gasped at the electric sensation. Roman's touch was deliberate, teasing, driving me slowly mad with desire.

"Roman," I breathed, arching into his touch.

He chuckled low in his throat, his fingers continuing their delicate exploration. "Patience. It's my birthday, after all."

I bit my lip, trying to suppress another moan as his fingers worked their magic. The anticipation was almost unbearable.

"You're so beautiful," he murmured, his voice rough with desire.

I let out a soft gasp as he worked two fingers in me, his thumb circling my most sensitive spot. The combination of sensations was overwhelming. My hips moved instinctively, matching the rhythm of his fingers. My breathing grew heavier, my heart rate quickened. A wave of pleasure washed over me. I knew I wasn't far away from climaxing.

Roman watched me intently, enjoying the sight of my passion. He could tell I was close. He increased the pace of his fingers, slowly building up a steady rhythm that sent shivers down my spine. My hips bucked wildly, seeking more, and he made sure to hit all the right spots.

It wasn't long before the orgasm hit me, knocking the air from my lungs.

I could feel his hardness pressing against me, hot and insistent. He was ready once again.

Roman reached over to the nightstand, his movements urgent. I heard the drawer open and knew he was getting a condom. He rolled it on with practiced efficiency, his eyes never leaving mine.

I watched as he positioned himself, ready to slide inside me. The anticipation of his entry was almost unbearable but also thrilling. With a deep breath, I reached down and guided him into me. He slid smoothly, filling me completely.

"God, you feel amazing," he whispered against my lips, his gaze locked with mine.

I smiled, wrapping my arms around him as he began to move inside me. Our bodies moved in perfect sync, like two pieces of a puzzle fitting together perfectly. I couldn't count how many times we had sex, but tonight it felt different. It felt like he was truly meant for me and me alone.

I dug my nails into his shoulders, only adding to the intensity of the moment. My eyes rolled back in my head as pleasure coursed through me with each stroke.

"Kaira," he groaned, his voice ragged with need. "I'm close."

"Me too," I whispered against his neck, my fingers tightening in his hair. "You drive me wild."

It was too much. He pushed deeper inside me, his hips bucking wildly as he let go. The feeling of his release was incredible, waves of heat and satisfaction coursing through me, tipping over the edge again. His body trembled against mine as he collapsed on top of me, our sweat-slick skin sticking together.

We lay there together for a long moment, catching our breath. I could feel his heart still pounding against my chest. "That was... unbelievable," he murmured hoarsely.

I kissed the side of his face. "Always is."

"Best birthday ever."

I couldn't help but smile. "I'm glad you think so."

"I haven't even unwrapped my gift all the way."

I let out a soft giggle. "Maybe you should finish unwrapping it then," I offered playfully.

Roman raised an eyebrow, his lips curling into a mischievous grin. "Don't tempt me with a good time."

He shifted slightly, propping himself up on one elbow to look down at me with affectionate eyes. With deliberate slowness, he traced his fingers down the side of my face, his touch sending yet another shiver through me. His fingers eventually reached the edge of my lace bra, toying with it teasingly. "I think I've found something else to unwrap," he murmured.

I slightly nodded my head to give him a silent invitation for him to continue. Roman's fingers expertly unclasped the bra, slow, almost reverently, as if savoring every moment. The fabric slid off my shoulders and fell away. He admired the view for a moment before bending down to kiss the newly exposed skin with adoration.

I closed my eyes and groaned. I was glad we could sleep in tomorrow because I had a feeling it was going to be a very late night.

38

ROMAN

The week had been nothing short of extraordinary. Every moment with Kaira felt like discovering a part of myself I hadn't known was missing. Whether we were making dinner together, stealing kisses in the hallways, or just sitting quietly in the library while she worked on her manuscript, everything felt right.

I had never felt so comfortable in someone else's presence. Sometimes, I would be working in my study and she would come in and sit in the corner working on her book. We didn't talk. We didn't have to. It was enough just to be in the same orbit.

I often found myself wondering how I ever managed before she came into my life. It sounded so cheesy, but I really did feel like she completed me. I never realized how empty my life was before she accidentally bid on me at that auction.

If I would have known how good life could have been with a significant other, I would have done it much sooner. Although I didn't think anyone else in my usual circles would have fit the role quite like her. Kaira was different. Humble. She wasn't impressed by the same things as the women I typically dated.

Maybe it was her authenticity that drew me in. She could see beyond the bullshit I wore like a shield, the wealth, and the prickly exterior I put up to keep people out. She challenged me, pushed me to be better, to think deeper. It wasn't just affection—it was a partnership.

I found myself spacing out, staring out the window. It was sunny. LA was pretty much through winter. I was looking forward to spring and then summer. Usually, that kind of thing wasn't a big deal to me, but Kaira had me looking forward to a lot of things.

Like Valentine's Day. It was only a couple days away, and for once, I was looking forward to it. I had big plans. Bigger than anything I'd ever attempted before. But before I could fully commit, I needed to clear my head and ensure this wasn't some reckless impulse.

That was why I decided to run it past the board.

I checked the time. I still had an hour before the meeting started.

Thinking about Valentine's and my birthday gave me an idea. I did a quick Google search for lingerie. Now that I knew my sweet, innocent little Kaira had a bit of a seductress side, I wanted to feed that side of her. I was hoping to get her wrapped in bows once again. I scanned the many, many options.

Finding the right lingerie took longer than I anticipated. Everything either seemed too extravagant or not quite right. I was looking at the lingerie and not the bodies or the faces of the models. I could picture her in each one. It was important to me that whatever I chose felt like Kaira—elegant, simple, with just a hint of daring. Finally, I stumbled upon a set that looked perfect: delicate lace in a soft shade of blush that I knew would look stunning against her skin. I smiled to myself, imagining her reaction, and quickly placed the order.

Once that was settled, my thoughts drifted back to the upcoming board meeting. The plan I had in mind was bold, something that could change everything.

The meeting room buzzed with low murmurs as I entered. They looked up, and as usual, the room fell silent. My team knew me well enough to recognize when I had something serious to discuss.

"Gentlemen and ladies," I started, taking my seat at the head of the table. "I need your input on a personal matter."

That got their attention. Personal matters weren't my forte—at least, not ones I brought into work.

"Personal?" one of them asked, eyebrows raised. "This is new."

I leaned forward, interlocking my fingers. "You all know about the arrangement I had with Kaira."

The room shifted uncomfortably. Of course, they knew. They'd helped orchestrate it to salvage my public image.

"Had?" one asked with concern.

"Have," I corrected. "Things have changed."

I saw the expressions. Disappointment. Resignation. This was exactly what they had expected of me. They were waiting for me to fuck this thing up.

"Changed how?" one asked with frustration.

I exhaled, glancing at the table for a beat before meeting their curious gazes. "I've developed feelings for her. Strong ones."

There was a moment of silence, and then a few snorts.

"You're joking," one said in a dismissive tone.

But I wasn't.

There was a round of groans and a bit of laughter.

When I didn't join in the laughter, the room grew quiet again.

"You're serious?"

"I am," I replied firmly. "And I think I want to propose to her. For real."

That set off a chain reaction of disbelief. Murmurs turned to outright protests, questions flying at me like arrows.

"Roman, have you thought this through?"

"What if she's playing the long game?"

"She could expose everything."

"You have no idea if her feelings are real."

My jaw clenched. I held up a hand, silencing the room. This wasn't exactly the response I was expecting. I thought they might be happy for me.

"Enough," I said, my tone commanding. "I know this sounds insane. I know it's a risk. But this isn't something I'm taking lightly. Kaira has been nothing but honest with me. If anything, she was the one hesitant to let things progress beyond the terms of our agreement."

Julia folded her arms, leaning back in her chair. "But how can you be sure? Feelings can cloud judgment, Roman. We're not saying this to discourage you—we're saying this because it's our job to look out for you and the company. You have always been very reluctant to get involved with anyone because you know you're a target. Your wealth and name alone draw a certain degree of attention."

"I appreciate that," I said. "But this isn't just about business. This is about my life."

"Your life and the company are tied together," someone pointed out. "If this goes south, it won't just be you who suffers."

His words sparked a flicker of doubt in me, a whisper of fear that perhaps I was being reckless. What if they were right? What if Kaira was just playing her role perfectly, a skilled actress who'd fooled even me? I knew her financial situation. She had been writing and I knew that was what she wanted to do, but until she got a publishing deal, she would have to work. If she was working, she wasn't going to have the same time to dedicate to the book.

Was she using me? If I fell for her, she would be financially set for life. She could do whatever she wanted. I knew money made people do some crazy things. The idea of Kaira using me for money was a hard pill to swallow.

But then I remembered her laughter. The way she'd lean into me when she thought no one was looking. The way her eyes lit up when she talked about her book or teased me about being an asshole with a heart of gold. The way I would catch her looking at me sometimes. There was no malice or nefarious intention in those looks.

"She's not using me," I said, my voice resolute. "Kaira agreed to this arrangement as a favor to me. She didn't come to me for money or fame. Hell, I had to convince her to stay when things got messy early on."

Julia studied me for a long moment. "You really believe this is real?"

"I know it's real," I said. "She's not someone who plays games.

And honestly? I don't want to be the man who lets doubt ruin something good. I've been that guy before, and I won't do it again."

The room fell silent, my conviction hanging in the air.

"You know the risks," Julia finally said. "If you're sure, then we'll back you. But don't go into this blind."

"I'm not," I assured her. "I know exactly what I'm doing."

That wasn't entirely true. I had no clue what I was doing but I was hoping my heart and instincts weren't going to lead me astray.

My revelation of my true feelings for Kaira left the room in a state of disbelief. More questions were lobbed at me. But through it all, I stood firm in my belief our relationship was very real and genuine. The Roman of three months ago would have faltered at the mere whisper of scrutiny.

The meeting dragged on, each argument met with an unwavering resolve. I had made up my mind, and nothing they said could sway me.

"That's all I have," I said and got to my feet. "I'll let you know if anything changes."

Back in my office, I leaned back in my chair and turned to the window. The conversation had left a lingering edge of uncertainty, but I wasn't going to let it derail me. I was not going to let my own self-doubt sabotage this thing with Kaira.

This was real.

Kaira wasn't using me. She wasn't pretending. If anything, she'd been the one keeping me grounded through all of this. She'd seen sides of me no one else had and still stayed. And when I pushed, she didn't just go along with it—she set boundaries, reminding me that this wasn't supposed to be complicated.

I thought about the way she made my house feel like a home again. The way she made me believe in things I'd given up on long ago—family, connection, love. I wanted to be the guy in her corner, cheering her on and encouraging her to finish her book. I hoped I could help her write another one. I wanted to use my connections to get her book in front of agents and publishers. I wanted to build her up. Help her dreams come true.

She had redefined my vision for the future. I found myself actually thinking about things like fatherhood. Me. A dad. The thought would have scared the shit out of me before. But not now. I knew Kaira would be a damn good mom. I didn't have any illusions I would be a good father, but I trusted her to guide me down the parenting road if things went that way.

Holy shit. What had this girl done to me?

Tonight, I was going to surprise her with a dozen of her favorite raspberry macarons. I knew she was probably deep into her writing. She was always doing stuff for me. Little things like leaving handwritten notes in my coat pockets or brewing fresh coffee just the way I liked it before I even mentioned I needed a caffeine boost. Small gestures that told me more about her feelings for me than grand declarations could ever manage.

This was a *real* relationship. It couldn't be all me taking from her. I needed to give and not in a monetary sense. I had to give of myself.

39

KAIRA

I had the house to myself. Well, as much to myself as it could be with a full staff roaming about. I spent most days alone. I caught up with Carla a lot more these days but she was working. I wasn't lonely, but I was a little bored. The estate was huge and there always felt like there was more to explore.

"Kaira?"

I turned to see Marilyn gesturing for me to come into the kitchen.

"What's up?" I asked.

She held up a deck of cards. "We finished early for the day. You asked if we had time to play cards earlier. Now, we do."

I grinned. "Yeah!"

We settled at the large table in the dining room. A few of the other staff members joined us, bringing in a coffee service to keep us nice and caffeinated. Marilyn shuffled with the expertise of a Vegas dealer, her fingers deftly mixing the cards in a rhythmic dance.

"So, gin rummy?" she asked, her eyes twinkling with mischief.

I nodded, eager to dive into the game. It was one of those old comforts from my childhood, something my grandmother had taught me on rainy afternoons. My parents and I still played the game when I went home for the holidays.

As we played, the conversation flowed easily. It felt nice to connect with the staff on a more personal level. They shared stories about working for Roman over the years, giving me glimpses into sides of him I hadn't seen yet.

"He's changed since you came, you know," Marilyn said casually as she discarded a card.

I had heard that several times. "Good. That makes me happy."

She nodded. "He smiles more. Laughs even. It's nice to see that side of him again."

I felt my cheeks flush slightly at her words. "He's been really great. I've enjoyed getting to know him better."

"We've all noticed," Marilyn replied knowingly. "You've been good for him, Kaira. He seems... lighter. More at peace."

Part of me wanted to downplay her comments, to dismiss them as exaggerations. But I knew Marilyn wasn't the type to just say flowery things. She was very blunt. And I knew she had a huge soft spot for Roman.

"I'm glad you think so. He really is a wonderful man, even if he tries to hide it sometimes."

Marilyn chuckled. "That he does. He's had his walls up for so long, it's been hard to get through to him at times. But you've found a way in." She gave me a fond look. "I don't know what the future holds for you two, but I hope he doesn't let this slip away."

We finished playing cards when it was time for them to get back to their own lives and responsibilities in the house. I made my way into the library to work on my manuscript, jotting down ideas until my wrist started to ache. I was hitting a bit of a wall. My story was falling flat. I needed to get my creative juices flowing again.

I set my notebook aside and leaned back in the plush armchair, letting my mind wander. As my gaze swept over the towering bookshelves lining the library walls, an idea began to form. Maybe I just needed a change of scenery to reignite my inspiration.

I left my notebook and laptop and headed outside to the sprawling gardens. The fresh air and sunshine instantly lifted my spirits as I strolled along the winding stone paths. I found a quiet, secluded spot near a burbling fountain and settled onto a wrought iron bench. I closed my eyes and let my imagination drift.

At least I tried.

It was stuck. The characters were hiding behind a brick wall in my mind. I sighed and opened my eyes, frustrated by my sudden lack of direction. The vibrant garden around me should have been the perfect setting to spark my creativity, but my mind remained stubbornly blank.

Giving up for the moment, I decided to simply enjoy the beautiful day. I tilted my face up toward the sun, letting the warmth wash over me. It was cool, but not cold. I listened to the bubbling fountain and found my thoughts drifting to Roman. I wondered what he was doing in that moment—probably sitting in his office and talking about money. I truly had no idea what he did at work. He always told me he was meeting this person or that one. It was reports and profit this and profit that.

To distract myself and hopefully give me some ideas for a scene I wanted to write, I indulged in the wardrobe Roman had generously stocked for me. I tried on different outfits just for fun. I finally settled on a sleek, fitted black dress that hugged me in all the right places. I styled my hair and did my makeup, imagining the look on Roman's face when he walked through the door. I wanted him to see me and stop in his tracks, to let the stress of his day melt away as soon as he laid eyes on me.

We didn't have any plans for the evening, but I wanted to keep him guessing. Dressing up would certainly make him wonder. Feeling daring, I took off my panties. I left them on his bed. When he came up to change out of his suit, he was going to see them. While we ate dinner, he was going to wonder if I was wearing anything underneath my dress. The thought made me smile.

On my way back from his room, I found myself pausing in front of what I had come to think of as the forbidden doors.

I stared at the double doors. They loomed there, tantalizing and mysterious, like the answer to a riddle I hadn't figured out yet. I had been given free rein of the house.

But not this one room.

Roman had been clear. "That's my space," he'd said when I asked about it. "Please don't go in there."

I respected his boundaries—well, most of the time. Just a peek. What could it hurt?

Curiosity was gnawing at me. I'd tried to rationalize it, telling myself it was just a man cave. Maybe a gym with expensive equipment or a movie room with leather recliners and a healthy porn collection. It wasn't really something to be ashamed of.

My imagination ran wild, like it did.

What if it was something darker? In some of the books I read, rooms like that held secrets—a mafia lord's torture chamber or a shrine covered in pictures of the unsuspecting heroine. It could be a sex dungeon or a room filled with monitors streaming hidden camera feeds throughout the house. It could be his serial killer lair or his secret scrapbooking workshop.

I laughed under my breath. *Okay, Kaira, let's be real. He's a vampire and that's where he keeps the coffin. He's not at work all day. He's slumbering in Transylvanian soil.*

The mystery tormented me. My hand hovered over the handle.

Don't.

But lord help me, I wanted to. The curiosity was eating away at me. Just a quick peek surely wouldn't hurt anything. He'd never know.

With a sharp inhale, I twisted the handle and pushed the door open, bracing myself for something freaky.

The room wasn't what I expected.

There were no whips, chains, or leather. No surveillance feeds and no vampire nests.

Sunlight streamed through a massive stained-glass window, casting colorful patterns across the hardwood floor. The air smelled faintly of oil paints and varnish. Several easels were positioned around the room. Some of the easels held half-finished works. Paintings lined the walls—landscapes, portraits, abstract explosions of color and emotion. They were breathtaking.

I stepped inside, my heels clicking softly against the floor. I had no idea Roman was an artist. These pictures were so... soft. So full of emotion. I felt love in these paintings. I had gotten to know Roman a little better, but I could not get my head around the idea he had created these masterpieces.

But then I noticed the plaques and framed articles scattered around the room. All of them bore the same name: *Rowena Kelly.*

His mother.

This was not his work. Part of me was relieved it wasn't Roman's artwork. I didn't want to think I didn't know him well enough to know he possessed this kind of passion and talent.

Rowena's work was stunning, alive with passion and joy. Each brushstroke seemed to hold a piece of her soul. As I moved through the space, I felt her presence—her warmth, her love, her unshakable spirit. It was as though the room itself was steeped with her essence. I had never met the woman, but I felt like I was getting to know her through her art.

I moved to stand in front of a particularly vibrant piece. It was a meadow bathed in golden light—I felt a lump form in my throat. Rowena had poured so much of herself into these works, only to be gone far too soon. I felt the weight of her absence and I had never met her. There was a hollow ache that wasn't even mine but Roman's. My heart hurt for him. How terrible for him that he lost such a beautiful soul at such a young age. I knew he would have been a very different man if his mother would have been able to finish raising him. Ruby was a great lady, but she didn't have the heart of a mother.

I was so lost in the art, I didn't hear him walk in behind me.

"What are you doing in here?" His voice was full of accusation and anger.

I froze, my heart leaping into my throat. Slowly, I turned to find Roman standing in the doorway. His suit jacket was off, his tie loosened, and his expression was anything but welcoming. His eyes burned with fury, his jaw tight.

I stammered, fumbling for words. "I was curious. I wanted to see what you were keeping in here."

"And you thought that gave you the right to invade my space?"

The anger in his voice made me flinch. "Roman, I'm sorry. I didn't mean to invade anything. I just... I couldn't help myself."

"That much is obvious," he snapped, stepping into the room. "I told you this was off-limits, Kaira. What part of that wasn't clear?"

Shame burned through me, hot and stinging. His silence was worse than his anger. He stood there, his chest rising and falling with barely restrained emotion. The room felt heavy, the warmth I'd felt earlier replaced by red-hot fury. I could feel his anger radiating off him in waves.

He ran a hand through his hair. The pain in his eyes was undeniable. It cut me deeper than any harsh word could. That look of betrayal on his face was brutal. I wanted to go to him. To wrap my arms around him and tell him everything was going to be okay. But I stayed put. The look on his face told me that was best.

Tears stung my eyes, but I blinked them away. He stared at me for what felt like an eternity.

My heart ached for him. I took a tentative step closer, reaching out. He stepped back, acting like I had some horrible disease. I realized he was more than just angry. He was hurt.

I did that.

40

ROMAN

The moment I saw the door to the studio ajar, I knew. My pulse quickened, a surge of heat spreading through me. It wasn't the good kind of heat, not the warmth Kaira usually brought into my life. This was fire, rage, betrayal.

I climbed the stairs, telling myself not to be angry, but it didn't help. Every step infuriated me. I had told her. I had given her access to my home. To my world. She could do anything she wanted. The gym, the theater, or the pool. I let her take over the kitchen, but that wasn't enough.

This was my place. It was my one connection to my mother. No one dared to violate this space. Marilyn was the only one allowed inside to keep it from getting covered with dust.

When I stepped into the room and saw her, I couldn't quite decipher the myriad of emotions pumping through me. She stood in front of one of my mother's paintings, her hand delicately brushing the frame. She looked so out of place there, in her black dress, her hair perfectly styled, a vision that could've taken my breath away if not for the scene surrounding us.

I wanted to grab her and kiss her like I normally did but I also wanted to grab her and toss her out of the house.

"What are you doing in here?" My voice came out cold and sharp, like a blade slicing through the quiet.

She spun around, her eyes wide with guilt, her lips parting as if searching for an excuse. "I... I was curious. I wanted to see what was in here."

I could feel the fury rising like a tidal wave, and I clenched my fists at my sides to keep it from overtaking me. "Curious? I told you this was off-limits, Kaira. What part of that didn't you understand?"

She flinched at the venom in my tone, and we stood watching each other in silence for a while the tension reaching a boiling point.

She blinked away tears. "I know I crossed a line, Roman, and I'm sorry. I didn't realize—"

"That's the problem," I interrupted, my voice rising. "You didn't realize because you didn't think. You didn't stop for one damn second to consider what this space might mean to me."

Her face crumpled, and I could see the tears flowing, but I couldn't stop. The words kept coming, harsh and cutting, like a flood I couldn't contain. I couldn't remember the last time I had been so angry. I was enraged.

"This room isn't just some part of the house, Kaira. It's sacred. It's the one place I've kept untouched, untainted, because it's all I have left of her."

"Roman—"

"Don't," I snapped, holding up a hand to stop her. "Don't try to justify it. You broke my trust, Kaira. The one thing I asked you not to do, and you couldn't even respect that."

Her lip quivered with tears spilling down her cheeks. She stepped closer, her hands outstretched as if to placate me. "I know I was wrong. I know I shouldn't have come in here. But I didn't mean to hurt you. I didn't realize how much this room means to you. I thought... I don't know what I thought."

"Clearly," I said bitterly, turning away from her. The sight of her standing there, looking so small and vulnerable, only made my anger worse. Not at her, but at myself—for letting her get close enough to have the power to hurt me like this.

"I'm sorry," she whispered, her voice breaking. "I was wrong, and I'm sorry. Please, can we just sit down and talk about this? Let me explain."

I turned back to her. The sight of tears streaming down her face clawed at my heart. But the anger, the betrayal—it was still too fresh. "What's there to talk about, Kaira? You broke my trust. That's all there is to it."

"I didn't mean to—"

"But you did!" I shouted, cutting her off. "You did, and now this place feels tainted. This was my sanctuary, Kaira. The one place in this whole damn house that was just mine. And now—" My voice cracked. I stopped, swallowing hard to regain control.

She was crying openly now, her hands clasped together as if in prayer. "Roman, please. I'll do anything to make this right. Just tell me how."

I shook my head, the frustration bubbling up again. "You can't. There's no fixing this."

I stared at her, the anger and hurt battling inside me. Part of me wanted to lash out, to push her away before she could do any more damage. But another part, the part that had grown so attached to her over these past few weeks, ached to pull her close and soothe the pain I'd caused.

Kaira was shaking, her shoulders trembling with the force of her sobs. "Roman, please," she choked out. "I never meant to violate something so sacred. I was just curious. Stupid and reckless, but not malicious. I would never do anything to hurt you. I know you know that."

"No, Kaira. I don't know that." I stared at her, the anguish and regret written all over her beautiful face. For the first time since we'd gotten to know each other, doubt began to creep in. Had she really been playing me this entire time? Was this all just part of an act to get close to me, to take advantage of my money and status?

The dark and insidious thoughts were like a cloud coming in. I had been so certain, so confident in her and in us. But now, as I looked at the violated space around me, that confidence crumbled.

"Just... just go to bed, Kaira. I can't do this right now. I'm going to say something I don't mean."

Her eyes widened, and she opened her mouth to protest, but I held up a hand to stop her. "Go. I'm serious. You don't know me well enough to know just how big of a dick I can be. Get away from me."

She hesitated for a moment, her shoulders shaking as she wiped at her eyes. "I know you don't believe me, but I'm sorry. I didn't mean to hurt you. I would never do anything that hurt you. I know you're angry. But just know I'm here for you."

I said nothing. I wasn't joking when I warned her. I knew I could wield my tongue like a vicious sword. I had the uncanny ability to cut people down with my coldness.

Without another word, she turned and walked out of the room.

I stood there for a long time after she left, staring at my mother's paintings. The beauty that once brought me peace now felt muted. It was all overshadowed by the weight of what had just happened.

When I finally left the studio and closed the door behind me, I heard it. The faint sound of Kaira crying in her room. It pierced through the walls, through my defenses, and straight into my chest. Hearing her in pain physically hurt me.

But I couldn't offer her comfort.

I made it to my own room, closed the door, and leaned against it, letting my head fall back with a heavy thud. My fists were clenched so tight my knuckles ached, but I couldn't bring myself to relax.

The storm was back, raging inside me like it hadn't in years. I hadn't felt this way since... since before her. Since before Kaira walked into my life and turned it upside down in the best and worst ways.

I should've been able to forgive her. To see past the mistake and focus on the fact that she cared enough to want to know more about me. But all I could feel was the sting of betrayal. The board's warnings playing over and over in my head.

What if they were right? What if I'd let my guard down too soon?

No. I pushed the thought away, shaking my head as if to physically dislodge it. This wasn't about my board or their warnings. This was about her. About us.

And right now, it felt like everything we'd built was crumbling. I couldn't tell what was real and what was just my imagination.

Did I get blinded by sex?

No. I was immune to that trick. There had been many a woman that tried to lure me, seduce me, and snare me with sex. That was not it. I went into this relationship with Kaira with my eyes wide open. I didn't believe she had a nefarious bone in her body.

I paced my room, running my hands through my hair as waves of anger and frustration crashed over me. She had violated my trust in the deepest way possible. It hurt because she was the first person I trusted in a long, long time. Maybe ever. I could feel I was making a bigger deal out of this than necessary.

The logical side of me knew that but I was feeling anything but logical at the moment. As usual, when I was spinning out, I needed to get my ass to the gym to keep myself from doing something stupid.

I jerked my shirt open, ignoring the buttons popping left and right. I moved to sit on the bed to take off my shoes when I saw a pair of black panties on the pillow.

My stomach clenched. Her being all dressed up and the panties on the pillow. She had been planning a special night for us. I didn't know how I felt about that.

Instead of dwelling on it, I kicked off my shoes, stripped, and put on my shorts.

I made my way down to the gym, hoping to work off some of this pent-up frustration. The second I stepped through the door, I could feel my muscles start to uncoil, the tension easing ever so slightly. This was my sanctuary, just as much as that studio was for me.

I wrapped my hands and started pounding away at the heavy bag. My punches were violent, far more than they usually were. Every thud of my fists against the bag intensified my anger. I pictured her face, her guilt and remorse, and it only fueled the anger.

With each strike, the rage and hurt roiled inside me, a volatile storm I couldn't seem to calm. Sweat beaded on my skin as I unleashed punishing blows against the bag.

There was a sick, twisting sensation in my gut that I couldn't shake no matter how hard I hit. I trusted Kaira—foolishly, it seemed. I let her into my world, let her see the parts of me I kept locked away from everyone else. And she repaid that trust by snooping around.

I understood it wasn't just the fact she walked into the room. It was a glimpse into a future with her. If I couldn't trust her to do that one small thing, how could I trust her with anything else?

With a final vicious combination, I stepped back from the bag, chest heaving. Sweat poured down my face and back as I tried to catch my breath. The physical exertion had helped burn off some of the anger, but an uncomfortable knot of uncertainty still lingered.

I wasn't sure if it would ever be gone.

41

KAIRA

I fled to my room, tears blinding my vision as I slammed the door behind me. My chest heaved with sobs. I pressed my hands to my face, trying to smother the sound. Roman's words replayed in my mind, cutting deeper each time. I felt like I had destroyed everything. I felt like I'd destroyed *us*.

Things were just starting to get really good between us. I looked down at the dress and felt ridiculous. This night was supposed to be all about us. I planned to seduce him and rock his world. That had certainly blown up in my face.

I collapsed onto the bed, burying my face in the pillow. The sobs wracked my body. His anger had been visceral, his words so nasty. I had never seen Roman so furious, so utterly devastated. And I was the cause of it.

Guilt and regret swirled through me like a storm. How could I have been so careless, so reckless? I knew that room was off-limits, yet I had barged in without a second thought, driven solely by curiosity. In doing so, I had violated Roman's trust in the worst way possible. I knew how guarded he was.

Just that very day, Marilyn had been telling me how much better

Roman was. She was so happy to see Roman coming out of the prison he put himself in.

And I sent him right back there.

I knew I had blown it. Roman was not the kind of man to forgive and forget. He wasn't just going to move on from this. I could feel that in my very soul.

I grabbed my phone and called Carla. She didn't answer. I tried again, my fingers shaking as I hit redial. This time, after several rings, she picked up. "Hey, Kaira, what's up?"

"Are you at work?" I asked, choking out a sob.

"Uh, no, but—"

I broke down completely, my words tumbling out in a mix of sobs and sentences. "Carla, I screwed everything up. Roman's furious, and I… I don't know what to do. I just need you. Are you at home?"

There was a pause, then Carla sighed. "I'm sorry, Kaira. I really am. But I'm not at home."

There was something in her tone that felt off. Oddly enough, she sounded a lot like Roman. She was guarded. Distant. I wiped my face with the back of my hand. "What's wrong?" I sniffled as I sat up.

"It's nothing," she said quickly. Too quickly. "Let's just focus on you right now."

"No," I said, sitting up straighter. I knew my friend well enough to know when something was wrong. She was definitely off. "What is it? Please, Carla, tell me."

Another pause. "I didn't want to do this over the phone, but… I feel like you've abandoned me, Kaira."

Her words hit me like a slap. "What?"

"Just forget it. What's up?"

"Carla, wait. What is going on? I called you…"

I realized before today, it had been a few days. I hadn't texted like normal. The last week I had been caught up with my book and Roman.

"Whatever, Kaira. It's fine. I know you've got shit to do. What's wrong? What did Roman do now?"

She wasn't asking because she cared. More like she was obligated to do so.

"Carla, please," I said. "I'm sorry. I thought we worked through this already. With you working and me here, it's hard to connect."

"You never call me anymore," she said, her voice trembling with restrained emotion. "You didn't even invite me to Roman's birthday party."

I cringed. "I didn't think you would be comfortable. It was all his friends."

"I'm your friend," she said. "I didn't think I had to remind you of that."

"Carla, no! I love you. You are my friend."

"I have to reach out to you just to get a response, and even then, it takes forever for you to reply. And when you do call, it's always about *your* problems or *your* life. It's like I'm just here when it's convenient."

"No, Carla, that's not true," I protested, my chest tightening with guilt. "I didn't mean to make you feel that way."

"That's what you said the last time I brought this up," she said quietly. "But nothing changed."

I felt like the air had been knocked out of me. "I'm so sorry," I whispered. "I never wanted to hurt you. You're my best friend."

"I know you didn't mean to, Kaira. But it still hurts. And it hurts even more having to point it out instead of you realizing it on your own. Twice. Not once, but twice. How would you feel if the roles were reversed?"

I swallowed hard, tears streaming down my face again. "I'll do better, Carla. I promise."

She sighed again. "What happened with you and Roman?"

I didn't even want to tell her. She didn't really want to hear it. I didn't blame her. The last few weeks had been all about me and my drama. And then when things started going really well, I abandoned her.

"I'm sorry," I said. "I shouldn't have called. I'm, well, I might be staying at the condo."

"What happened?"

"I don't want to dump on you."

"Kaira, just tell me," she said.

"I went into a room I wasn't supposed to and it was really bad. I think it's better for me to leave."

She was quiet for a minute. "I hope you and Roman make up. I really do. But... I think I need some space right now."

The line went dead before I could respond. I stared at my phone, the screen blurring through my tears. The loneliness that enveloped me was suffocating. For the first time in a long time, I felt completely untethered, like I was drifting alone in the dark.

I couldn't stay in the mansion. It was clear Carla didn't want me at my own condo. I was abandoned. I had only myself to blame.

But I couldn't stay in the mansion. I had to get away. I needed to talk to someone.

I didn't know who else to call. I had no one else. My fingers moved on autopilot, dialing my parents. It had been weeks since I'd spoken to them. That was just another thing to feel guilty about. I was a horrible daughter, friend, and girlfriend. I was batting a thousand.

But they were my parents and I knew they would love me regardless of my spotty contact. Since moving in with Roman, I had only reached out a couple of times via texts here and there. They weren't the type to keep up with the media, so I knew they had no idea about what had been going on. I could only imagine what their reaction would be.

My mom picked up on the second ring. "Kaira?"

"Mom." I couldn't say anything else. The lump of emotion was lodged in my throat.

"Sweetheart, is everything okay?"

The sound of her voice cracked something open inside me. The whole story came tumbling out. The contract, the fake engagement, the budding romance with Roman, tonight's fight—everything. My words were rushed and messy, interrupted by sniffles and hiccups, but I couldn't stop. I knew I was probably making no sense. My thoughts were all over the place.

When I finally finished, there was a long silence on the other end of the line. I had to check my screen to make sure she was still there.

"You did *what?*"

"I know it sounds bad," I said quickly, my face burning with shame. "But it wasn't supposed to get this complicated."

"You think?" my dad's voice came through the receiver, sharp with disbelief. "Why didn't you tell us any of this, Kaira?"

"Because I knew you'd try to talk me out of it," I admitted. "And at the time, I thought I could handle it."

"Kaira," my mom said, her voice softer now but still firm.

I took a deep breath and braced myself. Their reaction was about what I expected. "I know," I said with a sigh.

"This is serious, Kaira," Mom said. "You're playing with fire here, emotionally and legally. How could you get involved in something like this?"

"I don't know."

"If you needed money, you should have called us," Dad said.

"It wasn't really about the money," I said. "Well, only partially about the money."

"Was this some infatuation?" Mom asked. "Who is this guy? I've never known you to be so reckless. This is not like you at all."

I hesitated, wiping at my eyes. "I thought I was helping him," I said quietly. "And then it just... it became more. I didn't expect to feel this way."

My mom sighed. "Sweetheart, you need to get out of this arrangement. It's not healthy, and it's clearly causing you pain."

"The first thing you need to do is void that contract," Dad said. "Get out of that house. Get away from that man. You are not a…"

He didn't finish his sentence. He didn't have to. All three of us knew exactly what he was going to say.

The idea hit me like a punch to the gut. Voiding the contract would mean ending this... whatever *this* was with Roman. Could I do that? Could I really just walk away?

"I don't know if I can," I whispered. "I... I think I love him."

There was a stunned silence on the other end of the line. "Then you need to tell him that. But Kaira, if this is how things are now, you need to think about whether this relationship is good for you. I don't think it's healthy. I don't understand how or why someone would lose their temper over what you describe as a painting studio."

"It's hard to explain," I said.

"It sounded pretty clear to me," Dad said in a gruff voice.

"I hurt him, Mom. I crossed a line I shouldn't have, and I don't know how to fix it. It wasn't just a room. It was something very important to him. It's taken me weeks to get him to laugh freely and I ruined everything by walking through that door."

"Sounds like the guy is a real peach," Dad said. "Why would you want to be with someone like that?"

"Because he does laugh and smile and he's a good man," I said, feeling defensive of him. "I don't know what to do."

"You start by being honest," Mom said gently. "With him, with yourself, with everyone. No more hiding."

"I don't think he wants to hear from me," I said.

"Maybe not, but if you don't tell him how you feel, how is he ever going to know?" Mom asked.

I knew my mom was right. I had to be honest with Roman, even if it terrified me. I had to lay it all out there and let the chips fall where they may. Hiding behind the half-truths and falsehoods that started this whole arrangement wouldn't fix anything.

"Maybe," I said. "But I think I should give him some time to settle down."

"That's probably for the best," Mom said. "Why don't you try and get some sleep? You can talk to him in the morning."

We talked for a little while longer, but when I hung up, I didn't feel any better. If anything, I felt worse. I'd hurt Roman. I'd hurt Carla. I'd shut my parents out of my life. And for what? To pretend I was someone I wasn't, living a life that wasn't mine?

I curled up on my bed, clutching a pillow to my chest as the tears kept coming. I didn't know how to make any of this right. All I knew was that I felt broken, and the one person who might be able to put me back together was the same person I'd hurt the most.

After crying until I didn't have any tears left, I got out of bed and took off the dress that was now wrinkled.

I hung it up and put on my own clothes. I looked around the large closet filled with designer outfits. It was another reminder of my attempt to be someone I wasn't. The whole charade spectacularly exploded in my face.

42

ROMAN

I stared up at the ceiling in my bedroom. Alone. I was pretty sure I had not slept all night. Nothing I did would give me relief. It was like a form of torture. There was no escape. I had to wallow in the pain of betrayal. All the walls I put up to protect myself were in ruins and I felt exposed and vulnerable.

But not for long. I would never let myself feel like that again. I would never let myself be exposed like that. Ever. My arm automatically reached out to feel the empty bed. It had been way too easy to get used to having her beside me.

The decision to close myself off again was almost reflexive, a protective shell hardening around my battered heart. I rolled out of bed, my body heavy with exhaustion yet restless with stormy thoughts.

In the dim light of dawn, I walked over to the window and stared into the backyard.

I knew what I had to do. There was no way this thing with Kaira was going to work. Real or fake. Whatever it had almost been was never going to happen. It was a foolish plan from the very start. I had let myself get caught up but now I could see just how stupid it had been. I wouldn't repeat that mistake.

I showered and headed downstairs. I spotted one of my staff members. She was a newer one. I couldn't remember her name.

"Marissa," I said.

She jumped and spun around. "Sir! I didn't see you."

"Sorry to have scared you. I have a job for you."

"Of course." She nodded.

After telling her what I wanted, I walked to the kitchen to get some coffee. A lot of coffee. I leaned against the counter and stared at nothing. Recently, mornings were the two of us sharing coffee. Sometimes, she would make me breakfast, other times we would enjoy whatever the cook prepared.

But now, the kitchen felt void of warmth. The absence of laughter and light-hearted teasing was louder than any other noise.

My mind kept replaying the moments that led to this cold morning. How could I have been so naive? I allowed myself to believe in a fantasy, and now the reality felt harsher than ever. No more illusions.

I pulled out my phone to check my calendar. I hoped it was a light day. I didn't have the strength to deal with anything big.

That was when I saw it. The dinner reservation for tonight. For fucking Valentine's Day. It was a splash of cold water. I quickly cancelled the reservation, the action feeling final and painfully symbolic. It was supposed to be a celebration of us, whatever "us" might have been—real or imagined, it didn't matter anymore. A feeling of regret tickled at the back of my mind. Maybe I should have handled things differently. But it was too late for maybes.

I tossed the phone onto the counter with a clatter, rubbing my temples as I tried to shake off the headache that was building behind my eyes. The house was silent around me. I knew the rest of the staff would arrive or wake up soon.

And so would Kaira.

An hour later, I was in the foyer talking with another staff member when I felt the air shift. I knew what it was.

Her.

It was crazy that I could sense her before I saw her.

The moment I heard Kaira's soft footsteps descending, I raised my gaze. She looked wrecked. Her eyes were puffy and red, her complexion pale. She carried herself like someone who hadn't slept at all. She was wearing clothes I didn't immediately recognize. Black leggings and a hoodie that looked well worn. I realized they were her clothes. Not anything I had purchased for her.

It was a statement. She was making it clear she didn't want anything to do with me or the gifts I showered her with. That worked just fine for me.

I wondered if she'd spent the night crying. Judging by the way she looked, she had. Throughout the night, I had gotten halfway to her bedroom and stopped myself. I had listened to the muffled sound of her sobs. My heart ached to hold her, but I knew better. I couldn't let myself get sucked in. I knew I would be inclined to let my guard down and let her back in.

Anthony walked in behind me. He looked at me, then Kaira.

"Ten minutes," I said to him.

He nodded and walked right back out the door.

I stared at the contract amendments in my hands, the legal escape hatch I demanded my lawyers draft in the middle of the night. I knew people weren't happy with me, but considering what I paid them, they did what I asked.

The staff cleared out like they were fleeing an impending grenade explosion.

Kaira stopped in front of me, her expression guarded but resigned. "Good morning," she said quietly.

"I've had a termination agreement drawn up," I said and held up the paperwork. "This ends our contract."

She looked at the papers and then me. I saw the hurt. My shield was up. Her pain was not going to change my mind.

"Marissa will pack your bags, and Anthony will drive you home."

She nodded without protest, her lips pressed into a thin line. "That's fine," she said, though her tone betrayed her weariness.

I held the documents out to her, watching as she scanned the pages. "These release us both from the contract," I explained. "You're free of this mess. So am I. It will be like it never happened."

She took the pen I offered and signed her name with a steady hand, though her fingers trembled when she handed the documents back. "Is there anything else?" she asked.

I hesitated, glancing down at her left hand. The ring—*my* ring—caught the light, a cruel reminder of the facade we'd both worked so hard to maintain.

Her gaze followed mine. She seemed startled, as if she'd forgotten it was there. After a moment of hesitation, she slid the ring off and held it out to me. Her hand lingered a fraction of a second longer than necessary before I took it and put it in my pocket.

"I'll wait in the car," she murmured, brushing past me without another word.

Something in me snapped. I turned, compelled to say *something*, anything to explain this thing we had. Or didn't have. "This never would have worked anyway."

She stopped at the door and glanced over her shoulder, her expression a mix of hurt and disbelief. "I want to tell myself that too," she said softly, "but I think we both know it isn't true."

Then she was gone, stepping outside without a backward glance. I stood frozen, clutching the ring in my pocket as though it might ground me. The front door closed with a finality that echoed through the house.

Minutes later, Marissa came back down with Kaira's luggage, which, apparently, she had already packed herself. "She didn't leave much behind," Marissa said.

Anthony came back in the house. I saw the anger in his eyes but he didn't say anything. I knew what he was thinking. I knew Anthony liked Kaira.

"I'll take the bags," Anthony said.

I shouldn't have been surprised she had already packed. I supposed we both knew it was over. She would have left me if I hadn't kicked her out. Anthony grabbed the luggage from Marissa's grasp. He didn't wait for help or instruct anyone on what to do next. He just walked out, his shoulders rigid.

"She left a lot of clothes in the closet but I think that was intentional," Marissa said. "Should I pack them up?"

"If she didn't pack them, no."

She nodded. "Anything else?"

"No."

I stood by the window, watching as the car pulled away, shrinking into the distance. I thought I'd feel relief, maybe even satisfaction at reclaiming my house, my space, my *life*. Instead, I felt hollow.

"Is Kaira leaving?"

I turned to see Aunt Ruby at the top of the stairs, her silk robe flowing around her as she descended. She stopped midway, clutching the banister with a frown. "My maid just told me Kaira was leaving. That can't be true, is it?"

"Yes," I said flatly.

Ruby tilted her head, her brow furrowing. "Why?"

"Because."

"Roman, what is going on?"

"Nothing. It's over. That's that."

I heard her mutter something under her breath but I ignored it.

"I assume you won't be answering any follow-up questions?" she asked with her irritation evident.

"You assume correctly."

She frowned deeper, stepping closer. "But she and I were supposed to be discussing wedding planning today. I didn't get a chance to spend any real time with her. We had plans, Roman."

"Not my problem."

"We were going to create a Pinterest board for funsies and accidentally publicly share it so people believed—"

"Enough!" My voice thundered through the hall, silencing her mid-sentence.

Ruby's mouth snapped shut, her eyes wide with surprise. I rarely raised my voice at her, but I couldn't stomach another second of it.

"This is all bullshit," I said, my tone razor-sharp. "It always has been. I'm done indulging it. And so are you. Kaira is gone. Period. There is no fake engagement. It's over."

She opened her mouth to argue but thought better of it, instead retreating to the kitchen without another word. Her silence communicated her disappointment loud and clear, though.

I grabbed my coat and keys and slammed the front door behind me as I stepped into the cold morning air. It was colder than usual. Or maybe it just felt that way. A strong breeze brushed across my skin. The shitty weather felt appropriate—like a reminder of who I was before Kaira came along and thawed parts of me I'd thought were frozen for good.

The drive to the office was mercifully quiet. I ignored the Valentine's Day banners strung along the streets, the couples holding hands as they strolled, and the florists bustling with customers. Street vendors were on every corner trying to hawk their roses and other cheap items for those that were scrambling for last-minute gifts for their sweethearts.

When I arrived at the building, the media swarmed me as usual, their questions flying like arrows. But today, I was in no mood to play nice. They had gotten used to me smiling and dropping tidbits of information about me and Kaira.

"Mr. Kelly, what are your plans for Valentine's Day?"

"Is it true you gave your fiancée a giant heart-shaped ruby?"

"Have you chosen a wedding date?"

I stopped short, glaring at the reporters as they crowded around me. "Get out of my way," I snapped, my voice rough enough to make them hesitate.

They shuffled back slightly, murmuring among themselves as I pushed through the revolving doors. For once, they didn't follow me. Maybe it was the look on my face, or maybe they'd finally learned when to back off. Either way, I didn't care. Let them mutter. Let them speculate. It was all noise.

Once inside, I practically stomped toward the elevator. There were a few people waiting at the elevators but it was not a surprise that, when I stepped in, they were all suddenly not interested in riding in the same small box with me.

Once the doors slid shut, I leaned back and closed my eyes. I couldn't shake the image of Kaira's tear-streaked face as she handed me the ring back.

I'd done the right thing, hadn't I? I had protected myself, my company, my future. This was what the board had warned me about —getting too close, letting my guard down. Kaira had crossed a line, and I couldn't let that slide. I couldn't let *her* slide.

So why did it feel like I'd made the biggest mistake of my life?

43

KAIRA

Anthony kept looking in the rearview mirror but, thankfully, said nothing. I had no idea what Roman told the staff. I felt like I had been cut off. They were Roman's people. I had betrayed the boss and now I was on the outs.

"Are you okay?" Anthony asked quietly.

I offered a weak, watery smile. "No."

"I'm sorry," he said.

"It's okay. It's not your fault." My voice was barely above a whisper, the lump in my throat making it difficult to speak loudly.

Anthony kept his eyes on the road. "Do you have somewhere to go?"

I nodded, staring blankly out of the passenger window. "Yes, I still have my condo. I think."

I wasn't necessarily surprised Roman was throwing me out. I was going to leave anyway. But there had been a small part of me that hoped he would calm down and be willing to talk about what happened. I had been hopeful I would join him in the kitchen for coffee and he would be open to having a conversation. He would express his disappointment. I would apologize and promise not to do it again and we would move forward, together.

I should have known that was a pipe dream. Roman was not the kind of man that allowed for second chances. He had a hair trigger. While I didn't necessarily agree with his over-the-top reaction to me being in his mother's studio, I understood it when I put myself in his shoes. I knew how jaded he was. I had learned about his past and the way he kept everyone at arm's length.

And ultimately, I had made a mistake by breaking a promise. Now I had to suffer the consequences.

The ride to my condo felt longer than it should have. It was strange to go from the sprawling estates with iron gates and acres of perfect, lush green lawns to the crowded city streets. Buildings packed together like sardines. The only green was the palm trees.

It felt like shifting between two worlds in a single journey. This was probably what Cinderella felt like when she rushed out of the ball. As Anthony pulled to a stop in front of my building, I hesitated before opening the door, not quite ready to face reality. He offered to help me with my bags, but I declined.

"Thank you, Anthony," I said, forcing myself to sound normal. "It was nice meeting you."

"If you need anything..." he started, his concern visible despite his professional demeanor.

"I'm good. Take care of him."

"I'll do my best," he said with a nod.

Anthony pulled away when an impatient cab driver honked the horn. I stayed where I was, staring up at the building. I should be happy to be home. But what if Carla didn't want to see me? What if I wasn't welcome here anymore either? After our conversation yesterday, I had a feeling she was going to be less than thrilled at my return.

I had been a little homesick. It was the same brick and glass structure I'd always come back to after long days, the place I'd called home for years. My safe place with my cozy blanket on the back of the couch and my very basic bed. It wasn't a lot, but it was mine and it was comfortable and familiar.

But now, it felt foreign. Like someone else's home.

I trudged up the stairs, dragging my luggage behind me. Each step felt heavier than the last. When I reached the door to our apartment, I paused, my heart pounding. I wasn't sure if I should knock or just let myself in. It was my place. I was on the lease, but it didn't feel like I belonged.

Finally, I took a deep breath and turned the key.

The familiar hum of vacuuming greeted me as I stepped inside. Carla was in the living room, her back to me, headphones in place as she worked the vacuum over the worn carpet. She swayed slightly to the music, completely unaware of my presence. For a moment, I just stood there, watching her, trying to gather the courage to say something.

Eventually, she noticed me. Her movements slowed, and she straightened, turning off the vacuum. She pulled out her earbuds and tilted her head at me. "I thought you might show up."

I looked down at my feet, my voice barely above a whisper. "He kicked me out."

"Oh." Carla deflated slightly, her brows knitting together.

"What?" I asked, noticing the way her expression shifted.

"Nothing," she said quickly, but her tone betrayed her.

"Carla," I pleaded, stepping forward. "Please, tell me. We tell each other everything, don't we?"

She hesitated, crossing her arms over her chest. Finally, she sighed. "I thought you were here to apologize in person."

"What?" I was confused. "I did apologize."

She shook her head in disgust. "Yes, of course you did. Thank you so much for your time. I really, *really* appreciate it."

Her words hit me like a slap. "I—Carla, I'm sorry. I know I've been a terrible friend."

She shook her head. "Whatever."

"Carla, let's get some coffee and talk. I've been up all night and need some serious caffeine."

She rolled her eyes, which again surprised me. "Kaira, you didn't come here to apologize. You came here because things with Roman went sour. Again. That's the only reason you're here. You want to tell me all about the mean things he did. You want me to give you advice and tell you he really does want you and you should fight for him. Right? That's how this is supposed to go, right?"

Tears burned in my eyes. I blinked them back furiously. She wasn't wrong. I had been a selfish friend, caught up in my own drama while ignoring her. "I've messed everything up," I whispered. "I don't even know where to start."

Carla softened slightly, but she didn't move to comfort me. "I don't know what to tell you, Kaira. You've been so wrapped up in your life with Roman that you've barely noticed anyone else. You've seen our other friends do the same thing. We've sat on this very couch and talked shit about the stupid girls who go all in on a guy they barely know. And now, here you are, doing exactly that. Where's that girl who was going to conquer the world, huh? Where has she gone?"

Carla's words stung. She had a point. I had let myself get swept away by romance and drama, losing sight of everything else that mattered—my dreams, my ambitions, even my friendships.

"I know," I managed to say, my voice cracking with emotion. "I lost myself for a while there. I forgot who I was supposed to be."

Carla sighed again, her posture relaxing slightly as she looked at me not with anger, but with disappointment. "Yeah, you did."

I nodded, biting my lip to keep from sobbing. "I've been horrible to you. I've ignored you when you needed me."

"I didn't need you, but you were my best friend. We spent all our free time together and then you were just gone. You didn't think twice about me. I'm not mad that you had a boyfriend or whatever that was. I'm mad that you let his money and status change you."

Carla's words left me gutted, a piercing truth I couldn't deny. My eyes welled up as I gulped down the lump forming in my throat, feeling the weight of her disappointment. "You're right," I admitted. "I let myself get carried away with everything Roman represented. It was glamorous and exciting at first, but I lost so much of myself in the process."

"It's like you disappeared into someone else. The Kaira I knew wouldn't have done that."

I glanced around the apartment. This wasn't home. Carla and I would just keep going round and round. I didn't want to completely damage our friendship.

"I... I think I need to go away for a while. Give you some space. Get my head on straight."

She looked at me, surprised. "Where will you go?"

"To my parents' place in Philadelphia," I said. "Just for a little while. I need to figure out what I'm doing with my life. And you deserve better than what I've been giving you. If you want to rethink our living arrangement, I'll understand. All I ask is that you give me enough time to find another roommate."

For a moment, I hoped she would tell me to stay, that we could work this out in a day or two. But she didn't. She just nodded. "Maybe that's a good idea. I'll let you know if I find somewhere to go."

I swallowed hard, the lump in my throat growing. "Yeah," I said, forcing a weak smile. "Great."

I dragged my suitcases to my room. I wasn't going to bother unpacking. I closed the door behind me. The familiar smell of lavender and old books hit me, and for the first time in a long time, it didn't bring comfort. I sank onto the bed and pulled out my phone, dialing my dad.

He picked up after a few rings. "Hey, sweetheart," he said, his voice warm and familiar. "How was your night?"

"Terrible."

"I'm sorry," he said.

I took a shaky breath. I hated that I had to do this. I hated that I had to rely on my parents to bail me out of another mess. "Dad, I need to come home. The contract is over, and I'm broke, and I just... I need to be with you and Mom for a while. I can't be here."

There was a pause on the other end. I braced myself for disappointment. "You don't have to explain, Kaira. We'll take care of it. I'll book your ticket right now. When do you want to fly out?"

"Now. Yesterday."

He chuckled softly. "I understand. I'll text you in a few."

Tears welled up in my eyes again, but this time they were tears of relief. "Thank you," I whispered.

"Of course. We'll be here when you're ready," he said softly. "Hang in there, kiddo. This is for the best. You'll see."

After we hung up, I lay back on the bed, staring at the ceiling. I held up my hand. The ring had become a part of me. And now it was gone—just like Roman. The expression on his face when I walked downstairs this morning was brutal. He was so cold. He was just like the man I had met a month ago at that stupid auction.

My father was right. This was for the best. If he was that quick to dismiss me, it was never going to work. I couldn't be with someone that I had to worry was going to dump me if I opened the wrong door. It was better this ended now, before I was in even deeper.

At least that was what I was going to keep telling myself.

Desperate for a distraction, I started scrolling through my phone. That was when I saw it. A clip of Roman from earlier that morning, storming past reporters outside his office.

"Roman Kelly Roars at Reporters."

I hesitated, then clicked play. The video was only a few seconds long, but it was enough to make my heart ache. He looked furious, his jaw tight and his eyes cold as he barked at the reporters.

"Get out of my way," he snapped, his voice sharp enough to cut through steel.

But beneath the anger, I could see it. Pain.

This wasn't how things were supposed to end. Not for us. Not like this.

I dropped my phone onto the bed and covered my face with my hands. Why had I gone into that room? Why couldn't I have left it alone?

Tears spilled down my cheeks as I curled up on the bed, the weight of my mistakes pressing down on me. For the first time in a long time, I felt truly, utterly alone.

44

ROMAN

It had been three weeks. Three long weeks since I ended the contract with Kaira. Three weeks since I had truly slept. The house was not the same without her. Everything seemed to echo in the empty spaces she used to occupy. Everywhere I looked, I could picture her there. I actually fell asleep in her room one night, which was ridiculous because she had not slept in there for long before she ended up in my room.

Visiting the library was a form of self-torture. Sometimes, I would open the door and expect to see her sitting in the chair with her hair a mess and her laptop in her lap. I could almost smell her. I found a book on a table in the corner. It was one she had been reading. I picked it up and flipped through the pages. It was a sappy romance that actually made me smile because I knew that was her thing. She had told me about the book she was writing. Another implausible romance story.

But it was during the quiet nights that I found myself at the worst, replaying our last conversation over and over in my mind. The decision to end things was purely business at first. It was just another contract concluded in the long string of deals that made up my life. But every single day, the reality of her absence sunk in deeper. I had gone back to business as usual. It was the same life I had been living for years without any drama. Except, that old life wasn't sufficient anymore. The house felt off. Without her laughter echoing through the halls or her thoughtful looks when we talked about everything under the moon, it wasn't the house I had lived in all my life. I missed finding her cooking in the kitchen. I missed having coffee in the morning with her.

And today, it was going to be official. I had to give a statement to the nosy public about my love life. Technically, it was never supposed to be my actual love life. But somewhere, what started as a basic contract to save my ass turned into something real—then it had shattered me.

I reached for the blue tie. Blue was supposed to make me look honest or some shit. I buttoned my suit jacket, checked myself in the mirror, and sighed. It was time to face the world without her by my side. The press had been speculating wildly since she left, and today I would put an end to all the rumors. I would keep it professional, concise. The relationship was over. That was all they needed to know.

As I walked downstairs, I heard my staff in the foyer. They had all been giving me a wide berth the last couple of weeks. I knew more than one of them was pissed at me. They liked Kaira and most of them had taken her side.

I didn't blame them.

Anthony was waiting for me with the car. I was not in the mood to drive. I didn't trust my temper. I had saved my reputation with my fake engagement to Kaira. Adding a road rage incident to the mix would negate all of it, making it for nothing.

I slid into the backseat of the car. Anthony gave me a nod through the rearview mirror. "Ready, sir?" he asked, his voice neutral but I could detect a hint of concern.

"Yes, let's get this over with," I replied curtly. My thoughts raced as we drove toward the office where I would be holding the press conference. My mind was stuck in a loop, replaying every moment I had spent with Kaira, every laugh we shared, and every argument that pushed us apart.

By the time we arrived, the place was swarming with reporters. Cameras flashed as I stepped out of the car. I ignored the shouted questions and pushed my way inside. Several board members were waiting for me in the lobby. I was whisked away to the conference room where I was holding the press conference.

The PR team was waiting for me in a side room. Someone was fixing my hair while PR gave me notecards with my statement. They warned me about the questions that would come once I announced the end of my engagement.

I nodded, barely listening. I already knew what I was going to say, and no notecard was going to help me with the truth that was clawing its way up my throat. I had no intention of giving them any information about my life with Kaira. It was a mistake to drag her into this mess to begin with.

"It's time," someone said.

I nodded and took the notecards. Several board members and I walked into the conference room. The room was packed with reporters. The flashes of cameras felt like tiny daggers against my skin.

When I stepped up to the podium, the murmurs hushed, replaced by a suffocating silence.

I told myself to read the statement and call it good. I didn't owe anyone answers.

I cleared my throat, gripping the edges of the podium as though it could anchor me. "Thank you all for coming today," I began, my voice steady despite the storm inside me. "I have an announcement to make regarding my engagement to Kaira…"

The words stuck in my throat, but I forced them out. "It's over. We've chosen to go our separate ways."

The room erupted. Cameras clicked frantically, reporters shot up, shouting over one another. I held up a hand, signaling for quiet, and miraculously, they obliged. I had their undivided attention.

"I know there's been speculation about the authenticity of our relationship," I said, each word carefully measured. "And I won't waste your time denying it. The truth is it wasn't real. The engagement was a PR strategy—my strategy."

A gasp rippled through the crowd, followed by a renewed surge of questions. I ignored them, pressing on.

I heard the board members behind me suck in a breath. One stepped forward and put a hand on my arm as if to pull me away from the podium. The rumors had been circulating and the board wanted me to deny it. But I was tired of lying. If I lost future investments, whatever. I had money. I didn't need more.

I quietly shrugged off the hand on my arm and turned my attention back to the crowd that was waiting with bated breath for me to explain the situation.

"Kaira had nothing to do with the plan's conception. I made her an offer she couldn't refuse, and she agreed to help me. That's the truth." My jaw clenched. "If anyone wants to blame someone, blame me. I take full responsibility."

I looked out at the sea of faces, knowing full well how this would be spun in the headlines. I could almost see the sensationalist articles: *"Roman Kelly Admits Engagement Hoax!"* or *"Kaira Foster: Victim or Accomplice?"*

The thought made my stomach churn. "She's not at fault," I added, my voice firm. "Kaira is a good person. She didn't deserve to be dragged into my mess, and I'll regret it for the rest of my life. The plan was a bad move. It only hurt both of us. There are no winners here."

The room was silent again as I stepped back from the podium. "That's all I have to say."

An explosion of flashing lights and shouted questions erupted.

Despite the cacophony, I walked away with a mixture of relief and dread swirling in my chest. I thought it would be freeing to have the truth out there.

I was wrong.

My assistant was waiting by the door, wide-eyed. "That was... candid," she said as I passed her.

"That was the truth," I snapped, brushing past her.

My board members were waiting for me in the small room. "Give us the room," one of them demanded.

The assistants scrambled to get out. A few of the board members looked as though they'd aged a decade in the past hour.

"Roman, do you realize what you've just done? You've blown up your own empire. The brand. The trust. Everything!"

"And for what?" chimed in another. "To play the martyr?"

I held up a hand. "Spare me the lecture."

"No, Roman, you're going to hear this," my CFO said, his voice rising. "You're going to lose millions. Do you understand that? Millions. Our stock will tank. Sponsorships will pull out. And for what? To protect a woman who walked away from you?"

"She didn't walk out on me. We decided the whole sham was stupid. It was never going to work."

"It was working just fine. Why would you do that? You could have said she left you. We gave you a statement! You were supposed to say you cared about each other but realized you weren't ready to get married just yet. Mutual respect and blah, blah, blah! The lawyers drafted it beautifully."

My temper flared. "I'm past giving a damn," I said coldly. "But don't worry, I'll make sure your staggering salary remains untouched."

The venom in my tone silenced them. I walked away before I could say something I'd truly regret. Anthony was waiting for me. He said nothing as he started to drive away.

The drive home felt long. As he pulled into the winding driveway, the sight of the house felt more unwelcome than a refuge.

The place was quiet, as it had been since the day Kaira left. Too quiet. I'd caught the staff whispering about her a few days ago, reminiscing about her laugh, the way she brightened up the place. I'd shut it down immediately, barking at them to never speak her name under my roof again.

Now, nobody said anything when I was around.

Ruby was still giving me the cold shoulder, and honestly, I couldn't blame her. I'd exploded on her the day Kaira left, and she hadn't spoken to me since. I hadn't apologized either. What was the point?

The silence was suffocating. I was going to drive myself crazy if I stayed in the house another minute.

That evening, I met up with some old friends for drinks. The bar was loud and lively, but it didn't take long for me to notice the shift in energy. I knew it was because of me. Conversations were stilted, laughter forced.

Eventually, I couldn't ignore it any longer. "All right," I said, setting my drink down. "What's going on with you guys? Why is everyone acting weird?"

They exchanged glances, and I could see the unspoken agreement pass between them. Finally, Simon spoke up. "We're not the weird ones, Roman. You are."

I frowned. "What the hell is that supposed to mean?"

"It means you lied to us," Simon said bluntly. "To our faces. About the engagement, about Kaira. About everything."

"And let's not forget that you dragged a perfectly nice woman into your mess and then tossed her aside like she was nothing," Chloe added.

My jaw tightened. "That's not what happened."

"Isn't it?" Simon challenged. "Because that's what it looks like from where we're standing."

I looked around the table, hoping to find an ally, but all I saw were grim faces.

"You've been keeping everyone at arm's length for years," Simon said quietly. "Then Kaira comes along, and for a second, we thought maybe she was breaking through that rough exterior of yours."

"But you couldn't even let that happen, could you?" Chloe said. "You're so damn terrified of being vulnerable that you ruined it before it could go anywhere."

"Enough," I snapped, my voice sharp.

"No, Roman, you need to hear this. If you don't see all this as a giant red flag, you're in trouble." Simon took a drink. "I know you don't want to hear it, but real friends tell each other the truth, even when it's difficult."

They were right, and I hated it. Hated them for pointing it out. But mostly, I hated myself.

There was no cheering me up after that. I was a miserable drinking buddy and they gave up trying to get through to me. One by one, they called it a night, leaving me alone at the table with a half-empty glass and a gnawing sense of regret.

I couldn't run from the truth: I was the problem. And if I didn't fix it, I'd be alone forever.

45

KAIRA

The back deck of my parents' house had always been my sanctuary. Even with the backyard still dormant, it was beautiful. The sky was a little gray, but I didn't mind. I appreciated the stillness, something I hadn't realized I'd been missing until now. The chaos I left behind in LA with Roman and Carla had left me drained, disillusioned. Sitting here, wrapped in my old woolen blanket, I felt the threads of myself knitting back together.

There really was no place like home.

I had been here a couple of weeks, and while my wounds were scabbing over, I still wasn't sure what I was going to do with my life. My book had been left untouched on the laptop. I had no desire to write a love story. I was not feeling particularly loving.

Plus, the sight of the laptop reminded me of Roman. Every time I looked at the sleek machine, I thought back to the night he gave it to me. That led me to thoughts of him kissing me and us being in his bed. His birthday. So many good memories had been packed into a relatively short amount of time. When I was caught up in the moment, it felt like nothing could have gotten in our way. We were so happy.

And then it was just ripped away.

"Good morning."

I looked behind me and saw my mom standing in the doorway with her robe pulled tight around her.

"Good morning," I said.

"You're up early," she said.

"Couldn't sleep."

"Do you want some breakfast?"

"I'm not really hungry."

"I'll make waffles," she said. "I bet you'll be hungry once you see them."

"Thanks, Mom."

She drifted back inside, closing the door behind her.

I went back to my thoughts. Today, I felt like I was carrying the weight of my mistakes on my shoulders, and even the comforts of home couldn't shake it. I could hear my mother in the kitchen and the thought of thick, fluffy waffles and crisp bacon was tempting, but I was so rolled up in my own misery, I couldn't muster any excitement for the meal.

A few minutes later, the door opened and the scent of bacon wafted out.

"Good morning," Dad said. "Mind if I enjoy the fresh air with you?"

"Of course not."

My father sat across from me, sipping his coffee in silence. He didn't pry, not at first, but I could feel his eyes on me, studying the way I fidgeted with the hem of my sleeve, the way I stared out at the woods behind the house without really seeing them. My dad was one of those quiet, silent types. He didn't say a lot, but when he did, it was important.

Finally, he broke the silence. "You want to tell me what's really going on, kiddo?"

I shrugged, playing dumb. "What do you mean?"

He gave me that look, the one that said he wasn't buying it. "You've been here for three weeks, and you're still walking around like the world is ending. That isn't like you. You've always been resilient. This is different. This is much bigger. Talk to me."

I sighed and pulled the blanket around me. "It's complicated."

"Good thing I like complicated stories," he said, his tone light but his expression serious. "Start at the beginning."

So I did. I told him about Roman. At first, I couldn't stop myself from focusing on all the things about him that used to trigger me—the arrogance, the walls he kept up, the way he could be so cold and calculating. My father listened without interrupting, nodding here and there but letting me get it all out.

Then, without really meaning to, I started talking about the other side of Roman. The man who surprised me. The man who let me guide him through unfamiliar territory, who asked questions and listened when I answered. The man who opened his life to me, even when it scared him. The man who had achieved incredible things despite the pain he carried, the grief that seemed to hang over him like a storm cloud.

I told him about the library and how he had given me a laptop. I talked about the many, many hours we spent talking about nothing and everything. The patience he had when I talked about my book and bounced ideas off of him. Roman was not a fan of fiction or happy ever afters, but he always listened and somehow always had some really good insight.

"I thought..." I hesitated, trying to find the right words. "I thought, for a moment, that maybe I could save him."

My father set his coffee mug down on the small table between us and leaned back in his chair. "Kaira, you know that's not your job, right?"

I nodded, but my chest ached. "I know. It's just... I wanted it to be. I wanted to be the person who could pull him out of it. I loved watching him transform before my very eyes. Like a legit butterfly coming out of his cocoon. He blossomed. His friends saw it. His staff saw it. They always told me how good I was for him."

He reached across the table and took my hand in his. "Listen to me. Roman needs to save himself. That's not on you to carry. You cannot save anyone unless it's in a physical sense. You can give him CPR, stop the bleeding, or pull him back from getting hit by a bus. The stuff that's in here is not yours to fix." He dropped my hand and patted his chest and then his head. "That's not for you to fix. No one can fix that. I don't care if you're the best damn psychiatrist in the world. That comes from within. If he doesn't want to be the man you think he can be, that's on him. Not you."

The words hit me hard, but I knew they were true. Still, it didn't make it any easier to let go of the hope that things could have been different.

"I wish it wasn't like that," I said, my voice barely above a whisper.

"That's because your heart is so big," he said. "You care so much, and that's one of the things I love most about you. But sometimes, you care so much about others that you forget to care about yourself."

I went quiet, staring down at our hands. He'd always been able to see right through me.

"For once," he continued, "I think it's time you stop pouring into everyone else's cups and pour into your own. You deserve that, Kaira."

His words hung in the air, and for a moment, I didn't know what to say. Finally, I wiped away the tears that had started to gather in my eyes and looked up at him. "Thank you, Dad."

He smiled, that warm, familiar smile that always made me feel safe. "You've got so much to give, kiddo. But you can't give your best to anyone else if you don't take care of yourself first."

"I'll try," I said, and I meant it.

"Good," he said, leaning back in his chair again. "And remember, just because something didn't work out the way you wanted doesn't mean it wasn't worth it. This man—this Roman—he gave you an adventure. If that's all it is, so be it. But don't regret it. It's better to feel this, to go through this, than to feel nothing at all."

I nodded, wiping away another tear. "I've been guarding my heart for so long, Dad. I don't know how to let go of that."

"You already did," he said simply. "Something about him made you let him in. And if you can do that once, you can do it again—with your passions, your dreams, whatever comes next. You've got more room in there than you think."

"I don't know about that. I feel so empty. Hollow. I don't have anything left to give."

"You will."

I sighed. "Maybe. I guess right now the problem is I don't want to. I'm not interested in giving anything to anyone ever again."

He laughed softly. "You will. And don't worry too much about the butterflies. Metamorphosis is always a bit messy, but it's also beautiful."

I felt a smile tug at the corners of my lips—his optimism, stubborn as ever, had a way of making me see the silver lining. "It's just hard to see the beauty in the mess sometimes," I admitted.

"That's because you're right in the middle of it," he replied, shrugging slightly. "When you're knee deep in mud, it's tough to admire the landscape. Give it time, Kaira. Step back a bit, catch your breath. You'll see it eventually, the whole beautiful panorama, not just the mud."

I nodded slowly, absorbing his words.

"Life isn't always about holding on tight to what you have or what you want. Sometimes it's about learning how to let go and trust that's what's meant for you."

"If you love something set it free," I said, remembering a poster I had on my wall a long time ago.

He grinned. "Exactly. And if it comes back, it's yours—if it doesn't, it never was. But either way, you'll be okay. I know you. You might feel weak right now, but you're one tough cookie. Always have been."

"But what if I'm afraid?" I asked after a pause, looking into his eyes for some sort of reassurance.

"You should be. That's what makes it real. That fear means you're about to grow, about to change. It's the edge of your old comfort zone, stretching into something new."

I loved his combination of wisdom and encouragement.

I took a deep breath, letting his words sink deeper. "But change is so scary."

"It is," he agreed. "But it's also inevitable. And often, it brings with it things we never could have imagined when we were stuck in our old ways. Think about all the times in your life when a door closed. Didn't a window open somewhere else?"

I thought about it, the past instances flashing through my mind like scenes from a movie. He was right, of course.

"What do I do about Carla?" I asked.

He shrugged. "That one is a lot easier. She got her feelings hurt. I think it might have been a little bit of an overreaction but I don't know much about how you women navigate friendships. I'll go months without talking to one of my buddies and it's like a day has passed. You apologized. You've promised to be a better friend. If she chooses to end the friendship, that's on her. You can't control it, but I know you're a good friend. You had a hiccup. You were caught up in a unique situation. I bet you dollars to donuts it will happen to her one of these days. Then you can bust her chops right back."

"I hope so," I said. "Not in a mean way. I want her to experience that little bit of happiness I had. I just hope hers lasts longer than mine did. I'll probably get hurt feelings, but this little exercise has taught me a lot. I will give her grace."

He smiled. "Good girl."

For the first time in weeks, I felt a flicker of hope—not for Roman and me, but for myself. Maybe he was right. Maybe it was time to stop waiting for the path to open up in front of me and start making my own way.

Just then, the door behind us opened, and my mother poked her head out. "Breakfast is ready, Tweedle Dee and Tweedle Dumb," she called, grinning.

"I'm Tweedle Dee," my father and I said in unison, just like we had since I was a little girl. For the first time in what felt like forever, I laughed—a real, genuine laugh.

46

ROMAN

The house was oppressively quiet, a silence that had grown heavier with each passing day. I lingered outside the kitchen, listening to the muffled sounds of the staff going about their work. Pots clanged, water ran, but there was no laughter, no casual chatter.

Kaira had brought something to this house I hadn't realized was missing until it was gone. Without her, the house felt more like a tomb than a home. I hated it and I hated myself for creating it.

My choice to end the contract and essentially throw her out on her ass affected a lot more than just me. They were all feeling her loss. It had turned this into a house of mourning.

I glanced at my watch, realizing how much time I'd been wasting just standing there, lost in remorse. With an audible sigh, I stepped into the kitchen. The staff turned to look at me—some paused, some tried to offer a smile of greeting that didn't quite reach their eyes.

"Morning, everyone," I said, my voice hoarse. There were murmurs of "morning" in reply, but none of them held the warmth they used to. I couldn't blame them. They didn't want to look me in the eyes.

I poured myself a coffee and tried to act casual, but the tension in the air was suffocating.

"Could you all join me in the dining room?" I asked, trying to keep my voice even. "Whatever you're working on can wait. Bring a coffee, tea, whatever you'd like. I'll need about an hour of your time."

There were a few hesitant nods, but nobody moved. "Please."

Slowly, they filtered out of the kitchen, glancing at one another as if trying to figure out what this was about. They probably assumed I was about to fire them or scold them for allowing water spots on the glasses or a speck of dust on the shelves in the library.

They weren't wrong to suspect that was what was coming. The old Roman, the Roman before Kaira came into my life, would have done that. Hell, I did do that. I was meticulous and liked things a certain way. I hated when it wasn't done the way I wanted.

I followed them into the dining room, where the rest of the house staff had already gathered. I'd called ahead to bring everyone together. About fifteen to twenty people filled the space, their faces a mixture of curiosity and uncertainty.

I cleared my throat and stood at the head of the table. "Thank you all for coming. I know this isn't normal, and I appreciate you taking the time. We have some things to talk about. Please, everyone have a seat."

There was a shuffle of feet and the scrape of chairs as they sat down, their expressions guarded. I couldn't blame them. I hadn't exactly been approachable. None of them said a word. I was pretty sure a few of them weren't even breathing. I hated that I had made them feel like I was the big bad wolf and their jobs were always in danger.

I clasped my hands together, inhaling deeply before I spoke. "I want to start by apologizing. I know I've made this house feel like a battleground. I know I've made all of you feel like you're walking on eggshells, and that's on me."

The room was silent, but the tension eased slightly. Their expressions shifted from fear to confusion.

"For years, I've used this house, and by extension, all of you, as a shield. When things were hard, when the outside world got too loud, I took it out on you. I created an environment where no matter what you did, it felt like it wasn't good enough. And that's not fair. You deserve better."

Still, nobody spoke, but I could see the emotions on their faces. The uncertainty, disbelief, maybe even relief.

"I've been carrying around a lot of anger and grief for a long time," I admitted. "And instead of dealing with it, I lashed out at the people who've been there for me the most. That's you. You've been here for me in ways no one else has. When I lost my parents, you were the ones who kept me going. You tried to fill the void they left behind, and I've never properly thanked you for that. All of you stepped up when you didn't have to." I turned to the gardener. "When you insisted I help you in the solarium, I never really understood what you were doing. But now I see it was your way of trying to bring me back to life. You spent time with me and comforted me without offering the usual condolences."

"It was my pleasure," he murmured.

I looked at Marilyn, who had tears shining in her eyes. "And you, you have been a constant in my life longer than anyone else. You have been a mother to me and I have done a shitty job of showing you how important you are to me." I swallowed hard, feeling my own eyes start to burn with unshed tears. "I'm sorry for all the times I've overlooked that, taken your presence for granted, and for all the unnecessary harshness."

The room was heavy with emotions, a collective breath being held as if the walls themselves were waiting to exhale.

"I know apologies can't undo the past, but I'm here now, ready to make amends and move forward with a better understanding and appreciation of what each of you brings to the table."

A few people wiped at their eyes. I swallowed hard and continued. "I realize now how wrong I've been. Kaira—" I paused, her name catching in my throat. "She held up a mirror to me, and I didn't like what I saw. But she taught me something important: the only way to move forward is to face the truth, no matter how ugly it is."

I looked around the room, meeting each person's gaze in turn. "I've been selfish. I've used you all as my punching bags on bad days, and I am so, so sorry for that. I can't change the past, but I promise you, I will do better moving forward."

For a moment, the room was still. Then, Marilyn stood and approached me. Her eyes were shiny with unshed tears as she wrapped her arms around me. The hug startled me, but not as much as what she whispered in my ear.

"I love you, Roman," she said, her voice raw with emotion. "I've wanted to do this for twenty years. When you were little, you used to let me hug you. After we lost your parents, you recoiled any time I tried. Let me hug you."

I stiffened, unaccustomed to this kind of vulnerability, but as her arms tightened around me, something inside me cracked. I leaned into her embrace, resting my head on her shoulder. The discomfort of being seen so completely was almost unbearable, but I let it happen.

Marilyn pulled back slightly, cupping my face in her hands like she used to when I was a boy. "We've always loved you," she said softly. "We just didn't know how to reach you anymore. Why do you think we all stayed? It wasn't your sunny personality. We have all felt a responsibility for you. We loved your parents and many of us vowed to remain loyal to them. We knew they would want us to stick around. We needed to fill in the void they left. I know we can never replace your beautiful mom and dad, but we all want to try. You were such a beautiful, happy boy. We've always known he was still in there somewhere. When Kaira came into the house, we saw that little boy once again."

I nodded, unable to find the words to respond.

As I straightened, I noticed movement at the edge of the room. Ruby stood in the doorway, her arms crossed, her expression unreadable. For weeks, we hadn't spoken, the fallout of my explosion the day Kaira left still hanging between us. But now, as our eyes met, she gave me a small, tentative smile.

The staff began to murmur amongst themselves, some quietly

thanking me, others offering reassurances that they believed in my sincerity. But my focus was on Ruby.

"Ruby," I said, my voice steady. "We need to talk."

She nodded and gestured for me to follow her. I left the staff in the dining room and followed her to her favorite sitting room. She sat on the couch, her posture relaxed.

"Well, that was unexpected," she said.

I sat across from her, leaning forward with my elbows on my knees. "I had to do it. I've been a nightmare to everyone in this house, including you."

"You have," she said bluntly. "But why now? What changed?"

I hesitated, searching for the right words. "Kaira made me see things differently. She didn't put up with my bullshit, and she called me out on things I'd been ignoring for years. She made me realize that if I kept going the way I was, I'd end up alone in every sense of the word."

Ruby studied me, her expression softening. "She left an impression on you."

"She did," I admitted. "And now she's gone, and I've spent weeks pushing everyone else away, too. I can't keep doing that. I don't want to go back to that same cold and lonely place I was in before she came here."

She nodded slowly. "Roman, you've been hurting for a long time. Losing your parents, growing up the way you did—it's enough to break anyone. But you've always had this need to prove you could handle it all on your own. I know I should have been a better aunt. I wanted to, but you pushed me away. You were so capable and independent. I was wrong to think that's what I should have given you. I should have been around more. I left you alone for too long. You're not alone, Roman. You don't ever have to be. Not anymore."

"I know that now," I said. "Or at least, I'm trying to."

Ruby smiled. "I'm proud of you. For doing this, for apologizing. It's a start. A big one. Those people in that room would walk through fire for you. Most of them, anyway. I do hope you can appreciate that."

I nodded, feeling a weight lift slightly at her words, though the burden of my past actions still sat heavily with me. "I want to," I replied honestly. "I really want to start seeing things differently, Ruby. I want to believe that people care. Like really care. I'm jaded. I know that. I want to be different."

"They do care, Roman. More than you know. It's always been more than duty for them, for us. We stayed because we wanted to be here for you, because we care about you."

"Thank you for being so patient with me. I've spent the last month replaying every word and action I've made over the years. I feel like such an ass."

"Admitting you have a problem is the first step," she said with a small laugh. "You'll be better. I know you will. Take some time. I know your instinct is to chase after Kaira, but I think you need to let that rest a bit. Work on you. Heal. Then maybe there will be a chance."

I shook my head. "That ship has sailed. I'm not putting her through that again. I'm just glad for the time we had."

47

KAIRA

Nine Months Later

I stood in front of the mirror and looked at my reflection. Did I like what I saw?
Yes.
I was a confident woman.

At least that was what I was going to keep telling myself. I was a budding author launching my first book. This was my first step to success. I did it on my own dime and my own steam. Yes, I had some support from my parents and Carla, but this was mine.

I did this.

It had been a long nine months. The year felt like it dragged. Time seemed to slow down as I processed everything that happened at Roman's mansion, separating myself from that world and forging my path through the maze of self-publishing. Each step was a revelation, a declaration that I could make it on my own, without the shadow of Roman's influence looming over me.

I survived the media fallout after he announced our split and the fact that it was all fake. It had been brutal. Not something I ever wanted to live through again. Thankfully, I was shielded from the brunt of it in Philadelphia. And it wasn't long before someone else did something scandalous and Roman Kelly's fake fiancée was a distant memory.

I survived.

That was something I told myself every morning when I opened my eyes. I didn't just survive, I thrived. Getting kicked to the curb by Roman turned out to be the best thing to happen to me. I got taken down to nothing, and when I picked myself up, it was me who was the caterpillar crawling out of a cocoon. I liked the new me. I rarely looked at myself in the mirror and noticed my thick thighs or belly that could be flatter.

I adjusted the collar of my blouse, took a deep breath, and turned away from the mirror. Carla popped her head into my room. "You're going to be late to your own book launch."

"What do you think?" I asked. "Scarf or no scarf?"

Carla surveyed me for a moment before pointing decisively. "No scarf. Keep it simple. Let them focus on the author, not the accessories."

I nodded in agreement, dropping the scarf back onto my bed. Carla was right; today was about my work, my words. I took another deep breath and grabbed my purse.

"You look stunning, Kaira," Carla said, leading the way out of my room. She had been an enormous support through everything, almost like a sister I never had. Like sisters, we squabbled. After nearly two months apart, we were back to being best friends.

The drive to the bookstore felt surreal. I was about to present the world a piece of me, hidden in pages disguised as fiction. Carla and I were let in through the back. The eager staff told us there was a nice crowd and she hoped my hand was ready to sign lots of books.

I stepped out into the store and walked to the area that had been set up for me. My name was written in bold blue font on the posters Carla and I had made. I couldn't believe it was all happening.

The line at Barnes & Noble wasn't endless, but it was steady. Every new face brought a fresh wave of excitement and gratitude. As I scribbled my name on yet another inside cover, I couldn't help but feel the satisfaction of accomplishment wash over me. My debut book, a grumpy-sunshine, enemies-to-lovers romance, sat stacked in glossy towers around the table. Seeing my name printed across those covers still didn't feel real.

Beside me, Carla was in her element. She gestured dramatically to the piles of books, her enthusiasm infectious—or intimidating, depending on who you asked.

"Christmas is coming, people!" she hollered at a group browsing the sci-fi section nearby. "Don't you want to give the gift of romance? Don't you want to be a hero to your book-loving friends? This is Kaira freaking Foster! You'll regret not having this masterpiece on your coffee table!"

"Carla!" I choked out between laughter. "Relax! They're here to shop, not be barked at!"

She turned to me, feigning shock. "Relax? Have you met me? I'm your number-one hype woman. It's my job to make sure you sell out tonight."

I shook my head, still laughing. Carla's antics drew attention, sure, but it also made the whole event feel less overwhelming. I signed another book for a smiling woman who told me how much she loved the slow-burn tension between the characters. Her words stayed with me long after she walked away.

Carla leaned back in her chair and eyed the crowd like a hawk searching for its next prey. "That couple by the Christmas display," she said, pointing subtly with her chin. "I'm going to get them over here."

"Please don't." I tugged on her sleeve.

"Too late." She cupped her hands around her mouth. "Hey! You two look like people who'd love a spicy love story to cozy up with."

The couple froze, their expressions a mix of amusement and alarm.

"Carla!" I swatted at her, but she dodged effortlessly.

She grinned, completely unbothered. "Trust me, they'll thank me later."

Eventually, the couple did wander over, and to my surprise, they bought two copies. Carla made a show of claiming credit. I rolled my eyes but couldn't stop smiling. Who needed a publicist and agent and a big PR team that one of the big publishing houses would have provided? I had Carla. She was my secret weapon. And this way, I got to keep most of the money from my sales.

As the signing wound down and the crowd thinned, Carla leaned back in her chair, arms crossed smugly. "I think that was a very successful day for the future queen of romance novels."

I shook my head, but her words made my chest swell with pride. This past year had been the most challenging and rewarding of my life. I'd poured every ounce of myself into this book. It wasn't the story I'd initially set out to write, but it was the story I needed to tell—the one about heartbreak, healing, and daring to love again. I told myself and the characters that had grown very quiet since the breakup with Roman that one day, I would tell their story. But not yet.

"You did it, Kaira," Carla said, her voice softer now. "You really pulled yourself up by your bootstraps. I've never seen anyone work as hard as you have this year. You've had the most successful year of your life, and you deserve every bit of it."

Her words made my eyes sting. I smiled at her, my best friend who had stuck by me through every moment, good and bad. "Thanks, Carla. I don't know what I'd do without you."

"Well, for starters, you wouldn't have sold half as many books today," she teased, but there was a glint of pride in her eyes. "Seriously, though. You're incredible. And don't you dare forget it."

I glanced at the stacks of books, at the people still milling around with copies in their hands. For the first time in a long time, I felt truly proud of myself. I'd rebuilt my life, poured my soul into something meaningful, and it had paid off. But even as I basked in the glow of success, a quiet ache lingered in the back of my mind.

Carla must have noticed because she nudged me with her elbow. "What's that look for?"

"What look?" I asked, feigning innocence.

She raised an eyebrow. "That wistful, staring-into-the-distance look. Come on, spill."

I sighed, resting my chin in my hand. "I don't know. It's just... everything is great. My book is out, people seem to love it, I'm happy with where I am in life. But..."

"But?" Carla prompted.

I hesitated. I did not want to dump my problems on her. They weren't really problems. It was just a hint of sadness. "There's still something missing. Or someone."

Her expression softened, and she leaned closer. "You mean Roman."

I didn't respond right away, but I didn't need to. Carla had always been able to read me like a book.

"I hear he's going to be up for auction again," she said, her tone casual but her eyes twinkling with mischief. "They moved the event to Christmas this year. And this time, you can afford a ticket."

The laugh that bubbled out of me was more incredulous than anything. "Carla, that's insane. I can't just show up at a charity auction and bid on him like nothing happened. Especially considering how much he'll go for. I've sold a few books but I don't have a hundred grand lying around."

"You've sold a lot more than a few," she said. "Like a lot more."

"You know what I mean. I just, well, I don't want to reopen that wound. It's best I don't go back down that path."

"Why not?" she asked, as if it were the most obvious thing in the world.

"Because..." I gestured vaguely. "Because he's over me. He's doing great now. I've seen the headlines. He's all over the media, and he looks happy. He's clearly done a lot of work on himself, and I'm glad for him. But we weren't good for each other."

"A year ago, sure," Carla corrected. "Now?" She picked up one of my books and pointed at the animated male main character on the cover. "This guy? He might be your soulmate."

I rolled my eyes but couldn't suppress a small smile. "That's fiction, Carla."

"Maybe," she said with a shrug. "But fiction is inspired by life. And from where I'm sitting, it looks like Roman inspired a lot more than just your book."

I didn't deny it. Roman had been a catalyst for so much change in my life. He'd forced me to confront parts of myself I'd been avoiding, to take risks, to open up in ways I never thought I could. And even though things hadn't worked out between us, he'd left a mark on me that I couldn't ignore.

Still, the idea of seeing him again was terrifying. What if he didn't want to see me? What if he'd moved on completely?

"He's probably seeing someone," I said. "I showed him how good it can be with a woman and now he's probably found one that makes him happy. One that won't go into forbidden rooms."

She snorted. "Kaira, if you started every chapter in your books with 'he's probably happy without her,' do you think anyone would read them?" Carla tapped the book cover with a finger. "People crave hope. They want to see risks, they want grand gestures, they want love that conquers all odds. Maybe it's time you start living a little more like your characters."

I blew out a breath. She had a point. My characters always took chances, always fought for what they wanted. Could I really call myself a creator of such stories if I wasn't willing to take my own advice?

"Life does not always imitate art," I said.

"You don't have to decide now," Carla said. "But if there's even a small part of you that still wonders what could have been, don't let fear hold you back. Life's too short for regrets, Kaira. Just talk to him. Maybe you'll realize you don't have feelings for him anymore."

I nodded, letting her words sink in. Maybe she was right. Maybe there was still a chance to find my own happily ever after. But for now, I had my book, my best friend, and a life I was proud of. That was more than enough.

Wasn't it? I didn't need Roman.

Or maybe that was exactly why I was ready. I didn't need him. I made myself successful without his connections or support. Maybe now I could have it all.

48

ROMAN

I couldn't believe I was doing this to myself once again. I adjusted the bow tie threatening to choke me out. The Valentine's event had been moved to a Christmas event in the hopes of maximizing people's generous spirit. And to catch them before they blew all their money on gifts.

Not like that was likely to happen. The people that were scheduled to attend the event had money to burn. It didn't matter if they spent a ton at Christmas. They would have plenty left to do whatever they wanted—including buying a date with me and the other eligible bachelors.

"You look very handsome," Marilyn said when I stepped into the foyer.

"Tonight they required black tie," I complained.

"Well, it looks nice on you." She stepped forward and straightened the bow tie once again. "You'll be the one they all want."

"Until they get me alone," I said.

"Stop it. Any woman would be thrilled to get the chance to sit down with you."

I scoffed. "I don't know about that. I tend to turn them away once I start talking about the one that got away."

"Then don't talk about her tonight," she said gently. "This is a chance for you to meet someone new. I think it's time. You've come a long way. You're ready."

I knew that was what everyone thought, but that was not the way I felt. I was still hung up on Kaira. I wasn't sure I would ever forget about her. I wanted to, but I couldn't.

"I should go," I said. "Anthony is waiting."

And he was. He opened the car door for me. I slid in, trying not to dwell too much on how much I hated stuff like this. It was just a few hours and the money was for a good cause. I could suck it up for kids with cancer.

The ballroom was a hive of activity when I walked in. It was filled with the glittering elite of Los Angeles. The same characters that were always at these things milled about with champagne flutes in hand. They were decked out in their finest gowns and jewelry. I saw many familiar faces. And they saw me. I felt the eyes on me as I moved through the crowd.

Staff in sleek black uniforms darted between tables, balancing champagne flutes and hors d'oeuvres. I found a quiet corner at the bar, watching the interaction from a safe distance. A woman laughed too loudly at a joke beside me, her pitchy voice setting my nerves on edge. I ordered a scotch and turned slightly, trying to block out the noise. I took a sip of my drink and scanned the room once more, steeling myself to join the fray.

I mingled. Shook hands. Accepted congrats on my new business venture and said all the right things. It was like the same playbook with the same bits of conversation recited over and over again.

It wasn't long before a young woman dressed in all black came to retrieve me. I felt a tug in my gut, remembering last year it was Kaira who had been sent to find me.

"This way, Mr. Kelly," she said.

I followed her through the crowd to the same holding area as last year. It was bringing back a lot of memories—good and bad. I took my spot backstage, glad to be out of the ballroom with all the eyes on me. The break wouldn't last long but I would enjoy it while I could.

From my vantage point backstage, I watched the chaos with a mixture of amusement and disbelief. Had it really been a year since the last charity auction? It felt like a lifetime and yesterday all at once.

The buzz of conversation in the crowd was a dull roar. My name was already circulating in whispers, the anticipation palpable. I noticed the same two guys from last year were going up on the auction block.

"Gentlemen," I said, shaking their hands. "Good to see you back in the hot seat."

"Let's hope we survive another round."

The other billionaire grinned. "At least we didn't pretend to marry our bidder."

I smiled back, feeling a flicker of nostalgia. "If Kaira had bid on you, believe me, you might have tried."

Her name wasn't a secret—not after the media circus earlier this year—but it still had the power to make my chest tighten.

The first billionaire was introduced, his dating history poked fun at as the bidding war began. Numbers soared higher than last year, the energy in the room contagious. Maybe the organizers were onto something when they changed it to before Christmas. He was "sold" for an impressive figure. Then it was the second billionaire's turn. Once again, I was being saved for last, like the grand finale. No pressure or anything.

I watched the bidding, impressed to see him actually go for higher than the first.

Then it was my turn.

The emcee gestured for me to stand. I adjusted my jacket and rose to my feet. The applause was deafening, and I swept my gaze over the crowd, my expression carefully neutral. Faces blurred together, a sea of designer gowns and tailored suits.

My wealth, my business, and my looks were all listed as the many reasons people should bid on me. It was a little cringey, but it was part of the deal. I flashed my most charming smile and struck a few poses. Then the bidding started.

The numbers climbed rapidly, echoing around the high-ceilinged room. Each bid seemed to thrust me further into a spotlight I wasn't sure I wanted but couldn't escape. Fifty thousand... seventy-five... soon it was close to a hundred grand.

I stood there watching and happened to notice something. The crowd shifted.

A ripple passed through the room, heads turning in the same direction. The people in the back moved aside, creating a clear path down the center aisle. My pulse quickened as a figure stepped into the light.

It was her.

Kaira.

She wore a sparkling gown that shimmered with every step. Long gloves covered her arms and her red lips curved into a confident smile. Her dark hair was swept to the side, exposing the graceful curve of her neck, her collarbone, the perfect silhouette of someone who had walked straight out of my dreams.

Our eyes met, and my breath caught. She didn't look away, didn't falter. Instead, she smiled, bold and sure.

"One hundred and ten thousand," she said, her voice clear and strong, cutting through the murmurs.

The room went silent.

The number hung in the air, the same bid she'd made last year. The irony wasn't lost on me—or anyone else, judging by the collective intake of breath. Then the whispers began.

"Is that her?" someone murmured.

"I think that's her," another replied.

"His ex-fiancée," a woman nearby said.

"Fake fiancée," someone corrected, quieter.

"No, no, she's that romance writer now."

The auctioneer, to his credit, kept his composure. "Do I hear one-fifteen?"

No one dared to counter her bid. The room was transfixed, as if we were the only two people in it. The auctioneer's gavel came down with a sharp crack.

"Sold to the woman in the front row!"

Applause erupted, but I barely heard it. My gaze was locked on Kaira as I stepped down from the stage. People parted to let me through, the buzz of speculation surrounding us like static electricity. I barely heard them. Hell, I barely saw anyone else.

When I reached her, she looked up at me, her smile widening. "Before you ask, no, I didn't just spend more of your money."

I couldn't help but grin. "Good, because I was about to call my accountant."

Her eyes sparkled with mischief. "This time, I think we're worth the investment."

The words hit me hard—in the best way. She'd come back. After everything, she was here, standing in front of me, daring me to make a choice.

My grin turned into something softer, something real. "And what if I'm not willing to let this investment walk away again?"

The crowd, the noise, the past year—it all faded into the background. All that mattered was the look in her eyes, the hope and determination that mirrored my own.

"You're not going anywhere," I said, my voice low and steady. I closed the distance between us, cupping her face in my hands. Her gloves were cool against my skin, her lips warm and soft as I kissed her.

The room erupted in cheers, but I barely noticed. I was hung up on the way she melted into me like she'd been waiting for this moment as long as I had.

When we finally broke apart, she was smiling, her cheeks flushed. "So, what now?" she asked, her voice teasing but tinged with something deeper.

I took her hand, lacing my fingers through hers. "Now we leave," I said, glancing around at the gawking crowd. "I've got more important things to focus on than entertaining a room full of strangers."

She laughed, and it was the sweetest sound I'd heard in a year. Together, we walked out of the ballroom, leaving behind the noise, the past, and every doubt that had kept us apart.

This time, I wasn't letting her go.

"We're not sneaking out the back," she said.

"You said you were good for the money," I reminded her with a laugh.

"I am. Mostly."

"Did you rob a bank?"

She laughed. "Nope, but I just sold my book and got a signing bonus for my next one. Let's hope it doesn't flop."

"As if it would," I said.

We walked into a corridor meant for employees only.

I turned to face her. "I can't believe you're here."

"I wasn't sure I was going to come, but I wanted to see you. See how you were doing."

"Better now that you're here."

Her eyes searched mine, seeking sincerity, perhaps a hint of the cold, ruthless asshole I used to be. "I'm here for more than just that. I need to tell you something important."

My heart dropped. "What is it?"

"I've missed you."

Relief washed over me.

I laughed, the tension of uncertainty melting away into something warm and comforting. "I've missed you, too. More than you could possibly know."

Kaira squeezed my hand, her eyes shining with unshed tears. "Then it's really not just me?" Her voice was a whisper, vulnerable and filled with hope.

"Not just you," I confirmed, tightening my grip on her hand. "It's been a long year. Too many mornings wondering what could have been if things had gone differently."

She nodded slowly. "We've both changed, I think. Grown up a bit, maybe learned a few things about what we want. And what we can't live without."

I nodded. "I think you're right. And maybe this time around, we can do better by each other."

Her eyes sparkled again, that mischievous glint returning. "So, where are we going on our date? I believe I have you for the next few hours."

"Baby, you have me for a lot longer than that," I said. "I was going to take the lucky woman that bought me out to dinner, but I'm not interested in a seven-course meal. I'm only interested in dessert."

"Thank God," she said with a laugh. "Me too. Please tell me Anthony is around here somewhere waiting to take you home."

"He is."

"Lead the way, Mr. Kelly."

49

KAIRA

As we made our way toward the service exit, a flutter of nervous excitement danced in my chest. Every step I took alongside him felt surreal, like stepping back into a dream I thought had dissolved with the morning sun. Despite his reassurances, part of me still braced for the moment he would change his mind, the moment this bubble would burst.

Anthony was leaning against a sleek, black car, his presence as unassuming as ever but his eyes flickered with a hint of surprise as we approached. "Evening, Kaira," he greeted with a nod that was both respectful and slightly amused. "Nice to see you again."

"Evening, Anthony," I returned the gesture, feeling a small thrill at being included in this slice of his life again. "Nice to see you too."

Anthony opened the car door for us. As I slid into the leather seat beside Roman, I realized how much I had missed these simple moments—the comfortable silence, the shared glances, the underlying excitement of just being near him.

He settled next to me, our hands finding each other instinctively. The car pulled away smoothly, and the city lights blurred past us as Anthony drove us out to Roman's estate. I rested my head on his shoulder. I couldn't explain how good it felt to be in his presence again. My life had been full and busy, but it wasn't complete. He just had a way of making me feel whole.

Neither of us talked. I knew there was still a lot to say, but we had time. For now, I was content to sit here with him and just enjoy the moment.

"You look good in a tux," I commented.

He chuckled. "You're not so bad yourself in that dress," he replied, his eyes scanning me. "I mean it, Kaira. You look stunning."

I found myself blushing. It was as if no time had passed at all, yet everything had changed. I was more myself than I had ever been before, and from what I could gather so far, so was he.

When Anthony pulled to a stop at the estate, we both climbed out. It appeared the staff had already retired for the night. I looked around with memories flooding in. The last time I had been in the foyer was when he had kicked me out.

"Do you want a drink?" Roman asked.

I turned to look at him and slowly shook my head. "No."

"Me neither."

He took my hand and together we climbed the stairs. When we reached the top step, I was surprised to see the double doors open. I turned to look at him, questioning what had happened.

"I like to see her art," he said with a shrug. "I leave the doors open. Anyone who walks by here gets to see it."

I nodded, noticing he had cleaned up the place. It looked more like a gallery than an artist's studio. "I think that's a great idea," I said. "Her work is beautiful. It should be seen."

"I agree. I'm working with a gallery to display some of her pieces. I won't sell them, but I want the world to remember my mother and her amazing talent."

He had changed. I was so impressed. We walked by the room and into his bedroom. Nothing had changed in there. He reached up and undid his bowtie, letting it hang around his neck.

"Uncomfortable?" I asked.

"You have no idea."

I reached up and undid a couple of buttons on his shirt, giving the man room to breathe. His fingers wrapped around my wrist and stopped me.

"What is it?" I asked.

"I want you to know, there has been no one else since you."

The intensity in his eyes held me captive, a stark honesty that stripped away any pretense. "Me either, Roman."

He drew a deep breath, his grip on my wrist softening. "Kaira, I'm sorry for how things ended between us. I've had a lot of time to think, to understand where I went wrong."

It wasn't just an apology; it was a confession and an invitation rolled into one. His sincerity cut through the lingering doubts in my mind. I could feel the walls I'd built around my heart beginning to crumble.

"I know you've had your own journey since then," Roman continued, his voice low and steady. "I've followed your successes, always feeling pride mixed with a sense of loss. I just... I hope there's room for me, somewhere in your future."

The world seemed to hold its breath, waiting for my response. My thoughts raced, weaving past painful memories and future hopes. "You *are* my future, Roman."

I saw the flash in his eyes. Desire? Love?

It didn't matter because he kissed me and I had my answer. As our lips met again after so much time apart—craving each other's touch—I knew that there was no one else who could complete me like Roman did; no one else whose heart beat in sync with mine quite like his did. There was no one else who could challenge me yet inspire me like him; no one else who could make me feel safe yet drive me wild at precisely the same time.

Slowly we broke apart, breathless yet yearning for more. His fingers pulled at my glove and slowly peeled it down my arm before removing the next one. I slowly turned and moved my hair out of the way, silently asking him to unzip me.

I felt the cool breeze as it hit my bare flesh, sending shivers down my spine. Roman placed slow, gentle kisses on my neck and shoulders as he slowly eased the dress off me, taking it with him as he stepped away.

I was left standing there in just my bra and panties, feeling empowered. I wasn't the same shy woman as I was the first time we were together. I turned to face him.

His eyes burned with desire. "You are so beautiful." His lips brushed against my lobe, sending another shiver down my spine.

He reached around and unclasped my bra before gently lowering it to the floor. His hands traced patterns on my back as he kissed and nibbled his way down to my hips. I could feel myself melting into him, wanting him more than anything else in this moment—needing him like air itself.

My fingers trembled as I pushed his jacket down his arms. He shrugged out of it while I worked the buttons of his shirt, pulling it free from his pants. I was suddenly feeling frantic. I needed to touch him. I missed the feel of his skin under my palms.

I jerked his shirt open and groaned when I realized he was wearing an undershirt. He quickly pulled it over his head. Our bodies met again. His hard chest pressed against my soft curves, our hearts racing wildly together in time—as if we had never been apart despite nearly a year passing by since our last embrace.

Within minutes, we were both naked and stretched out on his bed. He kissed my neck, sucking my skin before running his tongue over the same spot. My body arched into him wanting more. His hand slid over my breasts before tweaking my nipple, sending shocks of pleasure through me. His other hand trailed down my belly before dipping into the wetness between my legs.

He pushed two fingers inside me. I gasped as my head fell back. "Roman," I moaned, grabbing his shoulders.

His mouth found my nipple and teased it with his teeth, sending shivers down my spine. He began to move both his fingers and his mouth in rhythm, pushing deeper, sucking harder. I threw my head back, feeling the climax building. It hit me like a wave, crashing over me, washing away any lingering doubts or fears. It had been too long. My body had been craving him for months.

He kissed me again, his tongue teasing my lips until they parted. He pulled back, just inches from my face. He ran his fingers through my hair, looking into my eyes.

"I love you," he whispered against my ear, his voice tinged with regret for the time we'd lost.

"I love you," I replied, feeling infinitely grateful for this chance to start over.

He moved his body over mine and then stopped. "Shit, the condoms. I'm not sure if they're expired."

I cupped his face. "Roman, I believe you when you told me you haven't been with anyone. I haven't either. I'm ready to trust you completely. I'm not going to get pregnant."

"You're sure?" he asked.

I nodded. "I'm sure."

"Damn, woman, I don't know how long I'll last. I've never gone this long without sex. I think I might explode at first contact."

I giggled. "Then we'll just have to keep doing it. I think we have a lot of missed time to make up for."

Roman slowly moved over me, guiding his hard length to my opening. He looked into my eyes, which were filled with love and respect. We locked eyes as he filled me completely. We both gasped at the sensation. Our bodies moved together in a perfect rhythm, as if they'd never been apart. He looked down at me with such love and adoration that it made my heart flutter.

He leaned in and kissed me softly while his hips began to move faster, driving him deeper inside me. I couldn't get enough of the feeling of being so completely connected to him. My nails dug into his shoulders, urging him to go faster, harder. He growled against my neck, taking my moans of pleasure as encouragement. I could feel the tension building within him, matching my own. I knew this was it. We were both going to lose control.

And then we did. Together, we climaxed. Our bodies shook with the intensity of it all as our love for each other consumed us in a haze of passion and desire. He kissed the side of my face, showering me with fifty kisses over my eyes and nose. I could feel his cock twitch inside me. It was one aftershock after another.

When he finally pulled out and tried to move away, I wrapped my arms around him, not wanting this moment to end anytime soon. I had never been so sure about anything in my life except for the fact that Roman Kelly was mine and I was his.

"I love you," I murmured. "I can't believe I'm here."

"I'm so glad you are," he said. His hand rubbed up and down my arm. "I have spent so many nights alone in this bed thinking about what I would do if I ever got another chance with you."

"Yeah? And what would you do?"

He chuckled. "That and then that again, but mostly, I would remind myself of what it felt like when you weren't here. I promised myself I would never take you for granted again. Every minute I get with you is precious. I'm not going to squander it."

"I took you for granted as well," I said. "I took a lot for granted. I don't want to do that ever again."

"Thank you for coming back to me," he whispered. "I don't think I could ever love anyone the way I love you."

He pulled the covers up over us, tucking me in close. It felt like we were in our own little bubble, protected from the outside world and its chaos. I closed my eyes and couldn't help but smile. This was exactly where I was supposed to be—in Roman's arms.

"I don't want to fall asleep, but I feel like I haven't truly slept since the last time I was in your bed," I said, my eyes struggling to stay open.

"Sleep. Let me hold you. We've got all night. And tomorrow. And the day after that."

I smiled but said nothing. I was exhausted. It felt like I'd been running a nine-month marathon. I could finally rest.

EPILOGUE
ROMAN

Six Months Later

Rome was even more magical than I remembered from my visit more than ten years ago. Granted, that visit had been during the height of my wild rebellion. I spent most of my time drunk out of my skull and chasing every woman that looked twice at me.

The cobblestone streets, ancient ruins, and the hum of life in the Eternal City felt a lot different with her as my traveling companion. Kaira walked ahead of me, her eyes darting between the architecture and the locals bustling through their routines.

The sun was high, casting a golden glow on everything it touched, including her. She wore a simple sundress, her hair hanging down her back, and a leather satchel slung over her shoulder—the quintessential writer in her element. She was wearing a floppy sunhat that really made her look like a tourist.

"You're staring," she said, glancing back at me with a smirk.

"Caught me," I replied, unrepentant. "It's hard not to. Rome looks good on you."

She rolled her eyes but couldn't hide her smile. "You brought me here to help with my writer's block, remember? Not to boost my ego."

I shrugged. "Can't it be both?"

She laughed. "You're impossible."

"What do you want to see next?" I asked her. "You're in Rome so when in Rome…"

"Cheesy." She laughed.

"But true," I countered playfully. "Come on, what's on top of your list?"

Kaira paused, biting her lip in thought. She pulled out a crinkled piece of paper from her satchel and unfolded it. "I was thinking the Pantheon first, then maybe we can head over to Piazza Navona?"

I nodded in agreement. "Sounds perfect."

As we walked toward the Pantheon, weaving our way through the crowded streets, I couldn't help but observe how natural Kaira seemed here. Perhaps it was the writer in her, forever in pursuit of stories and soaking up the atmosphere, that made her blend seamlessly into any backdrop, however foreign it might be. She wasn't snapping pictures or posing for selfies. She was doing her best to absorb all of it. She made notes here and there, but mostly, she was committing herself to the experience.

We reached the Pantheon along with what felt like three million other people, but she didn't care about the crowd. Kaira looked up in awe as we stepped inside. The shaft of light from the oculus overhead illuminated her face, highlighting her expression of pure wonder.

"Imagine all the history here," she murmured in a near whisper. "The stories these walls have witnessed."

I watched her as she traced her fingers along the cool marble, her eyes lit with a spark of inspiration. "Do you feel it?" she asked, turning toward me. "The weight of all those centuries?"

I nodded, taking her hand in mine. "It's incredible," I replied. "Every corner of this city feels like stepping back in time."

Kaira squeezed my hand and pulled me closer to the center of the

Pantheon. We stood together under the open oculus, bathed in a column of light.

"This is why I write. To capture even a fraction of this feeling in words."

I smiled, understanding her passion more clearly than ever before. "Are you thinking about making the leap into historical romance?"

She sighed. "No. I love to read them, but it would require a lot more research. I don't feel like I have the knowledge to do it justice. I'll stick to reading them rather than writing them."

"But I bet you could do a good job," I said.

She laughed as we walked out. "My biggest cheerleader."

Kaira checked her paper again, squinting in the bright sunlight. "Piazza Navona is next," she confirmed, folding the map and stuffing it in the satchel.

The walk to Piazza Navona wasn't long. Street vendors shouted out in lilting Italian, gelato stands boasted arrays of colorful flavors, and musicians added a soundtrack to our journey. Watching Kaira take it all in was easily one of the best experiences of my life. There was pure wonder in her eyes.

When she told me she wanted to write a book with her characters coming from Rome, I knew I had to bring her. She had never traveled. I felt like an ass because I had spent a couple of years traveling but I barely remembered the places I had seen. I had traveled to party, not to see and experience the places.

Kaira's face lit up at the sight of the fountains and sculptures that made Piazza Navona famously enchanting. She tugged on my hand with childlike eagerness. "Look at the Fountain of the Four Rivers! Isn't it magnificent?" she exclaimed, her words almost lost amidst the murmur of the crowd.

I leaned closer to whisper in her ear. "Every detail. Bernini really knew what he was doing."

She nodded enthusiastically, her eyes scanning every curve and crevice of the artistic masterpiece. "It's all so captivating," she said, pulling out her notebook and beginning to jot down thoughts hurriedly.

Watching her scribble rapidly, I felt an appreciation for her passion. She had this remarkable ability to see layers and meanings that I would have missed otherwise. I felt like I was seeing all of this for the first time. After spending an hour or so at Piazza Navona, I led her back toward the next stop. It was my plan, but she was unaware of it.

"I'm hungry," I said. "There's a rooftop restaurant I've been dying to take you to."

She arched a brow. "A rooftop restaurant? That sounds suspiciously romantic."

I grinned. "Maybe I'm just trying to butter you up so I can get a sneak peek at your manuscript."

"Oh, please," she said, nudging me as we turned the corner onto a quieter street. "Like I'd let you read it before it's ready."

"Hey, I'm the guy that gives you ideas."

"Too many ideas," she teased.

We continued to banter back and forth as we made our way through the winding streets, past stained walls and windows framed with lush greenery. We climbed the narrow staircase to the roof of the apartment we were staying in during our visit. Each step felt heavier, not from exhaustion but anticipation. I'd been planning this for months, and every detail had to be perfect. When we finally reached the top, I let her step out first.

Her gasp was everything I'd hoped for.

The rooftop was transformed into a private haven. A single table set for two was adorned with crisp white linens, candles, and a centerpiece of fresh flowers. String lights crisscrossed above. The panoramic view of Rome surrounded us, the city sprawling out in all its timeless glory.

"This... this is incredible," Kaira breathed, spinning around to take it all in. Her eyes met mine, wide with wonder. "Roman, there's no restaurant, is there?"

"Nope," I said, stepping closer. "Just us."

She laughed. "You really outdid yourself."

I pulled out her chair and gestured for her to sit. "Only the best for you."

Dinner was a feast of Italian cuisine, each course better than the last served by a single server I had hired. We talked and laughed, reminiscing about our first meeting, the wild ride of our fake engagement, and everything that had brought us to this moment. The sun was setting, the heat of the day finally letting up. The city glowed all around us as if it were alive.

The server brought our last dish, a rich tiramisu. I nodded, letting him know his services were no longer needed.

She took her first bite and groaned. "Delicious," she said, her eyes closed in appreciation. "Everything has been just perfect. I still can't believe I'm here. With you. It's magical."

"I wouldn't want to be anywhere else," I said.

"Thank you for this," she said earnestly. "For bringing me here, to Rome, to this moment."

"It's my pleasure," I replied, squeezing her hand gently. "But there's more."

Her eyes widened in surprise. "More?"

I reached into my pocket. My heart pounded, and for the first time in a long time, I felt nervous. But it was a good kind of nervous—the kind that came with knowing you were about to take a leap worth everything.

"Kaira," I said, my voice calm despite the chaos in my chest.

She looked at me, her expression softening. "What is it?"

I stood, pushing my chair back. Slowly, I lowered myself onto one knee next to her. Her hand flew to her mouth, and she let out a tiny gasp.

"Oh my God," she whispered.

From my pocket, I pulled out the ring—the same one we'd used during our fake engagement. The irony wasn't lost on me, but it felt right, like it had been waiting for this moment all along. It was a beautiful ring and it suited her. I had given it to her at the wrong time before, but now it was the right time.

"I know what you're thinking," I said. "The media is going to have a field day with this. They'll dig up every photo, every headline, and dissect the whole thing. They're going to assume this is another charade."

She laughed. "It'll be chaos."

"Let them," I said, holding her gaze. "Because for the first time, I don't care what anyone else thinks. Kaira, you turned my life upside down in the best way. You taught me how to be better, how to feel again, and you loved me even when I didn't deserve it. I can't imagine a single day without you. So, here I am, asking you—no PR stunts, no contracts, just us—will you marry me?"

Her eyes shimmered with tears. She slid out of her chair and knelt in front of me, taking my face in her hands. "Roman," she said, her voice breaking. "Yes. A million times yes. I was always going to marry you. You were always my happy ever after. I love that it wasn't a straightforward journey to this point. I fell in love with you the first time at that auction, but that wasn't the real thing. This is real. I love everything about you, even when you're cranky. I wouldn't change a thing."

Relief and elation crashed over me as I slid the ring onto her finger. It fit perfectly. It was finally back where it belonged. She threw her arms around my neck, and I pulled her close and kissed her.

We stayed like that for what felt like forever, wrapped in each other and the magic of the moment. When we finally pulled apart, her cheeks were flushed, and her smile was unstoppable.

"You're going to regret giving the media that much ammo," she teased, holding up her hand to admire the ring.

"Not for a second," I said, brushing a strand of hair from her face. "Let them say what they want. I've got the only opinion that matters right here."

Her laugh was pure joy. She kissed me again. "Let's finish this tiramisu and then go downstairs. I've got some thoughts about how I would like to celebrate our engagement. I don't want to risk getting kicked out of Rome, possibly Italy if someone in one of those windows happens to see us."

I laughed. "Now you're making me want to skip dessert."

"Oh no," she said as she picked up her fork. "I am not skipping one bite of this."

This was it. My forever. And for the first time in my life, I felt complete. I was whole. I had a real future. I was finally getting the dream I never thought possible. The dream I never knew I wanted.

THE END

ABOUT THE AUTHOR

Hey there. I'm Weston.

Have we met? No? Well, it's time to end that tragedy.

I'm a former firefighter/EMS guy who's picked up the proverbial pen and started writing bad boy romance stories. I co-write with my sister, Ali Parker, but live in Texas with my wife, my two little boys, my daughter, two dogs, three cats, and a turtle.

Yep. A turtle. You read that right. Don't be jealous.

You're going to find Billionaires, Bad Boys, Military Guys, and loads of sexiness. Something for everyone hopefully.

OTHER BOOKS BY WESTON PARKER

<u>A Wedding Bells Alpha Novel:</u>

Say You Do

She's Mine Now

Don't You Dare

Promise It All

Give Me Forever

Feels Like Love

Mine to Hold

Love by Accident

Two Become One

Love Me Not

I Choose You

All for Love

<u>A Faux Love Novel:</u>

Fake It Real Good

Fake It For Money

Fake It For Now

Fake it For Real

Fake It For Love

Fake It For Us

Fake It For Wealth

Fake It For Good

Fake It for Fame

Fake it for Fortune

Fake it for Glory

Fake it for Him

Searing Saviors Series:

Light Up The Night

Set the Night On Fire

Turn Up the Heat

Ignite The Spark Between Us

The Worth Series:

Worth the Risk

Worth the Distraction

Worth the Effort

A Wild Night Novel:

Between the Sheets

Under the Covers

Bad Boy Greeks Series:

Fake It For Me

My Favorite Mistake

Pretending to Be Rich

A Military Man Romance Novel:

Air Force Hero

Let Freedom Ring

Maybe It's Fate

All American Bad Boy

All For You

Guard My Heart

My All American Girl

A Bad Boy Bachelors Novels

Bad Boy Bachelor Claus

Bad Boy Bachelor Cupid

Bad Boy Bachelor Bunny

Bad Boy Bachelor Summer

Bad Boy Bachelor Thanksgiving

Bad Boy Bachelor Christmas

Bad Boy Bachelor Valentine

A Match Me Up Novel:

You and Me, Baby

Pull Me In

Never Let Go

A Last Time Novel:

My Last Chance

My Last Secret

My Last Song

My Last Shot

A Parkers' Christmas in July Novel:

Such A Hot Christmas

Standalones:

Captain Hotness

Hot Stuff

Deepest Desire

My First Love

My Last First Kiss

My One and Only

Mine Forever

Trying to Be Good

My Holiday Reunion

One Shot at Love

Always Been Mine

Caught Up in Love

All About the Treats

Good Luck Charm

Love Me Last

We Belong Together

Main Squeeze

Brand New Man

Made for Me

Follow You Anywhere

Show Me What You Got

Have Your Way with Me

Heartbreaker

Keeping Secrets

Going After What's Mine

Give Me the Weekend

Take It All Off

Backing You Up

Come Down Under

Need You Now

Desperate for You

Standing Toe to Toe

Take It Down a Notch

Take A Chance On Me

Spring It On Me

Come Work for Me

All Good Things

The Billionaire's Second Chance

Pay Up Hot Stuff

Bad for You

Showing Off the Goods

Our Little Secret

Runaway Groom

Love Your Moves

Rich Fake Witch

Fair Trade for Love

Match Me Up

Not Fake for Long

Dropping the Ball

Last First Date

Hometown Hottie

You Know You Wanna

Some Kinda Romance

Summer Nights

Can't Buy Love

Pick Me This Time

Come A Little Closer

His for the Holiday

Santa Baby

One Midnight Kiss

Valentine's Billionaire Auction

Made in the USA
Middletown, DE
10 June 2025